"Diplomacy's Stepchild"

"The Dreamsingers' War"

Part Two Of The

Ic'nichi - Human Chronicles

Continuing The

First History Of The Interstellar Concord

An Ic'nichi novel translated into human language

by,

Robert A. Boyd

1

*****

"A Note From The Human Translator"

Despite our best efforts, the translation software still has serious shortcomings, due in part to several Ic'nichi terms defying translation. These terms have, perforce, been expressed in phonetic form, and an addendum with possible meanings has been added to the end of this work. We continue to hope for progress in subsequent editions.

*****

"Those Innocent Beginnings Get You Every Time."
(Related by Learnéd K'deiTai)

"Emotions are the key." I rapped the chalkboard with my pointer to remind the audience of the diagram of the human brain, and to allow a moment for the echoes in the cavernous instruction circle to die down. "The humans are rational beings, of course, but they are far more prey to their emotions than we are. So to understand and communicate with them, one has to relate to them as if they are irrational."

It seemed almost as if the candidates were ignoring me, busy as most of them were scribbling notes. They were listening, all right. Human Studies was a much sought-after prize, and those who made the circle were both capable and motivated. That, and lurid tales of human behavior are always a popular subject.

"Rationality, or rather the lack of it, is fundamental to the human psyche, so to understand them, you have to grasp their world view. Reality is what they believe it to be, regardless of the facts. This effects everything they do, and it has shaped their culture in ways which can be hard to grasp at times."

I paused for another moment to let the echos fade, and idly pondered the high domed ceiling. I was still bemused at times to be standing there. It wasn't so long ago that we weren't sure we'd get off the humans' *er'trxxda* world with our ears. And now here I was, safely back home in the World Nest itself, teaching a course on the humans in one of the most prestigious Institutes on d'enchia. I could hardly believe it at times.

"This is not to say that the humans are evil," I went on. "Rather, their thought processes are so different from ours that their actions can be alarmingly erratic at times. But rest assured, as bizarre as they can be, they *mean* well."

Another pause. You wouldn't think a new 'Adjunct Learnéd' would be given the largest circle at the Institute—one of the largest on d'enchia, I understand. It was a work of art and an icon of academia: the polished wood, inlaid marble tile, and subdued light fixtures gave it a somber tone; dignified, steeped in culture, rich in history and tradition. It had lousy acoustics.

"As we discussed yesterday, fear and anger are the two strongest human emotions, and are closely related..."

"Learnéd K'deiTai?" A candidate in the second tier was waving her tail for attention. I squinted against the light; it was *her*, again. I was in no mood to put up with *her*, so I pretended not to hear and kept on. Hopefully she would take a hint.

"So in trying to deal with humans, one must..."

"Learnéd K'deiTai?" No such luck.

"...yes?"

"I have seen several references to humans relying on 'wise cracks', a form of humor, in unsettling situations. How do they apply humor in a crisis?"

"Hmmm, good question."

She was a sharp one, someone I was keeping an eye on for the Arbiters, and frankly she tested my nerves at times. Our Human Studies program was the first of its kind: so new, in fact, that we were still developing it. We hadn't the time to prepare so complex a topic, and we simply knew so *little* about the humans that the curriculum was severely limited. Whenever someone deviated from the prepared material, it usually left me stumped, and she was the worst of the lot at that. I would have preferred to put this off for another year or two, but the interest was there and the need was urgent, so I did the best I could. At times that meant faking it, outrageously.

"Humans use humor in a crisis to release tension by making 'wise cracks', as they say it. That relates to the terms to 'crack wise', and to be a 'wise ass', all of which refer to the human rectum, which is known as an 'ass' or a 'crack'." I paused to scan the rapt snouts on their tiered rings of belly cushions around me. They seemed to be buying it.

"We aren't sure of the origin of this, but it may have to do with the human reaction of losing control of ones' bowels when badly frightened. They make 'wise cracks' to avoid this loss of control, relying on higher reason—to be 'wise'—to overcome their instinctive fear, and thus maintain control of their 'cracks'."

More scribbling. I went back to my notes, hoping to pick up where I left off before she could start again.

5

"Learnéd K'deiTai?"

Sigh. "Yes?"

"But how does humor affect their emotional state, especially as they have such a difficult time at self control?"

The other candidates paused in their notes, and were paying close attention. These confrontations were becoming a daily occurrence, and they fully expected a show. I grabbed the first rational thing which came to mind. "Humor...is an intellectual process. One has to see the humor in a situation, devise a comment, and deliver it in a form that evokes humor in others, all of which requires logical thought. Being a 'wise ass' is a defense mechanism, their way of focussing their higher intellects to place reason over emotion."

More scribbling, and a few furtive glances my way.

"Learnéd K'deiTai?"

I resisted the urge to strangle her. *"Yes?"*

"Isn't humor considered a disruption of the defense mechanism? And if so, how does humor circle with the instability of the human psyche?"

'Ancestors!' I grumbled to myself. *'Where do they get this stuff?'* The program drew the sharpest minds, which was both a blessing and a curse. The prepared material was little more than an outline of what we knew about the humans, and the candidates' relentless curiosity made these sessions a daily challenge. Much of what we taught was being researched by them as extra credit projects, in fact. I did the best I could, drawing from my two and a half years as our Arbiter on earth, but their questions often left me stymied.

"Any...defense mechanism...short of obsessive-compulsive paranoia has to be considered 'disrupted' to some degree."

"But..."

"Remember, the humans are imperfect. Their defense mechanism functions despite their humor."

"From what you said earlier, they appear to depend on humor as part of their defenses. How is this contradiction resolved?" That was the academically correct way of accusing me of not knowing what I was talking about. My opinion of her, which

6

started out high based on her wit and curiosity, dwindled a bit more. The apprentices were watching avidly now. I sometimes wondered who they rooted for.

"Um...I..." Just then the gong rang, mercifully ending another day of mortal combat. The interruption gave me a chance to regain the initiative. "That is a significant issue in human psychology. You may research it for an extra credit paper."

"Sources, Learnéd?" The challenge in her tone was unmistakable.

I hedged, having no idea of what to suggest. "It's time you start developing your own sources."

That actually seemed to please her. "Learnéd N'detLeda in Aberrant Psyche published a paper on that recently. I'll ask him."

"Very well."

And on that note, the circle broke up, and the candidates started shuffling for the door.

"Ancestors!" I sighed once she was gone. "Is she one of *his* candidates?" No wonder she was such a knot in my tail. My opinion of her dropped another notch or two; the last thing this Universe needed was another overbearing *un'tdar* like him.

Once the last of them were gone, I slumped on the raised dais, too weary even to go to my seat cushion, and sat staring at the instruction circle around me. I was still bemused by how enormous it was. We were stunned by the number of applicants when the Human Studies program was first announced, and the Institute hastily rearranged their course schedule to open up this cavernous dome. Sorting through all the resumes was another monumental headache, as was a hurried printing of more texts. Even then, the number of well qualified candidates would have filled the sixteen circles of seat cushions that rose around me by three times or more.

What was worse, once we actually began the course, it soon became painfully clear how *limited* our knowledge of the humans was. It's one thing to deal with a crisis calling for cool deliberation and decisive action in the snout of possible interstellar war; confronting a circle of candidates with sharp, inquisitive minds likely to go off on Ancestors know *what* tangent is something else

7

entirely. But by time we realized how inadequate our preparations were, we were already caught up in the stampede: and when you're caught in a stampede, as everyone knows, all you can do is gallop along and hope for the best.

"Learnéd K'deiTai?" *Her* shrill voice cut through my fog, leaving me momentarily disoriented.

"Yes...um...?" For the life of me I couldn't remember her name.

She gave me an annoyed look. *"T'virDoma,"* she said, impatiently. *"T'virDoma, ab Clas'nch.* Your memory seems to be slipping, Learnéd."

"Never mind my memory," I snapped. Impudent *t'pithm'ig*; why do I put up with her, I wondered. "What can I do for you?"

"I want you to arrange with the 'Dark Grays' to get me temporarily assigned to the embassy on earth."

Not so much as an 'if you choose', and the glow in her eyes could only be described as hungry. My opinion of her dropped several more notches; the Arbiters were the *last* place for her. And as for sending her to the embassy, my Ancestors would disown me for even considering it. "Why would you want to go there?"

She offered a predatory grin. "The humans are fascinating, and I plan to make them my career, so I want you to arrange field study."

I shuddered at the thought. "I doubt if the defenders will make room for a half-trained first season candidate, considering the cost of transportation and supply. And field study comes in the third season."

"That's for *average* candidates," she said with a dismissive sneer. "I've worked hard at my studies, and you know my grades. I am ready for the challenge."

I admit she was right: she was as brilliant as she was conceited, and her grades were first finger all down the line. "Still, you have a lot to learn. You should focus on your studies for now."

"I would be ready *now* except that you've had to dumb down the instruction for all the *ordinary* candidates. This program really needs an accelerated study circle. It's a shame this is the only course of its kind available."

That finally knotted my tail. "You will forgive me for being blunt, young fem, but if you expect to pursue a career in the Arbiters, you will need to develop a more courteous nature!"

She gave me an amused look. "Why would I want to go into the Arbiters? Diplomatic service is *so* limited, *so* stodgy, *so* bogged down by rules and traditions. There are plenty of mediocre people well suited for that sort of drudge work."

"Thank you," I grumbled.

She ignored my dig. "Actually, I am thinking of diplomatic intelligence. Meeting the humans has opened up a whole new Universe, and there will be plenty of opportunities for someone with drive and ambition. I'm looking forward to matching wits with the humans. That's a career with a future!"

'And how will you fare against Admiral MacKenna?' I wondered as she walked away. The human Admiral ran us ragged with next to nothing for six long years during the Contact Crisis. *That* would be a confrontation worth seeing.

§

It was no surprise that I felt so weary after putting up with *her* through a day's classes. My tail was dragging as I headed for our grotto. Mind you, I *like* teaching, but the endless confrontations with that obnoxious...*un'tdar*...reminded me too much of all the nonsense my Aide and I put up with in the Arbiters. (I admit she did have a point about that.) Her on-your-snout personality and her condescending nature made it all the worse. She had a gift for irritation which she shared generously, and I was blessed with more than my fair share.

But despite the aggravations, we were doing well in life and building a promising career in academia. When we returned from earth, my Aide and I were deluged with offers from Institutes all around d'enchia; not to mention (at last count) 3,225 offers of egg-bonding. I was already determined to resign from the Arbiters, so the Institute offers came as a welcome opportunity. (I never responded to the others.) So after much discussion, we accepted a position with the leading Institute here in the World Nest, who assured us of their full support in developing our Human Studies program. We were only 'Adjunct Learnéds' of course, based on

9

practical experience at our embassy on earth, but the pay was decent, we were earning a fair amount of recognition in our new field, the work was a steady routine, and best of all there was *no traveling*. I even lived close enough to the Institute that I could walk.

Even better—and I bless my Ancestors every day for it—we *finally* had our own grotto. It wasn't a proper grotto, really, being a section of the outermost ring of the lecture circle which was partitioned to form an enclosed room, rather than a proper independent structure. It was not the largest, and was still mostly undecorated, and on an out-of-the-way side corridor, but it was all ours. My Aide made a start at decorating it with some human *objects' d' art* we brought back with us, which made it a popular place with the candidates, but aside from paint and furnishings, we hadn't had the chance to do much as yet.

My Aide was at his desk, busy with the last exam papers, something he was *'V'memb'Va* at, when I came in. "So, how was circle today?" he asked.

"About average."

He considered me skeptically. "You look a bit dragged out."

I turned to him with a weary sigh. "I had another run-in with that young *'v'thorble*. Ancestors save me, I think she may be a protégé of N'detLeda."

He made a vulgar noise. "*Another* one like him? Just what this Universe needs." He'd had his share of run-ins with her, and N'detLeda loomed large in our memories of earth.

"And it gets better. She told me she wants to go into diplomatic intelligence."

He blinked in dismay. "We'll be at war in no time."

"Oh, who knows? With luck, as obnoxious as they both are, they'll kill each other."

"More likely they'll start a purebred strain together. I pity the future."

"*Where* are the humans' battleships when we need them?"

I grumbled over to my desk, loosened my weskit, flopped comfortably on my belly cushion, and checked my computer station for messages. Aside from the usual trash, there was a note from one of my promising candidates posed a question about human anatomy. After some thought, I sent a message back suggesting some references and posing the matter as an extra credit project. Another note from one of the less hopeful complained about the study load. I almost erased it without bothering to answer, but decided to send him a brief note of encouragement. One can but try. That left only one personal note: from G'cetGian, the Eldest Arbiter.

§

"So, I trust you had a pleasant journey?" G'cetGian asked as I settled awkwardly on a belly cushion by the fountain in his grotto.

That seemingly harmless comment about wilted my ears. The last time he asked me that, I wound up being tossed in tail first as our replacement Arbiter-To-Humans. I still suffered nightmares half a year after returning from earth, and I'd spit in my Ancestors' eye before I'd go back there again.

"Well, it was only across the nest," I mumbled. I accepted a *V'liz* bowl, settled uncomfortably, and tried not to look nervous while part of me wondered what in *l'cc'vn* I was doing here. I was no longer connected with the Arbiters, and if there was any one person on d'enchia I had reason to fear, it was G'cetGian. Yet here I was: sipping *V'liz* and waiting nervously for the roof to fall on me. I must have been manipulated by him so often over the years that it became a conditioned reflex. My thoughts went off on a tangent as I wondered idly if the humans had a term for it.

He gave me one of those beatific smiles which made him seem so harmless. "And how are you two getting along?"

Back to the battle at hand. "Our course schedule at the Institute keeps us busy, and we have a couple of candidates who might interest you." My Aide and I were grimly retired from the Arbiters, and I had no desire to take up old habits. I hoped he would take the hint.

"That is good to hear, especially about those potential candidates," he said. "But it must seem so *dull* after your many adventures."

"I can assure you the program is proving quite an adventure in itself."

11

"And I know we can expect the best from our most experienced and illustrious veterans."

Wonderful: he was starting his flattery again. I may be conditioned to respond to his games, but I had also been here long enough to see him coming. "Our *experience* is proving invaluable in training the new generation. I daresay you can look forward to a steady stream of quality candidates in the future *if* the program is successful."

"That will be a blessing," he sighed. "Still, I suppose you miss the excitement, don't you?"

"A blood-crazed herd of alien fanatics bent on death and destruction *is* exciting; I wouldn't want your younger Arbiters to miss out on the adventure."

"Indeed? That sounds most dramatic: I would love to see it myself." He set his bowl aside and reached for the kettle. "More *V'liz*? Have you tried these sour rolls? I understand they are adapted from a human recipe." Not good. His hands trembled as he poured without awaiting an answer as I gingerly picked up one of the rolls as if it might explode. One does not refuse the hospitality of the Eldest.

"A minor side issue came up recently," he went on once we settled in. "The matter is being addressed by U'tdaPagrn there on earth."

"Well, I am pleased to hear the Arbiters are managing without us, now that we are gone."

"Oh, we're getting on, I suppose. Still, I am a bit concerned about U'tdaPagrn, since this is his first real occasion to negotiate substantive issues with the humans."

"U'tdaPagrn is a capable Arbiter," I countered. "Surely he can handle a routine matter."

"True, U'tdaPagrn is a fine fellow, fine fellow indeed." He paused to sip his *V'liz*. "But truth be told, he is rather *young* for such a heavy responsibility. V'koBilen insisted on using him, and assured me a year or two handling minor routine on earth would give him the seasoning he needs. He *is* doing well by all accounts, still, I can't help thinking that a quick look over his shoulder would be a good idea."

12

"And you plan to send us back there to second-guess him. You know that's poor form. And why drag us into it?" All this talk of earth was getting on my nerves, which made me rather snappish. "We're retired. We have our duties at the Institute. Surely U'tdaPagrn will benefit from handling this 'routine matter'."

"Quite so. He is doing a good job there, but we seem to be losing the *feel* of the place. He doesn't have anything like your experience, and I fear he may not be picking up on all the subtleties of dealing with the humans. It's not showing in his reports, anyway. This is a chance to take a quick look around, refresh the diplomatic equation."

"I am *confident* of U'tdaPagrn's ability, and of V'xoBilen's judgement concerning him."

"As am I." He eyed me closely. "Still, this is *so* important that the precaution is just common sense."

"But why us? We are *retired* after all, and I'm not anxious to jump into that pit of *er'trxxda* again. Don't you have someone else to send?"

"Oh, we're spread so thin these days..."

"Which is why our work at the Institute training a new generation of potential Arbiters is so important."

"...and I do appreciate your efforts. You do have some promising candidates, from all accounts. Still, we elders must carry the load for a bit longer until the new generation hatches, eh?"

"Honestly, Eldest, my Aide and I have done more than our fair share." I was starting to get a bit inflamed, seeing where this was headed. "We don't want to keep others from making their contribution."

"It's just a quick review: a few snout-to-snouts with key people, meet a few prominent humans, play the tourist, then back on the next supply ship. Honestly, if there was someone to fill my place here, I'd go myself." He gave me that dreamy smile. "It'd feel *good* to get into the field again."

'Right,' I thought. *'And the humans will make sense* that *fine day.'*

§

13

Long story short, he finally wore me down. It took enough *V'liz* to leave me jittery, and so many of those human sour rolls that my belly was aching, but he did it. *Why* do my Ancestors let these things happen to me?

It was getting late, nearly dark, by the time I got out of his clutches. I stood on the walk in front of the Arbiters' Circle, and wondered how I let myself get into this mess, and more urgently, how I was going to get *out* of it. Try as I would, I couldn't think of anything. I gave up: the only thing I could do was let my Aide know what transpired. Perhaps he could come up with a way out of this. I would have to catch him at home, which wouldn't improve his mood, and I could well imagine his reaction. He would absolutely bite his own tail over this—if he didn't bite mine.

§

"I will *personally* cast myself into the Uttermost Darkness before I'll go back there," my Aide informed me in no uncertain terms. "You must be *er'trxxda* to let that *vr'meol* hustle you so!"

That went better than I hoped. I couldn't blame him for being short-tempered: this wasn't the first time G'cetGian hustled me into some miserable adventure, and the memories of the *last* time were the stuff of nightmares. And it didn't help that I interrupted his dinner with an attractive middle-aged fem. "I'm sorry. You know how manipulative he is."

"And how limp your tail is! What about our candidates? What about the program? Things are still too loose for us to go galloping off at random, *especially* to earth!"

She watched for a bit, then sighed and discreetly slipped into the kitchen.

"It's just for a short time," I promised him.

"A short time on a planet full of homicidal *er'trxxda*! We were lucky to get out of there with our ears. We'd be *n'bna'nmn* to go back there again."

"Ah...well...think of it as an adventure."

He snorted in contempt. "Do you remember the human definition of an adventure? It's when you're having a bad time in a nasty place far from home. If that doesn't describe earth, what would?"

14

"It's just a quick review: a few snout-to-snouts with key people, meet a few prominent humans, play the tourist, then back on the next supply ship."

"That place is *not* my idea of a tourists' Paradise."

"We more or less have to go. The Eldest was right about needing to refresh the diplomatic equation..."

"Well I am *not* going, and that's flat!"

§

A lot of help *he* turned out to be, but at least he gave me a crumb to throw to G'cetGian. I wasn't surprised to find him at the Arbiters' Circle at this late hour; not with his work load and all the *V'liz* he consumed.

"My Aide flat-out refuses to go, no matter how much I argue with him," I told him. Not that I argued all that diligently: I was *so* relieved by this turn of events. I only hoped it would work. "I'm sorry, but it looks like we can't help you after all."

G'cetGian gave me a little sigh and that beatific smile. "I can understand his feelings." For a moment, that raised my hope that he would send someone else, but then he said, "However, I suppose that is all for the good. You won't really need your Aide, and it is best for someone to remain here to cover your Human Studies program. More *V'liz*?"

"Oh...um...well, thank you." He was already pouring as I spoke. I wasn't going to get any sleep that night anyway, so it shouldn't have mattered.

"And I still have a few of those sour rolls left," he added. "They are *most* curious, don't you agree?"

"I'm sorry to have to do this on such short notice," he said once we were settled in. "But I'm afraid circumstances have forced my hand."

"Not eleven days again?" I groaned.

"No, in fact. The next transport leaves for earth tomorrow." A pause to nibble a roll. "At least you won't be kept in suspense, eh?"

"But without my Aide..."

"Indeed. But he refused to go, so you will have to carry on alone."

15

"My work at the Institute..."

"And there is still the unanswered question of who sent that mysterious Protocol which got the negotiations started. Perhaps you will have some luck in sniffing out that trail while you're there."

"But...my Aide..."

"...will have his hands full overseeing your program while you're away, so his remaining here is all for the best."

"My Ancestors are plotting against me," I moaned. "Earth must be my personal Uttermost Darkness."

"But look at the bright side," he said with one of his beatific smiles. "You won't have anywhere *near* as much luggage to worry about this time."

§

Once I escaped his clutches, I stood on the walk in front of the Arbiters' Circle and tried desperately to think of something. At the rate this was going, it looked like I was to be the lucky recipient of an all-expense-paid holiday in the *er'trxxda*-infested cesspool of the Universe, unless I came up with a brilliant idea, fast.

Then I remembered that V'koBilen lived a short distance from there. He was semi-retired since his health took another downward turn, but it was early enough to catch him at home. It wasn't exactly brilliant, but I knew I could count on them, and it was all I had left.

§

V'koBilen was indeed home, preparing for bed in fact. Their grotto was in an older circle, had a comfortable, lived-in feel, and was decorated with her knitting and with those prints of human art which are so popular these days. He was dressed in a warm sleeping robe, listening to music and enjoying a late snack. He and his Aide greeted me warmly, and offered me *V'liz* and sour rolls, but his mood changed when he heard my litany of woe.

"Your Aide was right: you do have a limp tail when it comes to that conniving *M'mendoch*," he accused me.

"What?" I muttered in confusion. I only spoke with my Aide a short time ago, and unless he anticipated me and phoned over here... "When did he say that?"

"It's common knowledge all through the Service," V'koBilen said with an exasperated sigh, which left me wondering about my reputation among my former coworkers.

"Now love, don't fault K'deiTai," his Aide said. "We've had our share of run-ins with G'cetGian."

He gave her a guilty look, and nodded. "He tried to twist my tail on that," he told me. "So I can well imagine the pressure he put on you. Fortunately I was able to convince him that I am too old and ill to travel."

"Can you *please* talk to him? Get him to send someone else?"

"You know as well as I do that you might as well argue with the planet to stop rotating."

"But what am I to *do?*"

"You could simply refuse, you know."

"I tried that. It didn't work."

He gave me a disgusted look. "Then do like I did: develop a heart condition."

§

It's amazing how *useless* one's friends can be when dealing with G'cetGian. I cursed him for dragging me into this preposterous fix, V'koBilen and his Aide for not doing something to help, and my Aide for showing no sympathy for the condemned. Most of all, I cursed myself for having such a limp tail. V'koBilen was right: this was my own fault for not standing up to G'cetGian, not that I forgave him.

The local trolleys quit for the night by time I got out of there, so I had to walk—trudge—home, belly-aching and jittery. *Curse* the humans and their blasted sour rolls, too!

Honestly, right then I was bitter and frustrated and about used up. My Aide was right as well: I do have a limp tail when it comes to that conniving *M'mendoch. Why* do my Ancestors hate me so? More urgently, what could I do now that my supposed 'friends' covered their tails and left me dangling?

My one remaining hope was that the Institute Elders wouldn't grant me a release, which was not unreasonable since we had a full course schedule and our program was barely getting up to speed. Yes, the more I thought about it, the more confident I was that the

17

Elders would intervene. Of course they would: my responsibility now was to the Institute, not my former employer; our Human Studies was a vital curriculum developed at great expense and labor; we were right in the middle of the course; there were no other qualified instructors available. It was inconceivable that they would release me to go gyrating off at random to other worlds. That was reassuring, and I trudged through the center of the nest toward home with a weary sense of relief.

I should have known better.

*****

"Just Another Day At The Office"
(Related by Defender I'eiBida)

"You have your security pass?" C'traBenla was fidgeting nervously with my collar again, trying to get the Staff medallions more perfectly aligned.

"Yes, love," I mumbled. I was still half asleep, waiting patiently for my last bowl of *V'liz* to kick in, and wasn't entirely following her.

"And your meal money?"

"Yes, love." I was drifting off again.

"And remember that you need to meet with your Worthy today."

"Yes, love."

"And *when* do you intend to ask the Herd Guide about some bonus pay?"

"Yes, love."

"I'eiBida, I'm trying to help!" Her flare of temper dissolved into tears.

That woke me up at last. "C'tra, love..." I caressed her ears to try and reassure her. "You do help, a lot, and I appreciate it all."

She choked back her tears and gave me a hurt look. "I just want you to stand out in your new position. It means so much to you."

One of the many things I didn't think about when I asked her to bond with me was what would happen when she threw herself whole-heartedly into promoting my career. She's like that: get her focussed on a cause, and sparks will fly. Truth, I *was* grateful for her commitment, but her impulsive energy often created more smoke than traction.

"Love, they hardly notice, everyone is so busy." I nuzzled her ear the way she enjoys so much.

"Y-you look so nice in your new uniform." She started fidgeting with my collar again. "I'm so proud of you; one of the founders of the 'Dark Grays'."

"Well, I'm not so important as all *that*. They'd manage without me for, oh, a day or two, at least."

19

She gave a nervous chuckle and wiped a tear away. "I see you need your ego deflated again."

"I know I can depend on you, love."

She glowered at me fleetingly, then said, "I'ei, you really should ask the Herd Guide for some release time. You have enough saved up, and Ancestors know they owe us." She gave me a tentative smile. "We need to get away from everything."

"Mmm, I'd like that." I nuzzled her ear again just because it felt good.

"I was thinking we might take a few days at the Thousand Falls, perhaps."

That caught me by surprise. The Thousand Falls was one of the best romantic vacation spots on this continent, and not cheap. As tight as our finances were, I didn't see how we could afford it. But then...all those waterfalls...those pools and rapids of chill mountain run off...and her... I'd *have* to speak to the Herd Guide.

"Let me ask around and see if I can arrange something." Likely the humans would make sense before that happened, as hectic as things were at the Staff circle. One can but try. All those chill mountain streams... "Let's meet for mid-meal, after your appointment."

Even as I said it, I realized that was the wrong thing to say. We gave our first egg to the crèche three days ago, and she was not taking it well. She wilted a bit; the one thing she didn't need to be reminded of just then was the possession syndrome therapy program she was enrolled in. "Well...yes, I suppose," she said at last. "At your circle?"

"There's a new dining club opened near the 'Grays' circle here. I understand the *bv'nunma* is good." I'd have to sneak away early to catch the train back from the spaceport, but it would be well worth it.

She gave me a doubtful look. "Can we afford it?"

Now she was worried about finances. "We'll make do. We can put off that new sleeping pad until my next pay period."

We still occupied temporary quarters at the Junior Elders' Circle, where we landed after returning from earth. It was adequate if one isn't too picky, but it was run down, and the

20

furnishings left a lot to be desired. We were stretching my pay for the crèche fees for our first egg; luxuries were few and far between, so we made do.

"I was hoping we could get that soon," she sighed. She was still tender from her labor three days ago, and hadn't been sleeping well. "I guess we can save some extra and get a nicer pad next time."

"That's the spirit." I smiled and nuzzled her ear again.

"I live for you, love."

She did; really. I read somewhere that former *tra'taj* often become devoted to someone who treats them with respect and kindness. I did that right from the start when she arrived at our embassy on earth because it was simply the right thing to do, and it had an unintended impact on her. Truth, I hadn't thought about bonding with her until I asked her on a moment's impulse a few days before I returned home. I still hadn't gotten over my surprise that she accepted.

"So, are you all right?"

"I suppose." She sighed again, and turned her head away to hide her nervous expression. "I'm just worried about our hatchling."

Great. She was on *that* again. She conceived our first egg within days of returning home, and fretted over it ever since. Like I said, when she gets focussed on something, she goes all-out. It can be a bit overwhelming at times.

I nibbled her ear affectionately. "The crèches here in the World Nest are top rated. Our hatchling will have the best tutoring, and between your energy and my luck, it'll do well in life, I'm sure."

She settled a bit, and sniffed a few times as she eyed me. "I know," she mumbled at last. "I just...I want...we'll never even know if it was mal or fem." She looked me with that sorrowful gaze that came too often of late. "It's not all right. Not at all."

"C'tra..." I stroked her neck gently, and gave her a reassuring smile. "That's our way. That's the way we've always done it. Our hatchling will prosper, I'm sure."

Her tone turned hard and angry. "If it gets past the Egg Testers."

21

I backtracked hastily. "Love, don't fret over it. We don't produce defective eggs." I was starting to worry about her emotional state, which had grown more and more fragile since she labored. "We're a prime breeding pair if there ever was such."

She was silent for a long moment, then wilted. "I know. It's just...the humans..."

"They have their ways and we have ours. Besides, how could we care for a hatchling? Can you *imagine* trying to hatchling-proof this place? You saw the mess human hatchlings make. Do you really want to spend all your time cleaning up after one?"

"Ancestors forbid!" That got a laugh out of her.

Another domestic crisis under control, for now. I didn't need this, as tired as I was from all the work at Staff, but the costs of life bonding aren't always measured in coin. And, yes, I cared enough about her that I was willing to pay that price, but it could be wearing. "Are you all right, love?" I caressed her ears again to reassure her.

"Yes." She didn't seem quite so disconsolate now. "I just wish...I didn't feel so bad about it all." She gave my collar one last tug. "Now you trot! You're already late."

§

So I missed my trolley, again, which put me even farther behind. My Worthy was waiting for me in the rotunda of the 'Dark Grays' new Staff circle near the spaceport, and he was *not* amused. "There you are," he growled when I came trotting in from the train station. "Let's gallop. I need to get over to the Academy."

"Sorry." He fell in beside me as I trotted down the long curving corridor to our allotted niche. "Things at home."

His tone softened a bit. "She doing better?" As dismayed as he was at our bonding, he did like her.

"A bit." Honestly, I didn't feel chatty right then. We trotted along in silence for a while, dodging the endless stream of clericals and staff flunkies who are *always* going the other way, and picking our way carefully through the areas where they were still painting the place. Our work station was clear around on the far side of the circle (which seems consistent, somehow), so we had a goodly trot. I needed the exercise to work off some of my tension, anyway.

22

"How are those grade evaluations doing?" I asked as we struggled through another traffic jam at one of the entrances to the circle proper.

"Our herd is well above the curve, and we have a few who look promising. I'll know more after I've done the interviews, but we'll be sending two, perhaps three to the Leadership program. '

"Good." Some cheerful news for once. Sending candidates up to the Leadership course would be good marks on our file. "Did T'revNend get those papers graded?"

"Yes. He's all that keeps us going, you know." Fourth Degree Worthy T'revNend had been assigned to help us in our coursework at the Academy, and was proving a first rate administrator.

"Ah...yes. We'll have to give him a commendation."

"As soon as they get us the commendation forms," he grumbled as we fought our way clear of the crush. "How they expect us to build a new defender herd like this is beyond me."

§

Actually, the 'Dark Grays' weren't entirely new so much as we were expanding the Space Service defenders from a minor detachment into a separate herd in their own right. Our most visible sign of progress to date was our new 'Dark Gray' uniforms—for those whom Supply caught up with. Beyond those, and the few ships and existing resources of the Patrol, we had an empty egg.

The Chamber-Of-Ancients authorized a massive space mobilization after our botched contact with the humans, when we all feared we were at war with some sinister alien force of unknown size and purpose. Once we met the humans and got to know them, the Ancients redoubled that effort. Now, six years on, the fleet had grown from nine patrol craft, and was fast approaching thirty-two hulls, the limit agreed to in the First Accord with the humans. But hulls are one thing; crews, bases, supplies, and doctrine are something else entirely. Ancestors, we didn't even have uniforms to go round! It left us at a pounding gallop trying to hammer the raw—and I do mean 'raw'—material into some cohesive organization.

23

Our part of it was Human Analysis: trying to define the human threat and how to deal with it, and passing that knowledge along at the defenders' Academy and to Operational Plans. That was the theory: a lovely, innocent thing doomed to a cruel fate under the crushing heel of reality. The humans have an old saying, something about 'a riddle wrapped in an enigma', which is about the best description of them I've heard yet. For all that we lived among them and studied them for years, they bewildered us more often than not. And it doesn't help that the entire lot are homicidal er'trxxda. Our job was to figure them out before some incident erupted into a shooting war, Ancestors save us. It all added up to long days, quick meals, little sleep, and endless headaches.

Still, I shouldn't complain. We had it easy compared to those poor fools in Supply. Setting up a whole new defender herd (which hadn't happened in over two hundred years) created a paper blizzard beyond comprehension. Aside from our tasteful new Dark Gray uniforms, every requisition we sent up the trail was returned stamped with the dreaded 'Under Consideration'. That meant reports, schedules, attestations, analyses, reviews, reports on the reviews filled out on their own forms, endorsements of the reports on the reviews...you get the picture. Sometimes I think we should forget about developing stellar bombs, and turn our bureaucracy loose on the humans.

§

"I'eiBida?" The Staff Herd Guide ambushed us as we reached my desk. "The Eldest wants to see you."

That didn't sound good. "What did I do this time, sir?"

"Don't be so paranoid," he grumbled. My Worthy offered an exasperated sigh, but said nothing.

"I'm sorry I'm late..."

He gave me an irritable, bleary-eyed stare. "We all slip a bit now and then, but you, of all people, *can not* indulge in such slackness." He was the first one here in the morning, and the last to leave at night. How he got any sleep at all was beyond me. He

24

got in my snout and lectured me sternly, like he does. "Your work is too critical for this *cc'v'renk*! 'Punctuality is the key to success'; the Fifth Maxim of the defenders, *in case* you've forgotten. I want to see you at your desk on time from now on."

"Yes, sir. Sorry, sir."

"And as for the Eldest, don't go borrowing trouble."

"Sorry, sir, it's just I've had a few unhappy encounters with him in the past."

"Well this isn't one of them," he snapped. "I come to you wearing body armor, then you can worry. Until then, get your tail over there before his mood changes, at the gallop."

"Yes, sir."

He headed back to his grotto while my Worthy collected the report I was working on, gave me an exasperated ear twitch, and left me standing there wondering why I ever joined the defenders in the first place.

§

Needless to say, I was *not* reassured by the Herd Guide. The Eldest was a hard case at the best of circumstances, and things around here could hardly be described as 'best'. His grotto was at the main 'Grays' circle back in the World Nest, which meant another lengthy train ride. In the time it took to get there, I worried myself into a state.

Getting to the defenders' circle was one thing; getting *into* it was something else. If anyone in the 'Grays' had their tails straight, it was their largely ceremonial security herd *(l'cc'vn hro'n'nad t'pithm'ig)*. They *knew* they were first finger, the lot of them, and there was a certain amount of antagonism between us and all the passed-over 'Grays' anyway, which made for a chilly, proper reception.

One thing *did* change since I was here last. I well knew my way to the Eldest's grotto from traumatic memory, but they made me take a guidebook anyway. "So what do I need this *Bna'vwep* thing for?" I complained to the duty elder. The Ancestorless thing was *heavy*.

"Policy, sir," he said with a dismissive sneer. "We can't have *outsiders* wandering around lost; it cuts into our efficiency."

25

This must be the latest protocol *x'mnnb'* cooked up to annoy us by some flunky with too much free time on his hands. There was a stack of them from floor to ceiling, which he presided over zealously. And this *t'pithm'ig* lectures me on efficiency! *'Small tasks for small minds,'* as we say in the field force.

"You could put up direction signs, but that would make sense, and we can't have *that*, can we?"

"Far be it from me to make 'Grays' policy, sir," he said in prim righteousness. Bureaucrat. Nothing for it. I was told to sign out for it and lug it around wherever I went. "Don't set it down anywhere, sir. They tend to vanish."

I hefted the thing speculatively. "Might make a nice souvenir at that." He gave me a chilly glare, but since I outranked him, he limited his response to a frown as he waved me in.

§

That adventure passed, I was on my way after hesitating in the broad doorway to size the place up. The original structure was a single enormous room, larger than most warehouses, with the Eldest's grotto in the center and layer upon layer of work stations extending outward in concentric rings. Beyond that, five additional layers were added over the last two hundred and fifty years, each as packed as the first, and a sixth was under construction.

"Oy," I muttered as I surveyed the scene in dismay.

Ahead of me lay a perilous sea of glowing computer screens, buzzing telephones, yammering teletypes, scurrying technicians and clericals. The subdued rumble of office machinery and hushed conversations was deafening, and despite the ventilation, the air was acrid with the smell of hot electronics and packed bodies. They were forever trying to squeeze just *one* more work station into an area which already exceeded critical mess, so the few aisles were constantly changing as various departments fought for floor space. At least the doorway to the next layer was a distant guide beaconing me on. Thank my *Ancestors* we had our own circle near the spaceport! This place would make a respectable Nest in its own right.

§

26

The Herd Guide of the 'Grays' Staff was a full Ki-, which will give you some idea of the headway around there. Second Degrees were lowly scum in his territory, Staff specialist or not, and even the clericals resented my intrusion. The Herd Guide was a scrawny, dried up, flabby bureaucrat who hadn't galloped further than the cafeteria in years. Nonetheless he was a pettifogging stickler for detail, and his chilly demeanor always made me wonder if I'd wet myself.

"It's about time you showed up," he growled. That's one more down side to being the indispensable expert: you meet lots of important people who believe it's their job to make your life miserable.

"I came as soon as I got the message, sir."

"Well if you're expecting a medallion, we're fresh out." He gave me another disdainful sniff, then waved me past. "Well? Don't keep *him* waiting."

I was a bit miffed at his attitude, so I gave him the sharpest tail wave I could and muttered, "We who are about to die salute you."

"What?" He gave me a sharp look.

"Nothing, sir. It's an old earth expression."

Beyond that, the only barrier left was my own trepidation. I paused at the door to the Eldest's grotto, and give my uniform a last nervous tug or two while going over in my mind what he might want me for. I couldn't *think* of anything he'd be mad at me about. So I took a deep breath, and rang the gong three times.

Nothing.

I stood there for what seemed like forever, fretting myself into a tizzy. The muted rumble of voices and office equipment sounded like an approaching thunderstorm—make that a tidal wave. Honestly, for a fleeting moment, I wished I was back on earth. I was about to ring again when a muffled voice came from inside.

"Enter."

Here goes nothing.

§

The Eldest's grotto was large, austere, and brightly lit. The room was hung with subdued curtains, and the only furnishings were his desk, a couple of belly cushions, and the functional

27

fountain. The medallions of all the Great Nests of d'enchia hung around the room at eye level. There were some artifacts on small display stands along the wall: a chunk of twisted wreckage from our ill-fated Scout 114 (which had the misfortune to first meet the humans), a large wall map of the Ic'nichi and human spheres of space, and some odd items I couldn't take the time to ponder.

"Second Degree I'eiBida, fan D'chr reporting, Eldest." I hit a brace in the proper spot right in front of his desk, and gave him my best formal tail wave.

The Eldest was smaller than most fems, and stringy, but he was about as hard core as they come, and not someone you want angry at you. He was engrossed in a report when I came in, and gave me an absent-minded tail wave, but didn't even look up. From the paperwork scattered across his desk, it seemed his days were every bit as hectic as mine. As I stood there being uncomfortably ignored, it occurred to me how similar he was to the humans' Admiral MacKenna, and I wondered idly what that human would think of the scene outside.

Sitting off to one side was Fleet Elder H'rhAtor, the senior Ship's Eldest of our Patrol Service, recently appointed our first 'Admiral' commanding the vastly expanded fleet. I noticed, out of the corner of my eye, that he was also wearing the new 'Dark Grays' uniform. We made eye contact, and he favored me with a bemused ear twitch, but said nothing.

The Eldest finally looked up from his report. "Stand easy." Not that one stands easy in the Presence. "I have a job for you. I'm sending you to earth to have a look around."

"Sir?" *This* was out of nowhere! I looked uncertainly at the two of them, wondering what kind of trouble I was in now.

"The humans are up to something with those two battleships they were building," H'rhAtor explained, with a gesture at the document in the Eldest's hand. "We haven't heard anything definitive, but we can't afford to overlook this."

"You know the humans better than any of us," the Eldest added. "So you should be able to root out the facts."

"...um..." I was not thrilled about this; not at all. "Our duties at the Academy..."

"Your Worthy can handle that, and I've arranged for a substitute instructor to help him. It'll be a quick round trip, and we can manage without you for a day or two, at least."

"Um...yes, Eldest," was the only thing I could say.

§

Well: to say that I was unhappy is to strain the language. I paused to collect my wits once I was safely out of the building, and reflected sadly on what this turn of events would mean. The idea of going back to that miserable hole, with its higher gravity, and its intense weather, and all those *er'trxxda*, would wilt the stiffest tail. This was going to make a fine mess of our duties at Staff, which were already overwhelming us. My Worthy would not be pleased, and I could well imagine his peeved silence when he heard *this* one. I was not looking forward to the journey, either, or to the headaches and misadventures that I just *knew* would be waiting there. And on top of *everything* else, I was not looking forward to explaining this to C'traBenla.

§

"Earth?" C'tra was startled and shrill when I told her of this latest development over mid-meal.

"They're sending me to check out some rumors about the human Space Fleet. It'll just be a quick round trip."

She was not thrilled about this; not at all. "Your duties at the Academy..."

"My Worthy can handle that for a while, and they've arranged a substitute instructor for me."

She gave me a hurt look. "Honestly, I'eiBida, why do you let them do these things to you?"

"I'm sorry, love. I don't have much say about it."

The one thing I didn't need right then was a public scene. That new dining club was one large room crammed with small tables; more like a human cafeteria than a decent eatery, not that you'd know it from the waiters' attitudes. It was a short walk from the 'Grays' circle, so it was jam-packed with uniforms, all of whom seemed to be staring at us—at her. She was well known in defender Staff circles, and I was sure they were gossiping up a storm. (And the *bv'nunma* was dreadful, and overpriced, too.)

29

"I'll only be gone for a short while: in and out on the next supply ship."

"Earth?" She pondered that morosely as she chewed her *uf'thoka*. "I miss earth," she said at last, and eyed me speculatively. "We had some interesting times there, didn't we?"

"Interesting isn't *quite* the word that comes to mind!"

She stared off at nothing for a bit, then muttered something in *n'hroop* before she focused on me. "I'd love to visit earth again."

I could see where this was going, and tried urgently to head her off. "The weather there is terrible! And there's that higher gravity, plus it's a dangerous place. Remember how frightened and miserable we were?"

"Oh, it wasn't that bad, at least not toward the end." She got all dreamy-eyed. "It would be nice to go to one of the diplomatic socials, or maybe see *Señor* Vargas again."

In fact, this was alarming. She was warming to the idea fast. "It's a raw frontier. They're uncivilized."

"Hro'n'nad!" she snorted. "Geneva is a lovely place, and the humans are delightful people." She contemplated her bowl for a moment. "And my human affairs articles have been getting a bit stale lately." She looked at me again with the enthusiasm I knew of old. "I need to brush up on human culture."

"It's a hundred and eighty-two light years from here. It's a long and uncomfortable journey."

She started ticking items off on her fingers. "I can borrow a camera, so we can get plenty of new photos."

"Relations are still tenuous. It's a hazard duty assignment."

"And I'll take the red sequin gown for formal occasions."

"And you still haven't fully recovered from laboring."

"Or maybe the purple one?" Her enthusiastic grin told me I was in big trouble. "Oh, you know how strong I am. We need some time together, anyway. It'll be a working vacation for us." I was losing this argument fast, but there was no stopping her once she gets into one of her enthusiasms. This is what comes of life-bonding with a typhoon.

"And I believe Learnéd M'tinDegan is still at the embassy. I'm sure he has a lot to talk about!"

30

"I'm going there on defender business. I doubt if they'll let you tag along."

"Nonsense! I'm sure you can arrange it; you're on the *Staff*, after all." She gave me *that* look. "If not, I know a few people I can talk to."

I shied in panic. "All right, let me see what I can do."

§

"You want to take your *bondmate* with you?" The Eldest was not thrilled about this; not at all; on top of which he was peeved at having me show up on his doorstep again. "D'you think you're off on some *junket* like one of the Ancients?"

"No, sir." I had my arguments all rehearsed, although they didn't seem so iron clad under his icy glare. "But this is a covert mission, sir, and it'll look a lot less suspicious if I drag her along."

"Hmph! She's not exactly 'covert', you know."

"Yes, sir. That's the point. The humans won't suspect anything with the show she puts on. It'll look more like a diplomatic junket."

He was decidedly unimpressed. "This is official business. You want to take a romantic cruise, do so on your own time."

Wrong answer! The thought of C'tra's likely reaction goaded me on. "...well...sir...she has a lot of experience with the humans. She was close in diplomatic circles, used to work at the embassy. She might be able to sniff out trails I can't."

The Eldest was getting annoyed. "Do you realize what it costs to send one person to earth, not to mention two?"

"Yes, sir."

"But she's determined to go, isn't she?" He knew her all too well, having seen her in action as we made the social rounds after returning from earth.

"Yes, sir. I'm afraid so."

"*Why*, in your Ancestors name, did you life-bond with *her* anyway?" he grumbled. "Never mind; I really don't want to know." He sighed, then tried a different tack. "I hear she's not well these days."

"We gave our first egg to the crèche recently, and she's a bit down about it, sir. Going to earth will pick her right up again."

31

"Hmph. Congratulations on that," he grumbled. "But is she fit to travel? You'll be going on the embassy courier ship. That's a long, rough gallop." I must have looked surprised. "The regular supply ship left fifteen days ago. The courier is in for servicing, and will head back tomorrow. They'll get you there faster, and you can catch the regular supply run back."

"Which will make the journey that much shorter and less stressful for her, sir."

He eyed me in annoyance. "You've never been on our courier, have you? It's not a luxury liner."

"Besides, we can't risk her making phone calls to some of her political connections, can we, sir?"

That convinced him.

*****

"Unexpected Adventures"
(Related by Defender I'eiBida)

"This is delightful!" It might have been my imagination, but M'tinDegan's welcome sounded a bit frantic. No doubt he was thrilled to see old friends again since there were only a few of the original embassy staff who hadn't gone home. He was hopping back and forth like an excited hatchling, in fact. "It's good to have you back. We've made *so* much cultural progress since you left."

"Hello, Learnéd!" C'traBenla gave him a happy ear twitch. "It's good to be back."

"You simply *have* to try a new human food we recently discovered. It's called ocra, a regional delicacy..."

"Please!" I held up both hands to interrupt. "This is no time to think of food."

He hesitated, and gave me a concerned ear twitch. "I imagine you must be tired after your journey."

"Tired? My Ancestors should be here to pick me up any moment now. I can't *believe* I forgot how unpleasant the gallop from Singapore is."

Worse, that gallop lead me back to this pestiferous ruin of a private resort we inherited from the humans for our embassy. The place was still dingy and decrepit despite years of repairs and the efforts of the housekeeping staff, and that overbearing 'Gothic' architecture gave me a headache just looking at it.

"Did you take the direct weekly flight from Singapore?" M'tinDegan asked. "They started it after you left, and the new civilian P-wings are more comfortable than the military transports we used to travel in."

"If you can call four days sealed up in an aluminum box an improvement!" They *were* better than the peacekeeper C-wings, but it was still a dreary, cramped, exhausting trudge in an aircraft too small for all the Ic'nichi and their human APA escorts. And that was on top of the twenty days' travel from d'enchia.

"Oh, really, I'ei, where's your spirit of adventure?" C'traBenla chided me. "Think of it: we're back on earth where we first met. Isn't it romantic?"

I gave her a look and a weary sigh. "The Eldest was right: that old scout ship sure isn't a luxury liner. Thank my *Ancestors* that's over." She, however, was in top spirits. Space travel agreed with her, and she was tickled silly to be here again. I swear I will never understand that fem, for all that I love her.

It seemed the defenders were maintaining the traditions we started at the very beginning. Defender L'datMparn and his Worthy were there to meet us, and from the set of L'datMparn's ears, he was not happy to see me. "Welcome back, sir. I'm pleased to see you." The lying *cc'v'renk*. "So...ah...what brings you two here, sir?"

"I'm on a fact-finding matter," I told him brusquely. "And C'tra is here to brush up on human culture."

"Well, sir, I'm sure we can..."

He was interrupted by the thunderous roar of a large aircraft passing low overhead along the lake front toward Geneva's airport. It took me a moment to realize it was a human orbital shuttle.

"Ancestors!" L'datMparn gasped.

I studied it unhappily as it receded in the distance. "Do they normally come that close?"

"Ah...no, sir."

"They still limit themselves to Singapore," M'tinDegan added. "I can't imagine why they are here."

"An emergency landing, perhaps?" L'datMparn wondered.

"Well, unless they crash on the embassy, it's not our problem," I grumbled. I rather hoped it would.

§

C'tra and M'tinDegan were soon deep in the latest gossip, and L'datMparn made his excuses and left as fast as he decently could, so I headed on in by myself. The embassy's central foyer was all too familiar, with the humans' liaison office on the right side and the circular watch desk on the left. At least they'd removed that enormous chandelier which almost came crashing down on our heads, and which lay in a pile in one corner for most of our time here. The duty defender gave me a snappy tail wave when I came in. I looked him over, and was impressed by his sharp look and alert demeanor. I'll give L'datMparn that much credit: he ran a

34

tight herd, although the fellow's closed expression made me wonder how their morale was. The broad double doors to the ballroom were open, revealing a defender work detail scrubbing the floor. That was another disheartening sign, as floor detail is a favorite for defaulters with any Worthy.

Two wings branched off to either side, one leading to the cafeteria, the other to the Arbiter's grotto. I headed left toward the grotto just as a familiar figure came trotting into the foyer.

"K'deiTai?"

"Oh, I'eiBida?" He halted and pondered me uncertainly for a moment. "It's good to see you again. You're doing well, I hope?"

"No rest for the poor, downtrodden junior staff, I'm afraid."

"Try your hand at academia," he groaned. It was the same old K'deiTai in his rumpled wescott and baggy trousers, looking more tail-drooped and frazzled than ever, and in an odd way I was pleased to see him amid this herd of strangers.

"So what brings you here, sir? Are you assigned here again?"

"*Ancestors*, no! I'm just here for a bit of snout-to-snout for Eldest G'cetGian. I'm headed back home on the next supply ship."

"Have things been quiet here lately?"

"Yes, thankfully. There haven't been any disasters or crises..."

"I'eiBida..." C'traBenla came bouncing up with a couple pieces of her luggage, and stopped short at the sight of him. "...oh! K'deiTai!" She put on a forced smile. "What a surprise! And M'tinDegan too! All together again!"

He shied in panic, then gave her a sour look. "So what brings *you* here?"

"I'm here to update on human cultural matters," she answered his tone coolly.

"*You aren't assigned here again, are you?*"

She laid her ears back. "You don't need to worry about *that!*"

"I *always* worry when you're around!"

"If you want something to worry about..."

I grabbed his sleeve before they could come to blows, and dragged him toward the Arbiter's grotto as the clericals watched curiously. "I'm thankful you're here. I was sent here to look into something, and your advice will be helpful."

35

"But...I..."

"I'm sure U'tdaPagrn will want to see me," I said as I hustled him down the room. A quick backward glance showed C'traBenla looking hurt and confused. Better dealing with her later than settling a public brawl now. "And I'd like your opinion, too."

"I was on my way to mid-meal..."

§

The east wing of the embassy was pretty much as I remembered it. We tore out all the first floor guest rooms when we moved in, leaving a large open area spaced with vertical beams which was now filled to overflowing with clerical work stations. U'tdaPagrn's grotto was the former library at the far end. U'tdaPagrn sat by the tall windows overlooking the terrace, scribbling away at something with a harassed look. His desk was piled with papers and file folders, and the room was as dingy and worn as ever. It seemed like old times.

He greeted me with an unenthusiastic-but-pleased ear twitch. "Well, thank the Ancestors you're finally here."

"They were in a stampeding hurry to get me here, too, sir."

U'tdaPagrn gave me a worried sigh. "I'm not surprised. This battleship matter must sit uneasily back home."

"Are the humans landing shuttles in Geneva now, sir?"

U'tdaPagrn paled. "Was that what that was? No, they still limit themselves to Singapore." I understood why he seemed perturbed. The last time a human shuttle landed in Geneva, it was loaded with Space Marines coming to rescue us when the embassy was besieged by Anti-tech revolutionaries. Still, he seemed awfully jumpy. Earth service will do that.

"I was recently informed about the 'Dark Grays'." He gestured at my new uniform. "How are things going back home?"

"We're transforming from a peacekeeping force into a war fighting force. None of us are comfortable about it, but it has to be done. My lectures on human military history and methods were a shock to all."

"I read your reports." He shuddered. "Ancestors! These people scare me almost as much as they did K'deiTai."

K'deiTai made another sour snout, and sighed.

36

"I'm in Human Analysis now," I told U'tdaPagrn. "War plans, training, tactics, and opponent psychology."

He snorted derisively. "You have *your* hands full!"

"I doubt if I'll ever get the knots out of my tail. I don't know why they sent me here about this battleship thing. We have more than enough vital work to keep us busy."

"Actually, I requested you."

That surprised me. "I don't follow you, sir. L'datMparn has all our intel assets right in front of him. This is his duty, anyway."

U'tdaPagrn gave me a guarded look. "Candidly, I don't trust your replacement for something like this. L'datMparn is firmly in league with the hard-line herd back home. While he does his job well enough, I can't be sure of his reliability when the humans are involved. I'd rather have you deal with them, both because of your experience, and because I know you will be objective."

"What? He's gone political, sir?"

"So it seems. It's nothing overt, but it's definitely there. I was warned about him from back home, and we've all learned to keep our tails tucked up tight around him."

This was not good. We defenders have a long history of not getting involved in politics, but *some people* were picking up all sorts of negative habits from the humans. U'tdaPagrn hesitated and considered me closely for a moment, then added, "Another reason I asked for you is that you outrank him. That may come in handy if problems should arise."

"I...see." That was alarming, although I was careful not to show it. If U'tdaPagrn felt he didn't have complete control over the embassy defenders, then things must be seriously out of round. "So what do you have in mind, sir?"

"On this battleship matter? You have access to our intelligence assets, of course, and I have arranged for them to give you a complete update. You can call on them to do any searches or analysis you need. I will also arrange for you to meet with a human contact we have developed. That should be set up for you tomorrow afternoon."

"A human contact? Someone in deep?"

"Fairly deep." He gave me another uncomfortable look. "I'm

37

not thrilled with him, but he's L'datMparn's prize, so we might as well use him. In the mean time welcome back, I suppose. Go get settled in. I have some matters to discuss with K'deiTai."

"...but...mid-meal..." he sputtered as I left.

§

C'traBenla was waiting impatiently in the foyer amid our stacked luggage when I returned. "What is his *problem?*" she demanded. "Why did he have to jump on me?"

Great: I didn't need her going off on me along with everything else. "It was nothing, love. Don't knot your tail over it."

"He was rude!"

"That's how he is at times. You know how wound up he gets about human diplomacy."

She gave me a hurt look. "Can't he let go of the past? I didn't mean to do any harm."

"I know that, love, and so does he." I caressed her ears and gave her an imploring look. "Please...keep the peace. We'll only be here a short while, so let's not spend it squabbling."

She brooded on that, then nodded solemnly. "Yes, love."

§

I hunted up L'datMparn and had him assign a detail to haul our luggage to our temporary quarters, then we headed up ourselves. I wanted to stop at the Communications Circle on the second floor which, unfortunately, led us right past C'tra's old Cultural Attache office. When we left to return home, R'benTdan was the embassy's physical fitness instructor, but it seemed she moved into the Cultural Attaché spot as soon as we were gone. I shuddered at the thought of how our relations with the humans must have fared when M'tinDegan told me that.

The place was as cramped and cluttered as ever, with several sorting bins of the day's mail on the work table, and cases of envelopes and response literature tucked underneath. R'benTdan was busy with the steady flood of publicity requests when we arrived. She was as lean and athletic as ever, attractive if you like the predatory sort, and she was in a foul mood and ready to take on all comers. Her eyes lit up with an evil gleam when we came in.

"Well," she said to C'tra. "So you've returned to the scene of

38

your greatest triumph? It took some doing, but as you can see, I've managed to put the place in order since then."

Not a smart move to play on C'tra. "I can *see* that you've changed since responsibility was *forced* upon you," she replied coolly. "As I recall, your tail was the only thing you lifted back then."

R'benTdan gave her a frozen smile. "Sad to say I've been too busy with damage control, plus the pickings around here aren't the greatest. But then you'd know about that." She ran a hand over my shoulder. "Oh, my! I *like* these new 'Dark Gray' uniforms." She gave me a suggestive ear twitch. "They are *so* attractive. That look would turn any fem's head."

"Just be careful it doesn't come off," C'traBenla muttered with dripping sweetness. "It'd be a shame if you lost it."

"Well, I know you have things to do," I said quickly as I took C'tra's arm and herded her toward the door. "So we'll leave you to get on with it." The last thing I needed was for those two to get into a hissing contest: one more reason, if any was needed, why this assignment was going to be miserable.

§

Learnéds W'kiLap and T'apiDien were up to their usual antics when we got to the Communications Circle: herding it from the comfort of overstuffed belly cushions in 'the pit'. The place was busier than I remembered, with a couple hands of people assigned there for intelligence work. More desks and work stations had been crowded in, along with the mapmaking, instrument repair, and photo interpretation shops. The human teletypes were yammering away as usual, and four large screen televisions were displaying various news broadcasts. At least the place was cleaner than I remembered it.

"We heard you were coming back," W'kiLap greeted us.

"Oh? I'd like to know how, since we weren't informed of it until the day before we left."

"We have our ways." W'kiLap gave me a sinister leer.

"Our *mysterious* ways," T'apiDien added. "Spy stuff, you know."

"Yeah, I read about it in a cheap novel somewhere."

39

"Oooh, testy." T'apiDien gave W'kiLap a knowing ear twitch. "Sounds like you need some release time back home on d'enchia."

"He needs to wash that uniform, too. Talk about dingy gray!"

"And I'd swear he's putting on weight. Living high and fancy in the Staff are we?"

"It must be all those social functions; grazing the buffet tables, no?" C'tra chuckled at their banter, and her eyes gleamed.

"*Settling* into life-bonded bliss, no doubt."

"Some exercise is what he needs. I'm sure we can come up with a riot or a revolution..."

"...or a crazed bomber or two..."

"...or a panic-stricken human herd storming the gates..."

"...or even a diplomatic social."

"Go easy there! This is his first day back on the job!"

"Sink or swim." T'apiDien gave us a theatrical yawn. "He'll have to jump if he wants to run in this circle."

"All right you two," I groused. "I'm here about those two battleships, so let's cut the *x'mnnb'* and gallop."

"Oh, really, I'ei," she chided me. "You can be *so* serious."

"I'm here on serious business, love."

"We're already on it." W'kiLap headed over to their master work station at the end of the room and came back with a file folder. "U'tdaPagrn gave us the job weeks ago—strictly confidential, you understand. Our priceless L'datMparn doesn't know about this."

"Not that he can find his own tail anyway," T'apiDien grumbled.

I took the folder and leafed through it while C'tra and the two of them gossiped up a storm. There were several long range photos taken with our sky watch camera, shots taken from the courier, transcripts of intercepted e-mails and radio messages, and pages of written analysis. Skimming through it quickly, it looked like the humans were putting a substantial effort into those two hulls; enough that it was starting to affect their other construction. They obviously had some purpose in mind, but the one thing not included was some idea of what they intended for all their effort. That would figure.

40

"What is it about L'datMparn, anyway?" I asked after a bit. "Everyone seems afraid they'll crack their egg around him."

That sobered them both up, and they broke off their conversation with C'tra. "He's working for Ancient Z'keBalf," T'apiDien said. C'tra hissed at the name. "That's how he got assigned here: he's in league with the hard-liners in the Chamber."

I stared at them in dismay. "So he *has* gone political, Emm?"

"I'm afraid so," W'kiLap said. "It's nothing blatant, but you can tell. U'tdaPagrn doesn't trust him, and he's not very popular around here in general. There are rumors that he's informing on our people. There have been some *peculiar* unexplained policies implemented of late, and a couple of staffers were recalled for no reason we can see."

"And he's been reporting directly home without going through official channels," T'apiDien said. "Classified stuff even we don't have code keys for."

"Oh...great," I sighed. "That's just wrong. The 'Grays' have a two hundred and fifty year tradition of not getting involved in partisan politics."

"Well, all traditions come to an end, it seems."

"The Eldest will hear about this," I promised them.

§

Our luggage was already stacked against one wall of our assigned guest quarters on the third floor when we got there. C'tra started poking through it, but I was so weary and fed up that I flopped on the sleeping pad with a groan, and lay there watching her. "I don't know where you find the energy, love."

She paused and glanced at me. "You look a bit frazzled right now. Take a rest while I tidy up."

Ancestors, was I frazzled. Worse, this was one of those human sleeping pads with the metal springs in it, one of which was digging into my side; *so* typical of this whole adventure. The guest quarters are fancier than the rooms assigned to the staff, but new carpeting, paint, and improvised human furnishing couldn't disguise the two hundred plus years of this ancient crypt. At least we were near the staff lounge at the end of the east wing, so sanitary facilities weren't far away.

41

"All those stairs," I grumbled. Three flights of them, steep human stairs at that. "Up and down, up and down, every day. This gravity will ruin me for sure."

She came over and sprawled on the pad next to me. "We'll get used to it soon, love, like we did before."

"And to think the Eldest actually accused me of wanting to take a romantic cruise. You can tell he's never been here."

She gave me a little smile. "This *is* a romantic cruise to exotic, far away places off the beaten trail. You really know how to impress a fem."

That's one thing I love about her: for all her temperament, she comes through at moments like this which test so many service relationships.

"I'm sorry it's not the Thousand Falls."

She nibbled my ear affectionately. "We'll make the best of it," she purred. "What really matters is we're together. And as soon as you get through with your assignment, we'll spend some time playing the tourists."

I frowned at the memory of that file. "As soon as I get through with this assignment."

§

Another old tradition we started was still going strong. The welcoming feast began back during the early days of the embassy when every supply run brought urgently needed new snouts, not to mention desperately wanted fresh food. It became a tradition of greeting the newcomers, catching up on the gossip from home, and taking a break from the day to day tedium. That, and any excuse for a party is always welcome. In addition to the two of us, there were six replacement staffers and ten newcomers, which was all the excuse anyone needed.

The festivities started at evening meal, which was fancier and better attended than I remembered. There was quite a crowd, in fact. The cafeteria had changed since we saw it last. The original tables were replaced with some lower ones more suited to us, and the room redecorated in an Asian theme. The buffet was larger, with a new hot-and-chill bar piled with steaming goodies, plus a new drink dispenser.

I got off to a late start after matching ears over my mission plans with U'tdaPagrn and K'deiTai, and I was starving when I arrived. After twenty-four days on endurance rations, I *longed* for a good, hot meal. L'datMparn and his Worthy were there in full dress, which made them seem more out of place than usual, and there was a wide open space around them despite the crowd. They zeroed in on me the moment I appeared in the doorway, which was the last thing I needed.

"Good evening, sir. I trust you are settled in?" he greeted me with grating forced bravado.

"Managing." I wasn't in the mood for idle chatter with these two, *especially* with the buffet beckoning from across the room.

He exchanged nervous looks with his Worthy. "We were wondering if you heard about any policy matters which might affect this embassy, sir."

I paused and considered him at length, and noticed how anxious he seemed. They must be wondering if I was part of some countermove against his political tail-biting, and I was all too happy to take time out to stroke his paranoia. "Nothing I can discuss," I told him, severely.

"If it's a matter concerning this embassy..."

"I was sent to look into a *security* problem," I interrupted. "The matter is being addressed directly by the Staff."

"What might that problem be, sir?"

I gave him that chilly annoyed-superior-elder look. "It's a classified matter."

That worried him, although he tried not to show it. "Well, if I can be of any help, I will be happy to do so, sir."

"You have your duties," I said coolly. "This is a bigger issue which you don't need to know about."

"Ah...well, I will certainly make time tomorrow to consult with you on any local matters, sir," he said, carefully.

Good, I had his tail thoroughly knotted. "Tomorrow can take care of itself. For now, I am tired from the long haul, and I intend to have something to eat."

L'datMparn gave me a reproving look. "Yes, sir."

§

43

Nice try. No sooner did I lose L'datMparn, then Commander Lincoln Watanabi, the new Space Fleet liaison, intercepted me. He was average length, slender, and flawlessly groomed, and his complexion was so smooth that he seemed to be made of plastic.

"I am honored to meet you," he said, and bent over in some sort of greeting gesture. "It is a pleasure to greet one of the founders of interstellar diplomacy."

"Um...yes, pleased to meet you too, Commander," I muttered absent-mindedly. Across the room, the feeding frenzy at the buffet was in full gallop.

"I wonder how you would view the present diplomatic situation in light of the teachings of Sun Tzu?"

"Eh?" That stopped me in mid-stride, and I looked at him in confusion. "Sun Tzu?"

"A famed military thinker."

I had no idea what he was talking about. "I've...never met Sun Tzu, so I can't say."

"Indeed?" He offered just a hint of a smile at that. "You should read his work. I find his fifth principle especially relevant to the present strategic balance."

"Um...fifth principle?"

"Take, for example, the chrysanthemum: when subjected to drought, it withers, but recovers when given water."

"...chrysanthemum...?"

"Or perhaps the principle is best demonstrated by the seasonal migration of the ibis..."

...he went on like that for some time; the human had a rare talent for drivel while drawing me into the conversation in spite of myself. I was tempted to sluff him off, but a good rapport with the human fleet was essential, so I sacrificed for the cause. And a sore trial it was; I was *hungry*.

"...which is reflected in his victory at Ling Gni in 490 BC."

"Ah...."

"His eighth principle is demonstrated by the koi fish..."

He never let up; what it all meant baffled me.

"...which is the essence of his twelfth principle. Isn't that how your fleet views it?"

44

"...Um...we've...never encountered rivers in space..."

His snout lit up. "Ah! A brilliant metaphor! Then you grasp his ninth principle..."

Finally it got to be too much. The crowd at the buffet was thinning out, as was the selection remaining, and I was desperate. "...which ties in with Sun Tzu's fourth principle," he was saying. "Surely you can see the relevance in modern warfare?"

"You may be right, I'll have to read up on that." It was late, and my stomach was protesting. "If you will excuse me, Commander, I have matters to attend to." I cut out of there before he could bring up any more Sun Tzu, and headed for the buffet, which seemed as far away as d'enchia at the moment.

§

Agent Hyam Goldblum was the new APA liaison, and we collided about half-way across the cafeteria. I should know better. Like Commander Watanabi, he was average length and thin, but where Watanabi was smooth, his fur was dark, coarse, and seemingly uncontrollable. He was stoop-shouldered, and favored one leg from an old hatchling disease. For all that he was the Alliance's official spy in our midst, he was pleasant and easy to talk to. Too easy.

"My predecessor told me about you," he offered after we exchanged courtesies. "He said that if we should ever happen to meet, we could work together in confidence."

"Agent Roubidoux was a good friend," I said, wistfully. Across the room, the senior Banqueter was hanging the ladle over the buffet; the traditional sign that the kitchen was closed. I needed to get moving.

Goldblum looked around the room, then said, softly, "My superiors want me to find out about your visit here. You have a reputation at the Ministry, and they wonder why you have come back so soon."

I paused in mid-step, and gave him a nervous smile to cover my alarm. I had no idea that the Alliance Protective Agency took a particular interest in me, which was one more thing I could do without. "I didn't think anyone cared. It's a positive reputation, I hope?"

45

He grinned awkwardly in turn. "I suppose it depends on your point of view. Still, my superiors are pressing me about you. I hope you'll understand."

I was impressed by his openness as much as I was worried about the official scrutiny. I would have to be careful to avoid arousing their suspicions, but oddly enough, his candor gave me an idea on how to deflect that suspicion.

"About why I am here," I told him in a conspiratorial whisper. "My successor is not living up to *expectations*. There have been...questions...about some of his activities." He glanced curiously at L'datMparn, on the other side of the room. "Officially they sent me here on an inspection tour, but between you and me and the hidden microphones, I'm here to measure his tail."

Goldblum seemed confused. "Measure his... Oh. I see."

C'traBenla came drifting over with a plate from the buffet. "Where have you been, I'ei? You're missing late-meal." I stared longingly at that plate, which was *heaped* with exotic alien goodies; the aroma of fried onions was torment. "You really should try this ocra. It's delicious..."

"Well there you are, First Degree!" R'benTdan interrupted just as C'tra was about to offer me a bite.

"Oy," Goldblum muttered.

"It *is* First Degree, isn't it?" She crowded a bit too close for comfort, and gave me a blatant once-over. "It should be for someone as *capable* as you."

Goldblum sighed, but said nothing. C'traBenla gave her an icy glare. I took her hand to restrain her from doing anything rash. "As you noticed in my grotto earlier," R'benTdan snarked as she gave C'tra a cold smile, "Real quality shines through. Desperate effort isn't enough; it takes talent to do things right." She ran her hand over my arm suggestively. "I can see you appreciate *real* skill."

"*Some* people prefer quality over mere quantity," C'tra said. "Endless repetition becomes *so* tedious."

R'benTdan gave her a hostile look. "And some people expect too much from *amateurs*," she said in dripping sarcasm. "Is it any wonder they become disappointed?"

"You would know about disappointment, having seen so *much* of it." C'tra waved her plate in agitation, spilling a bit of sauce on the floor. My stomach protested in desperation. "*Someone needs* more than enthusiasm to get it right!"

"Someone with *professional* training, you mean?"

Wrong thing to say! C'tra lost it, dropped her plate, splattering those delicious goodies all over the floor, and tore into R'benTdan. "You *l'cc'vn vr'meol!* You're nothing but rancid *tra'taj...*"

Time to move before war broke out! I grabbed C'tra's arm and coaxed her away by main force before she could explode. "What are you doing?" she demanded as I dragged her through the onlookers. "Are you going to let that...that...*un'tdar* take such a tone with me?"

"She's trying to stir up trouble. You know how she is."

"I'll knot her tail around her neck and choke her with it!" she fumed. "The *nerve* of that *M'mendoch!*"

That was what I was afraid of. "Don't let her get to you, love. You're better than this."

She glared at me for a bit, then calmed down. "You're right. I'm sorry." She nuzzled my cheek affectionately. "But if you touch her, I'll have your ears, love," she murmured.

"I...ouch!...don't doubt that for an instant, dearest," I muttered through clenched teeth. I shouldn't have been surprised when she nipped my ear, seeing how territorial she could be. Still, that was unfair since I wasn't about to risk her love—or her temper—for a casual toss.

"It is so *stuffy* in here." She threw a venomous glance at R'benTdan, and headed for the terrace with me forced to tag along rather than risk a further confrontation.

§

She was soon engaged in another gossip-fest, and I made one more try for the buffet, which was starting to look rather threadbare. But as luck would have it, I ran into M'tinDegan and our two computer *'v'thorble*, who stuffed themselves and moved on to the *V'liz* and *'sti'eit* stage. "I'm glad you're still alive," M'tinDegan greeted me. "It looked like C'traBenla was going to destroy her and everything in between."

47

"Those two are poison," I grumbled. "They were when we were here before, and it looks to be even worse this time. I *really* don't need to be caught between the two of them."

"She's an ear collector," T'apiDien said. "She goes after those who aren't interested, and keeps at it until she wears them down."

"Wonderful." I winced from a hunger pang, which reminded me that I needed to gallop.

"There are even rumors that she's getting it with some of the humans," W'kiLap said.

That shocked me, halting me in mid-step again. "She wouldn't...? Who would start such a rumor?"

"I...wouldn't know, I'm sure." He ear-twitched in disdain.

"You can blame V'koBilen for her," T'apiDien said. "He has some eccentric ideas about diplomatic service personnel."

Those two should talk. "And to think I came here for matters of life and death," I sighed. "I sincerely hope our relations with the humans isn't as tail-knotted as this place is."

"Welcome home," M'tinDegan said with a sardonic grin.

"It *is* good to have the old herd back," T'apiDien said, wistfully. "Things have been so *dull* lately. No riots or revolutions or natural disasters; plenty of opportunities for you two to liven things up."

"Her in particular," W'kiLap added, and nodded toward C'tra.

"The one thing I am *not* looking for is any adventures. I just want to get this assignment over with as painlessly as possible, and get back to d'enchia on the next ship."

"A commendable philosophy. But remember our mantra..."

"...'Things never go just a *bit* wrong in interstellar diplomacy'..." the three chanted together.

"What's so curst annoying is all the petty intrigue going on around here," I grumbled as I turned to go. "It's just what we need; everyone snooping and prying into everyone's business."

"Worse than a diplomatic social," W'kiLap muttered.

"You want to keep your ears down around the Commander in particular," M'tinDegan said. "He's from the new fleet intelligence arm; something they created especially for us. Don't let his inane prattle fool you; he has a gift for wheedling information out of people unawares."

I halted again, and studied the Commander morosely. How much did I gave away in our little chat? "I swear I could write a book. It sure wasn't like this when we were assigned here."

"But then, we aren't under siege by the Anti-techs these days, so perhaps it's a fair trade off."

I sighed in frustration. "Perhaps. Now if you'll excuse me, I *really* want to get to the buffet."

§

M'tinDegan's ocra was all that was left when I *finally* got there, and it was cold and soggy at that. I wasn't impressed with it, but after twenty-four days on endurance rations, I wasn't picky. Plus I *knew* this was how the rest of my time here would go, so I resigned myself to the inevitable, and ate.

*****

"Unexpected Encounters"
(Related by Defender I'eiBida)

U'tdaPagrn had my meeting with his deep contact set up by the next morning as promised, so we borrowed an embassy car and headed to our rendezvous in Geneva. Despite my misgivings, he caught on at once to the idea of C'traBenla as diplomatic cover, and set the meeting at *Señor* Vargas' tailor shop. There was no holding her back in any event, so off we went.

As I remembered it, *Señor* Vargas' shop was everything you'd expect from a cheap human spy thriller: a run down little place down a quiet side street in an out-of-the-way neighborhood. The street was empty, and the neighborhood wasn't much. The building was shabby and worn, with a cracked concrete sidewalk and a couple of small trees in front of the dingy window. How he ever got involved with the embassy in the first place is beyond me. Things had changed since we were here last year.

§

"Oh!" C'traBenla let out a startled squeak when she saw our destination. *Señor* Vargas' new habitat was a large building on one of the main streets of a trendy shopping district. The front was all glass and ornate brick, with fine suits and gowns on dummies surrounded by samples of exotic cloth, jewelry, and accessories. A limousine pulled up to the curb as we were getting ourselves together, and deposited a matronly human fem who headed straight for the door without giving us a second glance. From the fixated look on her snout, it seemed that *Señor* Vargas' reputation as Clothier To The Universe made him a hot property among the smart set. Nor was she the only one; the street was crowded with arrivals and departures. Business must have grown indeed if he could afford the rent on this place.

"Thankfully he's still here," C'traBenla said. "I'd hate for this trip to go to waste." I supposed she meant the trip from d'enchia, which didn't help my sense of foreboding.

"That's good news," I grumbled absently as I looked around for any suspicious humans. The street was busy, and the sidewalks swarmed with Geneva's upper crust out to enjoy a mild spring day.

I tried to seem casual, which wasn't easy under the circumstances. If we were being shadowed, it would be hard to spot them in this stampede.

§

The inside was equally ominous: bright and colorful, well lit, music playing in the background, little wrought iron tables and chairs clustered around an expresso machine in one corner, definitely high-toned. The front of the store was lined with display counters supervised by a young human fem, while the rear half held racks of cloth and large tables where a couple hands' worth of people were hard at work. The room buzzed with the sounds of sewing machines and ringing telephones, and a swarm of customers were perused the accessories, discussed fashions with the staff, or were being fitted.

Señor Vargas was short and slender for a human mal, but what he lacked in size, he made up in sheer exuberance. 'Excitable' doesn't begin to say it with him, and his theatrics were well known among the embassy staff.

"*Madre de Dios*, but I have missed you, *señorita*...or is it *señora*?" he greeted us in grand style, arms open to welcome us. "Geneva has been so *quiet* since you left."

"*Hola, Señor* Vargas," she purred. "It seems you are busy these days."

"Busy?" That set him off. "*¡Si!* Busy by day, busy by night, busy on the weekends, busy on the holidays!" He threw his hands up in despair. "I work my poor fingers to the bone, and what thanks do I receive for my sacrifices?"

"You appear to be doing well," C'tra said, judiciously. "You must be pleased to have so many customers."

"*¡Si!* So *many* customers!" He grabbed two hands full of his fur in his angst. "But not one of them has the wit to understand my creations!"

"It seems that Geneva's elite have taken you to hearts. Surely they *must* appreciate your work to be so devoted."

"Geneva's elite? Bah! *¡Ciegos! ¡Sin eistilos!*" He grabbed a pile of half-finished dresses and hurled them at us in agitation. "They deserve to shop in thrift stores!"

51

C'traBenla gave me an amused ear twitch. They played this game before, many times. "The embassy staff have always appreciated your efforts, *Señor*."

"Bah! Your embassy is staffed by peons!" He went back to pulling at his fur while the employees and customers studiously ignored him. "Suits! Trousers! Uniforms! Peons!" he shouted. "How quickly my creations are forgotten!"

"I can assure you, *Señor*, your work has been *the* talk in social circles back on d'enchia."

That mollified him somewhat, and his snout broke into a grin. I'd heard some of the gossip going around those social circles, but didn't offer further details.

"The scarlet sequins..."

"Stops them in their tracks, every time."

He came back from wherever his dreamy state took him, and focussed on her again. "*Señora*, you *must* allow me to create a new treasure for you!" He grabbed her hand and tugged imploringly, which would get anyone else knocked on their tail. "It shall be my greatest creation!"

"Oh, I really can't..." she demurred with glaring false modesty. My poor knotted tail! Why else would she be here?

"*¡Si!* You cannot wear the same thing over and over. What is the drama in that? The passion? The grandeur? You were meant to make a statement! *How* can you do that wearing soiled rags?"

"Well...I'm not sure we can..."

"The softest fabrics! The finest lines! Here!" He grabbed one of the fashion magazines on a nearby table, shoved it at her, and pointed to a human model wearing a flowing gown. "Imagine this, pale blue and silver against your bronze complexion!"

I pretended to be bored, and watched the activity in the shop, looking for anyone watching us. Several of the customers were, but none of them seemed likely APA operatives. Perhaps they were enjoying *Señor* Vargas' show, which goes to say how *easily* humans can be entertained.

"Hmmm, that *is* pretty," she mused as she poured over the magazine. "But I know you are *so* busy, and I hate to be a bother." She loved to haggle, and was damned good at it. Hopefully she

52

could knock the price down to something our budget could survive. I ear-twitched an urgent caution to her, but she ignored me, as usual when she was on the prowl.

"Nothing else matters! These fools can wait. I implore you, *mi bella*! I shall dress you in flowing water! I shall crown you with raindrops!"

"Well, actually...our budget..." She pondered the magazine with a calculating set to her ears. I could hear the wheels going round and round in her head. *Our budget* indeed: this was going to hurt.

"A masterpiece! A treasure! Save me, *señora!*"

"I...uh...hmmm..." She perused the magazine some more. "I would love to, you do such fine work...but..." She closed the magazine with a despairing sigh.

Normally I would have tried to intervene, but she was unwittingly giving me the perfect cover for my rendezvous. So with visions of our budget in flames, I eased away and drifted toward the dressing rooms in the back of the building.

"A lovely velour, *señora*." He rushed over, grabbed a roll of light blue cloth off a nearby rack, and shoved it at her. "Soft as down! Can anything be lovelier?"

"Hmmm, oh, that is nice..."

I glanced around to see if anyone noticed me. The employees were all hard at work—they were well familiar with his gyrations —and I didn't see anyone who looked like a human APA agent. My paranoia was at an all-time high, driven by their increasingly verbal bartering

He snatched up another roll of darker blue. "And a cape of the finest wool, woven in *Espania* especially for you."

"Um...oh...that is lovely..." She fingered the fabric with feigned reluctance, but the set of her ears was not promising.

I pretended to browse among the piles of cloth as I worked my way toward the back of the building. Perhaps I could get her creation written into the intel budget as operating expense?

"And silver lace! The finest!"

"Hmmm..." She pondered the roll of trim he shoved at her. "With silver buttons?" The battle was begun in earnest.

53

"But of course!"

The workmen were busy at their tasks, and the customers were enjoying the spectacle. No one noticed me.

"And perhaps a touch of fine embroidery at the sleeves?"

"*Señora*, you have the soul of a poet!"

"But I don't know *where* you can find the time for proper fittings, not to mention our budget..."

"I shall *make* the time for you, *mi bella!* This is no task for lackeys! You shall receive my *personal* attention to every detail."

"But the cost..."

"Hang the cost! I cannot allow my finest customer to go without proper recognition. Pity me, *señora*! The honor of my humble establishment is at stake!"

"Well if we are to do you justice, there *must* be a contrasted lining, in light grey, of course," she said with mock severity. "The honor of your establishment cannot accept half measures, can it? But the price of such fine work..."

I couldn't stand it any more. All I wanted was to get this *over with* and get out of there before we wound up in debt for the rest of my career. I slipped through the curtain, and made my way down the narrow aisle of dressing booths to the booth at the far end.

§

The dressing booth was no more than a cubicle with a curtain over the doorway, a full length mirror on one wall, and a low shelf to sit on. It may have been adequate for the vertical humans, but it was far too small for us. I scrunched uncomfortably in one corner, tried to keep my tail from poking through the curtain, and waited nervously. I could hear the subdued murmur of voices and the occasional jingle of the door bell beyond the wall, punctuated by outbursts from *Señor* Vargas. I wondered distractedly how much damage this black operation would do to our budget...

This is serious, better keep focussed. I went over my questions once again, as I intended to keep this short and to the point, then *gallop* back to the embassy and home. Hopefully I could get the answers the Eldest wanted, and get *off* this world. Hopefully they would be good answers. Either way, they would owe me big time for this *x'mnnb'*.

54

For some reason I craved a huge bowl of *uf'thoka*, not my favorite at most times. But this wasn't most times, and I doubt if I could have stomached anything just then. *Stay focussed on the mission!* I was getting jittery. What could I do if I didn't get definitive answers? I'd have to get our two computer *'v'thorble* working on an internet search...I should have done that yesterday...

There was a faint noise, and my pulse jumped. I listened hard for the next few minutes. Nothing. I tried to relax without much success. The Eldest *better* come through with some serious release time after this. I worried about the diplomatic consequences of my getting caught. I worried about the answers, and what they could mean to diplomatic relations. I worried about C'tra out there all alone...with *Señor* Vargas and a room full of beautiful cloth...

It must have been only a few more minutes, although it felt like forever before I heard a soft noise from the next cubicle, and a pair of human legs dressed in neat trousers and shoes appeared in the gap under the partition. The trousered legs hesitated, fidgeting for some time before there was a single tap of knuckles rapping gently on the wall. It was our contact! I hesitated for a moment, then gave a single rap in turn. Harmless enough: nothing anyone would suspect unless they knew what to look for. I hate this spy nonsense, but considering how the human authorities would react if we were discovered, I couldn't be too careful. A moment of tense silence, then the shoes shifted uneasily, and two soft taps came on the wall. I answered with two taps in turn, as instructed. There was more anxious fidgeting, then the shoes moved out of sight. The curtain parted, and our contact entered.

"Pierre?"

"I'eiBida?" Agent Roubidoux was as startled as I.

*****

"An Ominous Development"
(Related by Arbiter U'tdaPagrn)

There was a knock on the door to my grotto, and K'deiTai and M'tinDegan came in. K'deiTai looked askance at me when he saw what I was doing. "Are you still fooling with that thing?"

I was a bit annoyed by the interruption, but also a bit relieved since it gave me an excuse to leave off that damnable human hand game. I had been at it most of the morning to the detriment of more important tasks, twisting the little plastic cube back and forth trying to get the colored panels lined up. It had been preying on my mind for months, and was slowly driving me *er'trxxda*.

"This *thing* is some kind of fiendish human plot!" I set it at arm's length on my desk and tried unsuccessfully to ignore it, again. "I can't put it down."

"Did you ever stop to think of what will happen if you get that thing solved?" K'deiTai asked, sourly.

"I'm sure I shall go stark, raving *er'trxxda,* and start foaming at the mouth and biting my tail. Not that I need to worry about *solving* the Ancestorless thing!" I hefted it in frustration and tossed it across the room. It bounced off the far wall but didn't break, again, more's the pity. "And what's worse is there is a young clerical in my staff who can whip through it in no time."

"Interesting." M'tinDegan gave me that thoughtful-scientific-musing look he used to poke fun at people's pretenses. "A most *curious* example of psycho-social interaction between species." He glanced at K'deiTai. "I'm sure this could become a valuable scientific paper on the stresses of interstellar diplomatic duty."

"I had my run-ins with that while I was here," K'deiTai grumbled. "I never did solve the *er'trxxda* thing."

M'tinDegan tisk-tisked, and gave me a sardonic look. "This could be serious. We may need to operate."

"Well you can start by cutting out the *x'mnnb'!*" I snapped.

"Who knows?" He gave me a sardonic ear twitch. "Perhaps they'll name a new neurosis in your memory."

"That's not *exactly* how I want to be immortalized in the history books!"

56

"Have you spoken to Learnéd V'NegNder about it?" K'deiTai asked.

"Oh, please, I have enough problems!" V'NegNder was our new embassy psychologist, and the life of the party when he'd been drinking. "And *please* remember to talk to V'koBilen when you get back. They need to be more careful about who they pick for duty here."

My Aide stuck his snout in through the grotto door. "You have a priority phone call from the humans."

"Oh? And what does the Chancellor want now?" I asked in weary resignation.

"It's someone from the human Defense Ministry."

"Well...why bother me with some routine matter?"

"They said it was urgent. They need to speak with you at once."

I looked to the other two uncertainly. "That's...out of protocol...isn't it?"

"Significantly," K'deiTai said. "The humans are very conscious of relations between their civil and military leadership."

I pondered that for a moment with an uneasy feeling, then reached for the phone.

§

My Aide looked at me expectantly when I came out of the grotto. "So? What did they want?" he asked as if he hadn't been listening on the other line. His rhetorical question was simply his way of digging for my reaction.

I hesitated for a moment, uncertain how to answer. "They didn't tell me," I said at last. "They just asked me to come over as soon as possible. They said it's urgent."

"Arbiter?" It was Agent Goldblum, head of the human liaison office. "I have the limo ready, sir."

"Thank you." Their giving their people an ears-up was another ominous development. "Do you know what this is about?"

"Oy, do they tell me?" He seemed perplexed; more reason to worry.

"Could it be some sort of trouble?" my Aide asked. "An incident, perhaps?"

57

"I can't think of any other reason for them to call. But something like that would be handled through the Chancellory." I brooded over the mystery for a moment. "K'deiTai, M'tinDegan, I want you to come with me. Your input may be useful."

"Certainly," M'tinDegan said. K'deiTai gave me a sour expression, but said nothing.

"Since this is from the Defense Ministry, should I alert L'datMparn as well?" my Aide asked, reluctantly. None of us was thrilled about bringing him into this.

"They wanted me to bring our defender liaison..." A thought struck me, and I reached for the telephone.

*****

"The Plot Thickens"
(Related by Defender I'eiBida)

"Pierre?" I was flabbergasted that Agent Roubidoux would be our operative. "What are you doing here?"

He seemed deeply embarrassed. "It is all your fault!" he cried in anguish.

"I...what do you mean? What did I do?"

He lowered his voice to an agitated whisper. "Do you not remember? When you first arrived at Singapore? How the Arbiter and the rest of you forced me to tell you about the Anti-techs?" I had to think for a bit before recalling how we pressured him into revealing the source of an embarrassing covert action on our first day there. "Your successor has blackmailed me for one moment's indiscretion!"

"I'm sorry, Pierre! I had no idea they'd do this. I noted it in my report, but I never thought they would use it against you." That was one more good reason to see about the priceless L'datMparn when we got home. I never did like him, anyway.

He considered me unhappily. "I cannot blame you, I'ei3ida. You were simply doing your duty. It is my own stupid fault for letting my guard down like that." I always admired his ethical sensitivity, but this was taking it a bit far, I thought. "I have given them a few minor matters under pressure," he added. "But I have avoided revealing anything significant. Do not ask me to become a traitor, I'eiBida."

"Ancestors forbid!"

He gave me a mournful smile. "I know you are my friend, I'eiBida."

"So...are you still at the embassy?"

"No. I transferred to diplomatic intelligence last month to try to distance myself from them."

"Well, if you get a chance to drop by, C'traBenla would love to see you."

"Ah, *La belle enchanteresse.*" He sighed, and gave me a dreamy smile. "Those were the good times. You two are doing well, I hope?"

59

"Quite well, thank you." No sense in laying my problems on him. "Look...this...may not be the best time to bring this up, but I was sent here to see what your fleet is doing with those battleships." Pierre gave me a pained look. "You know what a mess we're all in for if your Alliance has decided to renege on the First Accord," I hastened to explain. "If they are up to something, now is the time to call them on it, put a stop to it. No one wants a confrontation."

He studied me morosely, then let out a deep sigh. "You may reassure your superiors, I'eiBida. We cannot afford our present shipbuilding program, nor are the Chancellory such fools as to invite a war against your superior numbers. I hear they are doing upkeep on those two cores to protect them from hard vacuum."

This was as awkward as *cc'v'renk*. "Do they plan to complete them in the long run? I have to ask, Pierre."

"*Mon Deus!*" He hesitated, then lowered his voice again. "It will take us twenty years to complete the construction authorized by the First Accord! And even then we shall be outnumbered three to one!" Then he calmed down somewhat. "Ivan said something about building two large transports with those cores, later."

That made sense, seeing how critically imbalanced earth's fleet was. Their limited shipbuilding capacity was entirely committed to their defense forces. They had just three small transports, which weren't enough to sustain their two colonies, not to mention their embassy on d'enchia. They started construction on two huge warships while we were here the first time, but cancelled them as part of the First Accord. They were still in orbit, parked near their Space Dock, complete to the extent of the central columns, reactors, and engines, and one had part of its capacitor installed. Converting them into large transports would be both desirable and economical. Confirmation from Commander Rostokovich, the former embassy Space Fleet liaison, made it even more plausible. That was a huge relief, not just because we weren't faced with a diplomatic crisis, but also because my mission here was complete. It looked like C'traBenla and I could spend some time together after all playing the tourist for the next twenty days before heading back to Singapore and home.

60

"*Please* do not ask any more of me, I'eiBida."

"Of course, Pierre," I hastened to assure him. "I'm sorry about what has happened. I'll do whatever I can to..." My phone was buzzing. "...*l'cc'vn!* Yes? What?"

"Where are you right now, I'eiBida?" It was Arbiter U'tdaPagrn, and he sounded tense.

I hesitated, with an nervous glance at Agent Roubidoux, then answered cautiously. "I'm at the tailor shop, sir, like I mentioned yesterday."

"Very well." He caught my veiled hint at once. "I need you to report to the human Defense Ministry right away."

"Sir?" My attention was interrupted when Pierre's phone began beeping as well.

"Something's come up. They didn't tell me what, but they want to see me and our defender liaison right away. There must have been an incident."

Wonderful, *just* as things were looking up. I should know better by now. "At the Defense Ministry? Wouldn't this be handled through the Chancellory?"

"I don't understand it either, but they said it is urgent I don't like the taste of it."

"What about L'datMparn, sir?"

"I want you there instead, for reasons we talked about earlier." That was not good. U'tdaPagrn's distrust of L'datMparn must go deeper than I realized if he intended to keep the local defenders out of the circle on something like this. "Get over there right away, I'eiBida."

Agent Roubidoux interrupted. "I have to go, I'eiBida." I glanced at him as he was putting his phone back in his pocket. He seemed worried, too. "It is good to see you again." He gave me a nervous smile, then slipped out through the curtain.

I turned back to matters at hand. "Ah...yes, Arbiter. I'll be there right away."

§

C'traBenla and *Señor* Vargas were at it hot and heavy when I came out of the back room. "I'eiBida, isn't this lovely?" She waved the pale blue cloth at me. "It's so soft and..."

61

"Come on." I grabbed her arm and dragged her toward the door. "Something's come up. We're leaving."

"...what? I'ei...please excuse us *Señor* Vargas..." She protested all the way out to the street as I plowed grimly on. "...I'eiBida, what are you doing? Was that Agent Roubidoux I saw a minute ago?"

"I haven't seen him," I muttered distractedly.

"But he was right there...

"He was buying a suit." I hustled her toward the embassy limo, which was already running, with the APA driver holding the door open for us.

"But...my new gown..."

"It's lovely."

She finally rebelled when we reached the limo. "I'eiBida, *what* is this all about?"

"There's some sort of trouble. I want you with me until I can get you back to the embassy."

"Trouble? With the humans? What can it..." She was interrupted as another human orbital shuttle passed low overhead on final approach to the airport.

"Oh, great," I muttered. There must be something seriously wrong if they were landing shuttles, plural, in Geneva.

"Aren't they supposed to go to Singapore?" She turned to me and asked, "I'eiBida, *what* is going on here?"

"No time. Get in." I shoved her unceremoniously into the back, and snapped, "Take us to the Defense Ministry," to our driver.

§

Everything seemed ordinary enough when we reached the Defense Ministry. The building was one of those huge, ornate stone piles the humans favor for their public circles, with rows of cast stone pillars across the front, and statues of large, ferocious animals on either side of a broad stairway. The peacekeeper security was alert and cautious. I had to surrender my sidearm, but our embassy passes got us through the front door. We were met in the rotunda by a familiar snout.

"Commander Rostokovich! What is this all about?"

62

"I'eiBida! Good. I hear you are back." He seemed nervous, but pleased to see us. The sight of him, rugged and burly as ever, was reassuring in turn. If things were going bad, at least we had people we could relate to, and Ivan was a definite human-of-action. But right then he was agitated, pacing back and forth, slapping his fist into his other hand, his footsteps echoing off the ceiling. For all that I trusted him, his obvious tension worried me. "I wait for Arbiter to arrive, then I take you to the Admiral."

"What? MacKenna? He's here?"

That wasn't good either. The human Admiral was our number one nightmare, and with good reason. He was a soldier all his adult life, all through the Collapse, and the years of chaos which followed. He was ninety years old then, with over seventy years of military experience in every conceivable situation. He chased us in circles with next to nothing all through the Contact Crisis, and we on the Staff were in awe of his skill and cunning. He was old and feeble now, and pretty much kept to Singapore Space Port to avoid the headaches of dealing with the Alliance bureaucracy. Him straying far from home was good reason to worry.

"*Da.* He came yesterday in a shuttle. As soon as... There you are, Arbiter!"

I turned, and saw U'tdaPagrn and K'deiTai coming in the front door with M'tinDegan in tow, accompanied by their APA embassy security herd.

"Good day, Commander," U'tdaPagrn said, crossly. "What is this all about?" He and K'deiTai were both irritable, and I couldn't blame them. This whole mystery was a bit unnerving.

"You must speak to Admiral, sir. He will give you complete briefing." And on that ominous note, the Commander led us back into the building and up one of those damnably slow elevators to the Space Fleet circle.

§

The fifth floor of the Defense Ministry was the nominal center of the human Space Fleet, but it was half deserted since most of their essential functions were concentrated at Singapore safely away from the Alliance bureaucracy. A few offices were open, with a handful of clericals and a few Space Fleet peacekeepers at

63

various tasks, but most of the floor was deserted or used for storing records. The corridors were dusty and unlit, although faint voices came from a conference room which the Commander lead us toward down one hall.

U'tdaPagrn cornered me as soon as he could, and gestured furtively at the Commander. "Did he tell you anything?" he demanded in a hoarse undertone.

"No, sir," I whispered. "But what I've seen thus far worries me."

"Me too." He considered for a moment, then, "I hate surprises like this, *especially* when they involve the humans."

"What worries me is this irregular line of communication," M'tinDegan said. "We have process in place, why the deviation?"

"Good point. This doesn't sound promising."

K'deiTai paused as he passed. "What is *she* doing here?" he demanded.

"We were out together when I got the call."

K'deiTai gave her his best sour look, discreetly. "*Please* keep her under control!" he begged me. "This could be serious."

"I'll try, sir."

"This can't be good." He shook his head in dismay, then hurried down the hall after the Commander, with us following.

§

Admiral MacKenna was unimpressive to look at him. He was short and slight and shrunken with age, the tip of his snout was broken and healed crookedly many years ago, and there was an old scar on his left cheek. He moved with the painful stiffness of the old, and needed a stick to get around. He was seated in a chair when we arrived, attended by his Aide, Leftenant Hythe-Morrison, who fussed over him mightily.

He pondered us as we came in. "I know you," he said to me. "Can't recall the name."

"T'eiBida, sir. I commanded the embassy security detail during the First Accord negotiations."

"Yes, I remember now." His voice was rough and thin. I had to strain to hear him. "Getting too damned old, memory is going to pot. You stopped by my office in Singapore a couple times."

64

"Courtesy calls, Admiral."

"Hmmm, yes." He leaned on his stick, and stared off at nothing, lost in his musing. "We don't practice those niceties any more. Damn shame. It was different back when I was your age." He shook his head sadly. "This old world just isn't the same now, you know?" He came back from his reverie, and glanced at the other humans. "I believe you all know each other?"

"*Da*, Admiral," Rostokovich answered. Then to us, "I am on Space Fleet staff now."

In addition to Commander Rostokovich, there was another familiar snout: Night Eagle, now a lieutenant of the human Space Marines. "And I'm still plugging away with the 5001st," he added.

"I am pleased to meet all of you, but I am most concerned with this mystery," U'tdaPagrn said. "Can you enlighten us, Admiral?"

"All we know is what Captain Morgan told me," he grumbled. "She's got a wild hare up her ass. Last I looked, the 'Marco Polo' was coming in recklessly fast. They've probably rendezvoused by now, if they didn't plow into Orbit Dock. This is hotter'n hell, and it involves the humans *and* Ic'nichi, so she said. She insisted on meeting here rather than at Singapore to save you travel time."

That was not good. If the Admiral was our greatest nightmare, Captain Morgan came in a close second. She was the field commander of the human fleet, proxy to the Admiral, and according to the dossier I assembled on her, she suffered from severe psychological problems. She was a relentless, brittle, driving martinet, symptoms of what the humans call post-traumatic stress', and from the little I knew about her, she was not one to take lightly. If she felt four days' travel was too great a delay, then whatever her mysterious problem was, it must be bad.

"Couldn't this be handled by telephone?" U'tdaPagrn grumbled. "No doubt this has disrupted your operations more than ours."

The Admiral pondered for a bit, and his snout took on a worried look. "My guess is she feels this mystery is so hot that we can't depend on communications security. I can't see who she's trying to keep it from, though. I'm sure you could intercept any communications you wanted, but this is meant for you anyway."

"Is probably news vultures, sir," Rostokovich said.

MacKenna frowned. "Hmmm, yes. Which means she's worried about a panic if this mystery gets out."

"It seems to me landing shuttles in Geneva would raise more interest than a routine conference call," U'tdaPagrn said.

The Admiral sighed. "Believe me, Arbiter, *nothing* Captain Morgan or I do is considered routine by the media." There was a knock, and Agent Roubidoux came in. MacKenna eyed him wearily. "Glad you could make it, Agent. It just goes to prove what I've always said, the spooks are the last to know."

"I was in a meeting, sir." Pierre gave me a guarded look, which I returned. "May I ask what this is about, Admiral?"

"Sure, if you want to." MacKenna leaned on his stick with a weary expression. "But don't expect an answer until Captain Morgan gets here."

As the humans say, speak of the Devil and she will appear. The door opened abruptly, and the much discussed Captain Morgan came in. That was the first time I saw her in person, and she was a bit of a shock. She wasn't much taller than the Admiral, lean, middle-aged, and her steel gray fur was cut short. She was wearing human service utilities, and seemed ordinary enough— except for the icy chill in her eyes, and the tension in her posture. She was wound up like a spring ready to snap.

"All right, Captain," MacKenna growled. "You've raised stink from Singapore to d'enchia, dragged my Aide out of his comfortable office, and got the Geneva Airport Authority shittin' bricks. You want our attention, you got it. So give us your song and dance, and make it good."

"I received another message from J J Ballas, sir."

I happened to glance at MacKenna, and that clearly startled him. "Good enough," he muttered at last. "So what did he say?"

"It was a brief contact, like always, but...he...said..." Her voice drifted away, she sagged, and stared off at nothing.

"Captain?" MacKenna studied her uncertainly as she stared off into the distance. Hythe-Morrison reached out to take her arm. "No, don't," MacKenna cautioned him. We watched in nervous silence, wondering what was going on here as she stood there limp and motionless. It was several seconds before she stirred again.

66

"...they'as some new folks moving' inta th' neighba'hood, Honeylamb," she went on at last as she stared lifelessly at nothing. Her voice was completely changed: slower, deeper, with a soft, liquid accent; definitely a human mal. "They ain't nice folks, not like folks 'round heah."

I realized that my vision was blurring; Captain Morgan seemed to fade out of focus. I blinked my eyes to try to clear them, and her image shifted. Overlaying her was a faint outline of a human mal: large and heavyset, with dark skin and white head fur. He shook his head, and regarded each of us with sad eyes.

"They's gonna be trouble come of it." His voice came from her lips as she synched along with him. "You need t' get ready to fight 'em. An' you be sure t' tell them Ic'nichi folks. They's yo' friends, an' you can count on 'em t' help."

"Captain..." MacKenna said, but she ignored him.

"You be careful, Honeylamb." The image faded, she sagged again, then came back from whatever trance she was in. "...a-and then he...vanished before I could ask anything more."

The whole scene left us stunned. "Admiral, I am at a loss here," U'tdaPagrn said at last. "We need to be brought into your circle on this J J Ballas."

"Yeah, you do." MacKenna glanced at Captain Morgan, who was staring at the wall in a daze. "You all right, Captain?"

"...ah...sir?" She was groggy and disoriented, and looked around vaguely trying to see where that question came from.

"Help her." The Admiral's Aide and Night Eagle guided her gently to a chair. "Captain? You with us?"

Reviving from that trance was an effort on her part, but she was finally able to focus on us. "Um...yes, sir. It takes a lot out of me."

MacKenna watched her with obvious concern for a few seconds more, than settled in his chair, and turned his attention to us.

"Okay, then. About a year ago, the Captain here reported a contact with an unknown alien. She has had more contacts since then, but they have been few and brief. According to her, they appear as dream sequences or hallucinations. That...image we saw

67

must have come from her memory: an old blues musician named J J Ballas, who she knew as a child in the refugee camps. Apparently, they use that image to communicate with us, although this is the first time anyone other than her has seen it. Someone around here coined the term 'Dreamsingers', and you can see the connection."

"I...see..." U'tdaPagrn mumbled. "If I am not mistaken, Admiral, I believe this is covered under Part Fourteen of the Second Accord, relating to joint responses to new contacts?"

"An Accord which hasn't been ratified yet, not that you are wrong. I wanted to tell you as a show of good faith, but my superiors decided to hold onto it at the time since the First Accord hadn't been ratified then."

"Do you have any idea who these Dreamsingers are?" K'deiTai asked. "Or where they come from?"

"For that matter, sir, do you have any idea of their intentions toward us?" I added.

"First answer, no. We aren't even sure if this J J Ballas is one individual, or a representative of his race, or perhaps a racial consciousness. As to where they come from, the first contact was in a system in the border region well to the galactic north. It's a pretty remote area. Trouble is, there are no habitable planets in that system, so we can't say for sure where they come from." MacKenna paused and glanced at Captain Morgan, who was still recovering from her experience. "What do you make of their intentions, Captain?"

It took her an effort to pull her thoughts together. "Well, sir, the impression I get is amiable curiosity. I've gotten to know him a bit after several contacts, and I don't think they're a threat to us."

"How many contacts?" U'tdaPagrn asked.

She glanced at the Admiral, then said, "Four brief encounters with J J, prior to this. None was for more than a few seconds."

"Do you know why he contacted you and not the others of your crew?" M'tinDegan asked.

"No. Unless there was something special about me."

"Please think back, Captain. What was your situation at the time? Was there anything different about you at the moment?"

She brooded for a bit, then, "The first time he came to me, I was half-dead with exhaustion. We were on a deep patrol along the frontier, and were exploring an uncharted system. My crew and I all suffered from fatigue, and I thought I was hallucinating at first."

"What did you see, Captain?" M'tinDegan asked, softly.

"Just...vague glimpses..." She seemed shaken and lost at the thought. "Something seen out of the corner of your eye. When you look, it wasn't there. Anyway, these went on for several days while we mapped the system. Shortly before we left, I was in the astrogation dome. I...fell asleep...zoned out...I was exhausted. And he was there. It was only for a few seconds. We talked, nothing in particular, then he vanished."

"That sounds like some sort of telepathy," K'deiTai said.

"Indeed," M'tinDegan added. "Physical exhaustion may have opened your subconscious to them. We have a similar phenomenon: a dream state achieved after a long ritual of sleeplessness."

"You touched the Spirit World," Night Eagle said.

M'tinDegan nodded. "Or it is touching us."

She drifted for a bit, then, "We mostly talked about small personal matters. He knows a lot about me, about my childhood. He must have read my memories. I asked him about his people, but he said that wasn't important."

"That...doesn't sound like a danger," K'deiTai offered.

"Then why is he so evasive?" I asked.

"I don't know," Morgan said. "Shy, I guess." She seemed a lot calmer now, more sedate then when she came in. "He just doesn't seem hostile. I can feel his thoughts, and he's just curious, is all." She stared at nothing for while, then, "Although this last time, he seemed worried, too."

"Have you tried to contact him since?" U'tdaPagrn asked.

She glanced at the Admiral again, then said, "We went back there twice to try to reestablish communications, with no luck. We can't reach them, but they can reach me whenever they please."

"Even on earth, it would seem," I said. "So what do you make of this message, Admiral?"

69

"New folks?" He pondered her words unhappily. "He's warning us of a pending first contact which might go bad?"

"Moving in?" Morgan said, pointedly.

"An invasion!"

U'tdaPagrn turned pale. "Admiral, isn't that conclusion a bit premature?"

"Why else would they send us a warning?" MacKenna gave me a hard look. "Any idea what we may be up against, defender?"

"Sir? With every respect, sir, you humans have more experience at these things."

"But you people have far more time in space. What's your take on this?"

I had to ponder my answer; I still wasn't much of an expert on space travel. "An effective invasion force would need enormous logistics, far greater than anything we can do. I can only guess, but I would say any force large enough to sweep and secure this region would need as many as a hundred ships, at least forty of them combatants."

MacKenna turned to Rostokovich, and his voice snapped like a whip. "Commander, send a Code Black to Singapore, and inform them they have release of nuclear weapons. And make *damned* sure they know that does *not* mean the Ic'nichi! Also, send clearance for their courier to depart, and tell them to expedite the 'Marco Polo' for immediate departure." Then he turned to U'tdaPagrn. "Arbiter, your Chamber-Of-Ancients must be alerted at once. I'm ordering a general mobilization of our fleet, and I strongly recommend you do the same. Recommend to them that we join forces NINS."

"Yes, Admiral," U'tdaPagrn snapped. MacKenna's hard-bitten weariness had evaporated: he was all action now, with a no-nonsense driving force that pulled the rest of us along like we were trapped in a whirlwind.

"Admiral," his Aide intoned. "About those nuclear weapons..."

"You'll have your release within the hour, if I have any say about it." MacKenna's snout was as hard as ice, and his eyes shone with a cold fire. "T'eiBida!"

"Sir!"

70

"I want you to act as liaison for your forces. We'll need someone who is familiar with us, and can speak our language."

"Um...sir..." I glanced at U'tdaPagrn, who gave me a brief nod. "...yes, Admiral!"

"And what about you two?" He turned to M'tinDegan and C'traBenla, who were standing off in a corner. "What do you do around here?"

M'tinDegan seemed a bit distracted. "I am a sociologist, Admiral, part of the embassy scientific circle."

"And you?" MacKenna demanded of C'traBenla. "Are you on the embassy staff too?"

"I have been..." she mumbled.

"So you'd both know us pretty well. Good. I want both of you on our liaison team, too."

"Um..." I started to protest, but he cut me off.

"Commander Rostokovich!" He caught Ivan as he was heading out the door. "Take charge here. Put the liaison team together, arrange office space, communications, manpower, anything you need. You have my personal Class A priority on that."

"*Da*, Admiral!"

On that note, he struggled to his feet, took his stick, and headed for the door. "Dammit." I heard him mutter. "Here we go again."

§

Needless to say, this turn of events did not go over well with any of us, nor was the matter settled by any means.

"This is impossible!" K'deiTai cried. He and U'tdaPagrn were arguing while M'tinDegan stood off to one side watching them with pensive look. "I won't do it! I flat won't!"

"K'deiTai, you're the only Arbiter available," U'tdaPagrn pleaded with him. "I have my duties at the embassy, and if war comes, things here will be more hectic than ever. We need a representative to meet the Dreamsingers and these other aliens."

I tried to intervene. "I'm sure we can..."

"But I'm not an Arbiter any more! I retired. I'm a Learnéd now!" He waved frantically at C'traBenla. "And what can we expect to accomplish with *her* in the circle?"

"This wasn't my idea!" She was shaken and frantic.

71

M'tinDegan tried to soothe him. "Her energy and enthusiasm will be a big asset, K'deiTai. Remember how much she accomplished once she settled into the Cultural Attaché spot."

K'deiTai was fuming. "This is *er'trxxda*! I won't have her! She's a...a...a...menace to navigation!"

That got C'traBenla started. "You're exaggerating!"

"The Admiral wants her, and I'm sure he has good reasons."

"Perhaps we..." I offered.

"He doesn't know her!"

"He knows what we'll need far better than we do. We have to trust his judgment."

C'traBenla jumped into the fray. "I can too be helpful! Most of what happened back then wasn't my fault."

"And since when does he give orders to us?" K'deiTai was nearly hysterical now. "We don't even have authorization from the Ancients to do this!"

"And if he wants my help, that's his choice!" C'traBenla protested.

"Maybe we should..."

"Having us in a liaison herd makes sense," M'tinDegan said. "This *is* a first contact situation. Even if it is a hostile one, I can contribute a lot to our understanding of them."

"...perhaps..."

"But what about her?" K'deiTai yelled. "S-she's a...a..."

"DON'T say it!" she snarled.

I couldn't take any more, so I retreated out into the hall.

§

The Admiral, his Aide, and Commander Rostokovich were standing in the hall, distracted by the riot in the conference room. "So, what's all that?" MacKenna asked, and gestured at the door.

"Um...they're discussing procedural issues, sir."

He cocked an ear at the din. "It sounds like a barroom brawl in there." They were screaming at each other by then.

"Ah...yes, sir. It seems that way at times."

Then they came spilling out of the office, arguing furiously. "You have to, K'deiTai!" U'tdaPagrn insisted. "You're the only seasoned diplomat we have here."

72

"I'm retired! I quit! I don't know how I got into this in the first place! Ancestors forbid I should have to work with a...a...a...a...sliv-dancing *tra'taj!*"

Mercifully, they were yelling in our language, because I'm not sure the Admiral's heart could have withstood C'tra's reaction to that. It flattened my ears, I can tell you. I knew she could be salty when she got upset, but I was stunned. K'deiTai rocked back on his tail in amazement, then turned and stomped off with U'tdaPagrn trailing along, still arguing furiously.

M'tinDegan noticed the Admiral watching them, bemused. "Procedural matters," he muttered.

"You people must have some interesting Parliamentary debates." MacKenna turned to the others. "Anyway, Commancer, make arrangements with the Ic'nichi embassy to have some of their furniture and office gear brought over. We're all going to put in long hours, and they'll need crash space. Set up quarters and a liaison room, and arrange security with I'eiBida for them."

"*Da*, Admiral."

"Oh, and ask them about some of their food stocks, and some cooking gear. And provide any kitchen gear they'll need as well. '

"*Da*, Admiral."

MacKenna waved dismissal. Rostokovich saluted, and set off down the hall. MacKenna sagged once he was gone, and rubbed his eyes wearily. "God, I don't need this."

I was impressed by his attention to detail at a moment like this, and worried by how worried he seemed. "We have every confidence in you, Admiral," I said to try and cheer him up.

He glanced at me. "You do, huh? That shows how much *you* know." He sighed in what seemed like a state of near despair, then pulled himself back to business. "Well, we have a war to fight. Let's hop to it, defender."

"Yes, sir."

As he headed down the hall, I heard him humming to himself, some catchy tune that sounded like a march.

*****

73

"War Fever And Other Maladies"
(Related by Learned M'tinDegan)

I don't believe I have ever been as dismayed as I was when we learned that our two races faced the prospect of war against an unknown alien species. It didn't compare to our first contact with the humans as we weren't sure what their intentions were at the time, and as worried as we were, we didn't realize—then—just how bad an interstellar conflict could be. Needless to say, the humans took the matter seriously, and since we were in awe of their vast experience at war, we took it seriously as well.

Once Captain Morgan gave her stunning report, complete with the vision of the alien J J Ballas, Admiral Mackenna sprang into action. Within minutes, the whole building was in a stampede, goaded on by his lightning temper. Junior officers were running up and down the halls, a peacekeeper work detail was called in and set to rearranging furniture in several unused offices, the human fleet was placed on full alert, and defense assets were mobilized across the globe.

The Admiral hobbled relentlessly back and forth on his cane, snapping out orders which sent people flying. I followed at a discreet distance, fascinated by the sight of this frail elder who had transformed before our eyes into a dynamo. The legends about him are true: he was a natural leader and a driving force who never let himself or anyone else ease up for a moment. How he did it at his age, in his physical condition, was beyond me. I heard stories about humans accomplishing the impossible under duress: that must be the source of his strength. I could tell just from watching that he had an uncanny knack of tapping his deepest inner reserves on demand.

As for myself, I was in an agony of worry about the heavy role I would have to play in making war policy. For all my experience as a sociologist among the humans, they still bemused me at times, and I had no idea how I was going to relate to an unknown race who would be hostile and suspicious toward us to begin with. Honestly, I was haunted by the fear that I would offer bad advice at a critical moment which would lead to disaster.

J J Ballas was another question for which I had no answers. Thinking on the brief visitation, it seemed certain that his people were telepathic, which raised all sorts of questions about their mental and social structure. An important truth of sociology is that everyone has something to hide, no matter how trivial. Mental privacy, ones personal sphere, is key to so much of what makes us reasoning, social beings. Would telepathy remove that barrier, and how would it affect their culture and their world view? And how would that, in turn, affect their outlook on us? Would we even be able to relate to them? The Captain's trance and their need to reach into our subconscious suggested it would not be easy. I was lost on the matter, and as reluctant as I was, I saw no alternative but to consult with Learnéd V'NegNder on it.

Be that as it may, the immediate task was to get our two races on a war footing, which would not be easy since neither race had anything like a functioning stellar navy. The first order of business would be to develop a unified war policy. But to do that, the humans would first have to put their house in order, which would take some doing. So the rest of that day went to a chaotic scramble to turn the unused fifth floor of the Defense Ministry into a joint operations center so we could get on with the bigger job.

U'tdaPagrn went back to the embassy, leaving a fuming, miserable K'deiTai in charge, while C'traBenla showed the good sense to stay out of sight and not antagonize him. I was at a loss for how she wound up in this, and I spent a good deal of time thinking on how we could keep her contained. At least we had l'eiBida: if any defender could fill the crucial role of interracial military liaison, he was the one. He spent most of the morning in a circle with Agent Roubidoux and Commander Rostokovich, both of whom the Admiral assigned to the liaison herd, hammering together some sort of program.

"I knew it,' he grumbled when he came out of the conference room. He looked askance at me. "I knew something bad would happen if we came here. It's just my luck."

"None of us are thrilled about the possibility of war, l'eiBida, but we have to make the best of it."

"My Ancestors must be having a grand old laugh at me! '

"Look at it this way: if we do have to fight a war, you are the best possible choice for this spot. Your experience will be valuable to both us and the Admiral."

He gave me a sullen glare. "Wonderful. What more could go wrong?"

"Um, that does bring up an issue," I offered, delicately.

He nodded. "What are we going to do with *her?*"

"I don't suppose she could be evacuated with the nonessential embassy personnel?"

He made a rude noise.

"Well then, perhaps we can encourage her to take a role as official hostess. You know how she loves parties. It'd keep her busy and give her something useful to do."

He sighed and shook his head in exasperation. "Remember how she was back when we were assigned here? There's no chance that she won't meddle."

"I'ei, love!" Speaking of which, she came trotting down the corridor bubbling with all the impulsive enthusiasm we knew of old. "Isn't this exciting? I am looking forward *so much* to helping you with this assignment!"

I caught a fleeting look of panic in his eyes. "You didn't seem thrilled earlier."

"Well, yes, but the more I think about it, the more I want to take part. Just think: I'll be here by your side to help you in your duties. What more could we ask for? This is turning into a wonderful vacation!"

"Love, this is highly technical, and it involves delicate negotiations with the humans to draft joint policy. I know you want to help..."

She gave him an admonishing ear twitch. "And I can by taking care of all the little things so you can focus on the big picture."

Sad to say there was no denying her logic, although I'eiBida gave it an heroic try. "But..."

"I've already worked out our liaison office—how did you intend to get along with just that one room? I spoke to Commander Rostokovich, and he assigned some additional rooms for quarters and a staff lounge with cooking facilities."

76

"But..."

"You can't really expect our people to put in such long hours without hot *V'liz* and a place to sleep, do you? For that matter, the humans will need something as well, and I promised Ivan I would take care of that."

"But..."

"Learnéd W'kiLap will be over soon to help install the communications. I ordered new stationery printed up for us, and I put in requisitions for kitchen gear and bedding, which should arrive shortly."

"But..."

"I have to get back to the embassy and expedite the furnishings and supplies. Ivan promised to send some trucks, so we should have everything in short order."

"But..." But she was gone in a rush before he could get off another word of protest. We watched glumly as she vanished down the stairs, then he turned to me. "See what I mean?"

"Um...yes..."

"Ancestors preserve us," he grumbled. "As much as I love her, *how* are we going to get through this war with her around?"

"Perhaps we could turn her loose on the enemy?"

He actually considered for a moment, then shook his head. "No, that would be too cruel."

§

It wasn't long before all the commotion on the fifth floor drew the attention from higher up the feeding chain in the short, rotund form of the Defense Minister, the priceless Jacek Hogarthy. By all accounts, Minister Hogarthy was the laughing-stock of the human Cabinet, but he represented an important faction in the government, which is why we were saddled with him. He was excitable and vindictive, and his flabby jowls and whiny voice were the stock of comedians around the world. The peacekeeper leadership despised him, and he had an ongoing feud with the human Space Fleet. If any one human could offset MacKenna's military genius, he was it. He caught the Admiral in the halls near the elevator, and launched into one of his endless protests.

"Admiral MacKenna! What on *earth* are you..."

77

MacKenna rounded on him. "There you are! Where the hell have you been? I need release of nuclear weapons, now."

"...what..."

"I've issued a general mobilization order to the fleet. We may have a war on our hands, and I need release of nuclear weapons, pronto!"

The Minister turned pale. "What...?" Then he saw us standing nearby. "Then what are *they* doing here?"

"Not *them*, you idiot! We have a pending first contact, and our intel says they may be hostile. I sent a memo to your office; didn't you read it?"

"I don't have time to read all the paperwork crossing my desk!"

"You created it, you live with it. It's time to buff up, so get your thumb out and give me that release!"

Hogarthy got huffy at his badgering. "Now see here, Admiral! I find your conduct most unbecoming. *Most* unbecoming, sir!"

MacKenna gave him a mock dismayed look. "My...*God*, man! *How* do you cope with life?" He took Hogarthy by the arm and hustled him, squawking indignantly, down the hall to the elevator. "We're in a war situation against an alien force of unknown strength and clearly hostile intent. So you get off your dead ass and *get me that release!*"

Hogarthy retreated, too shaken to complain further for the moment. He would be back. "God, that's one thing we don't need," MacKenna grumbled.

"I gather you don't think the Minister will be much help in this crisis," I said. That was no surprise, since Hogarthy had a sorry reputation even among the Cabinet officialdom.

He gave me an annoyed glance. "I took a pain pill, but he keeps coming back."

§

The two trucks the Commander sent to the embassy returned loaded to overflowing in surprisingly short order, and a growing herd of peacekeepers soon had a steady stream of materials flowing up to the fifth floor. C'traBenla was all over the place organizing quarters, storerooms, staff lounges and liaison offices for both races. If anything, she was more hyper than ever.

"I'ei, love!" she said when we came on the scene. "I managed to get everything in one trip. The kitchen gear is all here, and we should have it set up shortly." She was trembling with excitement, chattering at a near-hysterical pace. "I talked with L'datMparn, and had him exchange one of the defenders you assigned for one who can cook. And I asked Ivan to expedite another refrigerator. We should have hot *V'liz* shortly, and meals by nightfall."

"It's beginning," I murmured once she left. I'eiBida nodded and sighed. The portents were ominous.

W'kiLap poked his snout around a nearby corner. "Is it safe to come out?" When we failed to answer, he emerged cautiously, lugging a hand cart loaded with communication gear and tools. "Did she get into some bad lemonade, or what? I've never seen her so hyper."

"She's off on one of her enthusiasms," I'eiBida grumbled.

"You should have seen her at the embassy. She had the place in an uproar."

"Everyone has their gifts: sad to say, that's hers."

The Admiral happened by while this was going on, and watched for some time, bemused by all the activity. "Remarkable," he said to me at one point. "Whoever that fellow is," he gestured at C'traBenla as she came charging past, "he knows his stuff." He watched for a bit longer, then asked, "What's his job at your embassy, anyway?"

"Her." I was mortally tempted to tell the Admiral the truth, since it was unlikely he would want a former sliv-dancer on a critical joint defense committee. "She..." *She* came charging past again lugging a case of frozen *rai'tru'na* berries: I faltered since it wasn't fair to speak without consulting with I'eiBida, and I didn't want to set off the scene she would make when she was sent away. "...she is involved with intercultural affairs."

The Admiral watched, bemused, as she shot past again, pausing for a moment to direct some peacekeepers delivering furniture before taking off for the stairs. "Intercultural affairs, eh? Damn, I wish I had lieutenants who could jump like that."

Just then, Captain Morgan showed up. "Admiral, I have the latest report from Singapore on the fleet's status."

79

MacKenna eyed C'traBenla for a moment longer, then turned to her. "Right. In my office, Captain."

§

Needless to say, all this activity sent Minister Hogarthy scuttling back for another round of complaining. He burst in on the Admiral, Captain Morgan, I'eiBida and me as we were discussing her report.

"Admiral, I *must* protest what's going on up here!"

"There are medications for that," MacKenna grumbled. "Therapy might help, too."

"We can't have them running loose in here! Who knows what they might get into."

MacKenna gave him an annoyed look. "They have more important things on their minds than pilfering office supplies, and if one of them does steal your fancy pen set, I'll buy you a new one."

"Who said anything about pen sets? I'm talking national security! You're giving these...*people*...carte blanche to the Defense Ministry!"

"I trust them. They have their priorities straight."

"Well I don't!"

"At least you admit it."

That confused him. "I mean I don't trust them not to go snooping around where they don't belong."

"Well then, post a watch on the lower floors."

"Post a watch..." Hogarthy was scandalized.

"That's right, post a watch. That's why we have all those guns, you know. And if you *don't* mind, I have important matters to attend to."

On that note, he struggled to his feet while Hogarthy fumed, took his cane in hand, and headed for the door. Hogarthy followed him out into the hall, badgering him as they went.

"This simply won't do, Admiral! You can't have them right here in the middle of the fleet's command center. Think of the risk...espionage...sabotage...terrorism..." He was working himself up into a fine lather over his self-imposed fears. "Who knows what they might do in the nerve center of our space defenses!"

80

"The fleet's command structure is in Singapore, where it belongs," MacKenna said, patiently. "The other services are dispersed, too. The only purpose this place serves is paperwork, and they're welcome to blow that up if they want."

"...blow it...if they want...!" He was apoplectic by then. "You can't be serious!"

MacKenna chuckled. "Sure I can. I have seniority."

Hogarthy was beginning to realize that the Admiral was making fun of him. "I don't appreciate your flippant attitude, *Admiral!* This is no place for *them* to be."

"This is a perfect spot for a liaison office. We have close access to both the government and the Ic'nichi embassy. Plus it will serve as a backup in case Singapore is taken out, and we can maintain communication with the fleet with all those radio links on the roof. Besides, this place serves no useful purpose otherwise."

"You are entitled to your opinion, I suppose..."

"Damn straight I am."

"...but you don't see the big picture..."

"The Admiral knows what he's doing." Unlike MacKenna, Captain Morgan was beginning to lose her temper with the Minister.

"...We're talking about policy matters far above his head!"

She gave him an icy look. "*He* is the expert, plus he's in command, so we'll listen to him."

Hogarthy got all huffy with her. "Personally, I'd say his expertise is overrated. You would do well, *Captain*, to listen less and think for yourself more!"

Something went 'click' in her eyes, and she cut loose on him. "That will be enough out of you! I will not have you spouting mutiny!"

He turned pale. "*Mutiny?* I was just..."

"Just suborning military personnel to disobey their superiors!" she roared. "According to Service Regulations, that's mutiny. And the penalty for suborning mutiny is death!"

"D-death?" Hogarthy cowered under her icy stare. "That's ridiculous! You wouldn't..."

"Don't push your luck," MacKenna muttered.

81

"If the Admiral says we set up here, then, dammit, we set up here! If the Admiral wants *them* here, then here they are! And if I hear you utter *one more word* of this seditious rot, I'll have you arrested!"

MacKenna was still leaning on his cane, bemused by this spectacle, as Hogarthy retreated post-haste. When he was gone, he let out an exasperated sigh. "I'd swear that boy spun out on the learning curve."

"Idiot!" she grumbled.

"That's Minister Idiot, Captain."

"He is indeed, sir." She ran her hands through her fur, scratching her scalp vigorously as if she was trying to wake up. "Well, if you will excuse me, sir, the communication gear needs repairs, as always."

"She *has* mellowed, sir," his Aide muttered to him after she left. "Even more than last time. Do you suppose those contacts are having some effect on her?"

MacKenna eyed her suspiciously as she headed down the hall. "Yeah. You may be right."

That comment struck me as ominous somehow, and I wondered what they meant by it. The only thing I could think of was her contacts with J J Ballas, which would be reason enough for concern. For that matter, perhaps it would be for the best: if that display was mellow, she must be a terror indeed.

§

It wasn't long before the air was scented with the aroma of boiling *V'liz*, which drew us to the staff lounge like a magnet. C'traBenla had rigged an electric heater under a large kettle which simmered with the thick, aromatic concoction, to which she was busily adding diced bits of this and that.

"Well, I see you're not so skeptical now," she said when we came piling in. "Sit yourselves down, and we'll have mid-meal in just a moment."

Truth, we were weary and famished from our efforts, and a break for a thick bowl of *V'liz* stew was welcome. The staff lounge was an unused office, minimal and drab, with faded paint and cracked floor tiles meagerly concealed by some throw rugs. A few human ottomans and a couple of low coffee tables were the only furnishings, and C'traBenla had her improvised kitchen set up in one corner next to the refrigerator. The aroma wafting from the *V'liz* pot made up for any shortcomings in the decor.

"This is a great idea, love," I'eiBida said.

She was busily dicing vegetables, and gave him a smug ear twitch. "So now perhaps you see my point about regular meals."

"Oh, I do, trust me. So what else can you prepare?"

"We don't have room for a regular kitchen, but I plan to improvise with this." She dumped a handful of chopped spices into the *V'liz* pot, then held up a large, shallow metal bowl which she had just unpacked from its carton. "This is a wok; the humans use them for stir frying, which I understand is fast and simple, as well as healthy."

"Oh?" I'eiBida considered the thing doubtfully. "So what sort of meals can this...wok...make?"

She picked up a booklet which came with it. "From what I see in here, we can use *uf'thoka* and rice, along with several human vegetables which have been cleared for our use." She showed him the booklet. "It will make a good light meal, anyway."

"Well that certainly sounds better than endurance rations."

She smiled at that. "I brought a few things over from the embassy, so let's see what we can cook up."

She set the wok on a large electric heater, then spent the next few minutes digging through the paperboard boxes she brought from the embassy. By time she pulled out a large bottle, the heater glowed, and the wok was smoking slightly.

"This is olive oil." She showed us the bottle containing a thick translucent liquid. "We use a bit of this, and fry the vegetables in it."

She poured some into the wok, which reacted with an ominous sizzling sound and a shower of spattering oil, which she retreated from in haste.

"It's smoking," I'eiBida said, uneasily.

She considered the bottle suspiciously. "This is what it says to use. I guess it's supposed to smoke."

"Yes, but that much?" The air in the room was getting thick.

83

She threw some diced vegetables into the heated oil; the spattering grew louder, and the fumes became thicker.

"Maybe we should stop to think this over."

"You are such a worrier," C'tra grumbled. "Eeepp! The vegetables are burning!"

"Aren't you supposed to stir it?"

"Perhaps it needs more oil." She emptied the bottle into the wok, and suddenly the room was filled with a sizzling roar and clouds of greasy vapor. "It's not supposed to do that, is it?" she wailed as she waved the fumes away from her snout.

"Do you have it too hot?"

"It's...(gasp)...supposed to be hot..." She threw a ladleful of rice into the wok, and retreated from the billowing smoke.

"We need better ventilation."

"Maybe I should have...(cough)...read the pamphlet," she muttered.

"Maybe you shouldn't...(wheeze)...put any more..."

...The fire alarm went off...

"...C'tra..."

"...Oh...*l'cc'vn*..."

...which triggered the sprinklers...

"...Turn it off!"

Too late: the wok burst into flames, creating clouds of billowing smoke which mixed with the fire suppressant spray to make a blinding fog.

"Everyone out!" We stampeded for the door.

"What the hell's going on in here?" Admiral MacKenna roared from the door. Bad timing on his part. All we cared about by then was exiting the room in a blind rush, knocking the admiral off his feet in the process. "Sergeant!" he yelled as he struggled to sit up. "That's a grease fire! Shut off the master valve!" One of his people took off down the corridor.

"Oh, there goes mid-meal!" C'traBenla whimpered. Fine time to worry about a meal.

"Let's get some fire extinguishers in here!" Someone helped the admiral to his feet, and he peered into the gloom, trying to see how bad it was.

"My stew!"

Another human came running with a fire extinguisher, and forced his way bravely into the boiling cloud behind the extinguisher's fog. He retreated, then came on again, hosing the wok which was now nothing more than a vague glow in the gloom. The flames died down, but sprang up again as soon as he shut the extinguisher off.

"My wok will be ruined!"

"Someone hit the circuit breakers!" MacKenna yelled.

The volunteer went back to hosing the wok, which died down again momentarily, but kept erupting anew. The lights went out, killing the heater just as Minister Hogarthy came bouncing up once again in a panic-stricken lather. "Admiral! What's going on?"

MacKenna ignored him, being busy at the moment. The fire extinguisher emptied, and the wok burst into flame again. The volunteer retreated, gasping for breath.

"Someone put a cover on that!"

"Admiral?"

Two humans rushed into the room with a heavy plastic floor mat and threw it over the wok, suppressing the fire just as the sprinklers shut off.

"Admiral!"

Commander Rostokovich came running, with Hythe-Morrison close behind. "Are you all right, sir?"

MacKenna seemed a bit winded, but no worse for wear. "Yes, I'm fine, Commander. Let's open some windows and get this smoke out of here."

"*Da*, sir!"

"*What* is going on here?"

MacKenna finally took a moment out for Hogarthy. "It's just a minor grease fire. No harm's been done."

"*Grease* fire? This isn't a restaurant! They can't be *cooking* in here!"

"I was just trying to provide hot food for our staff," C'tra cried.

Hogarthy turned on her in full indignation. "Look at this mess! What were you thinking?"

C'tra started to blubber. "I was just...trying...to help."

85

"I authorized them to set up some hot food service," MacKenna said. That was a lie, and I admired him for it. "We'll need it with the hours we'll be putting in here."

"I...I'm sorry..."

"Sorry? *Look* at this mess!"

"At least she's trying to help, which is more than can be said for *some* people!"

Hogarthy rounded on him again. "They could have burned down half the city!"

"It's a brick building, for crying out loud!"

"*Look* at the chaos and panic they caused! I had to evacuate the building! Do you *realize* how that disrupted our operations?"

"Interrupted the paperwork?" MacKenna was getting peeved. "Good Lord save us!"

"This is no laughing matter, Admiral!"

"Who's laughing? And if there's any panic and chaos around here, *you* caused it!"

Just then the fire wardens came clumping up the stairs in their heavy protective gear lugging axes, pry bars, and a thick hose.

"What? You called the fire department?" MacKenna demanded.

Hogarthy was bouncing in agitation by then. "Yes, I called them! The building was on fire!"

The fire wardens' leader studied the soaked remains of our mid-meal, including the priceless pot of *V'liz* stew which was now diluted with fire suppressant foam and overflowed onto the floor, then gave Hogarthy a contemptuous snort. "False alarm *mes amis,*" he said to his people. They packed up their gear and lugged it back down five flights of stairs with much grumbling and ill looks at the Minister.

"All right everyone," the Admiral said. "Show's over. Let's get back to work." The crowd of human gawkers began to disperse reluctantly. "Let's move, people!" They moved: they knew what to expect in his mood.

"*Admiral!*" Hogarthy howled.

"OUT!" Hogarthy retreated post-haste before his temper. That annoyance dealt with, he turned his attention to C'traBenla.

86

"I'm sorry!" C'tra whimpered.

The Admiral gave her a peeved look, then softened. "That's all right. You meant well. Leftenant!" He singled Hythe-Morrison out of the crowd. "Requisition a couple microwaves for these people."

"Yes, sir."

"Microwaves?" C'tra's already bedraggled look sagged even further, and she gave us an embarrassed glance.

"I *trust* you'll have this cleaned up in short order," MacKenna growled before he headed back to his office, leaving us there hungry, dripping wet, sticky with fire foam, and smelling of burnt olive oil.

§

We received word by late afternoon that our courier had left orbit and was on its way home to d'enchia. Soon, for better or worse, the war scare would spread to the home world. The Admiral was in his office laboring over war plans with a pad and pencil when we came to update him on that. How the Ancients would respond was a matter of great interest among us.

"I don't suppose you can give me some feel about how your people will react?" he asked I'eiBida.

"The fact that you're calling for help will make an impression, sir. I think we can expect a positive response."

MacKenna looked at him curiously. "Really? I didn't think I rated so high among your people."

I'eiBida hesitated, gave me a nervous look, then said, "Well, sir, if I may be candid..."

"Say your peace, mister."

"...ah...we on the 'Dark Grays' Staff have long been concerned about the danger your skill and experience pose, and here you are seeking help from us, your supposed enemies. Our leaders will take your alarm seriously."

MacKenna's eye ridge crept up. "I'm that much of a Bogeyman to you?" he sighed. "It wouldn't be the first time."

"I lead the analysis of your war record, sir, and we were amazed by how much you can achieve when you have so little to work with."

87

"Lord knows we have little enough," he muttered. He sagged wearily with his elbows on the desk, his fatigue showing.

"I am hazarding a guess, sir, but your warning should produce a substantial response."

"Well, we'll find out in another couple of months, I suppose." He struggled to his feet, then paused before heading for the door. "It's going to be a long couple of months."

§

A hand of the embassy defenders, who I'eiBida was careful to place on 'detached service', showed up at the Ministry to work our communications gear and maintain a standing duty watch. Minister Hogarthy responded to four unarmed defenders by posting teams of heavily armed peacekeepers on each floor by the elevators and stairs, and by arming the duty watch there on the fifth floor. MacKenna personally brokered an understanding between I'eiBida and the human duty officer, who seemed embarrassed by the Minister's hysterics, and the humans stored their side arms in the watch commander's desk.

"That man gives paranoia a bad name," he grumbled later. "It's not like I have anything useful to do around here."

"You put the idea in his head, sir." I'eiBida gave him a sardonic ear twitch.

"Don't remind me." MacKenna rubbed his neck with a weary sigh. Despite his driving will, the strain of the last few hours was showing. "So much for my life-long reputation as a military genius, I suppose."

"Not to worry, sir," his aide, Hythe-Morrison said, primly. "The history books are written by the winners, and thus far you've managed not to lose, somehow."

"Only to avoid your supercilious remarks!"

For all that Hythe-Morrison was 'terribly, terribly British', as someone once told me, he was a priceless asset to the Admiral, as any good Staff Aide would be. Despite the vast gulf between their ranks, they fussed and snipped at each other like an old life-bonded pair, and we could tell that MacKenna was genuinely fond of him.

"At least he knows how to make a decent mug of coffee," he said with a wry grin and a thumb jerked at Hythe-Morrison.

Hythe-Morrison turned 'terribly terribly' at that. "Four hundred years of Naval tradition will tell," he sniffed.

"We're making progress in spite of Hogarthy, Admiral," I said. "Once the threat becomes obvious, he'll back down."

MacKenna gave me a sour look. "Perhaps. But that's when the real fun starts. Trust me: this is only the beginning."

§

If it was only a beginning, it went along well despite the Minister's interference. Thanks to a monumental effort by all concerned, the fifth floor was effectively transformed into a war room by dusk. W'kiLap had the communication gear in place and linked to the embassy, the duty watch was set, and the mess in the staff lounge had been cleaned up. (The wok was given to one of the peacekeepers, who took it home to his bondmate.) It was getting late, and we were all tired and hungry when the embassy omnibus came to retrieve us, so we called it a day.

We ran into Captain Morgan at the elevator. Human elevators are abysmally slow, and we stood waiting in awkward silence while she stared straight ahead and ignored us. I could feel the tension in her: she was rigid, her snout tight, her jaw muscles working. I pitied the humans in her crew; she was ready to snap at any excuse, and I suspected she was a disciplinary terror to those under her. I'eiBida was uneasy, K'deiTai felt it too, and even C'traBenla was subdued. K'deiTai kept glancing at her curiously as the silent tension built up around us. Finally their eyes met, and they studied each other awkwardly.

"Honey...lamb?"

She bristled, and gave him a smoldering glare. "You don't want to know, Arbiter. Trust me." The elevator door opened, she marched in, whirled, punched the button, and was gone before we could find the nerve to enter.

"Are all their service fems that ferocious?" C'traBenla asked once she was gone.

"Ancestors!" K'deiTai muttered. "I hope not!"

*****

89

"The Gathering Storm"
(Related by Learnéd K'deiTai)

Learnéd K'deiTai, sen V'ran,
Ic'nichi embassy, Geneva, earth
275 Common, 12th v'venmn're

By this dispatch you are authorized to act as our Arbiter to the joint Ic'nichi-human defense commission, and to lead our delegation thereto. You are charged to cooperate closely with the humans in joint defense efforts when, in the opinion of yourself, Arbiter U'tdaPagrn, and our special council, bearer of this message, it is in the best interest of d'enchia to do so.

(signed)
The Most Ancient
By authority of the Inner Policy Circle

"Wonderful! As if I don't have enough troubles!" There was a time, I recalled ruefully, when I would have been overwhelmed by such recognition and the trust that dispatch placed in me. Right then I was ready to break down crying. "Why do these things happen to me?" I asked U'tdaPagrn, plaintively. "I pay my taxes, I'm a productive member of the herd; why do they always pick on me?"

"Really, K'deiTai," U'tdaPagrn grumbled. "Your whining is *cc'v'renk*. We all have to do our share in these troubled times, and you are no exception with your diplomatic experience."

I don't see what *he* was complaining about. *He* was the one squatting behind the big desk; this should be *his* knotted tail. But they always pick on me, curse their ears, and these last two months were a thankless, Ancestorless trial. I damned G'cetGian for hustling me into this, my own limp tail, the priceless Hogarthy, C'traBenla, J J Ballas, and all the rest who conspired to heap indignities and despair across my back. On top of *everything* else, the weather was as miserably hot and humid as only earthly summers can be. The windows in U'tdaPagrn's grotto were open, which helped a little, but the oppressive heat added a groggy fugue to my hapless angst. The light flooding in through the windows and the birds caterwauling in the bushes were so bright and cheerful that I couldn't stand it.

"My Ancestors hate me. They must." I wadded the dispatch up and threw it across the grotto in disgust. It landed next to U'tdaPagrn's human hand game, and his Aide scampered to retrieve both.

"Stiffen your tail!" U'tdaPagrn snapped. "This *r'vebbe* is unbecoming and counterproductive."

"And *what* do they expect me to accomplish with *her* in our circle? Ancestors save me from that *tra'taj*!" We spent those last two earth months marking time waiting for some response from d'enchia, which hadn't kept C'traBenla from stirring the pot with her endless enthusiasm. "Isn't it bad enough having a war on our hands? She's impossible!"

"Look," he said, evenly. "You might not care any more, but I want to live to retire, so *please* keep your temper and your opinions to yourself. We have enough to deal with without provoking her!"

I sighed in despair and hefted the bulky package of 'Instructions And Recommendations' which accompanied that accursed dispatch. "It's not like I need to worry about getting anything *done*. The war will be over before I get all this sorted out. We ought to use this *l'cc'vn* thing as a weapon." It was hefty enough to raise a serious bruise if thrown. "It'd be lethal."

"Right now we have more urgent matters. H'rhAtor and his staff will land shortly, so we need to get over to the Defense Ministry. He and the human Admiral want to match ears, and we need to be there."

"We might as well. It's not like I have anything better to do with my life."

There was a discreet rap on the door, and Agent Goldblum peeked in. "The limousines are ready, Arbiter."

"Thank you, Agent. Is the special representative ready?"

"I believe so, sir."

91

U'tdaPagrn and I pulled ourselves together and headed for the door, me lugging those Ancestorless instructions. "Look at it this way, K'deiTai," U'tdaPagrn offered. "Just think of the recognition your work on this joint defense commission will bring you back home in the Chamber."

"Oh, please!"

"All right, enough! We need to pick up this special representative and gallop."

"Well, hopefully it can't get any worse."

§

Actually, it could. The 'Special Representative' turned out to be Learnéd N'detLeda, of painful memory, who was waiting in the reception area amid a mountain of luggage which a detail of the embassy defenders were still adding to. And as if that wasn't bad enough, my nemesis from the Institute, T'virDoma, was with him. I should know better.

"What are you doing here?" I asked in dismay.

N'detLeda huffed in righteous indignation. "I was sent here by the Most Ancient to keep you from ruining everything." He waived a diplomatic credentials envelope at me. "It's all here in print, so try not to succumb to your fits of temper for once."

I took the envelope gingerly, but didn't open it. "And why is *she* here?"

"*She* is my protégé."

She gave me a superior smile. "Well, Learnéd, it looks like I'll get that field study after all." She handed me another credentials envelope, but by that point it wouldn't really make any difference.

"Why do these things always happen to me?" I complained.

"Probably because everyone else had the wit to duck in time," N'detLeda said.

§

On top of all our other problems, it didn't take long for the news vultures to sniff out what was going on. Eight starships in low orbit aren't easy to overlook, to say nothing of a *third* shuttle—the one bringing N'detLeda and other harbingers of ill fortune—landing in Geneva. By time we reached the Defense Ministry, it was under siege by a herd of network camera crews backed up by

92

an impromptu demonstration-cum-riot, backed up in turn by an excited mob which all but surrounded the building. The access driveway in the rear was kept open by the main force efforts of the Ministry peacekeepers and some hastily summoned gendarmes. Even so, we were forced to push our limousines through the herd with much revving of the engines and honking of horns.

"Like old times." N'detLeda eyed the mob uneasily. "At least they're consistent."

T'virDoma was pallid. "They're wild animals!" she gasped as she glanced nervously back and forth. There was a sea of hostile alien figures stretching away into the distance, and way the limousine rocked did nothing for her composure.

"You wanted field experience," I said with sour satisfaction. Someone broke a picket sign over the roof of the limousine, causing her to cringe in terror. "Welcome to earth."

The herd yielded reluctantly before our gendarme escort with much yelling, obscene gestures, and waving of picket signs while T'virDoma cowered below the window. When we finally reached the rear entrance, we were whisked from the limousines to the door by a peacekeeper escort. She hesitated when her turn came, watching the herd fearfully before exiting the limousine, then scuttled to the doorway between two human gendarmes. N'detLeda followed as fast as his dignity allowed while the demonstrators chanted and roared. At least they weren't throwing rocks—yet.

"*Borjemoi!*" Commander Rostokovich grumbled when we were safely inside. "Is not six hours since fleet arrived, and they are already rioting."

"How do they manage it?" Agent Roubidoux wondered, irritably. "Here they are with picket signs and everything. Have they nothing better to do in their lives?"

"If only we could come up with battleships as fast!"

"How are things here?" U'tdaPagrn asked.

"Not good, sir," Agent Roubidoux said. "The news vultures are in a feeding frenzy." T'virDoma's ears shot up at that. "I'eiBida is doing the best he can, but I am afraid he is being overwhelmed."

§

93

I'eiBida was in the press room providing the best rear guard he could, addressing an unruly herd of news vultures from a low improvised dais while C'traBenla hovered anxiously nearby. "This is purely a routine matter," he assured them frantically. "With the improved relations, it was decided to stage joint maneuvers between the two fleets."

"Why didn't you announce this beforehand?" they demanded.

"We're sorry about that. It seems there was a clerical error, and the announcement was delayed." There was more clamoring, the din so relentless that I'eiBida could hardly be heard as they tried to shout each other down. Then he spotted us in the wings. "If you will excuse me for a moment, I will consult with my superiors to see if there is any fresh news." With that he retreated off stage, herding C'traBenla before him.

§

"Joint maneuvers?" I asked when they reached relative safety. "That makes no sense at all."

He sighed, looking frazzled and overwhelmed. "It doesn't have to as long as it confuses them for the time being. It's better than telling them the truth."

"Hmmm. Speaking of confusion, an old friend has come to join us." I gestured to N'detLeda, standing nearby.

I'eiBida stared at him in dismay. "Wonderful," he muttered. C'traBenla's ears laid back, and she actually *hissed* at him.

"Well, I'm pleased to see you remember me," N'detLeda said. "So to dispense with the formalities, I am here to provide adult supervision at the request of the Most Ancient."

I'eiBida looked askance at me: I nodded morosely.

"I'eiBida," Agent Roubidoux called. "You need to get back out there. The news vultures are ready to riot."

"I see you have things galloping along in grand fashion," N'detLeda said, disdainfully. "Pity I wasn't called in sooner."

I'eiBida turned irate at that. "Well if you think you can do better, by all means, help yourself!"

N'detLeda hesitated, with a nervous look out onto the dais, then said, "Perhaps I should, if it isn't already too late."

§

The news vultures raised a blood roar when he appeared. "It is a genuine pleasure to be in Geneva again..." was as far as he got before they descended on him in force; yelling, shoving, pushing cameras and microphones in his snout, and behaving generally like news vultures do when on one of their hysterical rampages. The memories of the invasion rumors spread by the Anti-techs were fresh in their minds, and they were so agitated that I was afraid they would hurt him. I turned to I'eiBida, who gave me an amused look and a dismissive ear twitch, and I decided not to fret over it, as long as it was just N'detLeda.

"Regretfully, the announcement became a knotted tail," he managed once he fought his way to the surface. "You all know how bureaucracy is. We hope this won't cause any undue distress in the Alliance."

"But why maneuvers?" they demanded. "What's going on?"

"This exercise is an important first step toward a close working relationship between our two races on defense matters."

That set off another clamor. "Why this emphasis on defense?" they yelled. "Do we face another alien threat?"

N'detLeda backpedaled urgently on that. "This is simply a sensible precaution. Your own history shows the value of being prepared for any eventuality, something we have learned from you and taken to hearts."

That didn't help in the least. "Do you intend...is there any...absorb the human fleet...mutual defense pact...financial aid...security issues...your own..."

§

"He seems to have things under control," I said to I'eiBida.

"As much as anyone can, I guess. At least they'll eat him rather than us if they do riot."

"Do you think they will?"

I'eiBida stared at T'virDoma in surprise. "Who are you?"

"I'm his protégé, if you *must* know," she said disdainfully. "I'm here doing field research for my candidacy in Human Studies. I've seen references to humans practicing cannibalism; have you heard of them eating one of us?"

I'eiBida stared at her in confusion. "...Ah...not lately..."

95

"But it *has* happened, hasn't it? That human said they were in a feeding frenzy."

He turned to me in alarm. "Has one of our people been eaten?"

"No!" I protested. I was caught so off guard by this that I was swept up in his confusion. "...at least everyone's account for, as far as I know."

"Oh! She means the news vultures." He turned to her again. "That's just a..."

The crowd noise reached a crescendo, and N'detLeda retreated off stage at a barely dignified trot. "*Ancestors!*" he gasped. "They are...most enthusiastic..."

"Are you all right, Learnéd?" she asked in dismay. "It seemed like they were going to eat you!" He was disheveled, with two buttons torn off his vest. He had a couple bruises, and there was a scratch over one eye from an unfortunate rendezvous with a camera lens.

"Nonsense! Recall what I taught you about how excitable humans are. It was strictly routine."

"That...was routine...?" She listened to the pandemonium in the press room with obvious alarm.

Commander Rostokovich came on the scene. "Ic'nichi shuttle with fleet leaders landed a few minutes ago. They will be here soon, so we must move fast to get situation under control."

"Well then, let's get to it," N'detLeda said.

I'eiBida gave me a bemused look as they exited. "What have you been teaching them back home, anyway?"

"It isn't my fault! I can't tell her anything!"

§

As recently as three months earlier, an Ic'nichi battle force commanded by no less than Fleet Elder H'rhAtor arriving in earth orbit would have triggered a shooting war, and the thought of H'rhAtor and Admiral MacKenna sitting down at the same table to discuss common action would boggle the mind. But believe it or not, there it was.

The Fleet Elder and his staff arrived from the airport in the embassy omnibus escorted by a large force of peacekeepers and gendarmes. The crowd knew that omnibus on sight, and set up a

96

raucous reception. It took some time, and no small effort by the gendarmes to force their way through. By time they arrived at the rear entrance, H'rhAtor and company were a bit shaken.

MacKenna was positively bubbling with enthusiasm to meet his counterpart after all these years, which was not surprising with how he fretted over this situation for the last couple of months. "You're a sight for sore eyes, Eldest," he greeted H'rhAtor. "You and your fleet are about as welcome as Jesus at a monster truck rally!"

H'rhAtor blinked at him in confusion. "Um...thank you, Admiral. I am pleased to meet you at last, as well."

("What did that mean?" U'tdaPagrn whispered to me.)

("Some things are better off remaining a mystery.")

"Sorry about the reception out there." MacKenna jerked a thumb at the entrance. "Our people get a little carried away at times."

"Indeed?" H'rhAtor said, judiciously. "They seem rather excitable."

"Freakin' all-you-can-eat buffet out there," the Admiral grumbled. T'virDoma twitched all over at that. "But we have more important things to deal with."

Then, with grim inevitability, Minister Hogarthy came blustering in. "Admiral MacKenna! I hear you've set up sleeping facilities for the Ic'nichi on the fifth floor."

"And you've just now figured this out after two months?"

"We are not running a *gasthaus* here! They'll have to stay at the embassy."

"Our embassy is already full," U'tdaPagrn said.

Truth, even if we vacated the guest quarters, which would leave I'eiBida, C'traBenla, N'detLeda, and me dangling, there wouldn't be enough room for everyone. Moreover, once H'rhAtor heard the situation, he flat-out refused to impose his herd on the already overcrowded embassy.

"It's temporary," MacKenna offered. "There's plenty of room up there, and we need them on the ground for operational planning."

"But why here? Why not at Singapore?"

97

"Here we have close contact with the government and the Ic'nichi embassy, as well as the other services. Communications with Singapore are still spotty due to your penny-pinching budgets."

That got Hogarthy's back up. "Budget policy is not your concern, Admiral!"

"No, it's your concern. You cheap-skated us for years, and now we have a war on our hands, so you'll have to live with it."

Hogarthy looked H'rhAtor and his people over uneasily. "How many are you expecting, anyway?"

"Just a few. The Fleet Elder and his staff, six, altogether."

Hogarthy hesitated. "Well..."

"And some communications ratings," H'rhAtor said. "Enough for a round-the-clock watch."

"Um...how many is that?"

"Eight more, plus the clerical staff, of course."

"*Clerical* staff?"

"We didn't bring many since we didn't have the room on board, so that's only another eight."

"And the embassy security detachment," I'eiBida said.

"And a few for housekeeping and kitchen," C'traBenla said.

"And the liaison team," the Admiral said.

"Then they need to stay at a hotel!" Hogarthy cried.

"Too risky. You've seen the demonstrations; there are far too many nutcases out there."

Hogarthy bridled at that. "These are *our* people you're talking about, *Admiral!*"

MacKenna nodded. "Yes, exactly."

"Well...then arrange space for them at the defender barracks!"

"That means a drive clear across town. The security would be a major headache, and their reaction time in case of an emergency would be way too slow."

"I'm not allowed to win, am I, Admiral!"

"You're not trying very hard."

Hogarthy threw up his hands in despair. "Do what you please and be damned, then! It's not like you listen to me anyway!"

"Who was that?" H'rhAtor asked once Hogarthy left.

"My single biggest headache," MacKenna muttered. "The Defense Minister, my civilian overlord, God help us."

H'rhAtor considered the corridor Hogarthy vanished into. "Is he always like that?"

MacKenna nodded. "Some people are like Slinkies. They have no practical use whatsoever, but they bring a smile to your face when you push them down a flight of stairs."

"Um...Slinkies?"

"Yeah." MacKenna jerked a thumb in the direction of the departed Hogarthy. "Slinkies."

§

The humans made a festive occasion of their first formal meeting by holding a reception on the fifth floor of the Defense Ministry for H'rhAtor and company. I suspected that was the Admiral's doing as I understood he was a big one on protocol, and I knew him to be a master at psychological manipulation. There were buffets for them and us (ours supplied by the embassy), and all concerned were in dress uniform. Since we can't sit at human tables, the Admiral ordered the large table removed from the conference chamber and replaced with some of the low tables we used at the embassy. Seat cushions were in short supply on earth, so they improvised with some stumpy round cushions called ottomans while they made do with folding metal chairs.

Most of the morning went to formal introductions all round, and to each side cautiously sounding out their counterparts. Until recently, the people gathered in this room had worked on the assumption that they would only expect to meet in battle, should that misfortune befall us. Now they needed to meet each other as fellow professionals facing a common foe. That took some getting used to for both sides, and U'tdaPagrn, I'eiBida, M'tinDegan and I were all busy making introductions and soothing the rough edges.

C'traBenla was in her element, of course, socializing and flirting with the fleet staffers, and soothing tensions as they rose between our people and the humans. It was a repeat of her experience at Geneva diplomatic socials during our time here, and how she did so much to improve relations. As much as I hated to admit it, she might do some good after all.

99

One human stood out among all the uniforms; a well known news vulture named Antoine DuRochelle. He was average height for a human, heavyset and conservatively dressed, and he combined an air of pompous dignity with an unerring instinct for the story. He latched onto us back when we first came to earth, and C'traBenla courted him relentlessly during our time here, which resulted in much favorable if rather sensationalistic press coverage. He grew large in human journalistic circles with his reporting, and we were counting on him to help ease the shock of the pending war when we finally had to reveal it to the human public. As I understood it, he was here for background as a favorite of the embassy; discreetly, since we didn't want a riot when every news vulture ever spawned tried to fight their way in here.

He came on H'rhAtor, MacKenna, and me at our buffet, where H'rhAtor was sampling various earth foods and chatting with his opposite number. "Do you honestly think the risk of war between our two races is past, Eldest?" he asked after introductions all round.

H'rhAtor mused on that as he munched a celery stalk. "There are still doubts and tensions, of course, so one cannot entirely rule out anything. However, both myself and the Admiral feel that familiarity will reduce the tension, which is all to the good." MacKenna nodded to that.

"Do you feel confident that our combined forces can prevail in the event of war?"

"That is the big question, of course..."

"Admiral MacKenna!" T'virDoma came barging in with all her usual domineering bluster. "I wanted *so* much to meet you." I ear-twitched an urgent caution to her, but she ignored me. "I am a candidate in the Human Studies and Xenopsychology programs being taught back home, and I can't *wait* to interview you!"

"This is hardly the time or place," I said, sternly.

"Jealous, Learnéd? I am learning *so* much more here than in your course back home. No wonder you were unwilling to give me field research." The three of them looked askance at me as I wilted in embarrassment.

"I've studied everything we have on you," she said to MacKenna. "And I believe I know you inside and out."

"Do you?" MacKenna frowned, but kept his peace.

"Although I don't see how even *you* could build a cohesive military force out of that stampede outside. Is your entire society like those wild animals? How does your civilization manage to function?"

"We take long lunches."

"I plan to make a career with our diplomatic intelligence, and I am looking forward to matching wits with you."

"I wish them well," MacKenna said, evenly.

"And are *all* your news vultures cannibals?"

"Cannibals?" MacKenna muttered in surprise as I cringed again.

"They're the *worst* of the lot!" DuRochelle stiffened in resentment. "One of your people said they were in a feeding frenzy earlier, and it looked like they were about to eat my mentor, Learnéd N'detLeda!"

MacKenna gave DuRochelle a quizzical glance. "Shocking bad taste, I'm sure. I hope he wasn't too badly gnawed on?"

"Thankfully no. You people may not mind eating each other, but you should realize that we don't share your strange cultural practices. Eating one of us will surely increase the tensions between our two races."

I started to say something, but gave up, knowing her, and let her knot her own tail.

"No doubt," MacKenna said. "But you should be careful not to spread that opinion around too widely. You never can tell when it may reach the wrong ears, and what kind of reaction may result."

"You mean the news vultures, of course," she said, dismissively. "They would be *er'trxxda* to harm one of us. Rest assured something like that would provoke a strong reaction from our people."

H'rhAtor was following this with a bemused look, and gave MacKenna a cynical ear twitch. "Indeed, Admiral. Questions would no doubt be raised in the Chamber if she is torn apart and eaten alive."

101

MacKenna nodded grimly. "Which goes to illustrate an old truism on this world that one should never earn the wrath of the news media. There's no telling what it could lead to." He glanced at DuRochelle again. "Wouldn't you agree?"

"Indeed, Admiral," DuRochelle said, somberly. "Many have learned that lesson too late, to their regret."

"That goes to confirm what I feared," T'virDoma said to him. "You should suppress these news vultures for your own good."

"Many have tried over the centuries. Few are still alive."

"Well there you are! They were likely torn apart and eaten, if that scene in the press room was any indicator." She gave DuRochelle a curious look. "I don't believe I've met you. What do you do around here?"

"*Monsieur* DuRochelle is a good friend of your embassy, and a prominent member of the Fourth Estate," the Admiral said with a carefully neutral expression.

She gave DuRochelle a quizzical look and a plastic smile. "I am pleased to meet you...but I don't recall hearing of your Fourth Estate in the briefings we received. Are you a part of the Foreign Ministry?"

"No, madame, I am not," DuRochelle said, stiffly.

"The Fourth Estate is the news media," MacKenna said.

"*News media?*" She looked at the Admiral in dismay, then whirled on DuRochelle in panic. "You're a news vulture!"

"And one of the most notorious predators out there," MacKenna added. "He's as talented as he is ruthless. Thankfully he's on our side." DuRochelle, who knew an opening when he saw it, stared straight at her, and smiled.

T'virDoma turned pallid gray and shied back under his gaze. "I...I, um...nice to meet you..." She backed away anxiously, then retreated at an unsteady trot.

"Damn, I enjoyed that," MacKenna said with a hearty chuckle. "She needs to be quarantined for that terminal case of foot-in-mouth."

"You are a wicked human, Admiral," H'rhAtor said, lightly. "And please accept our regrets for that unseemly performance, *Monsieur* DuRochelle."

DuRochelle laughed. "Thank you, Eldest, but the Admiral handled that like an artist. Well, if you will excuse me, I must circulate." He paused and gave me a hard look as he went by. "You aren't planning to turn earth into a lunatic asylum, are you?"

"Honestly, we aren't, although it looks that way at times."

*****

"Another In A Distinguished Line Of Crises"
(Related by Learnéd M'tinDegan)

The roof nearly fell in on us the next morning when K'deiTai came to the embassy bearing bad news. "The Admiral just received an order direct from the Chancellor to demobilize the fleet and cease any joint operations with us," he reported to our hastily called advising circle in the Arbiter's grotto. "He said the Chancellor told him that 'we cannot take preemptive action against an unknown alien race who we haven't even contacted yet based on claims by another alien race we don't have formal relations with.'"

"He must be *er'trxxda*!" U'tdaPagrn said.

"This is Hogarthy's doing, no doubt," K'deiTai grumbled.

"That's still *er'trxxda*! Based on what little we know, we have to presume the worst."

"What is his problem?" N'detLeda demanded.

"He claims that the Alliance charter requires diplomacy as the first and preferred means of dealings between states," K'deiTai said. "To hear it said, he believes the Admiral is usurping civilian prerogative, and that the matter should be left to the diplomats."

"Even when referring to a 'state' they don't recognize, and have no contact with? Convenient."

"This Chancellor is a reactionary," U'tdaPagrn said. "The Anti-techs are one of the main factions in his coalition. He has precious little love for us, and I'm afraid he is knotting our tails on general principle."

"Great," I'eiBida grumbled. "Are *they* still around after that uprising?"

"Yes. A surprising number of their Populist wing slipped through the net, and more have joined them since. They are every bit as virulent toward us as before, and they exert major political influence with the government."

"Without the humans' stellar bombs, what chance do we have?" I asked in dismay.

"None," I'eiBida said.

"We need to pressure him," N'detLeda said. "Have our

intelligence dig up something we can use to force him into line."

"*You* must be *er'trxxda!*" U'tdaPagrn cried. "Can you *imagine* what would happen if we were caught blackmailing the Chancellor?"

"Well then, we simply have to be careful and not get caught," N'detLeda said reasonably, for him.

"Oh, yes, simply not get caught. That will solve everything. Besides, how can you be sure it would work?"

"Remember the crisis brought on by the Anti-techs when they released the 5th Office files? The Chancellor is a political creature; there are sure to be some embarrassing secrets tucked away in odd corners. And as a political *human*, he will do anything to avoid exposure."

"But there has to be some alternative!"

"I am not optimistic, and time is of the essence. We can look for alternatives, but we must do something, and do it quickly."

"Perhaps we can go public with this, enlist popular support?" I suggested.

U'tdaPagrn shook his head. "The common humans will panic. In any event, the Chancellor holds a slim majority in Parliament, and can prevent any action. And promising to keep them out of 'our' war will strengthen his grip on power."

"I've always wondered what it would be like to be the Autocrat of a world under siege," N'detLeda said.

"Hopefully we won't have to witness it!"

"Perhaps we could take this to his political opposition?" I suggested.

U'tdaPagrn shook his head. "You would still have a public panic, and they lack the cohesion to even try to oppose him."

"Is there any way we can bribe him?" I'eiBida asked. 'He is a *human* politician, after all."

"That may be our one real option, but I can't imagine what we can offer him."

N'detLeda gave that a contemptuous sniff. "Then we're back to applying discreet pressure."

U'tdaPagrn held up his hands in a cautioning gesture. 'It's still a dangerous ploy, and I don't see any way we can sway him."

"It's straightforward enough..."

U'tdaPagrn threw up his hands and walked away. "Whatever you're thinking, I don't want to know about it!"

§

We squabbled over it for a bit after he left, then gave up and went our separate ways. I'eiBida and I lingered in the lobby to commiserate over this newest disaster. C'traBenla came in while we were talking, and tried to comfort him.

"What can we do? he asked. "We need the humans, as weak as their defenses are. From what little we know about interstellar war, if the aliens are strong enough to invade this region, we will be hard put even with the human's stellar bombs."

"I honestly don't know. We need some sort of leverage with the Chancellor, but what it could be is beyond me." I was stunned by this setback, and the look on I'eiBida's snout was dismaying.

"It will work out, love." C'tra nuzzled his ear in sympathy.

"If we can't bring the Chancellor around, then I suppose we might as well pack up and head home," he sighed. "Our next line of defense is d'enchia itself. Things are not going to be pleasant these next few years."

That was simply too bitter a thought to be borne. I had no idea what to do, but I was determined not to let that happen. "Is there any way we can work around this?"

He shook his head. "Not unless the Admiral disregards the chain of authority, which is one thing I know he won't do. That could well lead to a mutiny against him, or to the Space Fleet being suppressed just when we need them the most."

"Look...love...stall for time," C'traBenla said. "You know how volatile these humans are. Give it some time, and things may change."

I'eiBida gave her a bemused look. "So now we're relying on the humans' *er'trxxda* world view?" He shook his head in dismay. "Ancestors, what a way to make a living."

"She is right, though..."

I was interrupted when R'benTdan came barging in. "Well there you are, First Degree!" She crowded up next to him, which made him decidedly uncomfortable. "Why so sad? You look all ear wilted and tail-draggy." She gave C'traBenla an icy look, and nuzzled his ear. "Perhaps it's the company you keep. You should get away from your *problems*, and relax for a while."

If *ever* there was an inopportune moment, she had a gift for finding them. She and C'traBenla sniped back and forth at each other for months now, and the mood between them was bitter. They hadn't come to blows yet, although there were a few near calls. U'tdaPagrn lectured them both sternly on several occasions, but we hardly needed to go looking for a war as we already had one raging here in the embassy. It made for no end of lively gossip.

I'eiBida tried to politely fend her off. "I'm doing well enough, thank you."

"And the company he keeps is everything he could possibly want, and then some!" C'traBenla snarled.

"Well, that would depend on how much he expects." She stroked his neck with one finger. "You need to set higher standards."

"And what would you know? Your standards are measured in minutes!"

"But I do have some to measure."

She went back to snuggling I'eiBida's ears, by which point he was leaning so far away from her that he was about to fall over. "Look...this really isn't the time..." he protested.

"I'm sure you can *make* time; some time when we can have a little privacy." She twitched a provocative ear at C'traBenla, who almost lost it. "That way we won't evoke any jealousies among the also-rans, will we?"

"...I'm...very busy with the defense effort..." He was being forced sideways, which put him up against C'traBenla, whose mood was equally forbidding. "I really don't want..."

"So much pressure," R'benTdan cooed while stroking his neck. "So many frustrations. No wonder you look so lonely."

"I'm happy with what I have, thank you."

I was a bit surprised to see him so timid around a predatory fem, which made me wonder what his and C'tra's relationship was like. He tried vaguely to fend her off, and she finally quit.

107

"If you get tired of your everyday *problems*," she gave C'traBenla a poisonous smile as she turned to go, "look me up. I can help you cope with all that *pressure*."

"Ancestors!" I'eiBida muttered once she was gone. "We have *got* to do something about her."

"I can offer a few ideas," C'traBenla grumbled.

He gave her a guilty look. "I need to get back to the Defense Ministry. Do you want to come along?"

"Later." She stalked off, leaving I'eiBida looking dejected and embarrassed.

§

I have heard that living through a battle gives one a huge appetite; perhaps so, since I was hungry all of a sudden. I skimped on first-meal that morning, so I headed for the cafeteria for something before heading back to the Ministry. It was midmorning, and aside from a few lingerers to be found here at any hour, the place was empty. N'detLeda was there, contemplating the buffet with its usual selection fruit and pastries. He glanced at me when I came in. "A sorry business, that," he said. "I don't know what we can do now."

I presumed he meant the Chancellor. "I'm no military expert, but I doubt we can do much without the humans."

He sighed. "No, we can't. Our herd instinct has played us wrong: with our level of technology, we should have developed stellar bombs over two hundred years ago. Without them, we're defenseless against a predator race like the humans." He started peeling one of the oranges and eating the sections with single-minded attention.

"Perhaps we should consider whether we're overreacting to the Dreamsingers' warning."

He gave me a doleful look. "I was given a complete briefing before we left d'enchia, and the 'Dark Grays' Staff concurs with the Admiral about the threat. That was why they sent H'rhAtor and every available ship."

"Not that I doubt the Admiral, but perhaps the Chancellor is right: can we be sure the invaders threaten us? They might only be a threat to the Dreamsingers."

108

"He *is* the expert, and in matters of bloodshed, I trust his judgment, as do the 'Dark Grays'." He munched his way through a second orange, then added, "I'm afraid blackmailing the Chancellor is our only option. Pity U'tdaPagrn can't follow that trail."

"Perhaps he can sway the Chancellor diplomatically."

"Don't count on it. Sad to say, there is only so much U'tdaPagrn can do. He speaks officially for the Ancients and our people, so he has to maintain certain *proprieties*." He selected a third orange, then turned to me again. "Diplomats are hobbled that way, which is why he doesn't want to try pressuring the Chancellor; not that I blame him." He considered his orange for a moment, then put it back and selected a couple grapefruits instead. "I don't know what we can do," he sighed.

"Um...are you going to eat all that vitamin C?"

"Yes. And then I'm going straight to bed and sleep it off."

§

Since there was nothing more to do here, I decided to head back to the Defense Ministry and do what I could for damage control. The APA watch stander in the lobby put in a call for an embassy limo, and I waited morosely for it at the front door.

C'traBenla came stomping up as I waited, and she was still in a foul temper. "The *nerve* of her!" She was boiling mad, in fact. "She's nothing but cheap *tra'taj!*"

"Ah...you're referring to R'benTdan, I presume?"

She ignored me, paced back and forth in agitation, her ears flat and tail stiff. "I'll settle matters with her, don't you doubt it."

"Um...I hope you won't...succumb to temptation yourself." She gave he a hard look. "That is, I understand how you feel about I'eiBida, and I'd hate to see you in trouble over something rash.'

She cooled a bit, although she was still in an icy rage. "You're right," she muttered. "But I'll settle with her, you can count on it! There are ways and ways, and I'll knot her tail yet!"

The limousine pulled up, and she stomped out to it. The APA security human held the rear door for me, and I started to get in, but then a thought struck me. There are ways and ways, she said. "I'll be back in a bit," I told him, and trotted back into the embassy.

§

The Communication Circle was busy, with teletypes chattering, and the clericals hard at work organizing the day's intelligence findings. T'apiDien and W'kiLap were in 'The Pit' huddled over some paperwork when I came in.

"I have a project for you that needs to be handled with the utmost discretion," I gasped before I had to pause for breath. Those stairs are steep, and I'm not a youngling any more. The two of them waited with interest, no doubt wondering what new mystery I cared to lay on them. "I need you to do a broad search for anything you can find on the Alliance Chancellor."

W'kiLap gave me a rude ear twitch. "You mean as in anything we can use to twist his tail?" I hesitated in surprise. "We heard he shut down the human Admiral."

I really didn't want to know how they learned that, seeing as we discussed it in private just a short time ago. "He is threatening the whole defense effort; we need to persuade him to back off. Can you do it?"

T'apiDien made a rude noise. "*Of course* we can do it!"

"It'll be a huge search, though," W'kiLap added, thoughtfully. "Things like that tend to be buried pretty deep. We'll need to write some special algorithms for it."

"We'll have a fun time defining the search perimeters, too," T'apiDien said to him. "We may need help on that."

"Hmmm, yes, we might." W'kilap gave him a knowing look, then said to me, "And how does the Arbiter feel about this? Or does he even know?"

"We discussed it at some length," I said carefully. "He didn't disapprove it."

"But he didn't approve it either?"

"He said he didn't want to know."

"Plausible deniability?" T'apiDien said, doubtfully. "That only goes so far, especially if this blows up in our snouts."

"This was N'detLeda's idea; we all heard him propose it earlier. If it does blow up, he'll take the blame."

They exchanged eager looks. "Oh, well then, no problem!" T'apiDien said.

§

110

Back at the Defense Ministry, I made a point of looking for I'eiBida to give him an ears-up about her. Perhaps it was my sense of defeat, but the place seemed shabbier and more forlorn than ever. The Ic'nichi and humans both seemed to move in weary slow motion as if they were just marking time. There was a sense of gloom in the air, and the place was grimly silent. I ran into I'eiBida in the conference room where they were pulling together an emergency meeting to see what could be done about the Chancellor's orders. C'traBenla was there, fussing with the coffee and *V'liz* pots, and I could tell she was still in a bad mood.

"Best be on your guard," I told him confidentially. "She is still upset with R'benTdan. I'm not sure what she's planning, but it won't be pretty."

He gave her a discreet glance. "Ancestors save me, I love that fem." He brooded for a bit, then said, "At least she's here and not back at the embassy. If we keep them separated, she'll calm down in time."

"I hope you're right." But I wasn't confident of it.

§

Our next conference got under way, and it was not a happy meeting. Everyone was tense and frustrated, and the gulf between the humans and our people was wider than the conference table. The fragile alliance between our two races, which we began to forge only yesterday, was sorely tested as we tried to cope with a crisis with no real solution. Even we supernumeraries gathered in the background around the edge of the room were worried. Try as they would, no one could offer a workable plan. Discussion soon gave way to recriminations, and tempers began to rise.

"You humans are supposed to be the warriors," one of ours yelled. "If you can't choose leadership that will lead, what good are you?"

"Your behavior is unacceptable, Third," H'rhAtor snapped. "The humans are not our enemy!"

The Third Eldest was sullen but defiant. "With every respect, Eldest, they hardly seem to be our friends either. And if this threat is as great as they make it out to be, then their desertion is hardly a friendly act!"

111

"This was the act of a politician, *not* the Admiral or his people! It is not fair to blame them for the tail knots inflicted by their civilian superiors."

The Third was in a temper, and looked ready to say something unfortunate. "True enough, sir. But the precarious state of our defenses overrides political niceties. The threat to us all is reason for them to grab tail and change their superiors' minds, or bypass them if need be, rather than sitting here moaning about it."

The Admiral bridled at that. "And would you go against the orders of your Ancients, mister?" he demanded.

"If the situation is desperate enough, sir," the Third said, forcefully. "All of us owe our first loyalty to our people. If this is as bad as you make it out to be, then it's our responsibility to defend them by any means necessary."

"That will be enough, Third!" H'rhAtor snapped.

C'traBenla was watching this from nearby, and I saw her ears snap forward, which worried me.

"He does have a point, sir," one of the other staffers said.

"We will not tolerate insubordination or talk of mutiny!" Captain Morgan yelled.

"I am *not* suggesting mutiny, *human*," the Third said, angrily. "But we—or rather, you—have to do something!"

H'rhAtor was on his feet in a rage. "Return to ranks, *Third!*"

C'tra finally decided to act. Before any of us could stop her, she barged right in. "Please excuse me, Eldest, but I think I can be of help here." H'rhAtor paused in surprise, then glanced at I'eiBida, who cringed.

"You've all just arrived after a long journey," C'traBenla went on in that oh-so-reasonable tone which was a warning sign to those who knew her. "And I'm sure your preparations before coming here must have been hectic. It seems that your Third...what's your name?" she demanded of him.

"Um...C'cheDmrek..."

"It seems that Elder C'cheDmrek suffers from a bit of fatigue. I'm sure he meant no harm. You know how tense everyone is these days. The *pressure* is getting to him, is all."

H'rhAtor pondered her doubtfully. "Perhaps so, but still..."

112

"It happens I know *exactly* what he needs: a visit to our physical therapist at the embassy. A good workout will take care of his tension, and help him *relax*." I'eiBida cringed when he caught her drift, as did K'deiTai. C'traBenla looped her arm around the Third's and half-dragged him toward the door, leaving H'rhAtor bemused. 'I'm sure you will feel *much* better...I'ei, will you call down and have the limo waiting? Ask for *R'benTdan*, and say that you have some *pressure* to work off..."

"I do not *believe* this," U'tdaPagrn muttered in disbelief.

"You don't know her very well, do you?" I said.

She was back a bit later, and there was evil glint in her eyes. "*What* are you doing?" I'eiBida demanded in a hoarse whisper.

"Not all diplomacy is handled over a conference table, love." She gave him a knowing look. "And it'll keep her hands away from where they aren't welcome."

"All right," he sighed. "But if she ruins him, they'll take it out of your pay."

§

The conference tried to pick up where we left off, but there really wasn't much to say. Without the blessings of the human authorities, there was little any of us could do, and little reason for the fleet to remain in human space. At least the tempers had cooled, and while there was still a degree of antagonism, it was under control for the time being.

"What a sorry mess," MacKenna groaned to H'rhAtor as the meeting broke up. "Hell of a note when our own leadership is the first enemy we have to defeat."

"I suppose all we can do is return home," H'rhAtor said. "But I strongly suggest we maintain active communication so we can continue our planning. If nothing comes of it, no harm will be done, but we don't want to be caught unprepared."

"True," MacKenna said. He considered for a bit, then said, "But let's stall for time. Stay here for as long as you can; we might still be able to talk the Chancellor around. We'll tell Hogarthy you're making preparations and wrapping up last minute details."

H'rhAtor nodded. "Agreed, Admiral."

§

We gathered in our lounge to talk things over, and *Monsieur* DuRochelle joined us shortly thereafter. "It is a sad thing *mes amis*," he said as he settled on one of the ottomans.

"Why is the Chancellor so dead set against us, anyway?" K'deiTai complained. "It's not like we haven't done everything possible to build good relations with your race."

"There is political advantage in fear. All politicians use it to some degree, and he is one of *those* who rely on it most because they have nothing positive to offer."

"We have a few like that ourselves."

"Can we talk him around?" I'eiBida asked. "Surely he can see the danger to your people."

"He is stubborn and opinionated," DuRochelle said. "And he has an inflated view of his adequacy. It will take a lot to change his mind."

"Hopefully the Admiral can convince Hogarthy to let us continue," K'deiTai said. "We should give him time to act."

"I sometimes wonder if there is greater hostility between the Admiral and his superiors than there is between our two races. I'm afraid his temper gets the better of him at times; he is not the most diplomatic of souls."

"Can't fault him, considering," I'eiBida grumbled.

"Perhaps we should release the story," K'deiTai said. "The public reaction may force the Chancellor's hand."

"I'm concerned that your people aren't ready for something like that," I said in turn.

DuRochelle mused on it. "Perhaps not. But we may have no choice. It may be our only lever to budge the Chancellor."

That reminded me of my conversation with our two computer *'v'thorble*, earlier. "We should explore all options before taking any rash action," I cautioned.

"I cannot sit on this story forever, *Monsieur*, especially as the Chancellor's actions imperil our people."

"I know, but please hold off a while longer. We don't know if this order will stand yet, and we don't want a panic if it can be avoided."

"True enough..."

T'virDoma came wondering in with a frustrated scowl on her snout. "Has anyone seen Learnéd N'detLeda?" she demanded.

"He is at the embassy," I told her. "He was feeling a bit under the weather."

"*l'cc'vn*," she grumbled. "I wanted to get his reaction to today's conference." She gave us all a frustrated glare. "These humans are almost *impossible* to understand, and there is so *much* gossip that it's hard to figure out *what's* going on around here!"

"Perhaps we could discuss current affairs over dinner," DuRochelle said in mock innocence.

T'virDoma flinched, then gave him a hard look and stalked off in a huff. Someone explained to her about her cannibalism gaffe of yesterday, and all and sundry, including the humans, had a fine time razzing her about it ever since.

§

It was late that evening when the three of us returned to the embassy after a long, trying day. Third Elder C'cheDmrek was waiting at the lobby entrance with Agent Goldblum for company when we arrived. He was ragged and disheveled, there were bite marks on his neck, and he favored one leg as he came down the walk in a flat-footed waddle. Evidently C'traBenla's therapy worked as planned: he was too weary and sore to be tense.

He paused when we met, and considered C'traBenla with a bleary-eyed stare. "Remarkable fem," he mumbled at last, before climbing painfully into the back of the limo.

"He seemed quite smitten by her," Agent Goldblum said as they drove off.

"Yes, I noticed the bruises."

"Oy. Well, if you will excuse me, sir, I have to fill out another incident report."

I'eiBida looked askance at C'traBenla once he was gone. "What did you have him say to get her going like that, anyway?"

She gave him a knowing smile. "You don't know everything about fems, my love."

"Perhaps that's for the best."

*****

115

"Unsung Heros"
(Related by Defender I'eiBida)

Someone was knocking persistently on our door, which dragged me out of a solid slumber. I lay there in a half-awake stupor, annoyed by the knocking, and wondering vaguely what that was all about.

"I'ei?" C'tra's elbow completed the ruin of my sleep, and I rolled over with an aggrieved sigh.

It took me some time to fumble my way to the door, still irritable and half asleep, and determined to give whoever it was a piece of my mind—if I could find it. It was M'tinDegan, dressed in a robe and looking like he was rousted out of bed as well. "What?" I asked him, plaintively.

"I just received a call from W'kiLap. He wants us to come to the Communications Circle right away."

"At *this* hour?"

"I don't understand it either, but he said it was urgent that we should come now."

"Can't this wait until morning?"

"Evidently not. He said they have some important news about a special project they're working on, and we need to come right away."

"I should have been an accountant," I grumbled. I closed the door and went to get my robe.

"Who was that?" C'tra mumbled.

"M'tinDegan. Something going on in Communications." She complained something inarticulate, and went back to sleep.

"I hope you appreciate how C'tra is going to knot my tail over this in the morning," I said as to M'tinDegan we trudged down the third floor aisle.

"It should be worth it," he promised me. That should have made me nervous, but I was still half asleep.

§

The Communications Circle was eerily quiet at this predawn hour, and deserted except for our two computer Learnéds and the last person I expected to see: our old nemesis Honoré Dassault.

116

"What..." I stared at him, flabbergasted. He was the same as ever; tall and spare, with a chill, remote demeanor. His fur was a bit thinner, and he trimmed off the fur strip under his nose, but there was no mistaking him after all the gyrations he put us through. "How did *you* get in here?"

"I believe we had this discussion once before, *monsieur*." he said with a thin smile. "My specialty, you will recall, is covert entry. True, your security has improved since my last visit, but I was not an invited guest then."

I turned on W'kiLap. "You let him through our security?"

"That was no trick," W'kiLap said, dismissively. "L'datMparn isn't the great expert he imagines himself to be."

"He let us design the upgrade, so it was easy to leave a few discreet peepholes," T'apiDien said with a snort of contempt. "He never saw it even with the plans right under his snout."

"*Great Ancestors* What were you two thinking?"

My dismay didn't faze T'apiDien in the least. "There was a lot of ground to cover, and his expertise helped speed the search up to a gallop. We're already getting results."

"...search? What search?"

"For embarrassing secrets we can pressure the Chancellor with to get him to back off on the war effort."

"*You plan to extort the human government?*" I was even more dismayed than before, if possible. "Do you have any *idea* what a smell that will make if it gets out?"

"The Chancellor won't say anything, and it was N'detLeda's idea to begin with, so he'll get the knotted tail if anyone does."

That mollified me somewhat. "Still, this is a desperate move if ever there was one."

"Not so desperate with the help of our friend here." W'kiLap gestured to Dassault.

"You need to get him out of here before someone sees him! If L'datMparn finds out about this we'll all lose our ears!"

"Not to worry. His defenders despise him enough that we had no trouble cultivating some key members of his herd these last few months. *Assuming* he shows any diligence at this hour, the night watch will keep him occupied."

117

"I should have been an accountant." I studied Dassault, bemused, then shook my head. "Have you three gone rogue on us, or what?" I asked M'tinDegan.

"Actually, I didn't know about him until this moment. But this is urgent enough that any step is justified. It's for their good as much as ours."

"I believe the humans call it 'tough love'," W'kiLap said.

"Not to mention it's some juicy gossip," T'apiDien added.

"But...but...why him?   Never mind that; *how* did he get involved?"

"You may recall I once said it is always wise to cultivate a variety of resources," Dassault said, severely.   "After our last encounter with the Anti-techs, your associates and I felt it best to maintain contact against future need."

"We haven't used him until now," W'kiLap said. "But bringing him in as a consultant proved to be a good choice."

"Indeed. The secret to successful covert snooping is knowing where to look, and the fishing, so to speak, has been most productive." Dassault allowed us another of his thin smiles. "This has proved most entertaining.   One cannot help but want to exercise old skills."

"The Chancellor has been a naughty human," T'apiDien said. "We're following a wealth of leads."

Dassault nodded in grim satisfaction.   "Enough that your problem should evaporate in short order."

"My Ancestors must be in hysterics," I muttered.   "Well since you're here, what have you uncovered?"

"It would seem, *monsieur*, that the Chancellor has certain *informal* interests in a number of major government contractors. He has received several stock options lately, as well as a number of expensive gifts, specifically access to a certain young lady of exquisite charm and dubious character. It all ties in suspiciously with the granting of some huge public contracts."

"It's buried deep behind several layers of front companies and bank accounts," W'kiLap said. "But it's definitely there. We're still digging up the details, but it's only a matter of time until we have the whole sordid story."

"And it gets better," T'apiDien added. "All this cover means he has a sophisticated organization backing him. If that were revealed, it would go far beyond his own corruption."

"Indeed," Dassault mused. "It appears the Chancellor has been bought by one of the multinational syndicates. Should the opposition learn of it," he offered another of his thin, humorless smiles, "it could bring down the current régime."

I pondered that for a moment. "That would do the trick, but will it get him to back down?."

"He'll do anything to avoid exposure, especially if he is as obsessed with power as most humans are," M'tinDegan said.

"You may rest assured of that, *monsieur*."

"Have they detected you?" I asked W'kiLap.

"Not as yet, we *think*."

I gave Dassault a bemused look, then turned to M'tinDegan. "I do not *believe* I'm doing this. If you've gone this far, you might as well go ahead and find what you can. But what*ever* happens, don't let them know it is us doing the snooping!"

§

Morning came all too soon, and with it the usual round of squabbling. It never quits on this planet. The atmosphere in the Defense Ministry was tense when we arrived. Apparently Admiral MacKenna spent the morning thus far trying to talk Minister Hogarthy around, and the results were dismal. By all accounts, the Admiral tried reasoning persuasion at first, and when that produced nothing, his mood descended rapidly and the tension rose accordingly. As we were going up in the elevator, we could hear him and Hogarthy shouting at each other in Hogarthy's grotto on the second floor.

K'deiTai looked askance at me and shook his head. "Not good," he muttered.

"Like we don't have enough of that at the embassy," I grumbled.

That curst elevator took *forever* to reach the fifth floor, and we were all itchy with the tension pervading the place by time we arrived. Needless to say, the first person we ran into was T'virDoma, who caught us in the staff lounge.

"There you are!" She was clearly in a mood. "It's about time you showed up. Things are falling apart around here, which doesn't surprise me with these *humans*."

"Well excuse us for eating and sleeping," I snapped at her.

"Learnéd N'detLeda is doing the best he can to cope with this latest crisis, so you need to get to it before things fall apart completely."

Ancestors, was I tempted. "You can tell His Loudness that we'll be along right away," I said, coolly.

"One would hope. And *you* need to get to work and simmer some *V'liz*," she added to C'traBenla. "Hopefully you won't set the building on fire again."

C'tra took exception to that, I can tell you. "Why me?" she demanded. "Can't you even heat up some *V'liz?*"

"*I* don't have time for *domestic* chores; that's why you're here. I'm busy doing important work." She trotted out before C'tra could react, leaving us to face her temper.

"That...*Bna'vwep!*" It took her a moment, she was so furious. "The *nerve* of that *un'tdar!*"

"Don't let her knot your tail, love."

K'deiTai retreated a step or two. "She's like that with everyone," he said.

"I'll teach her some manners!"

"Love...please..." She gave me a venomous look and stomped out. "Great," I grumbled. "Now we have two wars on our hands."

"And the invaders haven't even shown up yet," K'deiTai sighed.

I looked askance at him. "Are you sure about that?"

§

The first formal council of war got under way a short while later in hopes of accomplishing as much as possible before the joint effort was finally shut down. Admiral MacKenna sat at one end of the long conference table with the human staffers along the right side. H'rhAtor sat at the other end with his staff along the left side. Captain Morgan sat next to the Admiral, and we of the liaison herd hovered awkwardly in the background. The Admiral was a great one for protocol, so coffee and *V'liz* were served to all. The meeting got started once the servers withdrew.

120

"We have redoubled our shipbuilding efforts," the Admiral reported. "As is, we have three destroyers in commission, a fourth nearing completion, plus our five armed transports and scouts which aren't good for much more than reconnaissance and logistics."

"What about those battleships?" H'rhAtor demanded.

"If we divert all available resources, they'd be at least five years away from completion. In any case we won't miss 'em. They were the bright idea of the former régime."

"Four ships. Plus two squadrons the Ancients authorized as an expeditionary force. Twelve total. Against what?"

"Unknown. We have been trying to devise a reasonable worst case scenario, and the figures range from forty to over a hundred combat units."

"Probably larger and far better armed, as well." H'rhAtor was grim. "I suspect we shall miss your battleships before this is over, Admiral."

MacKenna gave a derisive snort. "Not hardly. So, what do you bring to the table?"

"We have eight patrol ships, a mix of new construction and more recent older ships, in two squadrons. More may join us if hostilities are prolonged. We also can call on seven ships suitable for logistic train and one for scouting forces."

"You really need more logistics, and especially scouts," MacKenna said. "We have both of ours committed, but they're nowhere near enough coverage, and both need servicing. Can't you expedite any more of yours?"

U'tdaPagrn, who was sitting next to me, gasped, and from the way the fleet staffers' ears laid back, I could tell they were alarmed too. MacKenna was probing into one of our most sensitive security issues; one that would be critical now, and which we couldn't avoid revealing. H'rhAtor considered him somberly, then evidently decided we needed to trust him. "No, Admiral. The eight ships I bring are all we have crews for." MacKenna's eye ridges shot up in their surprise gesture. "We are reshuffling the civilian fleet to free up transport ships, which will take time since we can't disregard our colony support program," H'rhAtor hastened

121

to explain. "We have some volunteers coming from the civilian sector, and a new herd has just graduated from the fleet circle, but we are especially short of command rates. We can hardly place raw Fourth Degrees in leadership positions. It appears we are not as adept at mobilizing as you are."

I gave an exasperated sigh and shook my head sadly. Training was a large part of my duty back home with the Staff, and all our efforts to date were still woefully inadequate. C'traBenla took my hand, and rubbed her snout against my ears reassuringly.

"Well, anyway," MacKenna went on. "As for armaments, our ships are all armed with gatling guns for defense, and each destroyer carries eight missiles. I have ordered the missile racks reinstalled on our scouts and transports." He paused and gave U'tdaPagrn a close look. "I can reverse that order if you insist."

H'rhAtor didn't bother to look to the Arbiter. "That will not be necessary, Admiral. We will waive that provision of the First Accord for the duration of this crisis."

"Thank you." MacKenna seemed relieved. "In that case, that gives us another forty tubes, seventy-two missiles total."

"Not bad," H'rhAtor said. "Our ships each carry twelve missiles, for a total of ninety-six." That produced a rumble among the humans.

"Let's just hope they're enough," MacKenna said. "Each of our missiles carries one nuke of a hundred kilotons yield."

H'rhAtor seemed confused. "A hundred kilotons, Admiral?"

"The equivalent of a hundred thousand tons of explosives."

H'rhAtor seemed stunned by that figure. M'tinDegan dove into his pouch for a calculator, and started working feverishly.

"I take it all your missiles have nukes?" MacKenna asked.

Again those of us in the room stiffened in alarm; what the Admiral was asking for was even more sensitive than our total fleet strength.

H'rhAtor agonized over what to say for some time. "No, Admiral," he said at last, fatalistically. "...we...do not have such weapons." The humans were stunned. "We know about them," he added, quickly. "But until we met your people, we had no idea anyone would be *er'trxxda* enough to make such things."

M'tinDegan handed his calculator to me and muttered, "A hundred kilotons, our measure." The number was appalling.

"Conventional missiles against nukes?" MacKenna said softly. "We out-gunned you all this time?" There was a long, tense silence as the two sides waited for the next move. H'rhAtor had just been forced to reveal our fatal weakness which would leave us helpless against the humans despite our larger fleet.

"They won't attack us," I muttered. "They have enough to worry about now."

"But what about tomorrow?" K'deiTai said, grimly.

Then the Admiral stood and looked around the room at the other humans. "What was said here stays here." His tone implied big trouble for anyone who disobeyed him. "*No one* is to breathe a word of this to anyone, *ever!*"

§

The conference broke for mid-meal, which was catered in the conference room by the human Ministry staff and a detail from the embassy. The mood was glum as we nibbled and argued among ourselves over how to cope what looked like a hopeless situation. Our people were tense after H'rhAtor's damaging revelations, and much of the muttering in closed circles was about how the humans might use that knowledge, and what we could do about it.

Some of the humans tried to be friendly, particularly Commander Rostokovich, who worked tirelessly to bridge the gap of suspicion and doubt. That helped some, but the idea of two forces created for the express purpose of fighting each other now joining hands against a common threat was simply too novel to be swallowed easily. Our liaison herd tried to soothe the frictions between the two staffs, but it was awkward and tense at best.

MacKenna and H'rhAtor took the occasion to slip away into the next room for some personal snout-to-snout away from the spotlight of their staffs. I noticed them leave, and my curiosity got the better of me, so I slipped out of the conference room and down the hall to the empty office on the other side. The connecting door was ajar, so I hovered close with my ears cocked.

"I...want to thank you, Admiral, for keeping confidence about our lack of nuclear weapons," H'rhAtor was saying.

I risked peeking through the crack behind the door, and could just make out the two of them. MacKenna sat in a chair leaning on his stick, while H'rhAtor stood in front of him. From the set of his ears, I could tell he was worried, as well he should be.

MacKenna eyed him with a disgusted look. "We have more important things to do than stabbing each other in the back. No sense in tempting those idiots down stairs."

H'rhAtor studied his snout for a tense moment. "They were right about you," he said at last. MacKenna gave him a raised eyebrow. "Our intelligence people told me you are one of the few humans in a position of authority whom we can trust. It is good to know that my faith in you was not misplaced."

"I'm grateful for your vote of confidence, Eldest." There was another tense silence. "Please understand, H'rhAtor, I am not a free agent. My loyalty is to my people and to the Alliance. If I must fight you, I won't hesitate, nor will I hold anything back. I will do my duty as best I can."

"I understand, Admiral. Your sense of loyalty is most commendable, and I will not expect you to do less than your best...if you must."

MacKenna brooded for a time, then his shoulders sagged. "All this fear and mistrust is bullshit. We have no reason to hate each other. From what I've seen of your people, we should be natural allies."

"I agree, Brian." H'rhAtor's ears settled, and his tail sagged in a gesture of confidentiality. "But until our leaders understand that there is no cause to fear, they will do so. Your people and ours are alike: they must have leaders to be fearful for them, and we in turn must be strong for our leaders."

"I like the way you put that. But how do we prove a negative?"

"There is no way, except for the passage of time."

MacKenna made a rude noise. "Don't hold out much hope, politicians being what they are." He sagged in his chair, brooding.

"This joint defense will give us a good start."

"Yeah. I'm afraid we may be so deep in it that we won't need to fear each other for a long time to come. Dammit, neither of our fleets is ready for war."

"Our patrol service was a public safety force until you came along," H'rhAtor said, confidentially. "Our ships' armaments were there mostly as a precaution; and frankly, they were badly out of date."

"Hell, until we met you, our space program was just make-work to keep our tech sector alive. We scrounged up old designs to improvise armaments during the Contact Crisis."

"Beyond that is the skills question. I admit I do not have any combat experience. We've never fought a space battle." That sounded like a confession and a laying down of a burden.

MacKenna shook his head sadly. "I've been a soldier all my life—ever since I was drafted into the Navy at seventeen. I have no idea how many wars big and small I've been in." He gave H'rhAtor a bleak look. "I heard your wars aren't much to write home about. I wonder if you can comprehend the horrors I've seen, that I've had a hand in."

"I've read the reports and seen some videos, but they don't begin to tell the story. In a way, I envy you, Brian. At least you know what you're doing."

"Yeah, I know. God help me, I know." That struck me as odd that this human who loomed so large in our darkest fears would be so troubled by his own abilities. He sighed, and stared off at nothing. "So much senseless bloodshed," he muttered. "All for the sacred honor of the cause. And it's always some self-righteous bastard who sends us off with bands and flags and bullshit to kill each other."

"I have read the histories of your famous leaders, and some of them make the fears all too real."

"Hold out hope if you can, my friend, but don't expect miracles from those sad-asses," MacKenna said, bitterly. "We may yet wind up facing each other some day."

"You are right, Brian," H'rhAtor said after a gloomy silence. "We are creatures of duty, you and I, and if we must fight, then we will. But as you said, your first loyalty is to your *people*, as is mine. Let us agree to remember that."

MacKenna eyed him, then nodded.

§

125

W'kiLap showed up by mid-afternoon with the latest news. "It's all here," he told our little conspiracy when we gathered in the conference room. He waved a human computer disc. "Facts and figures, names and dates, e-mails and fund transfers, enough to send the Chancellor and many others to prison."

"Ancestors!" I gasped as I looked around in alarm, even though the room was empty other than the three of us. "Hide that thing! Do you want the humans to find it?"

W'kiLap shrugged, and tucked the disc into his pouch. "I don't see what you're so worried about. We have the Chancellor by his ears, so let's get on with it."

Now that I was confronted with it, my tail was seriously wilted by the whole idea. "I hate to do this. It could cause no end of trouble between us and the humans."

"Right now the humans are the least of our worries, and the Chancellor is far more vulnerable than we are."

"This is completely unethical, even by human standards."

"The best methods always are. The point is that we have the Chancellor's tail, and can twist it as hard as we please. So what are we going to do about it?"

"We need the humans for the war effort," M'tinDegan said.

I scowled at that. "We can't do much without them."

"So we have no choice, really."

I shook my head in dismay. "We sure don't teach these things at the Academy. If we do this, who takes it to the Chancellor?"

"Um...good question," M'tinDegan mumbled as he and W'kiLap exchanged doubtful looks.

"We can't ask U'tdaPagrn; he'd never approve of it," W'kiLap said.

"And we can't expect him to officially involve the embassy in any event."

"N'detLeda, perhaps?"

I shied at that. "He's the *last* person we want to know of this! There's no telling *what* he and the hard-liners back home would use it for."

"Perhaps that human news vulture, DuRochelle?" M'tinDegan suggested.

126

"He would never squat on a story this big. He will blast it all over the networks, which would precipitate another government crisis at the worst possible moment."

"Aside from which, he's our threat to backbeat the Chancellor with," W'kiLap added.

"I can't think of anyone else. Any ideas?" They both shook their heads. "This is *er'trxxda*," I sighed. "This will never work, and it could make a fine mess of things. You don't even have a complete plan of action."

"It's our one realistic hope."

"Ancestors save us if *that's* the case. I have a bad feeling about this. We shouldn't use it unless we have no other choice. Perhaps the Admiral can still sway Hogarthy."

"Ancestors save us if *that's* what we're depending on," M'tinDegan said with a grim smile.

I shook my head in dismay, and turned to the door, but then paused and turned back. "What did you do with Dassault?"

"We paid him a consulting fee, and sent him on his way," W'kiLap said.

"Can we trust him with this?"

"Of *course* not. But he knows the value of what we dug up, so he'll hang onto it for now."

"I only hope my Ancestors are watching, because they'll never believe me otherwise."

§

There was another gloomy conference that afternoon, where the two sides started to map out the preparations needed, and it was soon obvious that we were in trouble. As inadequate as our defenses were, we were appalled by the sorry state of the human fleet, which existed on a bare-bones budget for years. They were desperately short of everything, much of which—such as cryonic gasses for their ships' systems—could not be quickly remedied. Their defense industry was a hollow shell, and their economy would be hard put to cover the costs of this war. In all honesty, about the only thing they could bring to the effort were their stellar bombs and their horrific aggressiveness, exemplified by Admiral MacKenna himself.

H'rhAtor and his staff returned to the fleet that afternoon, not wanting to complicate matters while the Admiral tried to change the Minister's mind. He and MacKenna agreed to stall the fleet's departure for as long as possible, and continue strategy discussions as best we could by radio. It was a sorry state of affairs, and the fifth floor of the Defense Ministry was shrouded in gloom when it came time to head back to the embassy.

"So what are we to do?" M'tinDegan asked as we were on our way down in the elevator. "I suspect it could take forever to bring the humans up to speed, and we aren't in much better shape, from what H'rhAtor said."

"You have no idea," I told him. "This is the worst logistics mess I've ever heard of: munitions, consumables, fuel, personnel— whatever a fighting fleet needs, they haven't got it, and they don't have the means to make it."

"Can we help them out?"

"With a few things; cryonic gasses, for one. But they're more or less on their own for most of it." I brooded on the sad state of affairs back home, and added, "We'll have our hands full, too."

"This is folly! If there was ever a need for our two races to work closely together, this is it. MacKenna and H'rhAtor need to stand snout to snout. Conferencing by radio is a poor second best, and runs the very real risk of a security breach. How can we plan for a major war like this?"

"Longer tails than mine can't answer that one," I said, somberly. "I haven't the faintest."

"We don't have any choice," he said firmly. "We *have* to blackmail the Chancellor."

I sighed. "I hate to risk it; it could make a dreadful smell if it goes bad. But you may be right."

*****

128

"Alarms And Excursions"
(Related by Learnéd M'tinDegan)

"*Mon Deus!*" Agent Roubidoux cried when we approached him about our plan at the Defense Ministry the next morning. 'Are you mad?"

"I don't like it either, Pierre," I'eiBida said. "But we have to twist his tail if we're to prepare your fleet for this war."

He glanced nervously up and down the corridor, then lowered his voice to a frantic whisper. "You would blackmail the *Chancellor?* Do you realize what you are attempting? Can you *imagine* what this could do to interstellar relations?"

"We have to risk it."

"And what will your own leaders say if this explodes on you? Aside from the diplomatic consequences, *think* of what this could do to your careers!"

"N'detLeda came up with the idea, so he'll take the blame."

That mollified him somewhat. "Even so, this is folly.'

"Perhaps," I said. "But we have no choice."

He brooded on it for a bit. "Perhaps. Regrettable, but the hour calls for stern measures, I suppose."

"Thank you for understanding, Pierre." I waved a human language transcript of the information we dug up at him. "But now we need someone to deliver this to the Chancellor."

Pierre shied in panic. "I certainly cannot do it! That would expose me." He gave I'eiBida a frightened look. "You promised not to force me to commit treason!"

"I did, and I'll keep that promise, Pierre," I'eiBida said, reluctantly, which made me wonder what that was about. "But can you suggest someone we can approach on this?"

He muttered something frantic in French, and looked around again. There was no sign of anyone in the area, except for the sounds of construction in an office at the end of the hall. Then he said, "I can think of no one who might have access, and whom you could count on. And, please, I do not wish to have anything further to do with this!"

"I can't fault you for that, but please keep this to yourself."

Pierre sighed in obvious relief, and studied us both closely. "I should report this. But you are my friends, and I know you mean well, folly though this is." He shook his head in dismay. "Who would believe me in any case?"

§

Admiral MacKenna came in a short while later after another morning of arguing with Minister Hogarthy. From the fury in his snout, it was plain that he fared no better than in previous days. It would seem that Minister Hogarthy was made of sterner stuff than he appeared to be if he could stand up under the Admiral's wrath.

I made a point of bringing him a cup of human coffee from the improvised staff lounge both to ward off the Autumn chill which pervaded the building and hopefully to ingratiate myself in some small way in hopes of learning the latest. "My guess is you had no luck, Admiral?" I asked as I handed him the mug.

"Yeah, he has a whim of iron," he grumbled. He slumped in his chair and stared at nothing, then took a sip of the coffee. "Thank you," he mumbled.

"What is his problem? He is the Defense Minister; doesn't he see the danger?"

He gave me a derisive snort. "This is nothing new. I went through this for years during the Contact Crisis." He fumed over his coffee mug for a bit. "He puts the 'petty' in petty bureaucrat. If it was just him, I'd mop the floor with him; but he borrowed a backbone from the Chancellor, and as long as he has that, there'll be no reasoning with him."

"Could you go over his head, perhaps? Surely the Chancellor will see that this is a critical defense matter."

"The Chancellor was all too happy to undercut the fleet to begin with, so we'll have no joy at that party."

"Is there any way you can work around him?"

He brooded on that. "Nothing I care to set a precedent for," he said at last. He took another sip of coffee, and stared dejectedly out the window at the bare trees. "The hell of it is, we'll be hard put together. By ourselves, we can't do much of anything. I hate to say it, but that asswipe is setting us up for a defeat in detail."

§

130

If I'eiBida and I were faltering after our encounter with Agent Roubidoux, the Admiral's gloomy assessment, which I'eiBida agreed with, stiffened our resolve. After some discussion, we decided to seek out Commander Rostokovich.

"Borjemoi!" Ivan said when we broached our plot to him. "Pierre warned me you were planning this madness, but I found it hard to believe. You are courting disaster with this, you know."

"It's N'detLeda's idea," I'eiBida told him. "So it'll his tail in the wringer if this gets out."

That mollified him, and he thought on it for a bit. "Do you have something solid to use against the Chancellor?"

I showed him the transcript. "There is enough here to bring him down, and we're uncovering more."

Ivan mused over the transcripts, with an occasional raised eye ridge. "Good. He is no *tovaritch* to the fleet, or to your pecple," he said at last. "Hopefully it will get rid of him."

"Hopefully it won't come to that. Right now we need someone to deliver this to him."

Ivan shoved the transcript back to us and held up both hands in a defensive gesture. "I would have no reason to speak with Chancellor, so it would be suspicious if I approach him. And it would implicate Admiral; I do *not* want to earn *his* anger!"

"So what do we do now?" I'eiBida wondered after he left.

"Honestly, I have no idea. They don't train sociologists for espionage and intrigue."

"How about sending him an anonymous e-mail?"

"That might work, but I get the feeling it won't be as effective as confronting him directly."

"Could Dassault do it?"

"I suspect he won't, seeing his obsession with secrecy."

"Perhaps he could suggest someone?"

"I'm not thrilled about delving any deeper into his world, but that may be our only option."

"That's the worst of all this," he sighed. "We must be in a sorry state if that's all we can count on to save us."

"No, the worst is we can't even count on that."

§

131

U'tdaPagrn was visibly agitated when he intercepted me upon my return to the embassy that afternoon. "There you are!" he snapped. "Where have you been?"

I halted and eyed him in alarm, wondering if we were about to be attacked by the invaders. "At the Defense Ministry. What's going on?"

"We have a new crisis on our hands. The embassy of the Dominions of Versailles has announced a reception for H'rhAtor and his staff. They'll be on their way down by shuttle shortly."

That was a relief! I could think of worse crises than a diplomatic social; although come to think of it, that would take some doing. "He's not one for diplomatic fluff, I understand. I imagine he was not thrilled."

"You suppose?" U'tdaPagrn gave me a vexed ear twitch. "I never thought anyone would use such language in an open transmission, even if it was coded."

"But who will show up on such short notice? These things normally take forever to organize."

U'tdaPagrn faltered. "I suspect this is aimed at the Chancellor. He needs the Dominions' support, so he'll surely put in an appearance. But why drag H'rhAtor into it?"

I pondered the implications unhappily. "This could upset the diplomatic equation. If the Dominions is playing their own game on the war effort, who knows how things might turn."

"That's putting it mildly. One thing we do know is this is a command performance by someone who takes an interest in our squabble with the Chancellor, and has the grunt to make waves, so we need to get over there as fast as possible."

§

The embassy of the Dominions Of Versailles was a monument befitting a powerful and prosperous member of the Alliance Of Nations. It's massive stone bulk was set in the center of a broad, flawlessly tended lawn dotted with trees and ornamental plants, and surrounded by an ornate iron fence. Despite the dormant plants and the Autumn chill, it was an impressive sight, glowing in the twilight. The gate guards saluted smartly as we drove up, and some embassy staffers were waiting to open the doors and escort

132

us into the hall. Despite the brave display, the place was largely empty. The bandstand was vacant, and the servants were still fiddling with the buffet. Even the area fenced off for the news vultures was bare.

K'deiTai was already there talking with I'eiBida when we arrived, and they seemed as perplexed as we were. "All I've been able to learn thus far is that this is a last-minute affair put on at the urging of someone from *our* embassy," K'deiTai told us. "But I haven't been able to find out who."

"It wasn't my doing," U'tdaPagrn said in confusion.

"*Something's* going on," I'eiBida said. "Is this a political move by N'detLeda?"

"If it is, I'll have his ears," U'tdaPagrn growled. "I'll take this to the Most Ancient in person."

K'deiTai agonized over that. "It's the only thing that makes sense, but thus far he hasn't shown up."

I'eiBida scanned the room with a morose look. "I don't see what good can come of this. There's hardly been enough advance notice to draw much of a crowd." As if to make a point, the staff were standing idly around, and there were only a handful of human guests, who mostly looked confused and a bit lost.

"Circles within circles," U'tdaPagrn said. "The Dominions are the single largest contingent in the Chancellor's coalition, and they haven't been happy with some of his decisions lately. Their hosting an official reception for H'rhAtor must be a warning to the Chancellor and his cabinet. Rest assured this evening will be a busy one. All the tail-shakers will have to appear."

I'eiBida nodded. "So, they're giving him a snap-to order. The Dominions is twisting his tail for some political purpose: the request from our embassy is just an excuse. They wouldn't bother to help us otherwise."

"But what's their game?" I asked. "Is this about the war effort, or are they simply using H'rhAtor as a *cause-célébre* to pressure the Chancellor about some domestic issue?"

U'tdaPagrn faltered as he considered that one. "No way to say, but if that's the case, this could damage our relations with the Alliance even further."

133

"I don't pretend to understand this *x'mnnb'''* I'eiBida muttered. "If this is N'detLeda's scheme, I don't see what it can accomplish, or why the Dominions would let him use them."

"Hopefully we can turn this to some advantage in the next few days," K'deiTai said. "Whatever's going on here, this could give us a small lever to use with the Dominions."

"If it doesn't make us into diplomatic poison." U'tdaPagrn scowled. "One can but hope for the best."

"*There* you are, I'ei!" C'traBenla came floating up with a plate from the buffet. "Isn't this exciting? I haven't been to one of these in the *longest* time. We'll have a grand time tonight!"

K'deiTai threw his hands up in despair and walked away.

I'eiBida looked at her in surprise. She was dressed to kill in her new blue velour gown and her latest jewelry finds, which must have taken hours of preparation. "What are you doing here?" he demanded.

"Attending the reception, of course."

"C'tra..." He gave an exasperated ear twitch, and his tail sagged. "This is official business. Something's going on with the Dominions, and it could be critical."

"All the more reason for me to be here stroking my contacts among the human politicians."

"Love...please...the situation is very delicate. I know you mean well, but..."

"But nothing! I spent two and a half years cultivating the Geneva herd, and now it's time to cash in. Who knows what a little smooth talk in the right ears might reveal?"

"It's not that simple. We may have a crisis on our hands."

"I would think you'd have a *little* more faith in my good intentions." She frowned at him, and her ears laid back. "In any event, this is the first real social event to come along since we arrived here, and I for one plan to have a good time!"

I'eiBida sighed, and looked her over skeptically. "How did you hear about this, anyway?"

She gave him a chilly look. "The Dominions' Cultural Attache and I are old friends; *of course* they would remember to invite me, which is more than I can say for *some* people."

K'deiTai came back once she left. "Why did you have to bring *her?*" he demanded.

"Have you ever tried to stop her when a party is involved?" I'eiBida grumbled.

§

The evening was indeed a busy one, although the herd drifted in slowly as humans rushed to get ready on such short notice. The Chancellor and a couple hand's worth of political cronies showed up all in a rush and looking decidedly out of sorts. The Dominions' Ambassador hardly had time to greet him properly before H'rhAtor and his staff arrived as well.

H'rhAtor was thoroughly put out by all this, but K'deiTai managed to intercept him before he plunged into the thick of it, and gave him our latest speculation about the political undercurrents. The Dominionois managed to put together a half-way respectable receiving line, with the Chancellor and his party pressed into service at the end, and H'rhAtor and company were welcomed with due ceremony. H'rhAtor was obviously not happy, but he knew the situation was delicate, so they kept their ears up and greeted the reception line with jaw-gritted courtesy.

"Good evening, sir," I'eiBida said once the worst was over. "I'm a bit surprised you went to all this bother."

H'rhAtor scowled at him. "Bunch of nonsense, but if there's any hope of salvaging the humans, we have to stiffen our tails and bear it." He pondered the Chancellor, who was making his way through the crowd on the other side of the room for the usual political tail-grabbing. "I just hope it does some good."

"Well...you never can tell with the humans, sir. We can't give up hope yet."

"Ancestors," he grumbled distractedly. "Have we finally been reduced to this?"

"Some things were not meant to be known, sir."

"That's the sad truth." He glanced at I'eiBida. "I don't suppose the Admiral will attend tonight? I would love to get off in a quiet corner with him."

"I suspect he hates these things as much as you do, sir."

H'rhAtor nodded morosely. "Points for him in my book."

135

"No sign of N'detLeda?" I asked softly once H'rhAtor drifted away.

I'eiBida frowned. "No, nothing. Where is he? Could something have happened to him?"

"One can but hope."

§

And so it went. The crowd grew slowly but steadily until there was a fair turnout. The buffet was busy, the news vultures were their usual nuisance, and the wine, champagne, and lemonade flowed. As expected, H'rhAtor and his people were the center of attention, to the Chancellor's displeasure.

We all circulated to work the crowd, keeping our ears up for any hint of what was really going on. From the comments I overheard, many of the humans seemed as perplexed as we were. One common theme we picked up on was the very real fear among those in the know. Word of the pending invasion had not leaked out yet—for a miracle—but a lot of the human political insiders figured *something* was going on, and even those not connected to defense matters were uneasy.

Despite our misgivings, C'traBenla kept out of trouble and spent the evening gossiping and flirting. I swear, to my lasting amazement, she could charm even human mals. There was a lively knot of humans around her wherever she went, which gave the event its one bright spot amid the pervasive gloom and confusion.

We got together with K'deiTai in an out of the way cul-de-sac to compare notes as the evening progressed. "No sign of N'detLeda?" I asked K'deiTai.

"No. I called the embassy, and he's still there."

"I don't understand; what is his game?" I'eiBida asked. "And why isn't he here to do whatever he plans?"

"N'detLeda plays by his own rules," I said. "But I honestly don't understand either."

"Well let us be thankful for small favors at any rate," K'deiTai grumbled, then gestured to C'tra, who was by the fire place in the center of a lively crowd. "Speaking of which, at least *she's* keeping out of trouble. We have enough problems right now."

"Indeed," I'eiBida muttered.

"We still have to talk the Chancellor into changing his mind, but I'm blessed if I see how."

I'eiBida and I exchanged wary looks. "I'm sure something will come up, K'deiTai."

"I hope so. We're running out of time." He gave us both a stern look, and shook a finger at us. "But whatever happens, don't you two try anything stupid. We have enough of that with N'detLeda!"

He drifted away, so we shelved the N'detLeda mystery and tried to come up with some ideas for our plot. The evening was getting on, and our maneuvering space was dwindling rapidly. We argued discreetly for some time, maintaining a polite front for any humans who wandered by, trying to decide who to recruit. Try as we did, and we considered every prospect, no matter how unlikely, we couldn't think of any humans we could count on to deliver our ultimatum without either exposing us or using the knowledge to their own advantage. And obviously no one from the embassy could do it.

"I hate to say this," I'eiBida said at last. "But it looks like we will have to speak to the Chancellor directly."

"What? Here? Now?"

"I'm afraid we have no choice. The fleet is scheduled to leave for d'enchia tomorrow, so one of us will have to deliver our ultimatum."

"I'm afraid you're right," I sighed.

"It gives me no pleasure, I can assure you."

"Well then, you need to get on with it."

He turned in alarm. "Me? Why me?"

"It's a defense matter; you're in the defenders. It's your job."

"This was your idea!"

"I'm with the embassy; we can't implicate U'tdaPagrn."

"We can't implicate the 'Dark Grays' or the human Admiral, either."

"I'm no diplomat. I wouldn't know where to begin."

"Neither am I, and K'deiTai won't do it."

"You make a stronger impression than I do, which will be important for convincing the Chancellor that we mean business."

"But you've been here longer, and have a better grasp of the language."

"My sociological skills are essential to understanding the aliens. You can be replaced, I can't."

"Thank you for that vote of confidence! C'tra will knot my tail righteously if I get us deported."

"We can bicker over this until the Universe ends," I said, evenly. "The only thing to do is match ears for it."

He agreed, reluctantly, and we proceeded to do just that.

"This could cost me my career," he muttered afterward.

"You lost, fair enough." I gave him a sympathetic pat on the shoulder. "It has to be done. It will cost a lot more than our careers if you can't convince him."

He gave me a jaundiced look. "*Our* careers? You owe me, big time. You can't *imagine* how much you owe me."

"No doubt." I made a sweeping gesture of invitation. "Shall we?"

He nodded reluctantly, and we headed across the hall to where the Chancellor was mingling with various political types near the fire place. Perhaps I should have remained discreetly in the background, but I went along to offer I'eiBida a bit of emotional support, and because I felt guilty and, honestly, I wanted to see the show.

It seemed that few of those there had any particular affection for the Chancellor; they were there strictly to curry favor by exchanging a few polite words, then moving on. We hesitated off to one side until the crowd thinned out momentarily, then I'eiBida took a deep breath to steady his nerves, and stepped forward.

"I beg your pardon..."

"Chancellor!" C'traBenla barged in at the *worst* possible moment with all her usual enthusiasm. "This *is* a pleasant surprise. I've wanted *so* much to meet you, and here you are."

I'eiBida hesitated, and looked at her in surprise.

"Indeed...madame," he said patiently. "I recall you well from when you were here before. I was a Chamber Deputy at the time."

"Well you have certainly *prospered* since then, I see."

I'eiBida's surprise turned to irritation.

138

The Chancellor slid easily into their small-talk mode used to politely tolerate a political outsider important enough to merit some brief attention. "So what brings you back to Geneva?"

"I simply *love* this world and your people. In fact, I recently received a small inheritance, and I am thinking of investing it here. Could you suggest any earth businesses I should look into?"

I'eiBida's expression changed from annoyance to confusion.

"You are most gracious, madame," the Chancellor said. "But that is not my field of expertise. Perhaps you should consult a brokerage."

She ignored him and prattled on. "I was talking to a friend the other day, Josephine N------, and she mentioned a construction company in the Dominions who received a *huge* contract for upgrades to the harbor facilities in Genoa. I find that most instructive, wouldn't you agree?"

A fleeting look of panic crossed his snout. "I..."

"And there is that new railroad bridge over the Rhine; a remarkable stroke of luck for them. They must be doing *something* right to land such a lucrative contract. I'm sure they are well worth looking into."

I'eiBida's expression changed from confusion to stunned amazement. From the way the Chancellor stiffened, I could see he was on to her ploy too. "Indeed, madame..." he began, but she cut him off abruptly.

"And that legislation which passed the Parliament recently will do the airlines serving Asia no *end* of good. They might be worth looking into as well."

I'eiBida gave me a look of near panic.

"I have also heard some interesting tidbits about the banking sector," she added. "I've always been fascinated with *international* finance with all those blind accounts and holding companies."

"But..."

"And there are those new shipping contracts for war supplies going to Singapore. They had a truly *remarkable* stroke of fortune, wouldn't you say?" she added, pointedly. "One wonders how they managed it. They must have put some *careful* preparation into their bids, no doubt. That sort of thoroughness is *telling*."

The Chancellor was fidgeting nervously by then, glancing around at the packed humans in the vicinity. "You don't think..."

"I've talked to any *number* of knowledgable sources, and they all tell me much the same story." She glanced casually at the news vulture DuRochelle, who was passing nearby; the Chancellor caught the subtle gesture, and his complexion paled.

I'eiBida looked dismayed.

"One can't help but admire their good fortune," she went on. "I'm sure if I discussed the matter more widely, even more *interesting* revelations would come up."

The Chancellor turned stone-snouted at that, trying to maintain a calm demeanor, but he was clearly worried. "You don't expect..."

"Of course, my interest in these industries would depend on whether earth gets involved in this war, wouldn't it?" She gave him a searching look, and while her tone was light, her ears were laid back in full aggression. "In that case, I would want to focus on defense industries, aerospace in particular, no?"

The Chancellor said nothing, but from his posture, he seemed undecided whether to explode or run screaming into the night. I'eiBida gave me a dismayed look as if he was beginning to understand how deep the hole she was digging was.

"I...don't suppose you could tell me what your government's policy is on this joint war effort, could you?"

"I...am not at liberty to..."

The coquette vanished. "I would *really* appreciate any *good* advice you could give," she said, firmly. "I wouldn't want to focus my interest in *unfortunate* directions, you understand."

The Chancellor hemmed and hawed uncomfortably, then, "Indeed, madame...I do understand...and you may turn your *attentions* to the war effort with confidence."

"Why, thank you Chancellor!" Her seeming innocence was back in force. "You are most kind! But I know you are busy, so I'll leave you to attend to matters of state." With that, she looped her arm around I'eiBida's, and half-dragged him away.

"What are you... What was *that* all about?" I heard him demand as they strolled toward the buffet pretending like they didn't have a care in the Universe.

"Really, I'ei, you are *such* an innocent." She gave him a smug look and a defiant ear twitch. "Most real diplomacy happens at these things; that's why the humans have so many of them."

His ears wilted, and he sighed, but didn't say anything.

"Now if you don't mind, I would like some lemonade, please."

§

The rest of the evening went about as those things usually go, although I was on edge waiting for the humans to arrest us. Instead, the Chancellor made his rounds as rapidly as he could, avoiding U'tdaPagrn in particular, to his confusion. At one point he came upon Minister Hogarthy, and they got into a discreet but furious exchange. That went on for some time, both of them keeping up an elaborate pretense for the crowd's benefit, before the Chancellor cut him off abruptly. Hogarthy threw a venomous look in our general direction and stomped out. The Chancellor left as soon as was politically expedient.

C'traBenla carried on as if nothing happened. She had a bit too much lemonade, and got into a raucous demonstration of some choreography from her days as a sliv-dancer, which livened up the scene considerably. I'eiBida and I hovered near the buffet where we could stay out of harm's way and nervously watch the goings-on. To say that we were shaken by her unexpected performance was the understatement of all time, and we both agonized over what her amateur enthusiasm might have unleashed.

"How did she find out?" I asked him when we found a moment of privacy.

"Ancestors alone know," he sighed.

"It must have been W'kiLap and T'apiDien. The three are close, and they're the only ones who know."

"And she got a knot in her tail, and came rushing over here to play at diplomatic intrigue." He shook his head in dismay. "Ancestors, that fem will be the death of me yet."

"But what about N'detLeda?"

He pondered that. "He must have known she was coming and decided to cut his losses," he said at last.

"Ancestors, I hope she hasn't wrecked our relations altogether."

"Well, at least things can't get worse than they already are."

"That's cold comfort, but you may be right."

H'rhAtor drifted by, and considered the bowl of lemonade on the human buffet. "How are you managing, sir," I'eiBida asked him.

"Well enough." He drew a cup of lemonade, sniffed it experimentally, then took a sip of it. "I hate these things, blessed waste of time usually. I've never been a politician."

"It keeps the humans occupied, sir."

"I did hear an interesting bit of news, though: it seems the Chancellor just changed his mind on the joint defense effort; right after talking with your bondmate in fact." He gave I'eiBida a curious look. "You wouldn't happen to know what that's about, would you?"

I'eiBida kept his ears rigidly under control. "She can be very persuasive when she chooses, as you know, sir," he muttered.

H'rhAtor paused to watch C'traBenla, who had a hand of young human fems doing a rough impression of a racy chorus number, to the crowd's delight. "So I see," he said at last. He finished his cup of lemonade, and gave I'eiBida a skeptical look. "We should be thankful she's on our side."

I'eiBida watched her for some time after H'rhAtor left. "It wasn't N'detLeda," he said at last. "This is her doing. She has the connections with the Dominions, and she certainly has the *l'fru'ng*. It's the only thing which makes sense."

I almost asked him if he was sure, but I remembered how she was when they were stationed here. He was right: it was the only answer which made sense.

*****

"Lurching From One Disaster To Another"
(Related by Learnéd K'deiTai)

The two leaders and their staffs got together at the Defense Ministry the next morning for their first formal strategy session since Hogarthy's order was lifted. I was morosely pleased at the change, if anything about this sorry spectacle can be considered pleasing, but I was confused no end over this sudden reversal.

The Defense Ministry was a scene of controlled chaos when I arrived. Hogarthy indulged in another fit of pettiness by appointing a large ceremonial peacekeeper bodyguard which, as to be expected, drew the usual herd of demonstrators. The peacekeepers were soon backed up by gendarmes, which only made things worse. By time we arrived, the demonstration spilled out onto adjacent streets, and their mood was turning violent. Once again we made our way to the back entrance by brute force, and were escorted from the omnibus to the building by an armed escort while the herd screamed and waved their picket signs.

My luck being what it is, the first person I ran into was T'virDoma. "Well, I see you survived this morning's native uprising," she greeted me with her usual superior air. "No doubt you are gathering loads of material to improve your program when this is all over?"

"Not enough to teach you anything," I grumbled.

"What set all this off, anyway?" I'eiBida asked.

"Oh, that was Hogarthy's doing," she said. "He turned this into a military spectacle, where we need discretion to avoid stampeding them. It amazes me how clueless that human is in particular."

I gave her an exasperated sigh. "No, he did it deliberately to discredit us, which you should know if you've studied human social behavior."

"At least now I can learn these things in the field rather than waiting for the next lecture."

N'detLeda came in just then. "Glad you could join us. Vacation all in and ready to get to work?"

I was in no mood for his baiting. "How are our media relations going?"

143

That sobered him up. He appointed himself our public relations speaker when he first arrived here, which we didn't object to since it kept him busy and out of the way fending off the news vultures in the press room. He soon regretted that decision, but we made him stick to it since it was no more than he deserved, and none of us wanted the thankless task. "Things are quiet for now. They're waiting to see what develops from this conference."

"Sharpening their fangs all the while, I suppose." T'virDoma gave me a surly look, but said nothing.

§

The fifth floor was busy as the Ministry staff made preparations for the conference, so we split up and scrambled to complete our own herd of last minute details. C'traBenla, thankfully, was soon preoccupied with the buffet. I made a mental note to check with I'eiBida and make sure she was kept under control and out of the way, if that was possible.

Agent Roubidoux and Commander Rostokovich intercepted me in the main hallway a short time later. To my surprise, Commander Watanabi was with them, looking as polished and artificial as ever.

"Good morning, sir," Ivan said. "Shuttle with your people landed at airport minutes ago. We should be ready to start shortly."

"Thank you, Commander." I was still brooding over this unexpected change of fortune, so I added, "What made the Chancellor change his mind, do you suppose?"

The two looked at each other. "We are hardly in a position to know the Chancellor's thoughts," Pierre said, cautiously, which struck me as ominous somehow.

"Perhaps he heeds new portents written in the dawn?" Watanabi suggested.

"Perhaps. And what brings you here, Commander? I thought the embassy was your assigned post."

Even his smile was remote and artificial. "Like the Koi fish, I must swim back to my roots in the proper season."

I was in no mood for his riddles. "I wish you would express yourself more plainly, Commander, instead of acting so mysterious all the time."

His smile vanished. "My apology, Arbiter. I came to the Ministry for a routine report, and thought I would take the time to witness this spectacle."

I felt a bit embarrassed in turn. "Thank you."

"And like you, I am perplexed by the changing winds." He gave the two a pointed look. "Indeed, the Chancellor himself has been blown off course. One can but navigate the seas of uncertainty and hope that the tides will be in his favor."

"I would not know about navigation," Agent Roubidoux muttered.

"Yet the astute man may find his way to battle by heeding the echos of the trumpet. No doubt the Chancellor's trumpet call has stirred many echos?"

"I did not get memo," Ivan protested. "How am I to know?"

"Am I the Chancellor's conscience?" Pierre objected.

"Indeed." He considered them with that irritating implacable calm which made us all so uncomfortable, then turned his attention to me. "If one is to find the nest of the Ibis, one must know the paths through the marshes. Don't you agree, Arbiter?"

"Um... Not knowing how the Ibis nests, I can't say."

"No doubt. But then, the hatchlings' cries will be heard, in time." With that, he bowed politely and strolled down the hall.

The other two watched gloomily as he left, then Pierre glanced at me. "You must always be wary around him, sir."

"Um?"

"He is from APA; I do not know which office." He sighed, and exchanged glances with Ivan. "For all his babble, he is a skilled interrogator."

"He uses that nonsense to baffle opponents," Ivan said.

"He's trying to unravel this mystery too?"

"*Da*. APA must be suspicious of Chancellor's change of heart."

Pierre nodded. "I hear they are probing everywhere all of a sudden. Your own security chief has been asking questions too."

If so, he hadn't said anything. I was disconcerted to learn L'datMparn was keeping such an important item from U'rdaPagrn. "Things have changed since I was here last," I complained. "It was never like this when you were in charge."

145

"*Oui.* He is among their best operatives. One never knows where his dissembling will lead you, or how much he uncovers. Always watch yourself around him."

§

I came upon M'tinDegan and I'eiBida in the conference room overseeing the last minute touches. I was still brooding over that run-in with Commander Watanabi, so I asked them, "What do you make of the Chancellor's change of position?"

"All for the good," I'eiBida said, fervently.

"Hopefully, we can make some progress," M'tinDegan added.

"No, I mean what made the Chancellor change his mind?"

"I'm sure he had his reasons."

"Any idea as to why?" I asked, suspiciously.

He was about to evade the question when the Admiral came in bearing a metal trash can, which turned out to be full of ammunition clips. "Damn-fool popinjay," he muttered. "Hogarthy issued his honor guard live ammunition, which could have touched off a major incident," he added to us. "Like I don't have better things to do than getting it all collected again."

"That sounds like him venting his displeasure at being overridden," I suggested.

"Yeah, that's about his speed." He hefted the trash can, which must have been a heavy load for a frail elder. "I get so sick of his petty bullshit. Sometimes I think we should just turn him loose on the enemy."

"We have our share too, sir," I'eiBida said. "I suppose it's inevitable no matter what race you talk about."

"You got that right," he grumbled as he handed the trash can over. "Here. Get rid of these, will you?"

"What am I supposed to do with this?" I'eiBida asked once he was gone. He hefted the trash can with both arms, and looked around for some place to put it down.

"Careful not to drop that," M'tinDegan said. "Could they explode?" I'eiBida hesitated, and examined them anxiously.

"Never mind that," I said. "What happened to change the Chancellor's mind? It's not like him, at least as he was during our negotiations."

146

The two gave each other guilty looks, and I'eiBida fiddled nervously with his trash can. "Um...we...persuaded him to reconsider," M'tinDegan said, carefully.

Something in his tone of voice, and in I'eiBida's neutral expression was ringing alarms in my mind. "How?"

"We offered him some sound reasons to change his position."

"What sort of reasons?"

"Um...reasons of a...ah...personal nature."

My ears stood on end in alarm. "You *blackballed* him?"

"Black*mailed*, and it was N'detLeda's idea, remember? If anything comes of it, his tail will be knotted."

That didn't mollify me in the least. "You must be *er'trxxda!* We can't do that! It's entirely outside of proper diplomatic protocol!"

"The humans do it all the time," I'eiBida protested.

"Well we are *not* the humans, in case you've forgotten!"

"And it worked; that's what really matters."

"In view of this crisis, we more or less had to," M'tinDegan added.

"*Why* do I endure this?" I gave them a bleak look. "Don't you two know better by now than to go meddling in diplomatic matters, *especially* like this? The Chancellor does not take kindly to threats, and his reaction is likely to be all too human. Who knows what sort of backlash will come of it."

"We're stuck with it now, I guess," M'tinDegan said.

"And the threat of exposure will hamper any action he might take," I'eiBida offered. "And if you don't mind, this thing is getting heavy."

"Never mind that," I snapped at him. As much as I was appalled by their stupidity, there was nothing for it now but damage control. "How much do you have on him?"

M'tinDegan pulled several pages of transcript out of his pouch and offered them to me; I declined to take them. "Plenty: bribery, corruption, conspiracy; we're digging up more details by the hour."

That set me back, as I didn't recall our intelligence being so thorough. "How were you able to do all that?" The guilty looks returned. "Well? How?"

147

"We had some help." I'eiBida's voice was a bit strained as he struggled with the trash can.

"Who?" More guilty looks. "*Who?*"

"Ah...Inspector Dassault..."

"You're associating with *him?* Have you gone *er'trxxda?*"

"Actually, he led the project," M'tinDegan said.

"My Ancestors must hate me. They must!"

"*l'cc'vn!* What do I do with this thing?" I'eiBida muttered.

I took a deep, shaky breath to calm myself, and tried to think it through. "I *suppose* any reaction by the humans will depend in part on how convincing your informant was," I said at last. "Who delivered your ultimatum to the Chancellor, anyway?"

"Um..." I'eiBida's ears twitched in dismay. "...she did."

I just gave up and walked away.

§

The conference got under way with the two staffs arrayed along opposite sides of the table, and the leaders at either end as before. Also as before, the liaison herd and various odd hangers-on were against the walls in the background. While our two species were supposed to be allies, the tensions were plain, and discussion soon gave way to argument, and then to recriminations.

"I don't see why we need you," one of our people said at one point. "Aside from your stellar bombs, you have an empty egg."

"It takes time and money to build ships," a human said. "We're doing the best we can."

"A sorry *'best'* it is!"

"At least we *have* nukes! Where are yours, if you're such a great fleet?"

"You humans are pretentious to call yourselves a star-traveling race!"

"*We're* not afraid to face the invaders!"

"That will do, Mister Singh, thank you!" the Admiral interrupted. The two staffers hesitated for a moment, then settled in their seats.

"Please forgive those unfortunate words, Admiral," H'rhAtor said. Then to his people, he added, "Do not make me apologize again."

148

"I would have sworn our relations were better than this," I said after that confrontation.

"They are tasked with the threat of war between our races," Pierre said. "If they can learn to trust each other, then the rest of us can as well."

"And if they can't?"

He sighed. "I only hope they can."

And so it went. H'rhAtor and the Admiral tried to limit the tensions by negotiating directly and only calling on their staffs for technical details. That worked to a degree, but each instance where someone was called upon had the potential for another outbreak.

"What do you think?" I whispered to M'tinDegan after someone made a telling point ending a rancorous debate.

M'tinDegan pondered for a bit. "They're all but paralyzed with suspicion of each other. You can feel the tension. I'm surprised they're making any progress at all."

"They are caught in a psychological dilemma," N'detLeda said. "They know they need to work together, but their distrust is too ingrained to overcome easily. That little display was symptomatic of the strain we all feel."

"A foolish waste of time and effort," T'virDoma griped.

I looked askance at her. "We're watching history being made; you could at least appreciate that."

"History gets made every day. We have an enormous stockpile of it already. What matters is the future."

"It wouldn't hurt to show a little enthusiasm."

"It wouldn't help, either."

§

The two leaders wrapped the conference up a short time later. Despite the tension and recriminations, they were able to hammer out a rough plan of action; notably a decision to provide the humans a tanker-load of cryonic gasses. That wouldn't solve their logistics problems, but it would make things a little easier for them.

The Admiral ordered more refreshments brought in, but it was the same as before: both sides awkward and distrustful. The two staffs kept a wary distance, congregated around their respective buffets in an ominous murmuring undertone. A few on both sides tried to bridge the gap, making strained, innocuous conversation with their counterparts. We kept busy applying oil to the gears of interstellar diplomacy, but that didn't help much. By then, I was a nervous wreck worrying about the consequences of their meddling with the Chancellor, and the tension in the room just made it worse. Being an Arbiter is bad enough: Ancestors forbid I should ever get caught up in interstellar diplomacy again, although with all these new first contacts, I was not optimistic.

"How do you do it?" I asked I'eiBida at one point. He paused and looked at me curiously. "I thought my work was stressful. How do you defenders handle things like this?"

I'eiBida shook his head. "Ancestors alone know. I sure don't. They never taught us how to socialize with dangerous aliens at the Academy; something we need to start, I guess."

"I'ei?" C'traBenla came over to interrupt us. "Do you know if we have any more of the humans' coffee? We're almost out."

"You!" I snapped. "You blackmailed the Chancellor!"

She gave me a cold stare. "That's right. And I got the humans back into the herd on the war effort, so a little appreciation would be in order."

"A little..." I choked up in frustration, and had to start over. "Can't you leave well enough alone for once?"

"I'm the only one of us who has no official connection with the embassy or the war effort," she lectured me. "So if your little scheme did fall apart, I was the only one who wouldn't create a diplomatic incident."

What dismayed me most was that she was right. "I swear you'll be my downfall," I sighed. "We should name a natural disaster after you."

"Typhoon C'traBenla?" She gave me an impudent grin. "That does have a certain ring to it, doesn't it?"

"I was thinking more like colliding galaxies."

§

I gave up on her and wandered away in despair, and my meanderings brought me to MacKenna and H'rhAtor, who were off

150

by themselves. Captain Morgan and M'tinDegan were there as well. "The most critical thing is to locate these aliens," MacKenna was saying. "Once we know where they are and what they have, we can come up with some sort of rational plan."

"There's an awful lot of Universe out there," H'rhAtor said, doubtfully. "We still haven't approached that region with our surveys, so even with your survey results, there is a vast unexplored zone to search."

"Can we combine our scouting efforts?" MacKenna asked.

"Certainly, but I am not sure what good it will do. We only have two long range survey ships, one of which is on the other side of our stellar sphere."

MacKenna paused in surprise. "Surely you have more than that?"

H'rhAtor gave him a rueful ear twitch. "We have been in space far longer than your people, Admiral. Right now we have several hands of worlds awaiting development, more than our colonization budget can absorb. Surveying has been a low priority for a long time."

"I wish," MacKenna grumbled. "So what can we do? We can't afford to go blundering around in the dark for years hoping to stumble onto the enemy fleet."

"Ask the Dreamsingers," I suggested. "There's no reason why they would withhold the information; we just need to raise the matter with them."

"Yeah, but the trouble is, we can't reach them," MacKenna said. "They have to come to us."

"Then perhaps we should send a ship to the system where you made contact, sir," I'eiBida suggested. "If we show up there, they'll figure that we want to talk with them."

MacKenna considered that. "Good point. They must know we need more intel, and showing up there will tell them we want to communicate."

"And we need to make formal contact and bring them into our planning anyway, sir," Morgan said.

"She is right," H'rhAtor said. "We should send a ship to that system. That is probably their home system, or the site of a major colony."

MacKenna shook his head. "No, there are no inhabitable worlds there; nothing but two gas giants and four airless rocks. We have no way of knowing where they come from." He turned to Captain Morgan. "Any luck contacting them, Captain?"

"I've tried sir. J J doesn't respond."

"They aren't very talkative, are they?"

"You may not have the mental strength to reach them," M'tinDegan said. Morgan gave him a venomous look. "Ah...that is, the human and Ic'nichi minds aren't geared for telepathy."

"Then I don't know what we can do," MacKenna said. "Looking for them at random would do no more good than looking for the enemy fleet."

"We must do something," H'rhAtor said.

"Yes, but what? How do we find them?"

I suddenly felt disoriented, vaguely dizzy, as if I was falling. The room faded to darkness, and I thought I was passing out at first. When my vision cleared, it took me a moment to realize that I was adrift in space, and another to notice that our conversation circle were all there.

"What the...?" MacKenna said in alarm.

"*Admiral?*" H'rhAtor looked around in near panic. "What is happening?" The rest of us were equally disconcerted by this bizarre vision.

A dull red star glowed like a dying ember in the distance, faintly illuminating a bright orange and yellow sphere which rotated seemingly beneath our feet. For all we could tell, we were standing in a circle in a high orbit above an alien world.

"A...gas giant?" MacKenna muttered.

"That *is* their home world, sir!" Captain Morgan said.

"They must be surpassing strange..." H'rhAtor mumbled as the vision faded, and we were returned to the conference room.

"Now *that's* communicating," M'tinDegan said in a shaky whisper.

*****

152

"Dawns and Departures"
(Related by Defender I'eiBida)

Once we learned where the Dreamsingers' world was, the Admiral ordered Captain Morgan to prepare for an immediate trip there. Once again, K'deiTai, M'tinDegan, and I were drafted to go along as representatives of our people. K'deiTai whined and moaned like he always did, while M'tinDegan and I took that bit of news stoically.

C'traBenla didn't. She panicked when she learned of our trip, and pleaded with me not to go as I tried to pack my field kit in our quarters. "I'ei, you're on the *Staff!* You aren't a field Elder! You have no business galloping off to nowhere!"

"It's just a reconnaissance. We're going to talk to the Dreamsingers is all."

"But the enemy is out there somewhere! You could be killed!"

I paused and nuzzled her neck to try to reassure her. "Love, I'm sure the Admiral will retreat at the first sight of them."

"I don't want to lose you, I'ei," she sobbed. "Please let me go with you. I-I want to be there with you, i-in case..."

"I can't, C'tra. The Admiral wouldn't let you go."

"You could at least ask him!" she snapped. "He listens to you; you could twist his tail if you really care about me!"

"C'tra..."

"It's not like I'm asking so much!"

Her pleading soon turned into an argument which only ended when I finally retreated to the defenders' barracks, and spent the night on one of their bunks, my mind in turmoil, hating her and longing for her. The worst of it was I understood what she was going through, and there was nothing I could do about it. I was the first mal in her life who treated her with respect; we were bonded; we were building a life together. And now all that, everything she ever longed for, was in danger of vanishing. I lay there, weary and restless, and wondered why I hadn't become an accountant. Being a defender is a lonely life at times, even when you're with the one you love.

§

153

I was groggy and stiff the next morning as I stumbled downstairs to the cafeteria. One thing I learned in the last few years was to stuff myself before going on long journeys, and I intended to put a dent in the embassy's food stocks. There was a hand cart piled with endurance rations, drawn from the old stock we first brought here, sitting by the cafeteria entrance waiting to be loaded on the omnibus. I eyed them uneasily, trying to decide whether they ruined my appetite or made me all the more desperate for a good, hot meal. I wouldn't have believed I would prefer the 'new and improved' rations.

C'trabenla was not in the cafeteria which, honestly, I was glad of. I was still sore over the fight last night, and I could well imagine her mood just then, so it was all for the best that we didn't bump into each other. Right then I had enough problems. The thought of going into space again, especially heading into a possible war zone, made me nervous and gloomy. I plowed into the buffet like a herd of rioting humans, and don't even recall what I ate for first-meal, aside from bowl after bowl of hot *V'liz*.

"This is impossible!" K'deiTai and U'tdaPagrn were arguing in the hall when I came out, while M'tinDegan stood to one side, quiet and pensive, with a kit draped over his back.

"K'deiTai, you're the only Arbiter available. I can't go. I have my duties here. We need an official representative to meet with the Dreamsingers."

"But I'm not an Arbiter any more! I retired. I'm a Learnéd now! I'eiBida, tell him!"

"Don't look at me," I grumbled. "I'm just a lowly rear echelon staffer who spends his days shuffling paper."

"A big help you are!"

"You get me out of this and I'll gladly return the favor."

"And don't forget old friends," M'tinDegan said.

U'tdaPagrn turned to me. "You better hurry, I'eiBida. The omnibus will be leaving shortly."

"Wonderful."

C'traBenla wasn't in our quarters when I returned for my travel kit. Honestly, I was starting to fret about that. Part of me was glad I didn't have to face her temper, but part of me wanted her more than ever. Even if she wasn't there, her presence was. My field kit sat on the bed pad all packed and ready to go, and a new set of camouflage fatigues from the embassy stores lay nearby. Ancestors, that fem leaves me bewildered at times. I dressed hurriedly, scribbled a quick note to reassure her, and headed downstairs.

§

The embassy omnibus carried us to the Geneva airport, where we would take a human shuttle into orbit. It was standing off in a remote corner when we arrived, venting fumes from it's fuel ports, and its turbines idling with a nerve-grating whine. The morning was chill and overcast, and the weather service was predicting snow over the next few days. We waited impatiently in the comfort of the omnibus while some humans quickly transferred our rations and baggage, then we braved the dawn to board. A chill rain started as we headed for the shuttle. Figures.

Human protocol is surprisingly similar to ours. The Admiral boarded first, followed by his Aide. After them came three of the Admiral's staff in order of rank. K'deiTai came next, as senior diplomat. He clambered up the ramp, then froze in the doorway with a dismayed look on his snout. I couldn't blame him for being scared; I was. He finally moved forward, and M'tinDegan went next as a diplomatic advisor. He froze in the doorway as well, looking toward the front of the shuttle. Then he looked at me with a bemused, unhappy expression, shrugged, and moved forward. Being a common staff Elder, I came last, curious as to what that was all about.

What it was about was C'traBenla, who was firmly planted in the corner of the area cleared for us with a travel kit tucked under her chest.

"What...C'tra..."

"I'm going, I'eiBida, and I *will not* discuss it." I knew better than to argue when she used that tone of voice.

The Admiral sat in one of the human seats watching all this, and while he couldn't understand what we were saying, her tone was unmistakable. He looked back and forth at the two of us, then raised one eye ridge, but didn't say anything. By then, the hatch

155

was sealed, and the humans were strapped into their seats. We hurriedly buckled our improvised safety harness as the queasy sensation of the shuttle's mass polarizer built up. I squatted on the deck opposite C'traBenla and stared at nothing, too bemused and worried to say anything. Well, at least if things did go bad, we would be together.

§

We rode up to orbit in chilly silence. Honestly, I'd given up by that point. She was determined to go, and it would take the humans' Space Marines to keep her there. In any event, I had more pressing matters at hand. This trip was an unprecedented chance to get a good look at human starships, and U'tdaPagrn gave me explicit instructions to make the most of it.

My first opportunity was aboard the shuttle. However, it was so similar to ours that there was hardly anything of importance to note. This was a passenger shuttle: the cargo deck was fitted with two rows of seats, with the forward rows removed for us. I carefully memorized the door controls and the access to the pilot compartment for later sketching. Other than that, there wasn't much to see.

We passed the humans' Orbit Dock as we looped above its orbit to reach the 'Marco Polo'. The humans made some big changes in the last year. Several new sections were added to the station proper, there were more more inflatable fuel tanks, and there seemed to be more small craft skittering around the area. I could just make out the humans' heavy lift vehicle in the distance, climbing from Singapore with a section of a ship's central column perched on it. The two unfinished battleships were nearby, and I was dismayed at my first close look at them. They were enormous, dwarfing three destroyers under construction. By my rough estimate, they would be as large as our largest colony ships. It was a chilling reminder of the potential threat the humans posed.

The shuttle maneuvered for docking, and the 'Marco Polo' came into view. This was my first chance to see the human ship which loomed so large in our history, and it was a bit disappointing. Their ships are smaller than ours, and the 'Marco Polo' looked tattered and weatherbeaten. The humans don't paint their ships, and this one was a patchwork of the central metal column marred by weld seams, and the dirty off-white habitat. Its minimal beauty was marred by protruding pipes, conduits, antennas, the improvised gatling gun mount, and various labels and warning signs stenciled here and there.

The pilots maneuvered us expertly into position, and we coupled with the docking collar with a gentle bump. The personnel hatch in the roof was opened, and the Admiral squeezed through into the ship, followed by his staff in order of rank, followed by us in turn. It was a tight squeeze: K'deiTai managed to struggle through, but M'tinDegan became lodged momentarily, and I had to give him a shove from behind. C'tra went next, then me. Getting our luggage aboard was a neat trick as well.

Most of the central column was taken up by an elevator which ran from the habitat all the way back to the drive pod. No one went down there unless the ship's reactor was shut down. The rest of the column was taken up with a tangle of pipes and cables; I figured repairs must be a major challenge, even seeing how agile the humans are in zero-G.

The elevator stopped in an air lock at the top of the shaft. Beyond that was a small room—the lowest deck of the habitat— with vacuum suits and space gear clamped to the walls. A ladder continued up from there through a storeroom, the crews' quarters, the ships common room, and the control deck at the top. That was an unwelcome surprise, as the elevators in our ships rise all the way to the top deck. The humans are able to climb up and down through amazingly narrow hatches which we could never manage under gravity. Thankfully we were weightless; it was difficult enough in zero G, and we are not designed to climb ladders.

A crew human lead us up to the next deck, the storeroom, part of which was cleared, and the humans' stores blocked into one section with a heavy cargo net secured to a grid of metal bars.

"I'm afraid the Admiral and his people have taken up what little extra room we have above, so we'll have to put you here," the human said. "This will be a quick round trip, so we cleared part of our supply bay for you. Your courier sent over some sleep sacks and a few essentials, so you should manage for a short time."

He left us to our affairs with that cheering news, and we examined our new home with no enthusiasm. Our rations were secured in a large mesh sack, and a cargo net held some sleep sacks and three of our vac suits. Aside from that, the place was bare and uninviting.

"Wonderful," K'deiTai grumbled. "Where are the sanitary facilities?" There were none, this deck being a store room.

"We'll have to use the crew's toilets," I said.

"If we can." He studied the ladder leading up to the next level. "We can't get to them while under acceleration. What can we do?"

"You can hold it in," I said, irritably. "Better than you hold your whining, I hope."

"There's nothing for it, K'deiTai," M'tinDegan said.

K'deiTai sighed. "There never is." On that cheerful note, we set to work putting our new home in order.

Something struck me odd as I secured my sleep sack, which lead to an unpleasant discovery. The surface of the outer hull was rough and uneven, and there were minor ripples and blemishes in it like it was made of cloth. I paused and studied it closely: it *was* made of cloth! I poked at it with one finger, but it was stiff—the outer hull was made of resin enforced cloth.

"It's a balloon," I muttered. K'deiTai looked at me curiously. "The hull was made by inflating a cloth balloon and spraying it with plastic resin!" I dug one finger into the edge of the rubber flooring to peel it away. "The deck is made of sheetwood!" I whispered to him.

"That's...not good?"

Then I noticed a discolored streak along the bulkhead. Patchwork: repairs done by spraying resin over weakened joints.

"This thing's as fragile as a soap bubble!"

We knew human ships were crude improvisations, but we were appalled to see how flimsy they were. After that disturbing revelation, we examined the rest of the compartment, and found much the same. The steel cargo posts looked like plumbing pipe and fittings, and M'tinDegan found a label from a fishery supply company on one of the cargo nets. The ladder running between decks was crudely welded out of steel tube, and the hatches were

158

simple lids with rubber gaskets closed by twist handles. For that matter, the decks could never remain air tight if the ship wasn't flooded with pure oxygen at very low pressure. What would happen if we suffered an explosive decompression was something we didn't want to think about.

"They expect to fight wars in ships like this?" M'tinDegan said in dismay. "They must be more dangerous than we realized."

"More dangerous to themselves," K'deiTai grumbled.

§

There was a delay while we waited for our courier to send over another sleep sack and vac suit for C'traBenla. We used the time to get organized, which proved to be a challenge. M'tinDegan and K'deiTai had no formal zero G training, and mine was minimal. Slinging a sleep sack in zero G is a neat trick, and we all struggled with nausea and dizziness as we worked. K'deiTai actually became sick, which added a cloud of vomit to our miseries. I cursed his weak stomach as I chased blobs of guck around the room with an absorbent towel.

"There!" I grumbled when I finished. "I should make you clean up the next time."

"I'm sorry," he murmured. "I feel better..." He paused and stared at C'tra, who was munching an endurance ration.

"Oh...*l'cc'vn*..." I muttered as I peeled off another absorbent towel.

Eventually one of the humans came down from above, continued to the deck below, and returned a short time later with the additional gear. C'traBenla grabbed her sleep sack and floated around effortlessly to set it up, to K'deiTai's disgust. We were pretty well settled into our storeroom-cum-quarters, and I was starting to wonder what the delay in getting under way was when we were startled by a loud buzzer. Then we heard a rumble as the ship's drive kicked in.

"Gravity," M'tinDegan said with relief as we drifted gently to the deck. "Thank the *Ancestors* for that!" He set to straightening up his sleep sack while he had the chance.

"This is going to be a long trip," K'deiTai sighed as he surveyed the tangled ruin of his sleep sack.

159

Once we got squared away, we took a pause for mid-meal, and settled in for the long haul. We weren't making more than an eighth-gravity: at this pace, it would take days to clear the system. Thankfully, our stock of endurance rations was there with us, since we couldn't reach the upper decks under even this feeble acceleration. What we would do when we needed to use the toilet was beyond me.

As I feared, it wasn't long before relieving ourselves became a problem. It wasn't bad at first, but the pressure kept building, and there was nothing for it but endure since the one human toilet was two decks above. Worse, there was no water, so thirst was another torment, and eating the preserved endurance rations was more of a trial than ever. Or perhaps we were better off without, considering.

We continued to accelerate for over an earth day, during which we grew increasingly bored and frustrated as we lay in our sleep sacks, which were the only comfort available. It was impossible to sleep while struggling to contain ourselves, so aching grogginess soon joined intestinal distress to make our lives miserable.

I was groggy with fatigue when the buzzing alarm came again, and the nausea of the mass polarizer swelled up in us. The lights dimmed as a heavy arcing sound came faintly from below, and the engines rumbled at full power. We all reeled under the increased thrust as the ship jumped into hyper-C. Then the engines shut down, returning us to free fall. We scrambled for the ladder.

§

Interstellar travel is mostly dull. Once the jump to hyper-C was done and the engines shut down, there was no vibration, no acceleration stresses, nothing. There were no viewports on our deck, not that there was anything to see outside anyway, and the constant background rumble of the ship's systems dulled the mind after a while. Add in the weightlessness, and it can be hard to stay awake at times.

We spent most of our time on the galley deck, which wasn't quite as claustrophobic as our quarters, and where we could mingle with the off duty humans. They were a bit reserved toward us at first, but loosened up within a day or so. I was impressed with their professionalism, and heartened by their desire for good

160

relations with us. They were worried about war with the mysterious invaders, but were calmly prepared for it if it came. As we figured originally, the humans could make very bad enemies, and very good friends.

One human was a devout follower of one of their mystical orders, and he and M'tinDegan got into long, rambling discussions about Zen. C'tra's outgoing nature soon brought her a circle among the human crew, especially the two female rankers. I socialized mostly with the Admiral's staff, while K'deiTai kept to himself and sulked.

Human ships are crowded. The Captain and the ship's physich were the only ones with real cabins, each just large enough to lay down in while under acceleration. The Elders had cubby holes covered with curtains around the edge of the second deck, mostly taken over by the Admiral and his staff, while the rankers' communal quarters were on the third deck.

Human ships were also under-crewed since they were simply too small and their life support too limited for more people. Their relentless workload was done in zero-G, which is not easy In addition to alternating watches, Elders and crew alike turned to for routine housekeeping and maintenance, which was an urgent, endless task. Personal needs took up time as well, so that a few hours sleep daily was the average. The crew quarters on the third deck were occupied around the clock, and quick naps were popular with those not doing anything in particular.

"I know space duty is demanding, but this is worse than I expected," I said to M'tinDegan at one point.

"I find it intriguing." He was busy scribbling in one of his notebooks. "As chaotic as the humans can be, they are also capable of greater structure and discipline than I believe our people are. They are more formidable than we thought."

"I just wish we didn't need to depend on them."

"I just wish I could understand them better."

"I just wish water wasn't so tightly rationed," K'deiTai grumbled. Everyone received enough to drink, but bathing and laundry were done as little as possible, which 'improved' the atmosphere no end.

"Look at it this way, K'deiTai." M'tinDegan gave him a wry ear twitch. "This ship could well fall apart, and we'd all be killed. Then your problems will be over, won't they?"

"I should be so lucky."

§

Six days under way, and we were gathered on the galley deck when Captain Morgan came drifting down from the control deck. She paused at the bottom of the ladder and seemed to collapse within herself in exhaustion and pain.

The Admiral was sitting at one of the tables enjoying a squeeze bulb of coffee, and eyed her with concern. "Headache, Captain?" he asked, softly.

Morgan sighed, and rubbed the bridge of her nose with two fingers. "Yes, sir."

"You should see your medic for something."

She shook her head. "It's all these extra bodies, sir. Our air filters were in poor shape when we left."

MacKenna pondered that with no enthusiasm. "Yeah, I've noticed. Can you tap the reserve oxygen faster?"

"We already are, sir." She yawned, and stared at nothing. "It doesn't help. The CO_2 is building up too fast."

That made me realize that we were all panting, a sign that the air was foul. "Will we make it, Captain?" I asked.

"Engineering says we will, but this won't be a joy ride." She studied us for a moment, and added, "You're crowding our one open space doesn't help, either." We were all aching and irritable from the conditions on board and the deteriorating air, and arguments broke out all too often.

"They're here for a reason, Captain," the Admiral admonished her. "We need them."

"Well they could at least stay down in their quarters so we could have more room!"

"We can't go showing favoritism to our allies," MacKenna snapped at her, irritably. "We're all in this together."

"And we won't be treated as inferiors," C'traBenla said.

The Captain looked her over. "Why are you along, anyway?"

"I'm his bondmate. I wanted to be with him."

"You're his *wife?*" She turned on the Admiral. "Why did you authorize *her* to come along?"

"It wasn't me," MacKenna protested, and turned my way. "Why did you bring her? I thought you were more responsible than that!"

"I didn't know she was along until we boarded the shuttle, sir."

"You could have told her to stay!" Morgan said.

"I tried that. It didn't work."

"You've seen her in action at the Ministry, Admiral," M'tinDegan said. "Trust me: one doesn't *authorize* anything with her." C'tra gave him an amused look and a defiant ear twitch.

"Wife or not, it was reckless and irresponsible for you to pull a lame-brained stunt like this!" Morgan yelled.

C'tra stood right up to her. "You *humans* make so much about your families that I would *think* you'd understand!"

"She's already here, Captain, so it doesn't do any good to complain about it now," MacKenna offered.

The Captain turned on him. "It's a matter of proper discipline, sir. I would think you'd understand *that!*"

The Admiral held his peace thereafter while they argued, neither one yielding the least, until they were finally worn down by the foul air. The Captain went up the ladder to the control deck simmering in anger while C'tra went the other direction, leaving us there embarrassed and distressed.

The Admiral glanced at me. "Your wife, eh?"

"Yes, sir. I'm sorry, sir."

"She sure has you pussy-whipped, doesn't she?"

"Pussy-whipped, sir?"

He glanced upward in the Captain's general direction, and sighed. "Never mind. I know the sensation."

§

In light of the tensions on board, we retreated to our quarters on the fourth deck. The air was a bit less foul down there, although we were all achy and short of breath. No sooner did we get there, then K'deiTai started with C'traBenla. "Of all the immature, irresponsible people, you are the worst. This is serious business. Can't you leave well enough alone for once?"

163

"I am aware of what this is, which is why I'm here," she snapped at him. "And I will do as I please, and I will not answer to *you!*"

"We have enough of that with T'virDoma."

"That one!" She turned on him with a chilly look and ears laid back. "*Never* compare me with *her* again!"

K'deiTai recoiled under her glare. "Sorry."

She fumed for a bit, then settled down. "Honestly, I'ei, I only came because I need you."

"I know, love." Despite all the hassles, I knew how lucky I was to have her. Life is never dull around her, anyway. This is what comes of life-bonding with a typhoon.

§

The Captain instituted an emergency conservation regimen later that day. All on board were restricted to their bunks except for a minimal duty watch, and required to exercise as little as possible. The engineering section shut down the ship's reactor, donned vac suits, and rode the elevator to the rear of the ship where they stripped one of the three filtration units and modified it to pass more air through its charcoal filters. The air was truly foul by time they were done, and the duty section wore oxygen masks.

When the engineers finished with that, they set to work on the next one, hoping to get them all done before the ship's reserve fuel cells were drained. Their work was hampered by everyone's groggy, weary condition, which made thinking hard and physical exertion a trial.

Despite that, all three units were running faster than ever by the next day, and the air slowly began to recover. It was a desperate field expedient held together with wire, improvised belting, and heavy tape. The engineering Elder fretted over the jury rig for the rest of the voyage. The shortage of CO2 cartridges did nothing to improve our peace of mind as well.

§

The Admiral sat at one of the plastic tables eating a zero-G ration when I came up to the galley deck a few days later, and he gestured me over. "So how are you folks doing?" he asked when I joined him.

"Well enough, sir. It's a difficult trip for everyone."

"You got that right." He cocked an eye at me. "I imagine you think this tub is a sorry excuse for a starship."

"We've been in space a lot longer than you have, sir. I'm sure our early starships were every bit as..."

"Crude?"

"Um...yes, sir. You'll improve in time."

He frowned. "In time."

"I am surprised you came along, sir. Isn't it unusual for the Fleet Eldest to go on a tactical mission like this?"

MacKenna considered me for a moment, then said, 'I get my start in the submarines. In the subs, the Captain and crew were one entity, everyone part of the whole. The Captain was always right there in the control room, making the decisions, putting his life on the line with the rest of us, far more so than in any other kind of naval vessel. I really don't see how a military leader can operate otherwise."

That was a bit of a revelation. "So...that was why you were at New Patagonia when our two squadrons confronted each other?"

"Yeah, lucky for everyone."

MacKenna was the one who realized what went wrong at the first contact, and had the courage to stop the looming battle when the missiles were already flying. I'm not sure I would have had that presence of mind.

"Are we going to get through this in one piece, sir?"

He sagged, and stared at nothing. "I don't know," he said at last with a weary shake of his head. "You never know until it's over, and sometimes not even then."

That dismayed me, which shows how we on the Staff respected him. "Well...sir...if anyone can do it, it'd be you."

"Yeah, miracles are my freakin' specialty, or so I'm told." He sighed, and rubbed his eyes. "God, I'm too old for this shit."

I was struck by how tired and bitter he seemed, which shouldn't have surprised me, knowing what I did about his service record. Greatly daring, I said, "Honestly, sir, you've done more than your share. You have to let it go. There will always be wars, and you can't fight them all."

165

"Wars and rumors of wars." He eyed me in weary resignation. "You don't know what it's like having people depend on you for their survival. Pray to your gods you never do."

"Um...yes, sir."

"Well," he sighed again. "We'll be there tomorrow afternoon." He shoved off the table and drifted across the room to the cubicle set aside for him. "We'll see what happens then."

*****

"Strange Encounters"
(Related by Learnéd M'tinDegan)

Sometimes I get a faint hint of what drives people to go into space, and I was having such a moment as we drew near our destination. A soft red dot glowed faintly ahead of us, set in a sky turned frosty gray with stars, and we could just pick out the system's six planets with the navigation telescope. Our present weightlessness added to the haunting, eerie sensation. We were a long, long, long...*long* way from home, or anywhere else. It chilled me and awed me at the same time.

"A red giant." Admiral MacKenna turned and studied the paper in his hand. "Four small rocky worlds with no atmospheres, and two gas giants." He gazed out through the transparent navigation dome again. "Not much of a system." Despite his pessimism, I think he felt the same sense of awe as I did.

"I never dreamed I would wind up in space when I graduated from the Institute."

He turned awkwardly to me, catching himself with one hand on the remote-controlled telescope which filled the cramped space. "I know what you mean. Hell, I can't believe it myself. Mister...ah..."

"M'tinDegan, sir. The sociologist."

"M'tinDegan, gotta remember that." He sighed, and looked at the distant star again. "When I was born, we'd been to our moon decades earlier, and had pretty well abandoned space travel except for satellites and robot probes." He shook his head in wonder. "Unbelievable."

Captain Morgan came drifting up through the hatch from the control deck. "Admiral? We're fifty hours from reaching orbit around the Dreamsingers' world."

"Hmmm? Yes, fine, Captain. Have you heard from J J?"

"No, Admiral."

"You may be trying too hard," I said. "As I recall, you were half asleep when he contacted you the first time. Perhaps you need to clear your higher thought processes so he can access your subconscious."

"Lord knows we're all tired enough," she said.

"You got that right." MacKenna nodded wearily. "Well, keep your eyes open, Captain, and let me know the moment you get a peep out of them."

"Yes, sir."

She returned to the control deck, and the Admiral went back to gazing at the stars. The vastness of that sky made me realize just how *tiny* our presence was in the Universe as my bemused thoughts roamed through that frosty night. Who knew how many intelligent races there were out there? Would we find the Ancestors out here as well, perhaps? How many races would we eventually meet? And what impact would they have on our culture? Ancestors know meeting the humans profoundly changed us. So *many* opportunities, so *many* challenges, so *many* potential enemies: it left me shaken to think of it.

"It's huge," MacKenna muttered at last with a sense of awe. "Infinite. It's too big for any man to grasp."

"Both our races are still new to interstellar exploration," I mused philosophically. "I suppose this will be a well-traveled backwater a thousand years from now."

"Hell, in a thousand years this'll be a slum. There'll be honkey-tonk joints and tiki bars all across this sector." He gave me a mock-disgusted look. "Interstellar karaoke. Forgive them, Lord, for they know not what they do."

§

Notwithstanding the Admiral's gloomy outlook on the future, we made orbit around the Dreamsingers' home world four days later. The ship was on full battle alert as it had been since entering the system, and Captain Morgan was under express orders from the Admiral to 'run like a sumbitch' at the first sign of trouble. The humans' tension and fatigue were plain in their tight voices and sagging expressions. While we Ic'nichi were able to rest, we were so worried that none of us could sleep for more than fitful snatches. We were all tail-drooped and bleary-eyed, and K'deiTai even stopped complaining.

"Braking complete, Admiral," Captain Morgan called down from the control deck to where MacKenna and a few of us waited.

The Admiral drifted over to the ladder. "All right, Captain," he called up through the ladder way. "Maintain full battle status, and get the capacitor recharged as fast as you can."

The ship traveled to this system in hyper-C, using most of their capacitor reserve to brake to a stop as we reached our destination. The last part of our journey involved the risk of meeting an attacker going in. Now that we were in orbit, we were vulnerable until the charge was built up again. The whine of the turbines was a constant background irritant, and the ship was as ready for battle as could be.

Once the drive was shut down, the Admiral and his staff gathered for a council of war. Captain Morgan and her elders were there as well, while the crew remained at battle stations. "So what now, sir?" she asked.

"That's a good one." MacKenna pondered for a bit, then said, "Have you heard anything? Even a hint they might be watching us?"

"No, sir." Captain Morgan sighed and stared at nothing, her fatigue showing, then pulled herself together by main effort. "Should we try the radios, sir?"

"That never worked before, sir," one of the humans said. "They may not have radios."

"Likely, but we don't have many other options," Morgan said.

"The enemy might hear if they're in-system, but I don't see any alternative." MacKenna considered some more. "What is the state of the charge?"

"We presently have thirteen percent on the capacitor, sir," the engineering elder said. "We're charging as fast as we can."

"That low?"

"We're way overdue for a major refit, sir."

"Not enough to jump." MacKenna shook his head in dismay.

"We'll need to recharge for another twelve hours before we can maneuver, sir; nearly thirty hours before we can make it into hyper-C."

MacKenna brooded for a bit, then, "All right, use the radios, but keep us on a heading that will allow us to jump straight out-system at the first sign of trouble—as soon as we're able to."

"Shouldn't we hold off until we have the recharge, sir?"

That would be the sensible move since we came here on a stealthy mission, and were nearly immobile with nothing but the ship's main engine. There was no telling where the enemy was or when they might appear or how well armed they would be. The 'Marco Polo' was hardly a warship.

"No," MacKenna answered after some deliberation. "We didn't see any hostiles on our way in, and I want to get this done and be out of here before someone shows up."

"Hopefully this'll do some good," Morgan said as the communications rating activated their powerful transmitters.

"They may be desperate enough to answer us this time," another human said.

"If they even have radios."

§

The next day went by in frustrating silence as we brooded over the mystery of contacting J J, and the ship's crew kept a nervous watch for any sign of an enemy. Contacting the Dreamsingers became an obsession for everyone as the day crawled by, and a running debate soon grew in the ship's galley deck.

"They probably don't have advanced technology, sir," the engineering Elder said at one point. "That chemical environment might be good for developing grown crystal technology, and perhaps some sort of plastics, but they won't have fire, which precludes any smelted or fused materials."

"No vacuum tubes, huh?" MacKenna frowned at the idea that they might be too primitive for us to reach out to them. "That doesn't help one little bit."

"Depending on the effective range of their telepathy, they may not have any form of artificial communication at all," I said.

"And we know they can reach earth, with a little help, sir," I'eiBida said.

"As for that, it's possible they have telepathic forums which serve the same purpose as broadcasting or theater. They may not even have a spoken language."

An alarm buzzer went off on the control deck, and we all but jumped out of our skins. *"Merde!"* the engineering elder

170

grumbled. "There goes one of the air filters. If you will excuse me, sir." He made for the ladder to the lower levels, swearing under his breath.

We reluctantly got back to the subject once the alarm shut off. "Perhaps we can improvise some other sort of communication," I'eiBida suggested. "They might be more receptive to radar frequencies, for example."

Captain Morgan considered that. "We could cobble something together, but it would mean taking the radars off line."

"Too risky. What about modulating the communication laser?"

MacKenna made a sour snout. "Even if they do respond, we don't speak their language, so they'll have to carry the whole load on translating."

"Which brings us back to depending on the Captain to act as a messenger," K'deiTai said. "And even that appears to be marginal."

"Yeah." MacKenna turned to me. "So how *do* we communicate with telepaths, anyway? If they have no technology, and they don't even speak, how do we get to them?"

I racked my mind trying to come up with an answer to that one. Sadly, all my sociological experience thus far was useless. The bulk of my work was among our own people, who at least used recognizable languages and a similar cultural basis. Nor did my experience among the humans help, since as bizarre as they were at times, they shared the same sort of the physical and social assets we did. This dilemma made me realize how *limited* my experience was, and the sweeping challenges we were only beginning to discover in interstellar relations.

"Other than the Captain, I am at a loss, Admiral," I admitted.

"What about the radios, sir?" Captain Morgan asked. "Should we turn them off?" All of us were increasingly worried about broadcasting our presence. For all we knew, long range missiles could be closing in on us even then.

"Not yet," MacKenna said, reluctantly. "Let's give them a little more time." That was taking a terrible calculated risk, but we had no other choice.

§

171

The waiting continued through the next day as the ship's radios blasted the planet at full power, and we nervously watched the sky for any sign of an intruder. The crew surveyed as much of the system as they could on our way in, but a solar system is vast, and it would be all too easy for a hostile warship to elude us.

The Admiral's patience, never plentiful, was exhausted late that afternoon. "Dammit! This isn't working. We've been barking up the wrong tree all along."

"Shall we shut down the radios, sir?" the engineering elder asked.

MacKenna scowled at him. "Yeah. Shut the damned things down, for all the good they do."

That brought a collective sigh of relief from both races. "So what do we do now, sir?" one of his staff asked as the transmissions were being secured.

MacKenna heaved a sigh of frustration. "Damned if I know."

§

We spent the next day in a sort of paralysis as we tried to come up with some other idea now that the radios were secured. Everything we considered—and we came up with some bizarre notions—seemed unlikely to work, or were beyond our limited technical means without cannibalizing the ship's systems. We kept trying.

The Admiral finally broke down on the fourth day, and asked Captain Morgan if she would agree to be sedated in an effort to let J J into her mind. "I guess we have to, sir," she said after some hesitation.

"I won't order you to do this," MacKenna said, softly. "I don't want to endanger your health, but we're out of options."

"Well, let's get it done, then," she said with some bravado. "We need to get back to earth and overhaul those filters."

The ship's physich was a young fem, a recent graduate from medical circle, and she was not thrilled with what the Admiral proposed. Her office was a cubicle on the galley deck which was barely large enough for a bunk and cabinets of supplies; the only one aside from the Captain to have a cabin, and that so it could double as a medical ward.

172

"What are we trying to do, sir?" she asked.

"We want her to be groggy, like she is physically exhausted from lack of sleep, but she still needs to be alert. Can you do that?"

The physich thought about that. "I can get that effect with a mix of pain killers and stimulants, but you're talking potentially lethal doses, especially in combination. This is dangerous, sir.'

"We have to, doctor," MacKenna said as he tried to hold back his frayed temper.

"But the risk..."

"It's all right, Maiko." Morgan laid a comforting hand on her arm. "We have to chance it."

The physich thought it over, and was not happy. "All right, if you insist. Perhaps if you clear your mind and focus on the contact, it would make the connection easier."

"And sit so you can look out the view port at the planet," M'tinDegan said. "That image might catch J J's attention."

The Captain strapped herself into a chair at the dining table where she could stare out the view port at the planet below, and waited passively as the physich mixed an assortment of medicines in a large hypodermic syringe, and fitted her with an intravenous tube.

"Are you sure about this, Captain?" she asked before beginning.

"Yes."

The physich started a steady hypodermic drip, and we waited silently for some reaction. After a bit, the Captain started nodding off, but kept pulling herself awake.

"Anything, Captain?" MacKenna said at last.

"...uh...n...nothing..." Her speech was already blurred, and she was having trouble concentrating.

The wait continued as the hypodermic dripped, and the Captain stared impassively out the view port, and the Admiral grew increasingly frustrated. "Why the hell doesn't he answer?' he complained at one point. No one replied; certainly not J J.

"This isn't working, sir," I said to MacKenna, quietly.

"It *has* to work," he muttered.

173

"She can't go like this much longer, sir," the physich said. She was growing increasingly worried about the Captain's condition as time passed. MacKenna fumed, but made no answer.

The wait continued. The hypodermic was running low, and the Captain was fighting to stay awake. "Dammit, what else can we do?" MacKenna grumbled.

Then, suddenly, the Captain's head came up. "J J?" She half turned in her chair, staring at nothing in the center of the room. "J J, talk to us." Her eyes were glazed and her speech slurred. "...please..." She sagged, drifting unconscious. And he was there.

What I saw was the same faint transparent image we saw back at the beginning: a large human mal, heavyset, with dark brown coloring and snowy white fur. It took me a moment to realize he was planted firmly on the deck as if he was under gravity, while we drifted weightlessly. He was dressed in rough workers' clothing, and had the same weary, weather beaten look as before. But this time he radiated a sense of fear which affected us all with scale-crawling dread.

"Well, ah see you'ah startin t' figure things out," he said, solemnly. "Ah'm glad yo come. We need t' do a power of talkin."

"Is she all right?" MacKenna asked.

J J glanced at her. "Don' you worry about Honeylamb. She's sleepin'. Yo' minds are too different, so we need her t' reach out to you. Ah let her sleep while we speak; that way she be all right."

"I...see." MacKenna eyed the two uncertainly, then pulled himself together. "Ah, J J, my name is MacKenna..."

"You'ah the leader of th' human space fleet. Ah know. Ah see you in her thoughts." He turned to us next. "An you'ah from the Ic'nichi. Ah'm mighty pleased to meet you all."

"Um...thank you, J J," K'deiTai said. "When you contacted us on earth, you said there was trouble coming?"

"Yeah." He shook his head, and looked at each of us with deep, sad eyes. "They comin'. They comin' soon." His gaze met mine, and I was struck with a deep sense of revulsion bordering on panic. "You need t' get ready. They'ah a bad lot, an' they up t' no good." His gaze shifted to the next person, leaving a sense of dread behind. "It's gonna turn right ugly when they get here."

"Who is coming?" MacKenna demanded.

"We don' rightly know who they are, 'cept we can feel their thoughts, an' they's plain evil through and through. They won't show no mercy t' anyone gets in their way."

"What are their objectives?" K'deiTai asked.

"We ain't rightly sure, their thoughts are so strange. Near as we can tell, they comin' to find themselves a new world an' kill off anyone they meet." J J furrowed his forehead in thought. "Or maybe its t' other way round. One thing we do know is there won't be no peace-talkin' with 'em."

"How many ships?" MacKenna demanded. "Where are they coming from? What sort of..."

Captain Morgan began spasming; mildly at first, but she was trembling on the verge of convulsions almost before we realized it. J J glanced at her, then held up one hand in a cautioning gesture. "She can't take no more of this. Ah gotta go. You take care, hear?" And he was gone.

§

The Captain was sent straight to her quarters at the insistence of their physich to recover from her ordeal. While she rested, we got together to mull over what little we knew, which wasn't much. Putting all J J's hints together, we started building a strategic picture, but it was as empty as space itself.

"Dammit! I wish they'd give us some plain talk instead of all these hints," MacKenna said. "Don't they realize we need to know more?"

"That may be part of their nature." I put a lot of thought and speculation into what the Dreamsingers were like over the last few days, and my conclusions were both fascinating and disheartening. "As telepaths, they must pass a lot of mental data directly, like we use body language. There was probably a lot of unspoken information in that vision, but J J might not understand how to communicate with non-telepaths."

"That must be what that eerie feeling was about," I'eiBida said. We all felt the fear and loathing in J J's eyes.

"Most likely. As J J said, our minds are too different for him to reach us easily."

175

"Thus their need for a human host." MacKenna nodded. "So how *do* we communicate with them?"

"I hate to say this," K'deiTai said, "but we need to sedate the Captain again, as many times as it takes."

"I'm afraid we have to," I added. "We need whatever information they have."

"And we need to decide in advance what questions to ask, sir," I'eiBida said. "With contacts that brief, we can't waste a second for idle chatter."

The Admiral have him an impatient look. "Already on it, mister." He didn't like putting Captain Morgan through any more of that, but accepted it reluctantly.

Their physich was another matter. She adamantly refused to subject the Captain to that ordeal again, and only agreed to do so under protest when the Admiral twisted her tail righteously. Even so, she wouldn't administer any more drugs until the Captain spent the night recovering, and as intimidating as he could be, nothing he said could sway her on that.

§

We gathered on the galley deck the next morning to reach out to J J again. Captain Morgan was pale and shaky, and had trouble focussing. Their physich was worried about her, but reluctantly agreed to administer the drugs again.

"Are you sure you're up to this, Loraine?" MacKenna asked before they started.

"I have to be, sir." She eyed the physich uneasily as she prepared the intravenous tube. "We need to reach J J."

"Any more of this will be rough on you, Captain," the physich cautioned her. "You are risking your health."

She hesitated for a long moment. "Whatever it takes, Maiko," she said at last.

The IV was inserted, and it wasn't long before she faded into semi-consciousness, staring vaguely through the viewport at the planet below. We settled in uncomfortably for what we expected to be a long wait.

"Dammit, I hope this works," MacKenna grumbled. "We can't keep pushing her like this."

Time drew out as we waited impatiently, the drugs flowed into her arm, and the physich fretted, but there was no sign of J J. The duty watch changed, and changed again, and still there was nothing. I'm sure the Admiral would have paced back and forth in agitation if we were under gravity.

"Ancestors, I hate this," I'eiBida said to me at one point. "The longer this takes, the closer the invaders get."

"There's nothing we can do," I told him. "We just have to wait and hope for the best.'

He stretched to work a kink out of his neck. "That's the worst of it; the waiting." He stared at nothing for a bit, then his attention shifted to C'traBenla, who floated listlessly in an out-of-the-way spot. She noticed in turn, and came drifting over to cuddle close to him. I left them to find what comfort they could together.

§

Mid-meal came and went with no new developments. The inactivity soon palled on us, and we wound up gathered off to one side to debate the matter among ourselves.

"Could it be as difficult for J J to reach us?" I'eiBida wondered. "He might be recovering from that last effort, like the Captain had to."

"That's possible," I said. "But I don't know what we can do for it."

I'eiBida idly watched the scene across the room, where the Captain continued to stare out the porthole, and MacKenna did a slow burn of frustration. "For that matter, it might be as simple as J J being asleep. We should have checked the planet's rotation before we started this."

"With our luck, it *would* be something that stupidly simple.'

"It might be a gender issue," C'traBenla suggested. "J J is mal; the differences between genders could be interfering."

"That is just an image," K'deiTai said, impatiently. "We don't even know if they *have* genders."

"She may have something," I said before she could take offense at his abruptness. "It seems the Captain is the only one J J *can* contact. Most of the crew are mals; they might not be able to receive telepathy due to a gender based mental structure."

177

"A hormonal difference?" C'tra wondered.

"I understand the Captain has reached the age where their reproductive process stops."

"Could that be it? K'deiTai asked. "That might explain why the other three fems on board can't hear anything."

"The Captain suffers from long-standing emotional problems," I'eiBida offered. "Her post-traumatic stress from her hatchling years may have altered her mind."

I nodded thoughtfully. "That could be it, too."

"I hate to say it, but we should have brought N'detLeda with us," K'deiTai sighed. "So curst *many* things that could go wrong, and we have no idea where to begin."

"There's likely little he could do anyway," I'eiBida said.

"What an intriguing culture," I said to myself as I reflected on what *little* we knew about the Dreamsingers. "Understanding them could be the career's effort for a *herd* of sociologists."

"Sad to say, we don't have that much time," I'eiBida said.

I paused to look at the Admiral and the Captain, with the bright yellow-orange planet peeking in through the viewport. "I wonder if we will ever open an embassy here?"

K'deiTai gave me his sourest look. "With my luck, that'd be where I'll wind up next."

§

Nothing. No results. Time passed, and the Admiral's patience was soon worn through. He grabbed the Captain by her shoulders, looked into her eyes, and shook her unresisting form. "Hello? J J? Are you there?" He shook her again. "It's Admiral MacKenna. We need to talk to you."

Nothing.

"Why doesn't he answer?" MacKenna complained.

"The Captain may be suffering some sort of psychic block," I suggested. "The drugs may have suppressed her mind too much."

"Shall I stop, sir?" the physich asked, anxiously.

MacKenna hesitated. "No. Keep going for as long as possible," he said at last.

"But she's in danger, sir!"

"It goes with the territory, doctor," he said, grimly.

178

The waiting continued as MacKenna fumed, Captain Morgan grew weaker, and J J remained adamantly silent. The physich became alarmed as her blood pressure dropped, her heart started fluttering, and she began nodding off. Finally, after half the morning had passed, she faded into unconsciousness. The physich defied the Admiral then, unhooked the tube, and began treating the Captain for her failing condition.

"How is she?" MacKenna demanded.

"She is in bad shape, sir," the physich said while reading her vital signs. The Captain was on oxygen, and her heart rate was fluctuating. "I will know in a few hours if she suffered any lasting ill effects. In any event, she *cannot* take any more of this."

MacKenna sighed. "Very well." He pondered the Captain, then gazed out the view port at the planet below, then turned to us. "We might as well head back."

§

It was another ten days' travel back to earth. Captain Morgan was soon back at her station, pushing her ship harder than I was comfortable with. She was remote and introspective after her traumatic visitation by J J Ballas, and was preoccupied with running her ship and driving her crew to make vital repairs

The mood on board was grim. MacKenna spent his days sitting by one of the small viewports in a withdrawn funk as he brooded over what little we learned. The crew were subdued since our limited success merely verified the threat without providing anything useful. As for us, we were depressed by the poor results, and relieved that our time in the cargo hold would soon be over.

We finally down jumped, and earth was ahead, faint in the distance. "Such a beautiful sight," K'deiTai said. "It makes one realize how *lucky* we are to live on such lovely, inhabitable worlds."

"Thank my *Ancestors* this will soon be over," I'eiBida grumbled. "When we get to Singapore, we should have them hose us down; we need it."

"I for one will be thankful to see the last of our endurance rations," I said. "I can't wait to get back to Geneva, and hit the cafeteria line."

179

"Not that I'm looking forward to it," K'deiTai said, somberly. "There's still a war to fight, and we are not ready for anything bigger than a clubroom brawl." He turned back to the viewport. "We Arbiters are supposed to prevent wars, not help prepare for them."

I noticed his lapse, but didn't mention it. "Good intentions, but sometimes you simply have to grab tail and do whatever needs to be done."

"Whatever," he muttered. He turned to look at me. "At least what comes next ought to be interesting."

*****

"From Bad To Worse"
(Related by Defender I'eiBida)

As if things weren't bad enough, we walked right into another crisis when we arrived at the Defense Ministry, in Geneva. Our first warning was a demonstration teetering on the edge of a riot going on outside despite the chill autumn rain. The gendarmes were out in force with more arriving, and several Ministry building windows had been broken by flying rocks.

"This does not look good," I muttered as we watched from the relative safety of the embassy omnibus. The sound of the mob was ugly and tinged with panic, and the air was heavy with the odor of riot gas.

"What is it *now?*" K'deiTai grumbled.

The gendarmes forced a passage for us, and escorted us inside where we found another near riot in the press room. N detLeda was fighting a hopeless rearguard, but the news vultures were so agitated that it looked like they *might* eat him alive.

"It reminds one of our early days," M'tinDegan said in disbelief; *deja vu*, as the humans call it.

Commander Rostokovich was the first human we ran into. "What is going on here?" K'deiTai asked.

"Arbiter! Good. You are back." Ivan seemed worried. "N'detLeda's protégé interrupted Ministry press conference two days ago. She let secret of aliens out."

K'deiTai's ears and tail wilted. "We're doomed!"

The Admiral came in just in time to catch that. "What did she say, mister?" he demanded.

"Ah...well, sir..." Ivan seemed more worried than before, if possible. "Minister was answering questions about Ic'nichi fleet and our mobilization when she interrupted. First she said Space Fleet is useless, and they will have to fight attackers alone..."

MacKenna raised an eyebrow. "First?"

"...*da*, sir. When they asked her about attackers, she said our intelligence has learned nothing of them, but that the Ancients sent their fleet to help..."

"Help *us?*"

"...*da*, sir. And when they asked her why they are here, she said Ic'nichi will have to save earth from destruction..."

"*Destruction?*"

"...*da*, sir, that's what she said. Then she said she could not see reason for Ic'nichi to come to our rescue. You can imagine news vultures' reaction. Then next day..."

"You let her back in front of a microphone after that, *Commander?*"

Ivan was sweating by then. "I am sorry, sir! There is no stopping news vultures now!"

"Or her, either," K'deiTai added in disgust.

The Admiral held his temper. "Go on, mister."

"Well, sir, yesterday, N'detLeda tried to calm them down. But when they asked him why she was talking about earth's destruction, he told them talk of hostile aliens on news programs are unconfirmed rumors."

"And?"

"And they did not buy that with Ic'nichi fleet here, and our own mobilization. Now they say we are covering up something."

"Great. That means our credibility is completely undermined!" Our hope of carefully releasing the story to avoid a panic had just been blown out of the water.

"*And* we face full-blown war scare, sir," Ivan added.

"That was the worst *possible* thing he could have told them," M'tinDegan said in dismay.

"There is more, sir. Then she interrupted Hogarthy again, and *lectured* news vultures! She said humans are all crazy people, and media are worst of the lot." K'deiTai buried his head in his hands with an anguished whimper at that.

"On the air?"

"Live, sir."

"Like it isn't bad enough already! On top of undermining our credibility, she'll turn the media solidly against us and the war effort." He sighed, and turned to us. "I take back every terrible thing I ever said about Minister Hogarthy. There really are bigger idiots in this Universe!"

"And she's one of ours!" K'deiTai moaned.

"Admiral MacKenna!" It was DuRochelle, looking frazzled and anxious. "May I have a moment, please?"

"How bad is it?" MacKenna greeted him.

"It is not good. You may not have heard since you were on your flight from Singapore, but she set off a world-wide panic. The stock markets are going mad, there is wide-spread rioting, and Parliament is in an uproar."

"This could turn the Chancellor against us again!" K'deiTai was coming unglued in a hurry.

"Likely so. His support for your efforts has been tepid at best. He is wavering on whether to reinstate his demobilization order, as many in his faction are pressuring him to do."

That meant our hold on him was crumbling; the only thing keeping him in check was our blackmail threat, and I had enough experience with the human media to know that the uproar over this would bury the scandal.

"How is the public taking it?" MacKenna demanded.

"With all the conflicting stories about, no one knows what to believe, so the rumor mill is running at top speed." DuRochelle was grave, and seemed to be on the brink of despair. "According to the latest, our fleet and the Ic'nichi are planning a joint coup against the Alliance."

"And they're buying that bullshit?"

"Some. Most believe that the rumors of hostile aliens are correct, and you are covering up the extent of the threat."

"Well, they're right about that, at least," MacKenna allowed.

"The public is on the edge, and the conflicting reports fuel their fears. You must do something, and quickly."

"All right, the first order of business is damage control." MacKenna turned to us. "Any ideas? Anyone?"

"Why not simply tell them the truth?" M'tinDegan asked.

"What? That we received a telepathic message from an invisible alien warning us of an enemy we have no firm knowledge of, and who haven't shown up after all this time?"

DuRochelle gave that a rueful smile, and shook his head. "That would confirm the coverup in the public's minds. It may tip the Parliament against you, too."

Inspiration came when most desperately needed. "What if we claim they are our version of your Anti-techs, sir?" I suggested. "We can say they are trying to stir up a panic."

DuRochelle mused on that. "It could help."

"But what about our fleet?" K'deiTai asked. "There's no denying they're here for something."

"We have the original story about joint maneuvers, sir," I said. "We can sweeten that by admitting that we are engaged in staff talks on defense policy."

"Make them think they forced a concession out of us," M'tinDegan added.

"That might work, Admiral," DuRochelle said, hopefully.

"Hell, it's all we've got."

"I shall see what I can come up with, *monsieur.* But what about these aliens? This war scare is real enough."

MacKenna mused on that. "They have reason to worry. We have to admit to it eventually, but is it wise to reveal it now with all this uproar?"

"If we don't, any future statement will contradict anything we say now," K'deiTai said. "That will undermine our credibility even further."

DuRochelle nodded. "Candor is your best defense, *mon* Admiral, and this is too critical a story to sit on it for much longer."

MacKenna shook his head in dismay. "All right. We'll go with the Anti-tech story for now, and start easing them into the threat with the defense talks admission. As for the rest, I'll get a formal statement to you first thing in the morning."

"Where is she now?" MacKenna demanded of Ivan once DuRochelle was gone. His cool demeanor under fire was replaced by cold anger.

"Arbiter ordered her confined to embassy, sir."

"I *want* her." His tone promised major earthquakes. "I want her *here*, pronto!"

§

T'virDoma arrived a couple hours later with an armed APA escort, and was promptly whisked up to the fifth floor and the Admiral's office. What followed was the most thunderous tail-knotting I could imagine, and I've been through a few in my time. *"Borjemoi!"* Ivan said as we listened to the Admiral storm. "I never heard of him so angry." His tirade carried throughout the fifth floor.

"She deserves it," I grumbled.

At one point, N'detLeda showed up and demanded—demanded, mind you—to speak with the Admiral, and was escorted to his office while we held our breath. There followed a minute of silence, then he tore into them again.

"Mon Deus!" Agent Roubidoux said. "He is worse than before."

"We should call fire department," Ivan said. "Building may burst into flames."

"If he can turn that wrath against the aliens, we shall be invincible."

Minister Hogarthy arrived just then, clearly intending to confront MacKenna about this latest fiasco. He hesitated in the hallway, listened to the racket coming from his office, turned pale, and retreated without saying a word.

The rest of us, Ic'nichi and human alike, were quiet and apprehensive; nervously busy, and thankful not to be the object of the Admiral's wrath. After what seemed forever, but was probably an hour, they were escorted out by two Ministry security guards. They were both pale and shaking, and T'virDoma was crying.

MacKenna came out a few minutes later, trembling and breathing hard, his snout livid, and he was winded.

"Are you all right, sir?" Ivan asked in dismay.

"I want them off this planet, mister!" MacKenna's voice was wispy and hoarse, but his eyes burned. "I don't care what it takes, ship 'em home!"

"Da, sir!"

§

Once the Admiral calmed down, we went into crisis mode to try to contain the damage. We monitored the news broadcasts while he was preoccupied, and it was clear that we faced a major public relations catastrophe. It was far worse than DuRochelle's brief report suggested: the economy was faltering, there were

185

demonstrations and riots everywhere, and the clamor for disarmament and even for breaking relations with us was loud and shrill.

"Amazing," M'tinDegan muttered in dismay as we watched the news coverage on a borrowed viewer. "I've never *seen* such pandemonium, even here on earth."

"It is as before we first contacted you," Pierre told him. "This is what comes of unfounded rumors of hostile aliens."

M'tinDegan considered him. "We really terrified you that badly?"

"*Oui*. You must do something, and quickly, lest the war effort collapses altogether."

Early that afternoon, H'rhAtor released a statement saying that the Ic'nichi were here for strictly routine matters, and did not anticipate needing to come to earth's rescue any time soon. It was a flat-out lie, but we couldn't afford the truth. Our people were ordered to remain at the embassy or the Ministry so our presence wouldn't stir things up even more.

Minister Hogarthy, true to form, was utterly useless. He issued a press release later that afternoon which managed to confuse the issue even more, and wished the whole thing off on us 'for further information'. However, he at least kept his distance from the Admiral, which helped.

§

"You humans never fail to amaze me," H'rhAtor said when he came calling on MacKenna. "Meaning no disrespect, Brian, but *how* does your civilization function?"

"Poorly," MacKenna snarled.

H'rhAtor pondered that for a moment, then asked, "How do you think this will affect the war effort?"

MacKenna gave him a sour look. "There *is* no war effort for now. The war is on hold until we can dig our way out from under this mess. We won't be able to plan anything rationally until we know how much damage this will cause."

H'rhAtor sighed. "Would it were so simple to put off a major war. Should we withdraw our fleet for the time being to reduce our presence?"

MacKenna shook his head. "Thank you, H'rhAtor, but that would just stir things up more. The best thing now is a show of calm."

"I don't pretend to understand you people. I'm not sure I want to. But you can count on our complete support in this, and in the war effort, when it gets to galloping again."

"*If* it gets started again." There was a hesitant tap at the door. "Come!"

A human communications rating gingerly entered and handed MacKenna a message form before retreating. "Well, it seems the Chancellor managed to pull his head out of his ass for once," he said as he read. "He issued a *personna non grata* writ on those two walking disasters."

"*Thankfully*," H'rhAtor replied. "If you need a ship to take them back to d'enchia, we will be happy to provide one."

The Admiral greeted that with a derisive snort. "Done."

§

If any of us expected to come through this unscathed somehow, we were soon disabused of such foolish notions. The Admiral pressed the four of us into coming up with some rational story to calm the public, with Ivan and Pierre to help. As he put it, we were to confirm the alien threat while dismissing any talk of war; confirm that our fleet was here to make mutual defense preparations while again neither confirming nor denying the alien threat; and make it sound like general mobilization on both worlds was purely routine. The Admiral would be graciously pleased to have it on his desk first thing in the morning. There was nothing for it, so we barricaded ourselves in the conference room with pencils and note pads, and hunkered down for the siege.

It was soon obvious that we faced a hopeless task, as each point we tried to make negated the other points. The day dragged on into evening as our frustration turned to desperation. The harder we struggled, the worse it got; anything rational would create even more panic.

"I never wanted to be a press flak," M'tinDegan sighed as we argued at length over one three-word phrase. "This goes against every principle of sociological study."

187

"*You* were the one in a hurry to get home," K'deiTai reminded him. "*I* knew something like this would be waiting for us."

"This is punishment for my sins."

"Look at it as exploring new areas of human culture," I said with a grim smile. "You can write a scientific paper on it." They all looked askance at me, but no one replied.

And so it went late into the evening. We debated; we discussed; we argued. We took a break for meals that none of us were hungry for. We analyzed; we negotiated; we deliberated. It was an exercise in futility and sorely tried self-restraint. Every time we thought we had something, a quick re-reading would bring up something elsewhere which shot it down.

"*Borjemoi!*" Ivan sighed as he sagged on the table after we finished *another* sentence. "War can be no worse then this!"

"And they give no medals for writer's cramp," Pierre added.

"This is useless," K'deiTai said. "We need to go the Admiral and tell him that what he wants contradicts itself at every point. There's no sense in continuing."

Ivan gave him a bleak look. "You will explain this to him?"

"Um..." K'deiTai's ears wilted.

Back at it. Spirits sagged; tempers rose; the trash can filled to overflowing with scrap paper. C'tra helped out as best she could with *V'liz,* coffee, and snacks coming in a steady stream. We drank a *lot* of *V'liz* that evening.

Despite it all, we managed to put something more or less coherent down on paper. It was mostly verbal nonsense which confirmed, denied, and confused everything, delicately seasoned with reassuring platitudes on the key issues. We were bone weary and hated each other after arguing over it for so long, but we did it. Minister Hogarthy would have been proud, and I defy the wisest human Learnéds to come up with anything better.

§

"It is done, *tovaritch,*" Ivan said after he delivered our opus to the Admiral's desk. "Our pardons have come through, and we may go."

"At least fighting the war will be easy after this," Pierre grumbled.

188

Ivan nodded morosely as we headed for the elevator. *"Da.* Tomorrow I will desert, and get some sleep."

"Capital idea," I said. "The worst they can do is send us to the fighting."

It was well past midnight when we left the Ministry. We were all weary, hungry, and jittery from all that *V'liz,* and I, for one, was about fed up with it all. The only humans we met on our way out were a couple of housekeepers, the security watch at the rotunda desk, and two weary and disgusted peacekeepers guarding the elevator.

It was raining again, with a hint of snow in the air. The chill night air was refreshing, and there was a brisk wind. The streets were deserted at this time of night, and aside from a bell striking the hour somewhere in the distance, the city was silent.

"Do you think it will work?" M'tinDegan asked as we waited for the limos to arrive from the embassy.

"I don't get paid to think," I grumbled.

"I suppose we shall find out in the morning," Pierre said. "It ought to be an interesting spectacle."

"At least nothing else can go wrong tonight," C'traBenla said.

"Don't *say* things like that!" K'deiTai admonished her. "Our Ancestors may be listening."

§

They must have been: as luck would have it, we ran into R'benTdan as we came through the front door of the embassy. She was dressed in a lounging robe, and was escorting another of H'rhAtor's staff out. They were both weary and frazzled, although he was somewhat the worse for wear.

She gave us a smoldering look as they went by. "Well, I see *you're* out partying late."

That ill-considered remark put C'tra in a venomous mood, which was *just* what I needed after my little day. "Well, I see your reputation continues to grow," she snarled in return.

R'benTdan laid her ears back. "At least I *can* build a reputation, which is more than can be said for *some* people!"

"You do have that gift...it *is* a gift, isn't it? I'm sure the gossip would sizzle if there were any *other* reason for your generosity."

189

"You would know about gossip, wouldn't you?" R'benTdan sidled up beside me with an evil look in her eye, and ran a hand suggestively over my shoulder. "And my generosity is always welcome, especially where it is so *desperately* needed."

Her forwardness was getting to C'tra, despite my embarrassed expression. "You would know about desperation, wouldn't you?" she said with an icy glance at me. "It's written all over your sagging jowls."

The gleam in R'benTdan's eyes said she was in an ugly temper and ready for a fight. "You would know about sagging, too, I'm sure." She ran her hand along my flank, and I recoiled when she caressed my inner thigh. "Is it any wonder things sag from lack of *proper* attention?"

"Look..." I tried to fend off her advances, without much success. "This isn't appropriate."

"All the better," she purred.

The human at the lobby desk was watching all this with obvious amusement, while our watch stander looked elsewhere and maintained a carefully neutral expression.

"I'm happy with C'tra...she's my bondmate..."

"Well if all you want is *breeding*, then I guess any dumpy old *NmFarg* would do. But there's so much more out there, if you just know where to look."

"He knows where to look," C'tra growled. "And he finds everything he needs there." The fight was going against her, which did nothing good for her temper. Her ears were laid back, a warning sign everyone knew.

"Really? He *needs* to set his standards higher." She caressed my ears again. "You'll be *amazed* at what's out there when you finally do."

"He'll need an appointment since what's *out there* is so busy!"

"Quality will tell, won't it?"

"I'm sure any *number* of people could tell, too, since *quantity* seems to be closer to the truth!"

Several more people were gathered in the hallway to witness the show. For all I knew, they were placing bets on who would survive.

I fended off another attempt at my thigh. "Look, I'm not interested! We've just returned from a long trip, and all I want is to go to bed."

She gave a theatrical sigh and an icy smile. "I suppose you *could* spend the night with *her* if you're too *frazzled* and *worn out* for anything better." She caressed my neck one more time, then sauntered toward the stairs with a blatant come-hither look over her shoulder. "Get a good night's sleep, defender. Tomorrow is another day, and you'll need your strength."

C'traBenla was giving me her icy glare when R'benTdan left. "What?" I protested. "I'm not interested in her!"

"Well you could have been a little more *dis*interested!" She marched toward the stairs with me trailing along protesting.

"She's a predator. I didn't do anything to encourage her. It's not my fault you two are feuding."

She turned and gave me a hostile look. "Honestly, I'ei, you need to stiffen your tail around fems."

§

C'traBenla was still mad at me when we *finally* reached our quarters, but by that point I was too weary to care. The embassy guest quarters were a welcome haven after everything I'd been through, even with C'tra in her current temper. I was on my guard to avoid doing anything which would set her off since I really didn't want to spend the night in the defender quarters again.

She dumped her kit on the bed pad, and stomped around the room putting things away. I eased off into one corner, trying to be as unnoticed as possible, and dumped my kit directly into the laundry bag. After six hands of days in space, my gear needed major attention. But right then, all I cared about was staying out of her way until she calmed down, and then getting some much needed sleep. Laundry could wait until tomorrow.

Then she paused and picked a sheet of paper up off the dresser. As she read it, her eyes grew wider and her ears came up. She looked at me after a bit. "Did you write this?" I had to think for a moment, then remembered that I wrote her a brief note before heading to the airport. I nodded, reluctantly, wondering how much trouble I was in. I *really* didn't need another argument right then.

191

"Love...this is *beautiful*." Her eyes turned all misty and her ears started twitching. "...'the way the light plays on your lovely scales, glowing with your rich bronze beauty'..."

Ancestors! Did I write that?

"...'entranced by your bold, exotic'..." She giggled. "...'and your'...I'eiBida! Really, love!"

What did I do? I didn't remember a thing I wrote; didn't even remember leaving that note until she found it. I was mortified.

"...'glowing with passion'... Oh, my!" She went on avidly. "Is that even *possible?*"

It must have been the stress of that morning. Yes, I was so distracted and upset that I poured my deepest angst out to her on that page without even realizing it.

"'...every time I look at you, I feel the overwhelming urge to'...Oh!" I cringed. She kept on reading more avidly as I wished I could melt into the floor. How much more was there?

"You would do *that?*" I cringed again. "I'eiBida, you *are* the naughty one!" She giggled and read that last part again. "Do you *really* feel that way about me?"

"Um...well...yes, I do." This was embarrassing. Thankfully we were alone; I'd hate to have our two computer geniuses get ahold of this. She went back to reading, giggling like a hatchling as I wondered just what I wrote and where the *l'cc'vn* I came up with all that. It must be the stress.

Finally, after what seemed like an eternity, she finished. She scanned the page again with dewy eyes, then folded the paper carefully and put in in her pouch. Then she came over and cuddled close to me. "I'ei," she murmured. "I had no idea you feel so strongly about me."

"...well...I...was just..."

"That was beautiful, love." She cuddled closer and nuzzled my ear. "I never realized you have such poetic hearts." She nipped my ear playfully, and added, "You really know how to charm a fem."

"...I...was just..." There was no way I could avoid saying it. "...just expressing my feelings to you..."

She reacted with a dreamy sigh. "Such beautiful feelings."

192

"I'm sorry about that scene in the lobby. She means nothing to me, honest."

"Not to worry, love. I'm not angry at you. We'll get through this, and I'll put a rare and righteous knot in her tail before I'm through." She nibbled my ear affectionately. "Maybe I don't show it at times, but I know you truly love me." She nuzzled my ear again, and murmured, "Which is why I love you *so* much." Then she...

*****

"What Goes Around"
(Related by Learnéd M'tinDegan)

Our supply ship came in a day behind schedule, bringing its load of food, mail, dispatches, news that ship 120, the fleet logistics ship, would appear shortly, and two familiar and unwelcome problems.

"As I expected," N'detLeda huffed as he handed over a diplomatic dispatch envelope. "The Inner Circle overruled you."

"Those *n'bna'nmn*," U'tdaPagrn muttered as he read the worst. "Don't they realize what a smell you two created?" His attempt to ship them home in compliance with the Chancellor's *persona non grata* writ had been scuppered by Chamber politics.

N'detLeda frowned at the memory of that fateful day. "It's not our fault the humans are so unstable. They need to learn how to control themselves." The crisis they set off two months ago was still reverberating around the planet. There were demonstrations in the street, riots in Parliament, and the stock markets were only beginning to recover from the shock.

"I suspect this is Ancient Z'keBalf's doing," K'deiTai grumbled. "He has no love for the humans."

U'tdaPagrn gave him a chilly look. "Then he's an even bigger *n'bna'nmn!*"

"Nonetheless, I am a special representative of the Most Ancient and the Inner Circle," N'detLeda insisted. "They want me to remain, so the Admiral will just have to live with it."

U'tdaPagrn wilted. "Wonderful. *How* are we going to explain this to him?"

"Err..." N'detLeda hesitated, at a loss for words in the snout of that daunting prospect. "I'm sure you can come up with something."

"This is your *Bna'vwep!* Don't expect me to save your ears!"

"And don't look to me for help, either!" I'eiBida added.

Just then T'virDoma burst into the Arbiter's grotto with his Aide protesting behind her. "There you are! What is the delay in assigning us quarters? It's been a miserable trip from Singapore, and I want to get unpacked."

194

"Patience, young fem," N'detLeda said, condescendingly. "Keep in mind that *average* intellects need time to adjust to the unexpected."

"And those two *tra'taj* are at it again!" She turned on U'tdaPagrn and lectured him. "Can't you keep the people working here under control?"

I'eiBida's ears wilted. "Um, excuse me," he mumbled, and hurried out.

"What I can or cannot do is no concern of yours!" U'tdaPagrn snapped at her. "Speaking of which, the Inner Circle *cannot* change reality by issuing diplomatic writs. You two are *cc'v'renk* on this world, and the human Admiral is the *least* of your worries. We have enough problems without you defying the humans' deportation order, so you need to tuck your tails under until we can get them to lift it."

"This is *er'trxxda!*" N'detLeda protested. "We are here for an important purpose, and we cannot let this diplomatic *x'mnnb'* get in the way."

"All the same, you two are restricted to the embassy until we can straighten this mess out."

"If it can be straightened out," I added.

N'detLeda sighed. "Then I *trust* you will take care of that right away? We have work to do."

"And we need to get unpacked," T'virDoma said, crossly, as they stomped out.

"Why don't my Ancestors just cast me into the Uttermost Darkness?" K'deiTai moaned once they were gone.

"We must have done something too terrible for that," U'tdaPagrn grumbled.

§

U'tdaPagrn called I'eiBida and me to his grotto a bit later, and appointed us to bring the unwelcome news to the Admiral. The day was a dead write-off anyway.

"Thanks for *nothing,*" I'eiBida said. "And we were just getting things under control at the Ministry, too."

"I'm sorry, but we don't have a choice," U'tdaPagrn said.

"C'tra will be impossible once they show up again."

195

Then a thought occurred to me. "Um...if the Chancellory refuses to lift the deportation order, those two will be confined to the embassy," I suggested. "If you don't press them on it, it will at least keep them out of the way and out of trouble."

I'eiBida gave me a grateful look, and turned eagerly to U'tdaPagrn. "You have to! *Please!*"

U'tdaPagrn nodded thoughtfully. "Yes, that would keep them out of mischief, wouldn't it? But it still means that the Admiral must be warned."

"Wonderful," I'eiBida groaned as his ears sagged.

"You're already drawing hazard duty pay, so what are you whining about?"

§

"They are back?" Commander Rostokovich said in disbelief when we told him. "Are your leaders mad?"

"They must be," I'eiBida said. "But we're stuck with them."

"What's worse, *we* have to inform the Admiral of this," I said.

Ivan gave us a pitying look. "I am sincerely sorry for that, my friends."

"Perhaps you could request political asylum," Agent Roubidoux said. "Your leaders can only ask you to risk life and limb."

"No," I'eiBida said. "An Ic'nichi's got to do what an Ic'nichi's got to do, I suppose."

"Then we shall pray for you, my friends," Ivan offered.

"Thank you." I'eiBida sighed, then looked at me. "Well, I guess we better get it over with."

§

"Politics, huh?" MacKenna took the ill news calmly. "You people are as messed up as we are."

"I am sorry, sir," I'eiBida said. "We tried to ship them home, but they bounced back with new endorsements from the Inner Circle. There was nothing we could do."

"Damned *politicians!* They're the same everywhere!"

"If it's any comfort sir, U'tdaPagrn won't press the Chancellory about the deportation order, so they will be confined to the embassy."

196

"That's something, anyway," MacKenna sighed. "Just keep them out of my road. And you, mister," he waved an admonishing finger at I'eiBida, "I'm holding you *personally* responsible for keeping her under control!"

"Um...I'll try, sir."

§

And of course Minister Hogarthy had to put in an appearance, as if our day wasn't hectic enough already. The Admiral admitted to us some time ago that they only had two hundred atomic weapons, most of which were ancient and of dubious reliability. A major effort was under way to refurbish their existing stockpile, and to construct new ones. He warned us to keep that strictly between our ears, since the humans were paranoid about such things, and learning that production had started again would bring on a major crisis. Having seen how panicky the humans were already, we took his admonition to hearts. Unfortunately, that didn't include one paranoid, panicky human in particular.

Hogarthy came trundling in, all lathered up over the latest development in the human defense effort, to interrupt our mid-afternoon joint conference. "Admiral, this latest scheme of yours —refurbishing those old warheads, not to say building *more* of them? This is beyond endurance!"

MacKenna considered him with a weary sigh, and rubbed his eyes with one hand while the rest of us waited expectantly for the battle to come. "Half those weapons are unserviceable," he explained with labored patience. "And the entire lot aren't nearly what we'll need to fight a major war."

"But...but...making new ones? You *really* want to play around with all that deadly radioactive material?"

"It's been sitting in those old reactors for forty years. Hauling it off planet will be all to the good."

"And why didn't you tell me about this? I only learned of it when I reviewed your budget expenditures!"

"We need to get the work done. If you'd listened to me back during the Contact Crisis, our defenses would be in far better shape." The Admiral was starting to get miffed. A couple humans in the background were making wagers.

197

"You clearly do not understand the political considerations!" Hogarthy lectured him. "The Intelligentsia are *adamantly* opposed to nuclear rearmament at any time for any reason."

"So you've been leaking top military secrets along with the rest of the gossip at your sewing circle?"

"Huh? No, of course not!"

"Then how would you know what anyone thinks?"

That stumped him. "Well...it's common knowledge..."

"And will the Intelligentsia fight the invaders with rocks and sticks after the fleet's been destroyed?"

Hogarthy must have finally realized that getting confrontational with the Admiral was bad strategy; he changed course and tried pleading with him. "Don't you realize the danger? Do you have any *idea* of the reaction if this gets out? It could end all our careers."

C'traBenla's ears picked up.

MacKenna knew full well what the public reaction would be, and he was not amused by Hogarthy's cluelessness. "Frankly, you can have this job with my blessings."

"Well if you can't think of yourself, at least think of me! You may not care for your career, but I do."

MacKenna snorted in contempt. "And what do you suppose will happen to your career if we run out of ammunition in the middle of a battle?"

"You have plenty of ammunition. All your ships have a full allotment of missiles..."

"And what will our fleet do for reloads, *assuming* any of them survive the first battle without nukes?"

Since whining wasn't going to work any better, Hogarthy abandoned it for his old habits. "You aren't seeing the big picture! There are political considerations which outweigh purely military matters. I would think you understood that!"

"I understand what we're facing better than you could ever hope to!" As we all feared, MacKenna was finally starting to lose his temper under Hogarthy's badgering. "Since I was put in charge of our planet's defense, perhaps you should *listen* to my experience in defense policy!"

"*We* make policy, *Admiral!* You'll do this without those *things!*"

"Then maybe we'll throw *you* at the enemy! You've certainly done enough damage here!"

"You're being sarcastic!"

"It beats strangling you!"

"Nonetheless, this is wrong! You need to learn to do without those terrible weapons on the highest moral principles!"

MacKenna stood and pounded the desk with his fist, which made Hogarthy draw back. "Moral principles be damned! There's only one principle that matters, and that's our survival!"

"You are impossible, sir!"

"Highly unlikely, anyway."

"Well since you are beyond reason, I *insist* that you put a stop to this madness! You have your orders, *Admiral!* If I hear any more of this, I'll...I'll take it directly to the Chancellor!"

"Well good riddance!" MacKenna snapped. "If he can stomach you, he's a better man than I thought." Hogarthy stomped out in a huff.

"I get the feeling he's going to be a problem," H'rhAtor said once he was gone.

"*Going* to be?" MacKenna gave him an annoyed glare before he sagged into his chair and rubbed his eyes. "Actually, you may be right."

§

It was late, as usual, when we returned to the embassy that evening; and as usual, we were all worn down and depressed over the state of affairs and Hogarthy's threats. Right then all I cared about was something to eat and a good night's sleep.

T'aiPiden and W'kiLap were waiting for us in the lobby. "So how goes the war effort?" T'aiPiden asked.

K'deiTai stared at him blankly for a moment before answering. "Things are still moving, but barely, and we have a long way to go before we'll be ready for any sort of fight."

"That's if Hogarthy doesn't interfere again," I added.

"That *hro'n'nad*?" W'kiLap snorted. "Why do the humans put up with him?"

199

"There's no accounting for taste, I suppose."

"True, but what explains the lack of it?"

"They are human, after all."

"Enough heroics for one day," I'eiBida grumbled. "I'm for bed." He headed for the stairs, then looked at C'traBenla, who had remained behind next to W'kiLap.

"You go ahead, love," she said. "I'll be along in a bit."

He nodded wearily and went along as the rest of us broke up and went our various ways, leaving her with our two computer *'v'thorble*. I didn't think anything of it at the time.

§

Ship 120 arrived in turn three days later, bringing a welcome supply of liquid hydrogen, oxygen, and helium for the humans, and drinking water, spare parts, and rations for our fleet. The cryo gasses did a lot to help the humans' logistics, although far more was needed.

They also brought the latest dispatches from the 'Dark Grays' Staff, which provoked another conference. "It seems we won't be getting any more ships for a while," H'rhAtor told us. "Staff ordered a hand of our more recent patrol ships to sweep the border region, which took up most of the available command rates."

"I can't fault them," MacKenna said, philosophically. "Having the ships here won't do much good if you folks get sucker-punched from behind." Despite that, he was clearly disappointed. "How soon will we know anything?"

H'rhAtor consulted the latest dispatch. "They have another ten hands of days before they are to report in. Any ship which sees something is to come directly here and alert us."

"Good. Someone back home is thinking."

"A second force of our slower, older ships is being assembled at d'enchia to support the planetary defenses. That way both home worlds will be covered, and we will bracket the area where your contact with J J Ballas took place, thus likely covering the threat axis."

MacKenna nodded. "If either home world is threatened, we can bring a relief force in quickly. How soon will they be operational?"

"Good question. Aside from the four presently on sweep, they have six more available, but they are short on crews. We can't place newly hatched Fourth Degrees in senior positions, and the rest of the fleet is already sadly depleted." He pondered the dispatch some more. "They are calling in volunteers from the outlying districts of our stellar sphere, but the travel time is long. I suspect it will be some time before those ships are good for much more than local defense."

§

Despite the gloomy reports from home, both sides were making real progress. The humans in particular were completing a major refit of all their ships, even though it meant scavenging parts from incomplete hulls. Their stocks of munitions were growing, and they were about to take delivery on another orbital shuttle, which would help tremendously.

Just as the news of the alien threat aroused panic in many quarters, it also spurred recruiting. Space Fleet had numerous volunteers from the other branches of the peacekeepers, and a major influx of recruits was starting to work their way through the training programs. They wouldn't be much help in the short run, but if this war went any length of time, the humans would at least have a ready supply of personnel to draw on.

The big question, of course, was whether those assets would ever be used with the political climate what it was. We didn't have much hope without the humans' stellar bombs, and I think all of us worried at length over what, if anything, the Admiral could do about Hogarthy's order. None of us were optimistic as we headed home to the embassy that evening.

§

It was snowing the next morning, and the embassy's antiquated heating system was hard put to fight off the chill which had everyone on edge. We gathered in the cafeteria for a somber first-meal, and I doubt if any of us were really hungry. I, for one, didn't eat much even though mid-meals at the Ministry were usually light. The prospect of losing our one real strategic resource, or even having the human war effort shut down entirely cast a pall over our gloomy little circle.

"Perhaps the Admiral can talk to Hogarthy, get him to change his mind," I offered at last.

I'eiBida was lingering over another bowl of *V'liz* and staring absently at nothing. "What good will it do?" he muttered. "Hogarthy is dead set against us."

"Surely he can do something?"

"The Admiral can't do anything without openly defying his civilian superiors," K'deiTai said. "And he won't do that. Going to the Chancellor won't help, and we don't dare make a public issue of it."

"I don't know what we can do without the humans," I'eiBida sighed.

C'traBenla laid a comforting hand on his arm. "Keep up your optimism, love. We've been through these things before; this will work out as well."

I'eiBida gave her a bleak smile. "Ancestors, I hope you're right."

§

The roads were in too poor a condition for the embassy limos, so we took the omnibus, which could plow through the drifts better. We were silent, caught up in our own thoughts made all the gloomier by the gray murk outside.

DuRochelle was waiting for us in the Ministry lobby, which was no surprise in itself, but after greetings all around, he said to C'traBenla, "You wished to speak with me, madame?"

"Yes, and thank you for a moment of your time." She took his arm and aimed at a quiet corner of the lobby. "I had a little matter I wanted to speak with you about...I'ei, you go on. I'll be up in a bit."

"What's all that about?" K'deiTai grumbled as they headed off.

"I'm afraid to ask," I'eiBida said.

§

The fifth floor was fairly busy even at this hour. We found Admiral MacKenna, H'rhAtor, Commander Rostokovich, and a few senior staffers loitering in the hall near the staff lounge. Their subdued mood did not look promising, and we could feel the tension in the air.

202

"How go things this morning, sir?" I'eiBida asked.

MacKenna sighed and glanced at his watch. "I suspect it'll hit the fan any..."

"*Admiral* MacKenna!" It was Minister Hogarthy, coming down the corridor nearly apoplectic in rage.

"...right on schedule."

Hogarthy got in the Admiral's snout, which was way out of character for him. "You overrode my order!"

"Damned right I overrode your order. We need every weapon we can scrounge up, and I don't have the time for your foolishness."

"Minister ordered work on nuclear weapons halted," Ivan muttered to us. We were stunned by what we never thought would happen: the Admiral had openly defied his superiors.

"This is mutinous! *Mutinous*, sir!" Hogarthy quivered in rage.

For once, MacKenna seemed on the defensive. "I did what I had to for all our sakes."

I happened to notice DuRochelle coming down the corridor with C'traBenla. He stopped in the distance and watched Hogarthy's gyrations.

"That is *not* for *you* to decide! The military is *subordinate* to the *civil* government. *We* decide defense policy!"

"It was your lack of coherent policy which forced my hand," MacKenna said, evenly.

"That is no excuse!" Hogarthy was trembling in mixed rage and excitement. "You are a mutineer, sir!"

I half expected them to come to blows over that, but MacKenna held his temper grimly in check. He knew he gambled once too often, and was trying to contain the damage. "What matters is the public's safety. We need those weapons if we are to have any hope at all."

"Utter *rot*, sir! It was raving militarists like you who made this world a charnel house! The Collapse turned you into a monster, and it's long overdue for you to be removed!"

MacKenna lost it then. "I was press-ganged into this *because* of my experience! The least you can do is allow me to exercise my judgment in this, which is far more than you'll ever have!"

203

"I never thought you were a wise choice even then, and you have tested my patience for the last time! I am going straight to the Chancellor with this! I'll have your commission before this day is out! You'll see!" He stomped off in a huff.

MacKenna's shoulders sagged as he watched Hogarthy go. "God, I don't know why I put up with this," he muttered at last.

"It seems you won't have to put up with it for much longer, Brian," H'rhAtor said, softly. "Please accept my sincerest regrets."

MacKenna glanced at him. "It was inevitable, I guess. Sometimes I wonder how I lasted this long with those fools."

"If nothing else, we will welcome your advice. I'm sure we can arrange for you to act as a consultant."

"We're gonna lose this war." MacKenna's snout was marked with bitter frustration. "He'll put some political hack in here, and we're gonna *lose* this war!"

"Your fleet is as sound as can be. We'll put up the best fight we can, of course."

"Don't kid yourself. Our chances aren't all that good under the best circumstances."

H'rhAtor sighed. "I'm afraid your temper has gotten the better of you once too often, Brian."

MacKenna scowled at that. "'fraid you're right."

I noticed that DuRochelle had intercepted Hogarthy by the elevators as he came stomping down the hall, and was showing him a folder of documents. Something about that stirred my suspicion, and I called the others' attention to them with a gesture.

Whatever DuRochelle showed him, Hogarthy was distraught over it. He stared at the documents in disbelief as DuRochelle lectured him sternly. We couldn't hear what they were saying, but Hogarthy was clearly trying to bombast his way out of whatever DuRochelle had on him, and DuRochelle was having none of it. They argued furiously for some time before DuRochelle cut him off peremptorily, and left him standing there. Hogarthy stared at us, shaking in anger, before throwing up his arms in despair and stalking away.

I'eiBida gave C'traBenla a suspicious look when she rejoined us. "What did he say to Hogarthy?"

She replied with a smug ear twitch. "Oh, I passed along a bit of *juicy* gossip; something about a press release in which Hogarthy takes full credit for starting a *massive* nuclear rearmament program, complete with budgets, photos, and all the rest. It ought to make a sensational news story, if it ever comes out."

K'deiTai was aghast. "You..."

"The soft voice whispering of political ruin turneth away wrath, as the humans say."

"The Sixty-*Fifth* Maxim of the Defenders," I said, bemused.

"Or should be," H'rhAtor added in dismay.

The Admiral looked at her, confused, then laughed out loud. "Talk about brinksmanship! *Damn* if you don't take the Blue Ribbon!" He shook his head in amazement.

"I'm afraid I am at a loss, Admiral," H'rhAtor said.

"His own party would hang him out to dry if the press ever got wind of that."

"Do you think he bought it, sir?" I'eiBida asked.

"Looks like he found it most entertaining, I daresay." MacKenna was bemused by her latest wild scheme, as were we all. "I suspect we don't need to worry about him for a while."

"See, love?" C'traBenla said. "Things work out in the end." She gave us a knowing smile, and went about her business.

The Admiral gave I'eiBida a sardonic look before heading back to his office. "Your intel people, hmmm?"

"Um...it would seem, sir." Evidently her years on the Geneva diplomatic circuit were put to good use. The forged documents those two computer *'v'thorble* cooked up had averted disaster.

"*Damn* if she couldn't teach us all a few tricks." MacKenna was trembling, almost giddy in relief. "If we ever go to war, *please* leave her at home."

"Ah...she's our secret weapon, sir."

MacKenna chuckled again, and glanced at H'rhAtor, who offered a blank expression. "Maybe we ought to surrender now."

"Why don't we just appoint her as the Arbiter-To-Humans, and go home?" K'deiTai grumbled once he left.

*****

205

"Portents"
(Related by Learnéd M'tinDegan)

Our next lot of bad news arrived a few days later, and U'tdaPagrn summoned us to his grotto to share the joy, bless him. "The Chancellor reversed the deportation order?" I muttered in dismay. "*What* was he thinking?"

"This is Hogarthy's doing, I'll wager," K'deiTai said. "That *un'tdar* has been a constant knot in our tails all along."

I'eiBida and I exchanged knowing looks, as we both figured this was a bit of payback by the Chancellor; something U'tdaPagrn hopefully didn't know about. "So what are we to do, sir?" I'eiBida asked. "The Admiral will explode when he hears this one!"

U'tdaPagrn looked pained. "Someone has to tell him."

"Not me!"

"Me neither!" K'deiTai said.

"I'm a civilian," I added. "You can't put me at risk!"

"A lot of help you three are!" U'tdaPagrn drummed his fingers nervously on his desk as he fumed over this latest setback. "Send N'detLeda in here," he said at last.

N'detLeda and T'virDoma appeared in short order, since they no doubt knew of this development already. "You will be pleased to know that the Chancellory reversed your deportation order," U'tdaPagrn told them when they arrived. "You are cleared to return to work at the Ministry."

"About time," N'detLeda huffed.

"That's no more than what we could expect from bureaucrats," T'virDoma griped. "*Human* bureaucrats at that."

"Indeed," U'tdaPagrn said, sharply. "I can't see rhyme or reason for this, but this is their world, so I guess we're *stuck* with it. So go on over to the Ministry and check in with the Admiral; he'll bring you up to date on their progress."

"Well, it's good to see that you're so enthusiastic," N'detLeda grumbled as they left.

We all breathed a guilty sigh of relief once they were gone. "Thank you, sir," I'eiBida said.

§

206

Not being complete *n'bna'nmn*, we gave them an hour's head start since that seemed to be the Admiral's maximum endurance. In fact once we arrived, we learned he took the ill news with surprising resignation, for him. N'detLeda and T'virDoma were pale and withdrawn when we trooped in. They gave us icy looks, but said nothing. Commander Rostokovich and Agent Roubidoux greeted us with bemused looks, but didn't comment. The rest of the humans and our fleet staff were pensive and silent, and even H'rhAtor seemed distracted. Perhaps we should have come earlier to witness the spectacle after all.

§

We turned to as best we could in the edgy atmosphere in the 5th floor, and as usual, we had our hands full. The 'Dark Grays' have nothing on human staff paperwork, which was all the more difficult with everyone so disconcerted as we were. At least, despite it all, the humans were making real progress on mobilization. Supplies were accumulating, their contractors were getting up to speed, and the general overhaul of the human fleet progressed rapidly. It wasn't much, but at least the humans were about as ready as could be.

Our little day was disrupted again when *Monsieur* DuRochelle appeared a short while later. "You cannot be serious!" he sputtered. "You let those *imbéciles* return? You let him give press conferences after what they did?"

"Oh, great! What is he up to?" I'eiBida asked in alarm. It was only then we learned that N'detLeda had returned to his old haunt in the press room.

"He is giving an update on our preparations, most of which should remain secret to avoid stirring a new panic!"

"Right on schedule, I see." I'eiBida shook his head in despair. Then he looked at DuRochelle sharply. "Is *she* there?"

"*Oui!* Thus far he has done most of the talking, but she seems determined to put in her opinion."

"We can't afford any more of *that!*"

"Then you need to move quickly."

"Try stopping her," K'deiTai grumbled. "There's no reasoning with either of them."

207

"And he'll think himself invincible with his new backing from the Inner Circle," I added.

"That...that...*sac pompeux d'air chaud* will create another catastrophe! *How* could your leaders be so foolish?"

"They must be in a race with the Chancellor to see who is more *hro'n'nad*," K'deiTai said, bitterly. "It's the only explanation which makes sense."

"Well they are certainly winning." DuRochelle pulled himself together. "What are we to do, *monsieurs?*"

§

"They are, huh?" was MacKenna's reaction to the news. "I thought I told you to keep her under control, mister," he snapped at I'eiBida.

"I'm sorry, sir! About the only way we can stop them is to shoot them."

"Well?"

I'eiBida was flustered. "Sir? I can't do that! They have direct authority from the Inner Circle..."

MacKenna gave him a disgusted look. "You have a lot to learn, mister." He summoned Hythe-Morrison, and sent him for Commander Rostokovich, who appeared promptly.

"You sent for me, sir?"

"Yes, Commander." MacKenna's voice was cool, and his eyes smoldered. "Go down to the press room and tell those *idiots* I would like to *consult* with them on our news coverage at their *earliest* opportunity."

Ivan saw the look in his eyes, snapped, "*Da*, sir!" and left at a trot.

"I hope you will give a thought to your blood pressure this time, sir," Hythe-Morrison scolded him.

"My blood pressure has lasted this long," MacKenna snapped. "You let me worry about it."

"As you wish, sir," Hythe-Morrison sniffed. "But please keep in mind that for an Aide to lose his principal to something which could be avoided leaves a black mark on the service record. I have no wish to return to line duty."

"You'll have a black mark on the seat of your pants!"

"Indeed." Hythe-Morrison was unimpressed, since they went through this routine regularly. "It wouldn't be the first time."

MacKenna gave I'eiBida a stern look once he left. "Watch and learn, mister."

The news conference broke up about a minute later. N'detLeda and T'virDoma appeared at the Admiral's door as we were leaving a short while thereafter, looking anxious and drawn.

"He wanted to see us?" N'detLeda asked the Admiral's Aide in a nervous murmur.

Hythe-Morrison gave them a chilly look. "He did indeed. Wait here, and I will tell him you have arrived."

The Admiral left them standing in front of his closed cffice door, quaking in nervous anticipation for almost an hour before their morale broke, and they scuttled away to the embassy.

"Can you believe that?" I muttered as they fled.

"I like it." I'eiBida was bemused. "You learn something new every day."

§

Life, such as it was, went on. The daily staff conference took place a short while later, and for once there was real progress from home to report.

"According to the latest dispatch, the scouts we sent out have seen nothing," H'rhAtor said. "As for the home defense squadron, two more ships are listed as ready for duty, another orbital defense platform should go on line soon, and our logistics are improving steadily. That gives us twelve ships guarding d'enchia, although I suspect they are still fairly raw."

"Well at least one of us is ready for a fight," MacKenna grumbled.

"As much as can be, at least. Honestly, we aren't much better off than you despite our greater numbers."

"I just *wish* we could find out where the enemy is!"

"Perhaps it is better that they have not appeared yet. An enemy who doesn't arrive is an enemy we don't have to face."

MacKenna gave him a frustrated look. "An enemy we can't find is an enemy who could come from anywhere at any time. Trust me: it's better knowing."

"Perhaps so, Brian," H'rhAtor said, somberly. "But the big issue is whether we will be able to complete our preparations, to say nothing of actually fighting this war with your civilian leadership what it is."

"Yeah, that's the big one. Hogarthy's been after the Chancellor, and the rumble we're getting is that he may shut us down again, especially after those two clowns showed up. I suspect he took that as a personal rebuke from your government."

"I suspect it was."

"And we're finally making real progress!" MacKenna pounded the table with his fist in frustration. "I *swear* I don't know why I bother!"

H'rhAtor considered him somberly. "Because you know you have to, Brian. You can't step aside and do nothing with this threat we face."

MacKenna gave him a sour look. "Yeah. Especially when I think of who they'd replace me with."

§

We were intercepted by the human duty officer when we left the conference room some time later. "*Herr* M'tinDegan? You haff a telephone call, sir." He gestured at the nearby watch desk.

"A call? For me?"

"*Jawhol.* If you please, sir."

I didn't know what to make of that. It couldn't be from the embassy. Who would call me here on a human telephone? I'eiBida and I exchanged dubious looks, and I went to answer it.

"*Monsieur* M'tinDegan?" the caller said. "I wanted to let you know your suit is ready. You may pick it up at *Señor* Vargas' shop right away."

"A suit?" I was caught completely off guard by this. "But I don't..."

"Rest assured, *monsieur*, it is waiting for you, if you could pick it up today before closing."

Then I realized the voice on the line sounded familiar. "I...ah...thank you. I'll be over right away."

"A *suit?*" I'eiBida griped when I hung up. "Don't we have more important things to do?"

"It was Dassault. I'm sure of it. He wouldn't call us here unless there was something vital to report."

"Dassault? What does *he* want?"

"I don't know, but he said I should come right away."

I'eiBida thought that one over dubiously. "Well, all right. But let's leave quietly. You go first, and I'll meet you at the back entrance in a few minutes."

I looked askance at him. "Isn't it bad enough that we have to put up with this spy nonsense from them? Aren't you carrying this a bit far?"

He looked around nervously. "I don't want C'tra to know we're going to *Señor* Vargas' shop."

"Oh."

§

It was late afternoon when we reached *Señor* Vargas' boutique. Even though the humans' holiday season was over, the place was as busy as always. "Curst foolish nonsense," I'eiBida said as we tromped through the recent snowfall which was only then being cleared from the walkway. It was a bit disconcerting to think that it was pre-summer when he and C'traBenla arrived here.

"Well, neither of us in an expert in espionage. This is how the humans behave, so I guess we just have to live with it."

"*Ancestors!* I should have resigned instead of coming to this pest-hole."

The scene inside was as frantic as always, with Geneva's smart set in herds for post-holiday fittings and alterations. *Señor* Vargas was preoccupied with a large human fem in a too-tight gown near the back of the room, waving his arms and carrying on as if catastrophe, or at least travesty had descended upon them all. Everyone else ignored them under the crush of business. We stood by the entrance uncertainly until a young human fem approached us. "I...ah...am here to pick up a suit," I told her.

She gave me a plastic smile, and waved to the fitting rooms at the back. "Of course, sir. You will find it in the booth at the end."

That in itself was odd, since they would never leave an important client to fend for himself like this. "Thank you," I mumbled as we headed for the rear of the building.

211

The booth she directed us to was a recent addition proportioned for us, which had been added to the end of the row of dressing booths. As I anticipated, Dassault waited for us inside, seated on the low bench. "*Bon jour, monsieurs.*" He gave us a small bow and one of his thin smiles. "Fancy meeting you here, of all places."

"Yes, fancy," I'eiBida muttered. We squeezed into the booth, which was a tight fit for the three of us, even though it was designed with us in mind. "So what's this all about?"

"So abrupt; you still do not appreciate the French soul, *monsieur*. I trust the *mademoiselle* is well? Did she accompany you, by chance?"

"Um...no, she didn't."

"Fortunate perhaps, as your family budget is already strained."

I'eiBida blinked in surprise. "How did you know that? And what concern is it of yours, anyway?"

Dassault waved the matter away. "It is a mere trifle. Uncovering secrets is my specialty, as you know, and I have come upon something interesting which you might find helpful."

That got our attention. "What?" I asked.

"It seems the Chancellor has run out of patience after the unexpected and unwelcome return of those two *parvenus*. He has decided to reinstate his demobilization order."

"I was afraid of that," I'eiBida said. "How long do we have?"

Dassault smiled again. "My news, my friends, is you needn't concern yourselves. The matter has been taken care of."

"How?"

"Such curiosity." He looked askance at us. "Those in our profession do not normally reveal such details. But it is no matter. We compromised the young lady who is the object of his desires..."

"His *tra'taj*?"

"...*Oui*. A most pragmatic fem, utterly mercenary and loyal to no one but herself. She gave us some interesting facts on the Chancellor's personal habits which will insure his non-interference."

I was a bit alarmed by that. "You didn't do anything bad to her, did you?"

"*We* did not," he said, sternly, as he took a photograph out of his jacket and offered it to us. "Rest assured that she was happy to cooperate when she saw the virtues of doing so."

"I wouldn't have believed that was possible, even for humans," I'eiBida mumbled as we studied the photo in wide-eyed dismay.

"Remarkable," I muttered.

"As you can see, the Chancellor has some *peculiar* tastes, which his paramour does not share. It made her most receptive to a *generous* offer."

That was a relief; I wouldn't want their sort of nastiness on my conscience, as fascinating as all this was from a sociological point of view.

"So you need not concern yourself with the Chancellor in the future," Dassault assured us as he carefully pocketed the photograph. "I asked you here to keep you abreast of developments. Now if you will excuse me, *monsieurs*, it has been a pleasure, but I must attend to matters." He stood and edged his way between us to the doorway, and peeked through the curtain, then turned to us again. "I regret, *Monsieur* M'tinDegan, that your suit is not quite ready. If you can spare a few minutes, *Señor* Vargas will give you a preliminary fitting." He bowed, and gave us another smile. "The bill has been taken care of, as a courtesy." With that, he left us there bemused.

"He worries me," I'eiBida said after a bit.

"That's his stock in trade," I told him. "Thankfully he's on our side."

"*He* is on his side."

"Well, it was worth the trip for that bit of news, anyway. *How* did they manage to do that? That *must* have been painful."

"I really don't want to know." We left the fitting booth and headed for the exit. "How did he know about our budget?"

"It must have been W'kiLap and T'apiDien."

I'eiBida gave me a bleak look. "Of course! That means the embassy security has been compromised!"

"They recruited Dassault for this project," I cautioned him. "I suspect they gave him that tidbit as an ears-up that he is working for them again."

213

He sighed. "I just hope they know what they're doing." He paused when we reached the main room and considered me. "Since we're here, do you want to get that fitting?"

"I might as well. I need a new suit."

"I wonder how he knew *that?*"

§

It was twilight by time we got back to the Ministry. The Admiral was still there, as busy as ever, so I'eiBida and I reported our latest news to him.

"He backed off, huh?" He eyed us skeptically. "So how did you learn that?"

"We...ah...developed it through some intelligence assets, sir," I'eiBida said. Neither of us was anxious to tell him about Dassault.

"That so?" He gave us a severe look. "I should ask you just what assets you are referring to, mister."

"...it...would perhaps be better if you didn't, sir."

"Damned spookery. I don't want to know anyway." He sagged, and rubbed his eyes. "Hell of a note when we can't even fight a war without our supposed enemies covering our asses."

"I can assure you we have earth's best interest in mind, sir."

"Whatever. War is a young man's game," he said with a sigh. "Sufficient unto the day."

§

By time I got back to the embassy and ate a skimpy late-meal, I was exhausted. It was nearly midnight when I finished cleaning up and reached my quarters, and I sank onto the bed pad with a weary sigh. The Admiral was right: war is for those much younger than me. I lay there for a while, staring restlessly at the clock by my bed, unable to sleep. After brooding on it, I decided fatigue and worry were the cause; hardly a surprise with the threat hanging over us. I sighed, cleared my mind, and tried to go to sleep...

...I was standing in a deserted hallway. I gazed around in surprise, wondering where I was and what was happening. The hall seemed familiar...then I recognized it as part of the main ring at the Institute where I was apprenticed so many years ago.

'This must be a dream', *I realized. It certainly seemed so, despite my apprehension. The hall was dark and deserted, curving away to the left in both directions. The faint light from the street lamps outside did little to dispel the gloom, but oddly enough, I could still see clearly.*

But there was a surreal, undream-like feeling as if somebody was watching me from near by. I stood gaping at the shadows while that feeling began to get on my nerves. "Hello?" The faint echos were my only answer.

I started walking along the hall, trying to find someone or some familiar landmark. The place was silent and faintly eerie, but oddly comforting. I well remembered this hall, and those hopeful, challenging days. I half-hoped I would run into old Learnéd C'dbrTen: it would feel good to show him that his pessimism about me was wrong. After a while, I realized that the hall was endless, circling forever back upon itself. I passed one closed instruction circle after another, all the same, all comfortably familiar academia, all vaguely disturbing.

That feeling nagged at me, making me uneasy. I thought it was just a dream at first, but the longer I walked, the more it seemed like someone was watching me. The eerie tension was amplified by the gloom. I went on for the longest time trying to ignore it, but I couldn't. Finally, I looked up and down the deserted hall, and I began to sense this was no dream. There was nothing, but after I started walking again, the feeling was there; an undeniable presence. That was foolish: no one would wait in ambush for me here in the Institute, even in my dreams, so there couldn't have been anyone in the shadows. But there was.

Finally it got to be too much. I paused again. "Who's there?" There was nothing in the shadows but that ominous feeling that someone—or some thing—was watching me. "Hello?" Then I had an inspiration. "J J Ballas, is that you?"

"You the smart one," a deep voice said from behind me. "You seem faster than th' others at figuring what's what."

215

I turned, and he was standing a short distance away; no shadow image this time, but a solid figure. He was enormous, his head brushing against the high ceiling, and his bulk made him seem even larger, although his formidable presence was softened by the sad look in his eyes. I thought at first that his size was my fearful reaction before I realized he was far larger than any human could be. Then I recalled that his image came from the human Captain Morgan; a hatchling's-eye view. He must have failed to correct for my adult perspective.

'So they aren't flawless after all,' *I thought.*

He shrugged, and shrank in size until he was merely a large human. "Ah guess maybe so. You the smart one, all right. You the one that likes t' understand people. Ah can feel it in yo' thoughts. Tha's good. Tha's mighty good."

I considered him doubtfully. "Then you must know we're concerned about your warning. Can't you be more open with us about the threat?"

"It ain't so simple as you think. We'ah trying, but we don' know how t' explain it. It's gonna be bad, and that makes it harder t' tell." With that, a sense of foreboding swept over me. J J was worried, even scared.

"How soon?"

He frowned: I could see his expressions clearly even in the dark. "Real soon. We're wonderin' if you got the strength an' the courage to do what has-ta be done."

"We have a saying: 'Courage is laid by desperation...'"

"...an' hatched by hope." He smiled, which made me feel good. "You Ic'nichi ain't so weak as you think, sometimes."

"Well, we try."

"An' the humans ain't so strong as they think, sometimes." He considered me closely as that ominous foreboding returned. "This-here's gonna be a tough fight, and they's worried about how poorly their fleet is. They be countin' on you to set a good example fo' them."

"Ah...well, we will certainly..." He was gone...

...I awoke with a start, and I lay staring at the bedside clock for a long time as I tried to calm myself and put it all in perspective. I had a pounding headache.

§

Naturally, I reported the matter to Admiral MacKenna first thing the next morning.

"Dammit, why can't they give us some solid information to work with?" he grumbled. "If they want our help, why play guessing games with us?"

"It may be J J didn't think of it," N'detLeda said. He was clearly intrigued by that visitation, and I knew I was in for an exhaustive interview once I finished with the Admiral. "We are dealing with an alien mindset, so who knows what their mental processes are like?"

MacKenna gave him an icy look, which made him draw back. "Yeah, alien mindsets are a bitch, aren't they?" He dismissed that petty annoyance and turned to the rest of us. "Any thoughts on what to do?"

"The Captain still seems to be our best point of contact," I said carefully, since I didn't want to get caught in whatever schemes they dreamed up. "As much as I dislike the notion, we have to ask her to do the drug regimen again."

"Yeah, I figured that."

"And we must have our questions lined up and ready to go, sir," I'eiBida added. "We can't push the Captain like that very often, so we have to make each second count."

MacKenna eyed him. "Good point. We'll have to do that."

"*If* she's willing to risk it, I hope, sir?"

"I'm sure she will, knowing her." He turned to Commander Rostokovich. "Send an alert to Singapore for the 'Marco Polo' to prepare for another mission to the Dreamsingers' world. Details will follow shortly."

"They are about to start their long overdue refit, sir," Hythe-Morrison said.

"It can't be helped. We need to follow up fast, from what J J said. They'll just have to patch her together one more time." He turned to Ivan. "Get that message out, mister."

217

"*Da*, Admiral." Ivan seemed enthused by this turn of events.

Then MacKenna looked at me, which I didn't need. "It seems you're on J J's mailing list. If you have any further contact, let me know at once."

"Of course, Admiral."

"Should he go with Captain Morgan, sir?" Ivan asked

"What did I do to you?" I grumbled. I was not thrilled by the idea of another expedition into a war zone in that rickety barrel.

The Admiral pondered me for a moment as I wished fervently that I could disappear into thin air like J J. "Mmmm...no," he said at last. "We need him here as a backup if J J needs to get word to us in a hurry. Or if Captain Morgan is no longer available," he added, somberly.

§

The orders were sent to Singapore, which brought Minister Hogarthy out of his hole emitting a cloud of bluster. As always, it was not the high point of our day.

"Admiral, all these missions galavanting off at random simply won't do. The fleet budget is already strained to the breaking point with all your requisitions, and these *supposed* enemies your *supposed* alien warned us of have yet to appear. Seeing that there is no immediate threat, you need to calm down and go back to your regular mapping routine."

"Just because they aren't here doesn't mean they aren't coming," MacKenna said, reasonably. "And I, for one, don't want to wake up some morning and find earth under siege. We're thrashing around in the dark here. We need to know more about their numbers, location, technology. We need to know where they are and what they're up to, at a minimum."

"We cannot have the fleet gyrating all over space looking for enemies who may not exist! That will make a fine mess of our budget, sir! I countermanded your order to the 'Marco Polo', and I will thank you to stick to your regular mapping routine. *If* our ships encounter hostile aliens, then we can reexamine our policy."

MacKenna was understandably angry at Hogarthy's meddling. "This is no time for penny-pinching! We face an unknown threat, and we need to size them up at least."

218

"In my opinion, Admiral..."

"I don't give a flying purple *damn* for your opinion, mister! There are hostiles out there, and us finding them will cost a lot less than them finding us.'

The Minister bristled at that, showing a remarkably stiff tail to the Admiral's temper. "Nonetheless, *Admiral*, you have your orders from the proper *civilian* authority, and you will be expected to carry them out to the letter!"

"Your Minister of Defense doesn't seem to share your concern," I said once he was gone.

MacKenna gave me a contemptuous snort. "*He* is about as pathetic as an inflatable dominatrix." That's what he said, and to this day I don't understand a word of it. Human idiom can be a challenge at times, so I'll record it, and let the reader puzzle over it.

"So what are we to do, sir?" I'eibida asked.

"Perhaps we can release our courier to you, if it will help," K'deiTai said. It's a former scout ship, and newly overhauled."

"But how are we to maintain communication with d'enchia?" I asked in dismay. "With this war crisis upon us, we don't dare lose contact with our fleet."

"We could use the 'Marco Polo' as a temporary courier," Agent Roubidoux suggested.

"No. We would have to clear them with d'enchia traffic control before they could approach the home world," I'eiBida said. ' The 'Conestoga' is the only human ship cleared to enter the system. Without advance clearance, they might be fired upon, especially with the war tension like it is now."

"Could we use one of our ships as a temporary courier?"

"We need to keep the fleet concentrated," H'rhAtor said.

"Oh, t'hell with it," MacKenna said at last. "Sometimes I wonder if the human race can govern itself." He fumed silently for a bit, then turned to Commander Rostokovich. "Send a coded alert to Captain Morgan confirming the mission to the Dreamsingers' home world. Detailed orders will be sent shortly."

"*Da*, Admiral."

"You *do* realize you will get in trouble for defying your superiors again, sir?" Hythe-Morrison asked, pointedly.

219

MacKenna rubbed his eyes with two fingers, and vented a weary groan. "Hell... The worst they can do is cashier me. I'd love to see 'em do that!"

§

"Ancestors! And I believed our bureaucrats were bad!" K'deiTai groaned once we were safely tucked away in our liaison office. "I swear that Hogarthy makes me wish we still had 'Big Jim' Frobeshure to deal with."

I'eiBida gave him a sour look. "Maybe we can surrender to the invaders?"

"Would you want this lot surrendering to you?"

I'eiBida's ears wilted, but he made no reply.

*****

"A Moment Of Truth"
(Related by Learnéd K'deiTai)

We were immersed in one of those all too frustrating progress sessions when one of the human telephones buzzed, and the Admiral's Aide answered. "Yes? He's right here." He handed the phone to MacKenna. "It's for you, sir."

MacKenna listened in silence, then said, "Right. Monitor them closely." He handed the phone to his Aide and looked around the room. "Orbit Dock just picked up a distress beacon from the 'Marco Polo'. Triangulation puts them in the outer fringes of the solar system."

Rostokovich considered that doubtfully. "'Hudson' is the only ship with maneuvering reserve to help them, and they are out of system now."

MacKenna turned to H'rhAtor. "Can your ships reach them?"

"Yes, but while they can take the crew off, they couldn't retrieve your ship. Ours don't have the fuel to tow your ship back to the inner system in any reasonable length of time."

"Admiral?" I said. "Our courier is a former long range scouting and mapping ship. I will ask Arbiter U'tdaPagrn to order them to leave at once, if it will help."

H'rhAtor nodded. "That type of ship has far more maneuvering reserve since they expect to make multiple jumps."

MacKenna gave me a look of gratitude. "Thank you, Ambassador."

§

On which note, the meeting broke up. I was in the corridor chatting with I'eiBida and M'tinDegan when the Admiral returned.

"It's all set," he announced. "Your courier will be leaving shortly and should reach them tomorrow." He turned to I'eiBida. "Come on, mister. We're headed for Singapore."

"Sir?"

"It looks like they had a run-in with our mysterious invaders. I want the straight poop from them NINS, and H'rhAtor wants you to be there." Then he glanced at M'tinDegan. "You're the sociologist?"

"Yes, Admiral."

"Good. You'd best come along too. Our people may have learned something which can help us understand the invaders." He headed for the door, then turned back to me. "You should come as well, Ambassador." *Just* what I needed.

If we thought we were hard pressed before, we were mistaken, as this first sign of the enemy accelerated things into an outright stampede. The Admiral paused just long enough to unleash a flurry of orders which set everyone jumping before we headed for the airport. "All right, let's get the hell out'a Dodge," he said when he was finished. "Did you get us transport?" he added to his Aide.

"Indeed, sir. The embassy's omnibus is standing by, and I was able to requisition one of the executive aircraft."

MacKenna's mood lightened a bit at that. "Good! At least we travel in comfort." He turned to us with a wry grin. "That's the only reason I put up with him: he knows how to look after *Numero Uno*."

Hythe-Morrison turned up his snout and gave that his usual superior smile. "And you benefit indirectly, as usual. Clever of you, I'm sure."

It was clear and cold, excellent flying weather at least. Our aircraft was waiting for us, and its two crew humans saluted the Admiral smartly. "You ready?" he demanded.

"Yes, sir," the senior said. "We're all set to go, and we have refueling stops and relief crews lined up en-route."

"Good. Singapore direct, and step on it." And we were off.

The executive plane, used by Alliance officials, was a far cry from the usual run of military aircraft. It was sleek and modern vehicle, and richly appointed, but too small for five humans and three of us. Despite the comforts, it was a cramped three day journey, made all the worse by the minimal facilities that simply weren't designed with our people in mind. The on-board toilet, in particular, was a tight fit for humans, and there was no way we could squeeze into the tiny compartment. Each leg of our journey became an endurance test as we waited impatiently—sometimes desperately—for the next stop where restrooms were available. The Admiral was in a stampeding hurry, so we were only on the

222

ground long enough to refuel while we *galloped* for the nearest facilities. We never *quite* had an accident, but at times it was close.

What was worse, we left so quickly that none of us had a chance to grab clothing or rations. The Admiral and his people made do with sandwiches and coffee delivered on the flight line, but peacekeeper rations are heavy with earthly animal proteans, which is inviting disaster. The only readily available food for us was that old standby from our original mission here: rice. The humans have a thousand recipes for cooking the Ancestorless stuff, but we had to make do with eating it raw right out of the sack. *Big* mistake: raw rice absorbs body fluids, making restroom stops all the more urgent.

"I swear the Uttermost Darkness holds no terrors," K'deiTai griped.

"Unless there's rice there," I grumbled.

And so we endured: sleeping on the floor wedged between seats and waiting desperately for our next landing. While en-route, we received word that our courier reached the 'Marco Polo', and that they were able to maneuver. By time we reached Singapore, they were back in orbit, and the human crew had been evacuated.

§

Our arrival in Singapore was *not* triumphal: we were exhausted, aching, smelly, and suffered massive constipation. If I *ever* see rice again, I will surely go *er'trxxda* and kill *someone!* If the Admiral shared our discomfort, he didn't let it slow him down. We scrambled to keep up with him regardless of our physical condition.

Singapore was far busier than I remembered it. All six human shuttles were hard at work ferrying supplies and materials into orbit, and the vertical launch facility in the distance was preparing their heavy lift vehicle to boost an engineering pod for a new ship. Trucks were on the move everywhere, and stacks of cargo waited under tarps on the flight line. A ship was being unloaded in the harbor nearby, and another C-wing came in right behind us. Singapore offered precious little infrastructure for their fleet, but the humans performed miracles with what they had.

The base hospital was a dreary slab-fab construct decorated in government modern, but it was well equipped since the Admiral insisted on taking care of his people. The entire crew of the 'Marco Polo' were affected by whatever hit them, and had been evacuated ground-side by time we arrived. The worst cases were restrained and under sedation, and the rest were in rocky condition.

"They have four dead, and two more catatonic, sir," the human physich said. "The rest are shaken and demoralized, and a few are borderline insane. As near as we can tell, they were hit with some kind of projected death wish. Two of the dead suicided, and the other two just keeled over."

"Projected *death wish*?" MacKenna exchanged uncomfortable looks with us; clearly caught by surprise. "Some sort of psychic weapon? How can you *project* death wish?"

"I don't know, sir, but that's the best description we have thus far."

The survivors greeted the Admiral with unconcealed adulation. For all that he was a relentless taskmaster, he gave them a sense of pride and purpose which they sorely needed at the moment. That sense was severely strained: the haunted looks in their eyes and on their snouts was disquieting. According to the physichs, some of them would be able to return to duty soon, others would require prolonged therapy, while a few were so traumatized that they would be useless for further service. All of them looked like they would be limited to administrative duty in the future. The Admiral took a few minutes to encourage them, talking to each one in turn, although he was eager to see Captain Morgan.

§

The Captain was in a darkened room, curled up in one of the beds, trembling and staring at nothing. She hardly noticed when we came in, and stared at the Admiral with a look I hope never to see again. MacKenna sat at her bedside and caressed her forehead. "Captain?" She twitched when he touched her, and looked at him with uncomprehending horror. "Loraine? What happened?"

She struggled for words, and was unable to speak at first. The more she tried, the more she trembled, as if the memory of the attack was too horrible to bear. She kept trying doggedly, and the story came out bit by bit. "We never...past the outer world." She gasped for air, and clung to the Admiral's hand with a death grip. "I...I...f-flat-lined the capacitor...took us far enough..." She drifted off and went into another fit of shuddering.

MacKenna bent over her and stroked her hair, surprisingly gentle with her. "It's all right, Loraine. You're home now. You're safe."

"I...we..." She curled up even tighter, shaking and crying.

"Admiral?" Their physich was back. "She needs to be sedated, sir. She needs to rest."

MacKenna confronted him angrily. "I need her report, doctor. You can wait your turn."

"Sir, I've seen this several times already. The longer she focusses on what happened, the more she deteriorates. She's useless to you now, sir."

He took the physich's arm and herded him out into the hall. "Can you help her?"

He hesitated, with a quick glance at the Captain. "I don't know, sir. We have some psych heavyweights coming in...anti psychotic drugs...shock therapy, maybe." He considered for a moment. "They'll know a lot more about this than me. Hopefully they will figure out something.'

"Well, at least we know where they are," MacKenna said. He glanced at his Aide. "Call the field, have a shuttle ready. We're headed back to Geneva, pronto."

§

The need for swift action and the Admiral's temper notwithstanding, it was late that day before a passenger shuttle could be freed up for our use since all of them were hard pressed by the demands of their mobilization. If the traffic supervisor hadn't been more afraid of the Admiral than anything else, we likely would have been out of luck.

The trip back to Geneva was every bit as uncomfortable as our journey to Singapore, with the added annoyance of a multi-G takeoff. At least the trip was mercifully brief. As timing would have it, we arrived back in Geneva in mid-afternoon. And as luck would have it, Minister Hogarthy was there to greet us with his usual warmth and good cheer.

"Admiral, this is too much!" he sputtered as he pursued us through the Defense Ministry lobby. "The Geneva Airport Authority is complaining about all these shuttle landings."

"I don't have time for you," MacKenna grumbled as he pushed through the security gates.

Hogarthy followed him, still protesting. "I am your civilian superior, *Admiral!* You will *make* time if I require it! Why did you have to use a *shuttle? Think* of the cost! And you left that executive plane in Singapore. We have to pay the daily usage, and our budget is already a disaster. *When* do we get it back?"

MacKenna finally turned on him with fury in his eyes. "You'll be lucky if you get it back at all! The enemy has arrived! We are preparing to meet them, and I'll be *damned* if I'll take the time now for budgets!"

Hogarthy froze, and turned ghastly pale. "The enemy?"

"That's right. And I'm not sure what we can do against what they have. So if you will *excuse* me, I'm busy trying to save the human race from extinction!"

§

"How bad is it?" was H'rhAtor's greeting when we arrived on the fifth floor.

"Not good," MacKenna said. "They're at the Dreamsingers' home world. They're hitting it hard with some kind of psychic weapon. Our ship must have caught the fringe of it, and it all but wrecked them."

H'rhAtor's ears wilted in dismay. "Did they learn much about the hostiles?"

"No. They never had the chance. They were lucky to escape."

§

An emergency staff meeting was called soon thereafter. "But how do we fight them, sir?" someone asked once the Admiral gave his report on the 'Marco Polo's casualties. "Unless they chanced onto an outlying picket ship, this psychic weapon must have planetary range."

"This is an unknown technology," one of ours said. "I don't think we have any defense against it."

226

"Good point." MacKenna turned to H'rhAtor. "We better face facts here. The only way we can engage the intruder is up close and personal. So how do we get past this mind assault?"

"Surprise, sir," H'rhAtor's Second said promptly. "We will have to come out of jump right on top of them and hit them with everything we have before they can react."

MacKenna looked at him, bemused. "You sure you never attended Annapolis?"

"We must pick off as many as we can before they can hit us with that mind assault, then retreat, sir," a human said.

"Ambush 'em." MacKenna nodded thoughtfully. "Operate like a guerilla force with hit and run raids. Wear them down or draw them off the Dreamsingers' world. I like it."

At that, H'rhAtor raised an objection. "If you plan to go to their aid, I must ask if this is an appropriate course for us to take."

"What do you mean? We know where the enemy is. Now's the time to hit them while they're preoccupied."

"As much as I sympathize with the Dreamsingers, our mandate is to protect our two races. Going to their aid exceeds our authorities, and would convince the intruder that we are enemies. Can we commit our races to an expeditionary war?"

"They need our help!"

"I agree, Admiral. But we are not free agents: we must have good reason to commit our forces to battle, and the aliens do not threaten us directly. Nor can we be sure they intend to attack us."

"How can you know that?"

"I cannot, of course. But if they mean to conquer the Dreamsingers' world, then our worlds would be useless to them. Our leaders will question any action we take on that basis, especially if our losses are severe, as I suspect they will be."

"Yeah, that's true." MacKenna fumed over the matter. "But if they do plan to attack us, having the Dreamsingers on our side is better than nothing, no matter how weak they are."

"A weak ally is better than no ally, certainly." We could tell that H'rhAtor was looking for an excuse to commit our fleet to battle. From the expressions on the snouts around the table, we all wanted to.

"Dammit, it's the right thing to do, and you know it!"

H'rhAtor brooded on that. "You are correct."

"And if there's one thing I've learned over the years, it's to assume the worst when dealing with warmongers. Can we take the chance that they won't turn on us next?"

H'rhAtor sighed. "A telling point, Admiral. I withdraw my objection."

"Then a large scale raid appears to be our one real option: jump in, pick a few off, then retreat." MacKenna mused for a bit. "We'll set up a rendezvous point where our ships can rearm, then hit them again at random intervals."

"But we cannot waste time hunting for targets, sir," one of ours said. "The chance of finding something close to pick off when we come out of hyperspeed is not good."

"Our only hope would be to come out in some sort of grid array so that we covered a broad area of space," a human said. "Someone should get lucky then."

"Um...Admiral? Can we do it?" I was appalled at the notion. "I don't know much about maneuvering starships, but can you hold formation jumping at light speed?"

"If any ship is off by the tiniest margin, it could be a disaster," U'tdaPagrn said.

"Yeah." MacKenna pondered the matter glumly, then turned to H'rhAtor. "What do you think, Eldest?"

"It is a matter of timing, calibration of our times and thrusts, and a great deal of luck. Realistically, we will have to operate as three separate squadrons, each within its own arrival zone. Still, I am not optimistic."

That produced a round of brooding silence.

"Perhaps we could drop into the outer system and release our missiles at just below light speed, sir," one of the humans suggested. "One of them striking at .99 C would incinerate any ship by its sheer inert mass."

"Um...no." MacKenna said. "If you miss, it'd wreck havoc on the planet. And at that range, there's no way to spot targets, or to correct for gravity flux, dust, and so on, especially as you'd be in a Godawful hurry to launch."

228

"At that close to C, the mass would be horrendous," another human said. "The missiles couldn't maneuver without mass polarizers."

"And our guidance systems aren't up to maneuvers at that speed, on that scale, anyway," someone else said.

"Neither are ours," H'rhAtor added. "And it would take a year or more to design something from the egg."

"So we're back to a direct assault," MacKenna said. "But can we do it? Can we maneuver as a fleet at light speed, and maintain any sort of pattern?"

"Given meticulous preparation..." H'rhAtor agonized over it. "...I would say it is possible."

"Hell, that's the best we can hope for."

§

Captain Morgan made an unexpected appearance two days later, arriving in the borrowed executive plane, which set Minister Hogarthy off again. We first learned of her arrival when the peacekeeper security called to report the furor on the first floor. Hogarthy's antics pushed her too far, and she rounded on him with a tirade which sent him running for dear life. She looked shaken and drawn, but functional when she arrived on the fifth floor, which I can only describe as a testament to her iron will.

"You shouldn't be here, Captain," MacKenna said as she sagged into a chair in his office. "You're in no shape for duty, especially for combat."

"I'm no worse off than I usually am, sir," she said, evenly. "And right now, you need everyone you can get." The haunted look in her eyes was disquieting to all of us. "J J needs me, too," she added.

"What about your crew?"

"There are a few who can manage, and Personnel is scraping together enough replacements to get the 'Marco Polo' back in action."

"I'm not thrilled about sending you out with a scratch crew, and we won't have time for you to do a shakedown. Orbit Dock will be lucky to complete your repairs in time as is."

"We're at war, sir. We have to make do."

MacKenna eyed her doubtfully. "And you're AWOL from the Singapore hospital."

She gave him a stern look. "Arrest me if you like, Admiral, but unless you do, I'm in this fight."

MacKenna nodded thoughtfully. "Welcome back, Captain."

§

Now that the enemy had appeared, the most urgent question was what their numbers were, and what was happening at the Dreamsingers' world. The humans sent the cargo ship 'Conestoga' to reconnoiter, since the crew of the 'Marco Polo' were badly traumatized by their attempt to enter the system. The Captain of the 'Conestoga' came up with a clever idea (one we have since copied for our fleet): they came out of jump in the debris field of the outer system just below light speed, and dropped a weather satellite reprogrammed to focus in on the Dreamsingers' world as it tore past. They then jumped back into hyper-C, ran ahead through the system, and rendezvoused with the probe as it came out the far side.

§

"Nothing," MacKenna muttered.

We were gathered in the conference room to view the eagerly awaited video, which was proving to be a disappointment.

"We haven't reached the Dreamsingers' world yet, sir," Captain Pytel said.

The video image was not impressive. All the probe could pick up was a faint wash of starlight compressed to a near flat accretion disc by the terrible speed.

"Whoa!" MacKenna jumped as a blur of light shot across the screen. "Play that back."

And there it was: the Dreamsingers' world. But all we could see was a smudgy blur of light.

"Um, Admiral? What is that?" I'eiBida pointed to a dark spec overlaying the planet's disc.

MacKenna studied the image closely, but there was nothing discernible. "Commander Rostokovich, let's have the science boys see if they can clean this image up."

"*Da*, Admiral."

230

I'eiBida interrupted. "If I may suggest, Admiral, our computers are well adapted to this work, and our two computer *v'thorbel* are among the best. Perhaps they can pull something off this."

MacKenna pondered him for a moment. "All right."

§

Two days later, they brought the image back, and I have to say those two *v'thorbel* did a magnificent job. Somehow, they corrected for the speed-induced compression and the velocity blur, pulled the focus in, and blew it up enormously. The result was startling—and alarming.

"How big do you think that is?" MacKenna asked.

"According to our calculations, it is about fifty human kilometers in diameter," W'kiLap said, judiciously.

We stood in nervous silence around the large blowup image laying on the conference table, afraid to say the obvious. Finally, the Admiral took the plunge. "Their world doesn't have a moon, does it?"

"*Nyet*, Admiral."

It was a beautiful, crystal clear image. The Dreamsingers' world was a gaudy, fuzzy sphere in banded colors, slightly egg shaped from the gravitational tug of its star; typical of a gas giant world. The object orbiting it was black, smooth, hard-edged, and perfectly round. Fifty kilometers in diameter We could see its shadow on the planet's atmosphere.

"Good...God," MacKenna said, aghast. "How can we fight that?"

We all stood silently for some time, stunned by the reality of what we faced. Our worst nightmare was a fleet of overwhelming numbers and power, but a single ship large enough to have its own gravity was beyond anything we could have imagined. We were appalled, and I think all of us felt a bitter sense of hopelessness right then.

"I hope to God there's just one of those," MacKenna said.

"If there are more, we might as well not worry about it," H'rhAtor said, hollowly. "We will exist or not by their whim."

"Maybe." The Admiral's grim determination came to the fore again. "But we have an old saying: 'It ain't over 'til it's over'."

231

"What good can we do against that, sir? Even with our nukes?" a human asked, bleakly.

"God..." MacKenna mumbled. "I don't know. But we have to do something."

"Brian..." H'rhAtor said hesitantly. "They are simply too large and too powerful."

"Dammit, I know!" MacKenna fumed, and I swear he was afraid. "But we can't sit here and do nothing!"

"We have to help them, sir," one of ours said.

"How?" a human asked.

"It would be suicide..."

"What is wrong with her?" someone interrupted.

Captain Morgan, who was standing in the background, was having some sort of crisis: her eyes tightly closed, trembling, fists clenched, sweat pouring down her snout. "Are you all right, Captain?" MacKenna asked in alarm.

"It's...them..." she muttered through clenched teeth. "J J...they're suffering...they're...dying...being crushed...they're pleading for help..."

Our doubts vanished in that instant. "Tell them we're coming, Captain," MacKenna said. She didn't respond, so he took her by the shoulders and shook her. "Do you hear me? Tell them we're coming!"

She held on for a moment more, then sagged in his arms. "...They...know, sir..."

He held her tenderly for a bit longer as she trembled, then helped her gently into a chair. There were tears in his eyes when he faced us. The room was deathly silent: we could well imagine the horrors the Dreamsingers were enduring.

"When do we go, sir?" one of the humans asked at last.

MacKenna glanced at H'rhAtor. "We sail in seven days."

"We will be hard put to be ready," H'rhAtor said.

"So will we, but the Dreamsingers can't hold out for ever. Ready or not, we sail in seven days."

That settled it, for all of us.

*****

232

"Standing On The Brink"
(Related by Defender I'eiBida)

In a way, being committed to battle was a relief; not that we were thrilled with the prospect, but at least the suspense was over. Admiral MacKenna's decision to launch the combined fleets sent us scrambling for last minute preparations, and our days were more hectic than ever.

As part of that, the Admiral and H'rhAtor moved by shuttle to Singapore, where the center of the action was. K'deiTai, M'tinDegan, and I were chosen for the liaison field team, which brought on another crisis between C'traBenla and me.

"I'eiBida, *please* let me go!" She was frantic, in tears, and clung to my arm with desperate strength as I was trying to pack my field kit.

"C'tra, I can't. Not this time."

"I'eiBida...I don't want to lose you!"

I paused, took her head in both hands, and nuzzled her ear to reassure her. "You won't. I promise."

"How can you say that? You're going off to war!"

I understood why she was so frantic. She knew what we were up against, and I didn't have much hope either. Her world was coming apart before her eyes, and I felt ugly inside because of her torment. Did human fems suffer like this when their mals went off to their endless wars?"

"C'tra...I have to go. Our people need me to be there." I felt guilty saying that, since she knew she couldn't demand I put her ahead of my duty to our race.

She fought back her tears and gave me a momentary look of resentment before she sagged in despair. "Please..." she murmured. "Be careful."

I held her close and nuzzled her ears. "I will, love." As if it would matter in such a gigantic battle.

It took a lot of coaxing to get her panic under control, but she still looked stricken as I hefted my field kit and left. In spite of myself, I felt ashamed.

§

233

It was chill and wet at this early predawn hour, fitting for the moment, and the rest of the embassy was just stirring. We ate a hasty first-meal in the cafeteria, although I was too distraught to eat much, and then the embassy limo was waiting for us. U'tdaPagrn saw us off in the lobby.

"Good luck to all of you." He was somber and strained, as were all of us. "We're all wishing you the best."

"I'm going to have to resign from my resignation," K'deiTai grumbled. "*What* will it take to get them to listen?"

C'traBenla came down as we were leaving, and stood in the background looking lost and forlorn. I wanted to comfort her, but couldn't think of what to do or say. Best get this over as quickly as possible. I took U'tdaPagrn aside as we left. "We're going into battle against an enemy the size of the World Nest back home," I said confidentially. "If I don't make it back, watch over her." He glanced at her, and nodded.

It was raining when we left. We had a shuttle to catch.

§

It was the height of the monsoon season and raining steadily when we arrived in Singapore, which didn't help our somber mood. After our soggy departure from Geneva, it seemed like the whole world was drowning in chill despair. Singapore was busier than ever, with equipment, supplies, and technicians boarding the shuttles in a steady stream. As we drove away from the loading area, I noticed a C-wing off-loading a shipment of guided missiles —brand new from the manufacturer. A load lifter was busy at another aircraft moving pallets of red-painted auto-feed drums of gatling gun ammunition. The effort over the last few months to mobilize the human defense industry was starting to pay off.

It was late when we arrived, so the three of us took up temporary quarters in our new transit barracks. The place was a bare, functional dormitory, with a small cafeteria, some offices, and a badly overworked embassy staff. It was serving as temporary quarters for our fleet personnel on ground duty, and was packed to overflowing. They managed to find space for us, and we settled in for a sleepless night.

§

234

The two leaders got together for a final conference the next day. We were as ready as could be, which was not saying much, but the sheer size of the enemy called for a fast rethink of our battle strategy. All of us were exhausted from our disrupted sleep patterns, but there was no time to adjust.

"We're going to need our nukes to take that monster out," MacKenna said as he considered the blow-up image of the black sphere. "So it looks like we'll have to lead the attack." He turned to H'rhAtor. "We don't know what sort of defenses they may have other than that mind attack, so I recommend the Ic'nichi forces take a defensive posture ready to deal with any smaller ships they have. If nothing shows, you can take targets of opportunity."

H'rhAtor nodded thoughtfully. "A sound plan, Admiral." Then he gave MacKenna a wry smile. "Far be it from me to keep you from grabbing all the glory on this one."

"Hell," MacKenna grumbled. "There'll be plenty of fun for everyone."

Six days to go.

§

Preparations continued, made all the more urgent now with a battle strategy to prepare. We three were largely superfluous for the moment, although we stayed close to advise on our respective fields. Of the three of us, I had the most wearing schedule as I pitched in to help H'rhAtor's staff draw up our plans. For me that meant acting as liaison to the human staff to help coordinate with their planning. It was a monumental task which needed to be done in days, which only made it worse for everyone.

I was running on V'liz and nervous energy I ran into Commander Rostokovich and the Admiral in the corridor on the evening of the third day. "Good evening, sir," I said to MacKenna. "And how are you doing, Ivan?"

Ivan yawned, then stared vacantly for a bit before answering. "We put in long hours, my friend. How goes it with you?"

"I thought the paperwork back home was bad. Little did I know."

Ivan chuckled. "Perhaps we should let paper shufflers do the fighting if we ever go to war, *nyet?*"

"Trust me: it would be Armageddon."

"Death by a thousand paper cuts. First side to run out of forms would surrender." He turned to the Admiral. "If Universe made sense, all wars would be fought that way, sir."

MacKenna laughed at that. "Well...yeah. But if this Universe made sense, it'd be *so* damned dull."

We watched as he hobbled away. "He is right about that," Ivan said at last, somberly.

Four days to go.

§

Two days later, separate briefings were held for the senior ship's elders of each race. The meetings were held in a conference room at the Space Port headquarters. I attended both, and was struck by how young and inexperienced they seemed, and by how few there were. In our case, the Eldests (commanding), First (operations), and Second (engineering) elders of our eight ships didn't even fill the conference room. The scene was poignant and unsettling; everyone nervous but willing to do their part, waiting with feigned impatience, whispering nervously among themselves. You could feel the tension. Everyone knew we were about to do something we had dreaded and trained for for years, and the slim numbers reflected how limited our fleet assets were.

The picture of the black sphere, and H'rhAtor's description of its size and armament produced an ominous rumble from the gathering. "We don't know what defenses they may have other than this mind assault," H'rhAtor told them. "But that mind weapon is formidable. Our one real hope is to hit them by surprise."

The projector flashed a diagram on the screen, and H'rhAtor spent the next few minutes going over our deployment. "We will attack in a flat front. The humans will be in the center, with four pairs of our ships in a circular flank formation around them."

"The sheer size of the target means that the humans must make the primary attack with their stellar bombs. Our mission is to protect the human ships from any enemy escorts until they can hit the target. If the defenders have any secondary ships, we will focus on them. If there are no secondary defenses, and the humans

236

fail to destroy the target, then we must do the best we can with our conventional weapons. After that, we will cover the humans' withdrawal if needed."

"Why do we have to cover them, sir?" someone asked.

"Because their ships have the equipment and technicians to handle stellar bombs; ours do not. If this first attack is unsuccessful, we will need them to continue the fight." That produced another ominous rumble. The revelation of our secret lack of stellar bombs was almost as disturbing as the enemy we were about to fight. Just because we were allies of necessity didn't mean we could discount the humans as a potential threat in the future.

"Any ship which is no longer able to fight is to withdraw at the Eldest's discretion. If you can't do any more, save yourselves."

The briefing finally broke up, and the fleet personnel filed out in grim silence with no more than an occasional murmured conversation. The Admiral attended our briefing, although he couldn't understand our language, and spent the time silently watching, gauging our people. "What do you think, sir?" I asked as he was leaving.

He sighed, and gave me a grim look. "I've seen worse, and lived to tell of it."

Two days to go.

§

We received a welcome addition when our brand new cruiser number 168 arrived the next day. H'rhAtor and MacKenna were thrilled with the addition of twelve missile tubes and two defense gatling guns, not to mention the command control systems fitted to make the ship into a squadron leader. H'rhAtor transferred his command to ship 168, and their still-raw crew had their hands full meshing with the rest of the force. Admiral MacKenna chose the 'Marco Polo' for his flagship since the humans didn't have any command-equipped ships. The humans somehow pulled together a scratch crew to replace their losses, and Captain Morgan was somehow able to mold them into something resembling a trained herd. I suspect the Admiral wanted to keep an eye on her after her recent encounter with the black sphere, as well as for any link she could establish with J J Ballas. Since most of our people were weak on human language, the three of us would go along to do double duty as translators.

One day to go.

§

Finally all the planning and scrambling was done. For better or worse, we were ready for battle. I went to the Officers' Club late that afternoon, drawn to the comfortably familiar surroundings. The place was decorated in early government issue, with subdued lighting, drapes, and inexpensive furniture; much like the service clubs back home. The bartender had *'sti'eit* and lemons for use in drinks, but I resisted temptation. They didn't have *V'liz,* which annoyed me no end for some reason. The place was busy but quiet, everyone enjoying a last brief moment of calm before heading out to the fleets.

I went off to an out-of-the-way corner of the verandah, and stood watching the rain and brooding about tomorrow. The weather was chill, and the rain came in torrents. It reminded me of our first time there, when we hastily evacuated by air ahead of a typhoon. I stood for a long time watching the headlights of passing trucks glitter on the puddles, reflecting on the past and wishing we were back home where I had no greater worries than the endless paperwork and C'tra's possession syndrome. Right then I was feeling pretty low.

Commander Rostokovich came wandering by, and stood watching the rain and sipping a mug of coffee. After a while, he turned to me. "Are you all right, my friend?"

"As well as could be, I suppose." There was a gloomy silence, then, "Have you ever been in battle?"

"*Da.* I was in maritime forces before I came to Space Fleet. We fought pirates, smugglers, slavers; a month did not go by without some sort of action." He studied me for a moment, then said, "This is always the worst part. The waiting. Once the fighting starts, you will be too busy to be afraid."

"I hope so. Dying can't be any worse than this."

He snorted derisively. "Dying is the easy part." He was silent for a bit, then said, "*Borjemoi.* I wish I could go with you."

238

I turned to him in surprise. "You *want* to go?"

He considered me somberly. "This will be one of the great battles of our history which will decide the fate of our people. I am a soldier; it is my duty. I am ashamed not to be part of it, even though I am needed here."

It occurred to me that the human peacekeepers weren t so very different from we defenders after all. "If they get past us, you may well have your chance when they come here."

There were tears in his eyes. "And if that evil day comes, I will shout your name when the battle is joined." He drifted away after a bit, and left me standing there watching the rain and remembering.

§

And then everything was ready. Morning came all too soon after a sleepless night. It was still wet and miserable when we met for a hasty first-meal, then were taken to the landing field in the large van used by our people transiting on their way to Geneva. Most of the fleet personnel were already aboard their ships, and the few remaining in the van with us were silent, each of us lost in our thoughts.

There were shuttles from each fleet waiting for us. A small herd of humans, last minute additions, waited to board their shuttle. The Admiral was among them, although he was too preoccupied for any small talk. Commander Rostokcvich was there as well to see us off.

"I wish good luck for you," he said somberly. "I hope you win, and more than that, I hope you all return to us."

"Thank you, Ivan," I said in turn. "I hope we can settle things so that you won't have to deal with them here."

We boarded the shuttles without ceremony, but then a big sendoff would have been grotesque.

§

The 'Marco Polo' was familiar to us now, although more crowded than ever and showing signs of recent, hasty repairs. A couple of video camera operators were along to record events, and the ship's young physich was assigned an even younger surgical assistant. Night Eagle and some of his marines were there as well.

I couldn't imagine what a few marines could do in a battle of such magnitude, but the Admiral wanted them, and we needed to depend on his judgment. Night Eagle was bemused by it all, but solemnly pleased to be there.

Many peacetime luxuries which made life in space bearable were removed to cope with the press of bodies. The microwaves and coffee pot were left behind, and the galley deck converted into quarters with sleep sacks hung everywhere. At least logistics wouldn't be a problem since we were going on a brief out-and-back mission, rather than a lengthy patrol, but the odd corners were clogged with spare parts and repair materials. We brought along our supply of endurance rations, but we would have to eat them cold; not that it mattered, *especially* with the number twelve ration.

"Wonderful," K'deiTai grumbled as we sized up the niche set aside for us. "To think that I've been reduced to this. My Ancestors must have abandoned me."

"Think of it as our second off-world embassy," M'tinDegan admonished him with a rueful grin. "That will make a notable addition to your list of accomplishments."

K'deiTai gave him an icy glare. "So would committing the first murder in an interstellar embassy!"

"What's to cry about?" I said. "It's such a cozy, intimate place." Our sleep sacks were three high from floor to ceiling, with just enough space between the next stack to squeeze by. "It's not like our first time on earth when we slept in an aircraft hanger. No drafts here."

K'deiTai shook his head in dismay. "I swear when we get there, I'll defect to the Black Sphere. The worst they can do is drive me insane."

It took several hours to get everything set. We departed with no fanfare; each squadron headed out on their own for a designated rendezvous point on the edge of the system. From there, we would jump as a group; our next destination: the Dreamsingers' world. The humans had four destroyers, two armed transports, and a scout ship; we had a cruiser, eight patrol ships, and our logistics ship. It wasn't much to take on an opponent the size of a small moon.

§

It took us ten days to travel from earth to the Dreamsingers' system, and flying in formation like we were proved impossible. This was the first time starships of either race had traveled in groups, which produced no end of unpleasant surprises. Theoretically, we were all traveling at the same course and speed: in practice, that was only a theory. Even minute variations sent ships swinging wildly as changes that might take days to see at sublight were enormously amplified at multiple light speeds. The ships gyrated dangerously in relation to each other, and the humans almost came to grief as the 'Tartar' narrowly averted a collision with the 'Conestoga' shortly after leaving earth. The humans tried adjusting their courses to guide on the 'Marco Polo' at first, but the variations were too minute for their controls.

Our fleet was having similar problems, although our ships seemed to be better at fine tuning their courses. Still, both fleets were forced to reduce speed and move their ships farther apart until we covered a sizable chunk of space. After that, things went smoothly enough, but the bridge crews were constantly on alert, and made endless minor course changes, which was wearing on all concerned.

That was the worst of it, but there were other problems. Even though the ships were traveling in convoy, and thus were supposed to be stationary to each other, our radio communications simply didn't work. The engineering staff argued about it at length, and came to the tentative conclusion that even though the ships were all but stationary to each other, radio messages sent between them were somehow being left behind at our hyper-light speed. That didn't make much sense, but I was too preoccupied to wonder about it.

We limped along as best we could, hoping that the other Captains would make the right moves on their own initiatives. We could see them clearly, with the two Ic'nichi squadrons around us at a distance. Beyond that, there was absolutely nothing. At hyper-C, the rest of the Universe was effectively beyond the speed of light, and thus invisible. All we had to navigate by were the gravity wells of nearby stars, and those were detectable only by our instruments; a Universe of nothing but black holes.

As for us, we had no duties for the moment, and nothing to occupy our minds but waiting and worrying. I don't think I have ever felt as low as right then. We waited quietly since none of us had anything to say or the energy for random gossip. I fretted over what was to come, and wished with all my hearts that I was with C'traBenla.

§

I climbed back up to the galley deck after visiting the toilet in the crew quarters when we were five days out, which can be hazardous with the ship constantly maneuvering as it was. Sure enough, the maneuvering thrusters kicked in for a brief burst, and I hung precariously to the ladder until they shut down again. The Admiral was sitting at one of the portholes gazing at the empty sky. "Have you ever been in battle?" he asked when I passed him headed for our ration supply.

"Sir?"

He turned at looked at me somberly. "Have you ever been in battle before?"

"Um...not to speak of, sir. Most of my career has been spent in peacekeeping or on the Staff. My only real combat was a brief incident when I was in the 'Green-And-Tans'. I was in the ranks then, and it was nothing more than what you call skirmishing."

He considered me for a long moment, then shook his head. "You have no idea how lucky your people are."

There was a long silence punctuated by the endless hum of the ship's systems, then I asked him, "Are we going to win this, sir?"

"Hell, I don't even know if we're going to *survive* this." He brooded for a bit as I watched uneasily. "But then, the goal in war isn't to survive," he said at last. "And all too often winning is just a pious hope. Why should this be any different?"

*****

"Cry Havoc"
(Related by Defender I'eiBida)

Best intentions notwithstanding, the fleet was badly scattered when we downjumped in the outskirts of the Dreamsingers' system. It took nearly a week for the squadrons to reform, which had everyone agonizing over the delay while the Dreamsingers needed us so desperately. Our other big fear was that the black sphere would be alerted to our presence, and we would walk into a trap. Hopefully our remote location in the systems' outer debris field would keep them from seeing us.

MacKenna called H'rhAtor as soon as his flagship was in range, and they conferenced by radio. "We need a change of plan," he said. "These course gyrations are far too severe at high speed."

"There is also the danger of natural debris closer in," H'rhAtor answered. "Neither of us normally operates at light speed so close in to a system."

"Yeah, there is that. I recommend we come in at just above the speed of light. That should make station keeping a lot easier, and we'll still be effectively invisible to them. It won't help much against natural obstacles, but we'll just have to take our chances."

"That seems workable, Brian. However, I am not sure how much good it will do. No matter how carefully we time our jumps, the buildup delay in our mass polarizers makes precision jumping all but impossible. From what I saw of your maneuvers, you suffer the same problem."

"Yeah," MacKenna grumbled. "But what else can we do?'

It took over a second for the vast power stored in our capacitors to reach full discharge. If it wasn't for the superconductive cooling, the systems would be vaporized. Even at just above light speed, there was no way we could be sure of coming to rest near the spot we aimed for, which not only killed any prospect of a coordinated attack, but posed the very real hazard of hitting the planet as well. It was a potentially crippling weakness which didn't matter in ordinary stellar travel.

"I can't see any other option," H'rhAtor said, reluctantly. "So I suppose we will have to depend on luck."

"I'm afraid so," MacKenna said. "As imperfect as it is, this is our only chance to hit them by surprise. I sure as hell don't want to wait until one of our worlds is besieged, and I suspect we may need the Dreamsingers if any more of these monster ships come around, so we have to act now before they get exterminated."

"Very well, Brian, I concur. Best of luck to you."

"And to you, Eldest."

§

Despite the urgent desire to get the battle over with, it was another two days before the fleets were sorted out and arrayed in their starting positions. In the mean time, our navigation telescopes spotted the black sphere orbiting the Dreamsingers' world, so we at least had a point to aim for. We also used the time to recharge the capacitors, which made sleep that much more difficult with the reactor turbines and the constant whine of the generators going full blast all the time.

As the time for action approached, the Admiral decided that we could come up to the bridge to witness the battle first hand. That would be a neat trick: the bridge was claustrophobic when all stations were occupied, and the Admiral, Captain, and the duty elder floated in the small clear area around the ladder between the lower decks and the navigation dome above. Despite the crowd, I managed to pull myself up the ladder and hover right behind the Admiral to watch, while M'tinDegan poked his head up through the open hatch. K'deiTai chose to remain below, not that there was any more room for him anyway.

The bridge was lined with control stations and view screens, each with a heavy duty crash couch for one of the ship's crew. The place was dimly lit with red battle lamps, which made it almost impossible for us since we can't see as far into the red as humans can. The faint lights of the touch screens helped, but the bridge was still shrouded in shadow. The air was thick and stale, and tense with rising fear.

I was fascinated as the humans made their preparations. Their ships were ramshackle improvisations, but they handled themselves with cool professionalism. Captain Morgan kept everyone galloping as the weapons were checked and the

244

navigation laid out. The crew went over their systems to make sure everything was in order, and planned out their emergency procedures with finicky detail. As the 'zero hour' approached, the crew paused to eat a final meal of zero-G rations, and then the Captain led an invocation to their Ancestors to protect them and grant them victory. Finally, the crew left their stations a few at a time and dressed in vac suits, including the ponderous environmental packs. We put off doing that due to the crush on the galley deck. It took the humans some doing, but they completed their preparations and returned to stations, and we waited anxiously as the 'zero hour' approached.

§

"Start the clock," the Captain said at last.

The duty elder pressed a button, starting the official clock which would control the events to come. "The clock is started, Captain."

"Stand by on the drive."

The duty pulled a key on a short chain out of his tunic, and inserted it in a slot in one control panel. "Drive standing by."

The tension was rising fast; everyone focussed obsessively on their stations, acting with jerky, nervous movements, their voices tight, their responses clear and precise. The stale air was tainted with the odor of electronics and fear.

"Navigation?" Captain Morgan snapped.

"Course plotted and programmed, Captain." That was hardly necessary since the calculations were made days in advance and checked countless times, but the tension was so great that some release was needed.

"Other ships standing by?"

"They're all slaved to our counter, Captain. They report ready." Captain Morgan was trembling. All of us were.

The Admiral was pressed up against the ladder opposite me, giving what little space there was to the Captain and the duty. I could tell from his tension that he was as nervous as the rest of us. "Is it always like this, sir?" I asked him quietly.

He didn't look at me, but stared straight ahead at the main view screen. "Yes." he muttered. "Every time."

245

"One minute to zero" the duty said at last.

"Capacitor?" Captain Morgan snapped.

"Fully charged, and coolant is on line," one of the crew said. "Ship is presently at Condition Epsilon."

"Set condition Delta."

The helm technician made a few adjustments to his controls. "Condition Delta set, Captain. Ready to maneuver."

"Fifteen seconds," the duty said. The tension in the crowded bridge was unbearable.

"Arm the drive."

The duty turned the key he inserted earlier. "Drive armed, Captain."

"Five. Four. Three. Two. One. Zero!"

The lights dimmed. There was a heavy arc rumble as the capacitor discharged into the mass polarizer, reducing the ship's mass to near zero as the engines kicked in. Where we limped along at an eighth-gravity before, now the ship bucked and groaned under full acceleration. The Universe ahead of us flattened, split open, folded back, and vanished behind us as we passed light speed.

"Six hours, twenty-three minutes, thirty-five seconds," the duty said as the rumble of the engines faded.

"Recharge the capacitor."

"Recharging," the engineering technician said. "Presently sixty-eight percent available."

"Acknowledged."

I watched their instruments nervously, trying to estimate how close we were to the Dreamsingers' world. There was nothing out there except the planetary black holes which only our instruments could detect, and which we wanted to avoid hitting at all cost. The other ships around us were visible, and as we feared, our neat battle array started falling apart almost at once.

"We're lagging behind some of them, Captain," the helm said. "Shall I adjust our speed?"

"Negative. Maintain station and let them adjust on us."

"Six hours," the duty said.

§

246

Once under way, there was nothing to do but wait while the fleets raced into the system. The bridge settled down into a tense routine, everyone marking time until the moment we came out of jump. My back started aching from my cramped position, so I eased down the ladder and joined the other two on the deck below. "It will be a while yet," I told them.

"I wish we could get this over with," M'tinDegan said with a wain smile. "I've never been as scared before in my life."

"You're not the only one." Right then both of them needed the moral support of my example, not that I was any less frightened. "You'll manage. Speaking of which, we need to get ready.'

That meant wrestling into the vacuum suits borrowed from our fleet now that we had a bit of room to work with. Vac suits are clumsy affairs despite generations of design effort that went into making them as easy to get into as possible. While trained fleet personnel might be able to do it, we had a miserable time with the bulky things in zero G.

"Thankfully I'm not in the space service," M'tinDegan sighed. "I'd hate having to squeeze into these things all the time."

"I don't think they make them in your size." His years of sedentary life at the embassy showed.

"The worst thing is that if we need these, they probably won't matter," K'deiTai grumbled as he fastened up his sleeve connections. "I hate to think what will happen if this junk heap takes a hit."

"Five hours," the duty said over the intercom.

"It doesn't do any good to fret, K'deiTai." I was concerned that his pessimism would affect others, including me. "You need to think positive."

He sighed. "I am *positive* we are in trouble!"

"What *ever!*" Honestly, some people.

§

"Four hours," the duty said.

"Why is it taking so long?" K'deiTai grumbled from below.

I was back at my station on the ladder behind the Admiral, and looked down the ladder way at him. "We are well into the system now, but there's a long way to go yet. Be patient."

247

"This Ancestorless suit itches."

"There's nothing I can do about it," I said, curtly. "And remember to use your relief bladder before the battle starts, or you'll *really* itch then."

"Um...I forgot to hook it up." He withdrew and began pulling his suit apart, muttering to himself all the while.

§

"Three hours," the duty continued his monotonous chant of doom.

I clung to the ladder, watching the humans as they waited restlessly, and brooded. I wasn't optimistic about our chances; too many things were going wrong, and our combined fleets were badly outmatched by the black sphere to begin with. My thoughts drifted to C'traBenla, and I comforted myself by recalling all our good times together. I was incredibly lucky, despite her impulsiveness and her temper, to win her love. She bore an egg with me, and stood by me through the endless headaches of my career. That meant a lot, especially now. I wanted desperately to be with her, and begged my Ancestors to get me through this in one piece. The thought of her having to face the future alone was unbearable.

§

I came back down some time later to see how the others were doing, and to grab a quick snack.

"How can you eat at a time like this?" K'deiTai asked.

I paused in my number fourteen endurance ration, which I wasn't enjoying anyway. "Self discipline. I need the energy for the battle ahead."

"But how can you eat *those* things at a time like this?"

"Self discipline," I sighed.

"Two hours," the duty said.

§

"Sixty minutes," the duty said.

The Captain keyed the general announcement channel. "All stations go to Condition Beta." Around us, a last few adjustments were made to the controls as we went from cruising to standby battle status.

"Rotate the ship." The helm used the maneuvering jets to turn the ship end for end so we could use our engines to decelerate. We could see the rest of the fleet matching our turn on the view screens.

"Thirty minutes," the duty said when the maneuver was done.

"Secure the recharge."

The engineering technician adjusted his controls, and the steady whine of the generators dimmed. "Recharge secured, Captain. We have eighty-two percent."

"Dedicate thirty-two percent to the downjump, hold the rest on standby for emergency maneuvers." That wasn't much. We would come out of jump into a major battle with hardly enough power to get us under way if needed.

Time crawled on. The tension on the bridge was unbearable. MacKenna was rigid, watching everything with quick, spasmodic movements of his head.

"Fifteen minutes," the duty said.

"All stations go to Condition Alpha," the Captain said. "Vacuum preparations for all hands." Around the bridge, the crew sealed their helmets and activated their environmental pods.

"Weapons?"

"Gatling gun armed and ready. Spare ammunition standing by. Electronic countermeasures active. Missiles one through five ready, six through eight on standby."

That caught me by surprise; why were they holding three of our precious few missiles off line? I pulled myself further up the ladder and peered over the weapons technician's shoulder: five of the eight lights representing our missiles were green, the other three yellow. "Um...Admiral..." He silenced me with an urgent wave of one hand.

"Ten minutes."

"How does the fleet look?" MacKenna asked. He and Captain Morgan were the only ones with their helmets still open, so they were able to speak directly to each other without the others hearing.

"We're scattered from hell to breakfast, sir," the Captain said. MacKenna cursed, but said nothing more.

249

The tension ratcheted up notch by notch as the clock wound down. I was trembling, and my arms ached from my strangle hold on the ladder. My nervous funk brought to mind all the tense moments we endured during our first tour on earth. As bad as the siege of the embassy was, this was far worse; we were going into battle against a foe that frightened the *humans*.

"Five minutes."

"God, they're scattered all over the sky," MacKenna grumbled as he studied the view screens.

"Worse than ever, sir," the Captain said. "Let's hope the other captains will modify their downjump by a few seconds to trim their positions."

"That's risky this close to the planet, but it's all they can do."

"We'll lose a lot of firepower otherwise."

"Yeah. And we still have the downjump to get through."

"Sixty seconds."

The Admiral and Captain sealed their helmets and activated their environmental pods. I hastily snapped my snout cone shut, and glanced down the ladder at M'tinDegan and K'deiTai. Both had their suits sealed up. M'tinDegan hung on the ladder just below me, watching the action from deck level, and K'deiTai was on the deck below fiddling with his suit controls.

"Stand by," Captain Morgan said. She was rigid, her jaw muscles flexing with tension, watching the screens with beady-eyed obsession.

"Thirty seconds."

"Bring up the navigation system. I want a fast position check the instant we downjump."

"Yes, Admiral."

"Ready..." The counter was winding down rapidly. "Five. Four. Three. Two. One. Now!"

The engines kicked in so hard that the whole ship groaned under the strain. The thrust caught me by surprise; I slipped, and clung convulsively to the ladder to keep from falling. The nausea of the mass polarizer came up again as the Universe exploded behind us, overtook us, wrapped around us, and closed ahead—and the enemy was there.

"Where are we?" MacKenna demanded. A quick look at the view screens showed the enemy almost on top of us; a dull black shadow blotting out half of the Dreamsingers' world. Our jump was nearly perfect, although the rest of the fleet was scattered all over the area. The 'Zulu' was closest, having all but rammed the sphere. The 'Marco Polo' was not too far off, but the rest of the human ships were as much as several light-seconds away.

"We only have three ships in range, sir," Captain Morgan said.

"Dammit, we have no choice," MacKenna snarled. "We're in range. Do it."

The Captain was on the general fleet channel at once. "All ships commence fire, fire for effect!"

"Commander Ivan Rostokovich," I murmured, remembering a promise he made to me. We watched in tense silence as they launched our five missiles.

It took nearly a minute for the message to reach all the ships. Eldest H'rhAtor acted on his own to get his ships in action, but they were scattered every bit as badly as the humans. Instead of a concentrated volley, there was a loose barrage as ships fired at varying ranges and times.

"This is totally fucked up!" MacKenna muttered. "If they have any defenses at all, they'll pick our missiles off one at a time."

And so it proved. The intruders must have been surprised by our sudden appearance, but they reacted swiftly. A laser beam, faintly visible in the thin outer planetary corona, reached out and touched the first missile launched by the 'Zulu'. It exploded. The 'Zulu's next missile was neutralized as soon as it left the rack, and the ship itself was quickly under fire from several laser mounts.

"Dammit, get out of there!" MacKenna yelled.

"They got one of our missiles!"

The 'Xanadu' was firing, and more lasers reached out to intercept their missiles one by one. The 'Zulu's engines came on, and it started pulling away from the sphere amid a cloud of leaking air and loose debris. They launched their third missile, which managed to get a short way from the ship before it too was exploded. The 'Zulu' was struck by several large pieces of the missile, and drifted slowly to one side as its engines faltered.

251

An alarm went off, and one of the control panels went dead. "We're hit, Captain!" the operator cried. "Navigation is out!" That was when I realized we were taking fire ourselves.

The alarm rang again, and our vac suits began slowly billowing out. "Hull breach!"

"They got another one!" Our ragged barrage was being chewed up by the sphere's defenses.

"All stations, damage control report."

"That's our last missile!" The hull clattered as we were struck by the debris of our final shot.

I was starting to lose my nerve. This had gone on far too long; the element of surprise was lost, and we weren't doing any real damage to the sphere. This battle was shaping up to be a disaster. "Admiral, perhaps we..."

And then it hit.

I could never, in my entire life, have imagined the sensation which swept over us like a tidal wave. To this day, it still gives me nightmares. Everything I had ever done, ever said, ever thought, ever believed was an obscene lie. I was disgusted with my very being, horrified by my species, ashamed of living. I was foul, filthy, a disease. I was worthless, degraded, meaningless. I wanted to die. I needed to die. Dying was my only salvation, my only way of apologizing to the Universe for the sin of my existence. I sobbed hysterically from grief and shame. A part of my mind told me this was all the aliens' mind attack, but as the seconds ticked away and I wallowed in my degradation, it was harder and harder to believe what my mind was telling me.

I tumbled helplessly, spasming, retching, crying in bitter shame. Around me, the humans were equally helpless, some of them screaming in terror, others moaning and sobbing as they thrashed helplessly against their seat harnesses. I caught a flash of light on one of the view screens, but didn't realize until later that it was the 'Zulu' exploding with a blinding flash as their capacitor shorted.

Captain Morgan tumbled helplessly in the center of the deck, unable to control herself. "H-h-h-el-lp me, J J," she gasped.

"Honeylamb..." The voice was a faint, ghostly echo.

"Please...J J..."

"HONEYLAMB!"

And he was there, for just a moment, standing over her with his back bowed under the weight of the alien attack, shielding her. She sobbed, struggled to orient herself, and pushed across the bridge to the weapons console. All the lights were red, the missiles expended...except the three we hadn't fired earlier. She hit those three lights all at once, and the ship shuddered as the last missiles leapt from their rack.

"Hurry, Honeylamb!" J J was reeling as if from a searing fire.

Captain Morgan grabbed the trigger assembly and squeezed with both hands. There was a ripping sound in the background as the ship's gatling gun sprayed.

"Ah can't..." J J was gone.

Morgan sagged as the mental attack renewed, but clung desperately to the trigger until the gatling gun was empty.

We learned later that the reason Captain Morgan hadn't fired the three missiles at the start of the battle was because they were a new specialized human weapon: space mines. When she finally did fire them as a last desperate resort, it turned out to be just what was needed. The mines were fitted with stealth technology, and once their booster stages burned out, they were next to impossible to detect. Nonetheless, the sphere aliens were soon aware of them, and several of their defense lasers swept the area trying to knock them out. But again, Captain Morgan did the right thing by hosing the planetoid with all their gatling gun ammunition, which created a cloud of interference. The mines were strobe lit again and again as the alien defenses picked off the gatling gun shells one by one. Then one of the mines was struck, detonating it with a blinding flash. The alien's fire faltered for a moment, then returned with renewed fury. Hundreds of bullets were flashed to vapor, hundreds more impacted harmlessly on the planetoid. The second mine was hit and detonated, and the defenders focussed on the final mine...

...the final mine sensed a target within range, used its tiny maneuvering thrusters to turn to it, and the closing stage rocket motor fired. A dozen defense lasers turned to stop it, but were stymied by the rain of gun shells. The beams picked off dozens of shells, then hundreds, drawing closer and closer to the missile. Soon it was too close for most of the defense batteries to lock onto it, but the few which still could fired at it with relentless fury.

One of the lasers clipped the missile, causing it to spin out of control. It drifted onward by inertia, all power lost, and detonated with a blinding flare that lit up the side of the alien planetoid.

Aboard the 'Marco Polo', we all collapsed as the alien mind assault abruptly cut off...

*****

"Fiddler's Green"
(Related by Learnéd K'deiTai)

...The next thing I knew, I was laying in a field of soft grass. I was stunned by the *horror* of the alien mind attack, so the sudden change of scene left me dazed and disoriented. I lay there for some time, I don't know how long, staring up at the brilliant blue sky and the soft, billowy clouds, and wondered vaguely what happened. Did I die? I remember wanting to with all my soul; did my Ancestors grant my wish? But if they did, would they accept me after all the foul, degraded things I felt about myself? Would we gallop for all eternity through the rolling meadows and verdant marshlands of *a'vemn'vb'li*, or was I doomed to the Uttermost Darkness as something too loathsome to exist? The rational part of me said that was a result of the alien mind attack; that I should shrug off those doubts; that we must have destroyed the black sphere and freed our minds. Those feelings and doubts haunted me nonetheless, and I couldn't quite shake them off. I lay on my side and wept in shame and self loathing.

I finally fought the despair off enough to pull myself together and wonder what happened. Perhaps my Ancestors would be coming for me soon...or perhaps this place was some fiendish creation of the black sphere...

...That thought chilled me as my inflamed imagination conjured up all manner of horrible fates to befall their prisoners. I rolled up on one elbow and gazed about, and it took me a while to realize the others were there too. J J lay on his back, no ghostly image this time, but a solid figure, staring transfixed at the sky. That was a vast relief...unless they captured him too? Captain Morgan lay by his side, with MacKenna opposite. I'eiBida, M'tinDegan, H'rhAtor, and the rest of our expeditionary force were scattered around them.

Captain Morgan was the first to recover. "What..." she gasped. She struggled to sit up, and sat leaning on her arms, shaken and disoriented. "Where...J J?" She rolled over, struggled to her knees, grabbed the old man, and shook him anxiously. "J J? Are you all right?"

"Wha...? Where are we?" M'tinDegan asked.

"Lawd," J J moaned. "You done it."

"What happened?" M'tinDegan repeated.

"You done it. You kilt 'em. You kilt 'em all."

"J J...Admiral!" She spotted MacKenna lying nearby and panicked. One look said it: he was as pale as a cloud, utterly rigid, staring at nothing with wide open eyes. Dead.

"A-a-admiral!" Morgan broke down, scrambled over J J and clutched MacKenna's limp body, sobbing hysterically. "Nooo!"

"J J? Can you do something?" I whispered.

J J looked over at MacKenna, then struggled to roll up on one elbow and reached out to him with a trembling hand. His hand sank into MacKenna's chest; he gasped and his back arched in an agonized spasm. J J withdrew his hand, then brushed it over and through MacKenna's head. MacKenna shuddered, then lay still, breathing in ragged gasps. J J sank back with a groan. "Thas all ah can do."

"Admiral!" Captain Morgan shook him by his shoulders. "Are you all right?"

Mackenna groaned, and stared vaguely at the sky for a long time. "I'm...alive?" he mumbled at last. He didn't sound convinced of that. Captain Morgan broke down and cried, clinging to him. He held up one shaky hand and caressed her cheek tenderly. "I'm all right, Loraine."

"Are you still with us, Brian?" H'rhAtor looked pretty ragged himself.

"I...guess." He stared at nothing for a while, too listless to do anything. "Did we win?" he asked at last.

"Yes, Brian. One of your missiles shattered the sphere."

"Good."

"T'eiBida? Where are we?" It was only then that I noticed C'traBenla, U'tdaPagrn, Commander Rostokovich and Agent Roubidoux off to one side. C'traBenla was naked, U'tdaPagrn a sleep towel, the others in underwear. It must be the middle of the night back in Geneva, and they were snatched out of a sound sleep. "T'eiBida! What happened?" She was on her feet, shaking him on the edge of panic.

I'eiBida groaned, curled on his side and vomited, then looked at her vaguely. "C'tra?"

"*Where are we?*"

"Don' you worry, little lady," J J assured her. "This heah ain' no place in particular. It's jus' a place in yo mind."

"Huh?" She glanced at J J in confusion, then reared up and looked around.

That caught my attention, so I took a good look at the surreal landscape as well. We lay under the canopy of a grove of trees next to a small lake surrounded by low, rolling ground covered with lush grass sprinkled with colorful flowers, the whole ringed by dense forest. The sky was a flawless blue, with puffy clouds and an orange sun—our star, I realized—overhead. The day was warm, and a there was a gentle, cooling breeze from nowhere. And over it all was a feeling of calm and peace like I had never known before. It was enough to bring tears, it was so lovely.

"It's...beautiful..." C'traBenla whispered.

"We...seen it...in th' Admiral's mind." J J sounded weary, as if he had borne a terrible burden over a lifetime. "You-all need a touch of healin', an' it's easier fo' us t' call you heah than t' go to each of you."

That was a stunning thought: the Dreamsingers could capture our consciousness and bring them here—to whatever metaphysical 'here' this was—over interstellar distances.

"But...where are we?" C'tra asked again.

MacKenna struggled to a sitting position and gazed around. "Fiddler's Green," he muttered at last.

"Admiral?"

"I...know this place." He stared at the lake uncertainly, then began singing in a low, quavering voice:

"Halfway down the trail to Hell
in a shady meadow green,
are the souls of all dead troopers camped
near a good old-time canteen.
And this eternal resting place
is known as Fiddler's Green."

257

"I wondered what you used to hum all the time, sir," Pierre said.

"I...learned that when I was a kid...it stuck in my head ever since." He tapered off and stared at the lake, bemused.

"Who were they?" I'eiBida was the next to recover his wits. "The black sphere, where did they come from?"

"They was like us," J J said. "The same kind a' life, anyway. We don' know where they come from, 'cept they came a long way. They wanted t' take our world from us." He strained to sit up on one elbow, and looked at us one by one. "But you kilt 'em. You saved us. We'ah greatly beholdin' t' you fo that."

"You had us fight your war for you?" MacKenna demanded.

"We suffered great losses," H'rhAtor added. "Our leaders will want explanations."

J J pondered the Admiral for a moment with sad eyes. "They would'a come fo' you, after. They was jus' pure mean, right through. They hated anythin' wasn't their kind." His gaze shifted to H'rhAtor. "We wasn't strong enough to hold 'em off, an' we can't make weapons like you do." His gaze shifted to take us in one by one. When his eyes met mine, I could feel the depth and tragic wisdom in his words. "You couldn't take 'em without us t' help. So we did the only thing we could: we fought 'em, all of us, together."

MacKenna pondered that in silence, then exchanged looks with H'rhAtor.

"He is right," H'rhAtor said.

"Yeah," MacKenna said at last. "Damn."

"You could have been honest with us, J J."

"Ah know. An' a'm sorry fo' dragging you into this, but you wouldn't have helped us 'cause yo fleets weren't ready. We had to survive, ya know? We'll make it up t' you, in time."

MacKenna and H'rhAtor exchanged looks. "We keep this to ourselves," MacKenna said. H'rhAtor nodded.

I noticed M'tinDegan was nursing one arm, which had an ugly welt across it. Once called to my attention, I saw a large bruise on his neck, and a patch of blood on his torn tunic. "Are you all right?" I asked him.

"I guess," he muttered as he tended to another welt on his leg.

"Were you injured when we got hit?"

He gave me an exasperated look. "I'eiBida landed on my head, and knocked me off the ladder. I wound up falling three decks before I could catch myself. How I managed to slide through those narrow hatchways without breaking something, I can't imagine."

I glanced at I'eiBida, who gave me an embarrassed ear twitch. "Sorry," he mumbled.

"What was that weapon of theirs?" H'rhAtor asked. "That...feeling..." We all shuddered at the memory. "It was horrible, like...dying..."

"They was willin' us all t' die," J J sighed as he sank back again. "Tha's how we fight, with feelin's. They got them a machine that pulls all their hate together an' shoots it out. We couldn't stand agin' that, an' neither could you."

"Death wish, as a strategic weapons system." MacKenna shuddered and curled up in a ball. "God, I thought we were bad."

J J sat up on one elbow again and looked at him. "You a troubled lot. You got a whole lot a' fear in you. But you can get over it if you try. You be mo' like the Ic'nichi, an' you'll be okay."

"Lord, I hope so," MacKenna mumbled. He lay on his back and stared up at the trees overhead.

"If you can help bring peace between our two races, that will make up for this," H'rhAtor said.

"Ah...guess it would," J J sighed. "We'll keep that in mind."

We lay there for a while, not saying anything, content to enjoy the warm sun and the cool breeze, luxuriating in the unreal sense of peace, thankful to be alive and that our war was over.

"I feel...different," MacKenna said after a bit. He turned to J J again. "What's happening to us?"

"We doin' some healin' fo' you." J J sounded more weary than ever, and his snout was creased with pain. "We're helpin' you get rid of some of what happened heah. That'll give you a head start on the rest of it."

"You're absorbing our pain?" M'tinDegan asked in wonder.

J J considered him for a long moment, his eyes filled with suffering. "Ah guess...you could say that."

259

I thought about it, and realized the terror of that experience was faded, remote, like the memory of a horrid dream. It was unnerving to think that the Dreamsingers could still reach out to us and alter our memories after what they must have endured. A fleeting thought crossed my mind that they could be every bit as dangerous as the black sphere, if they chose to. I realized too late that they were reading my mind, and half-expected that thought to be whisked away. I was oddly relieved when it wasn't.

"What about you, J J?" Captain Morgan asked. "Are you all right? How about your people?"

"We suffered," he said, sadly. "We been hurt real bad. But its ova now. You'll be okay now, an' we'll get ova it in time." He sagged, and lay flat on his back. "Lawd," he sighed. "It feels so *good* to see the sky again."

*****

"Counting The Cost"
(Related by Defender I'eiBida)

The alien sphere was breaking up, torn apart by the shock and thermal stresses of the stellar bomb, and the explosive decompression which killed all on board. The cloud of debris was spreading, which made it hazardous for ships in the vicinity, and even more so for people in vac suits, but MacKenna and H'rhAtor wanted bodies and technology, so a goodly part of those who survived the battle were drifting through the wreckage, collecting.

The control deck of the 'Marco Polo' was busy, with a full watch cobbled together out of the functional survivors despite the strain on everyone. Many had died under the mind barrage, many more of us were out of commission, and all of us were affected to some degree. Yet by the bridge clock, the battle lasted less than five earth minutes.

The capacitor was recharging, work parties were repairing battle damage on the decks below, and even though there were no more missiles and precious little gatling ammunition, the ship was at full battle alert. Despite exhaustion and battle fatigue, no one was getting any rest including Captain Morgan, who drifted in the center of the command deck nursing a bulb of coffee and fighting to stay awake. The fragile alliance between us and the humans was already starting to fray, and she and H'rhAtor were forced to clamp down on their people on more than one occasion.

I spent most of the time since the battle in the control deck for want of anything better, and kept myself occupied by taking an inventory of recovered items, passing occasional summaries to H'rhAtor, and other busywork. Despite my exhaustion, I was too frazzled by the after-battle let-down and the horrors of the mind attack to risk sleep. I was taking a break at the moment, and idly watched the action on one of the view screens. The alien sphere was a black semi-circular mass with one side fragmented, stark against the brilliant colors of the gas giant world beyond. The breakup was slowly spreading, the debris field becoming thicker and wider. The blinking suit beacons could just be seen as they moved cautiously through the wreckage. The planet in the background was crossed by faint streaks of light as bits of junk hit the atmosphere. I've never been a poet, but it had a tragic, awesome beauty. I was bemused by the sight, and by the thought of our improbable victory, and by the realization that I would live, and would soon go home to C'traBenla.

I missed her desperately right then. At least she saw me when we were in J J's dreamworld. It was a big comfort that she knew I was all right. Our time in Fiddler's Green was all too brief, and I regretted not having the chance to reassure her. My thoughts drifted back to that verdant meadow green: her image was clear and sharp in my mind even though the rest of it—and our reason for being there—was just an ominous blur.

The com-link squawked something, bringing me back to the here and now. The humans around me were alert but weary, their voices subdued and their actions carefully deliberate. Long stellar voyages are draining with the cramped conditions and endless workload; wartime operations doubly so as I was learning. I reflected that this would be a priceless experience when I returned to my Staff duties.

Captain Morgan stared at nothing, floating limp near the central ladder, then shook off her drowsy state. Having tasted the strain of command, I understood how she felt as she went through one of those convulsive open-mouth gestures they have when tired.

"I am no expert on human medicine, Captain," I said to her. "But you look exhausted. Perhaps you should rest."

She gave me an icy glare, then wilted and shook her head. "I can't, not with the Admiral out of commission."

"You are the only senior rank left for your people. Not much is happening right now; you should get a bit of rest."

"I will manage, thank you," she said curtly.

I made a mental note that she seemed unable or unwilling to delegate her responsibilities: a serious weakness if she was forced into prolonged war operations. Old habits never die.

"Marco Polo, we've got an intact body for you," Night Eagle's voice came over the com-link. He muttered something in Sioux, then, "Ugly bumbuck. I wouldn't want to meet this in a dark alley."

262

"There he is, Captain." The radio watch stander was using the Marco Polo's navigation telescope to track the Lieutenant's beacon. A pair of suited humans jetted in our direction towing an inert mass. Whatever it was, it was large; larger than a human, and from how it quivered, it didn't seem to have any bony structure. As they drew up to the ship and braked with their suit jets, the flaccid corpse billowed out. "Jesus, it's a giant jellyfish!" she said.

"Add it to the collection," Morgan mumbled, referring to an esoteric assortment of junk wrapped in a cargo net floated nearby. The two sides had agreed to pool their findings, which kept things from erupting thus far.

Boredom and hunger were setting in, and I was weary enough that sleep didn't seem so frightening after all. Plus I was curious about the Admiral's condition, now that she mentioned him, so I excused myself and struggled through the narrow hatchway to the galley on the next deck down.

§

The decks below the galley had been breached and were still under repair, so the wardroom was converted into a makeshift hospital for the nine members of 'Marco Polo's crew who succumbed to the mind attack. Two of those were catatonic, while three were incapacitated but slowly recovering. The remaining four would need prolonged care before they would be whole again, if ever. One of those was the ship's physich: her assistant wasn't much better off, and had his hands full. Two more died for no apparent reason, and were packed in the ship's refrigerated stores for the time being. From comments passed between the human ships, it seemed the rest suffered as bad or worse, and I hated to think of what the situation in our fleet must have been.

The Admiral was one of the 'Marco Polo's casualties. He floated in a zipped up hammock strung above one of the tables, heavily sedated, trembling and staring at the wall with a look of icy dread in his eyes. Whatever calming effect the Dreamsingers' netherworld offered, it didn't entirely carry over into our reality.

"How are you doing, sir?" I asked.

He stared at me with a hollow look. "...I'm...alive..." From his tone, he seemed surprised, even dismayed.

263

"Yes, sir, you are alive, and we destroyed the black sphere, and we'll be going home soon," I told him firmly. He needed the reinforcement. "Earth is safe. You accomplished your mission, so you can take it easy now."

"Paid my dues," he mumbled. "God...I'm too old for this."

Captain Morgan drifted down through the hatch, so I eased back to give them some privacy. "How do you feel, sir?" she asked.

"Has...has there been...any word from J J?" he whispered.

She shook her head. "No, sir. Nothing."

"You have to keep trying." He gripped her sleeve with a trembling hand. "I have to know if they made it."

"I will, sir," she said, tenderly. "You need to rest. Everything is going smoothly, and I'll tell you the moment I hear anything from J J."

I realized then that she was deliberately pushing herself to exhaustion in the hope that J J would contact her again. I sincerely hoped he would.

§

K'deiTai floated curled up in one corner sobbing softly. "How are you doing?" I asked.

It took him a while to focus on me, and longer to answer. "I am still here...I suppose." He gasped and shook all over. "I never...would have believed such horrors...can exist."

"Well they don't any more," I said to reassure him. "It's over and done with."

"For now." For once, his pessimism seemed well founded.

"We'll all go home soon, and you can go back to your teaching. You should have quite a few important lessons to pass along to your apprentices."

"You and me both," he sighed.

"And as for diplomatic matters, I'd say this war has enhanced the Admiral's standing with the Alliance, and the cooperation of our two fleets will break down a lot of barriers. Improved relations are sure to come of it."

K'deiTai shivered and stared at nothing. "I suppose. Honestly, I couldn't care less."

M'tinDegan was also among the casualties, floating in a sleeping sack in an out of the way corner staring at nothing. After our abrupt return from J J's dream world, he came down with such a severe bout of nervous trembling that I needed to delve into our limited medical supply to sedate him. That was nearly a day ago, and while he seemed calmer, he was nowhere near whole.

"How are you doing?" I asked him.

He considered me for a long moment, then muttered, "I suppose I will recover, in time." His gaze drifted, and he sighed. "I'm not so young any more."

"Nonsense. You're only as old as you feel."

"That old, hmmm?"

"And you are a genuine war hero, something our people don't have many of. The *tra'taj* will stampede at the sight of you."

He gave a derisive snort. "But which direction, I wonder?"

I decided privately that I would try to get him enrolled in the Sacrificials; not that he was a defender, or that his physical injuries were so severe. Still, he deserved it for all the work he put in, and for the trauma he endured.

"So how are you doing?"

I thought on it for a bit, since I wasn't entirely sure how I felt. "Relieved to be alive." I said at last, somberly. I brooded on that question for a long time, since it seemed so important for some reason. "At least I begin to understand how the humans cope with their wars, I suppose."

"I wish I could," he sighed. "But I'm not entirely sure they understand it."

"I feel...different," I said at last. "I'm not sure how or why. '

"This was your first taste of real battle. My research among the humans shows it changes one's perspective on life and death."

"Maybe. I guess fear isn't such an unknown now."

"The humans say you 'met the elephant'."

"I guess I did," I sighed. "What is an elephant?"

"They were huge terrestrial animals; awe-inspiring I can understand why the humans are so taken by them."

"I'd like to see one when we get back to earth."

"They're extinct now. They died out during the Collapse."

265

"Figures." We were silent for a bit, each lost in our musing on what we went through, and what it did to us. "I understand the humans will send a ship back to earth with the wounded soon," I said after a while. "I can arrange for you to go along, unless you would prefer to go home with our fleet?"

He pondered that for a bit. "No, I'll go back to earth. The research site is as much of a home as any sociologist has, you know. Earth is where I can do the most good for both species."

"I'll be glad to get back to my duties in the Staff," I said with a weary groan. "This has been a miserable, Ancestorless adventure if ever there was such."

"Well, one good thing *has* come of it. I finally know what it feels like to fight an enemy which scares the humans." He cracked a feeble smile. "It ought to make a sensational scientific paper."

"You intellectuals are all alike," I chided him. "Always thinking about your papers and your journals. You need to get your feet on the ground and start living life."

"But just *think* of how N'detLeda will fume! Let's see him top *that* one!"

"Oh. Yes, he'll be furious, won't he?" That would be worth seeing.

§

The Admiral was in such bad shape after the battle that he was transferred to the 'Xanadu' when they headed back to earth with the human wreckage of the brief, horrible encounter. Our liaison party went along, but it took some effort to squeeze us in, since the 'Xanadu' carried thirty wounded and disabled humans in need of immediate medical attention despite the Dreamsingers' efforts to clear our minds. They had to borrow a few crew from the 'Marco Polo', since two thirds the 'Xanadu' crew were disabled as well. The 'Marco Polo' fared better than the rest of the fleet, with half of their crew disabled. I suspect the reason they got off so easy was J J's intervention. Be that as it may, we were thankful to see the end of the war, and to be headed home. Hopefully, now that the crisis was past us, life could return to normal.

*****

266

"It's A Living, I Suppose"
(Related by Learnéd K'deiTai)

"I ought to send the entire lot of you back to d'enchia in irons," U'tdaPagrn said in flat-eared anger. "*What* were you thinking? Do you have any *idea* how much damage this will cause to interstellar relations?"

In fact, our return from the war was *not* triumphant. U'tdaPagrn learned about their blackmailing the Chancellor while we were gone, and no sooner did the embassy omnibus deliver us to the main entrance, than we were summoned into his grotto for a righteous tail-knotting. W'kiLap, T'apiDien, and C'traBenla were already there, looking somber and strained.

"You *blackmailed* the Chancellor! In *all* my years of diplomatic service, I have *never* heard of anything like this!"

If there was any good news, at least N'detLeda and T'virDoma twisted some tails and hitched a ride home on the courier as soon as they learned of our victory, so they weren't there to witness our debacle.

"And what's worse, you were consorting with Honoré Dassault! If there is a worse human to conspire with, I can't imagine who it could be!"

"We needed his help," W'kiLap protested.

"You might as well have invited the Anti-techs to infiltrate our security!" Work was under way even as he spoke to remove the back door those two *'v'thorble* created, not that that was his only angst. "And *you*, K'deiTai! Of all people..."

"I had nothing to do with this!"

"You were at the reception; you could have told them not to!"

"I tried that. It didn't work."

"Well you *certainly* could have warned me about it afterward so I could provide damage control. As is, our prolonged silence on the matter implicates this embassy. The Chancellor has worked himself up into a state, and there'll be no reasoning with him now."

"Um..." My ears wilted as I remembered, belatedly, that I forgot about the matter in the press of affairs. "...I thought I told you. Sorry."

"As if it makes a difference now!"

"How bad could it be since the Chancellor has to keep his part secret," M'tinDegan said, defensively.

"It'll be bad: the Chancellor made it plain there will be major repercussions over this, and that *un'tdar* has a talent for vindictiveness. And as to keeping it quiet, *we* are the ones with the knotted tails, since any public disclosure could get this embassy shut down!" U'tdaPagrn went on to vent his angst in some decidedly undiplomatic terms, finishing with, "You may have wrecked four years of diplomacy with this *x'mnnb'!*"

"We did what had to be done," I'eiBida said. "We were helpless without the humans."

"I'll grant you that. But your methods were entirely unacceptable."

"And we did it to save the Dreamsingers from extermination! The Black Sphere people would have come after us later, and it took everything we had plus the help of the Dreamsingers to defeat them."

"We don't know that, but even so, still it doesn't justify your actions." U'tdaPagrn fumed at us for a bit, then asked, "Have you heard anything from them?"

I'eiBida shook his head sadly. "No, sir. No word from J J. Nothing." M'tinDegan echoed that.

"Ancestors help them," U'tdaPagrn muttered. Then he turned his attention back to us. "Until further notice, you are all confined to the embassy. I'm going to ship you home, where this matter will be referred to the proper authorities. Ancestors alone know how long it will take to untangle this mess you stirred up!"

§

Agent Goldblum and Commander Watanabi were in the lobby when we came by, plainly wanting news of the war. "So how was the battle?" Goldblum asked.

"Oh, it could have been worse, I guess," I'eiBida said, wearily.

"It's over, love," C'traBenla said to comfort him. "We survived, and we'll be going home soon."

"A sunrise tinted blood red is preferable to no sunrise at all," the Commander offered.

268

I'eiBida eyed him suspiciously. "You're starting to make sense."

"The fish finds wisdom in the water, as the bird does in the air, is it not so?"

"I suppose. Now, if you will excuse us..." He and C'traBenla headed for the cafeteria.

Talk of good timing, R'benTdan came by a moment later with another fleet staffer in tow. *He* favored us with a weary nod and a bemused sigh; *she* looked the worse for wear, and the pleasant front she showed her latest conquest was thin and brittle.

"I know what she's trying to do," she growled at us once he was gone. "She's trying to humiliate me. She thinks she can wear me down by throwing one mal after another at me until I'm forced to turn them away."

"Shocking," I said. It seemed C'traBenla ran wild through the support staff which remained behind at the Ministry during our absence. For a moment I *almost* pitied R'benTdan.

"But I'll show her!" she snarled in frustration. "I won't let some washed up fourth-finger ex-*tra'taj* get the better of me!"

"I...admire your determination."

"Oy," Goldblum sighed. "The paperwork!"

Not that she noticed. "She's afraid I'll steal her bondmate, as if I'd want her leftovers," she fumed. "She thinks she's oh-so-clever, that she can wear me down and make me admit she's better than me, but I won't let her!"

I knew C'traBenla was insecure about her bond with I'eiBida, but this seemed far too subtle for her, since her style was more toward mayhem with blunt objects. I gave W'kiLap a speculative glance, wondering if *someone* was goading our physical therapist on, and moreover, *what* could set her off like that.

I was about to say something when we were interrupted by a new arrival, another fleet staffer, and a decidedly plain and unimpressive one at that. "I...ah...came over to see someone named R'benTdan," he said, awkwardly. Goldblum threw up his hands in despair.

Her mood changed as if someone threw a light switch. "Yes, that's me," she purred. "How can I help you?"

269

He looked her over with an appreciative eye. "I'm told you are the physical therapist here?"

She slid her arm around his and gave him an eager ear twitch. "You have some stress to work off, don't you?"

"Yes."

"Understandable." She turned and dragged him toward the stairs. "It must be *difficult* spending so much time in space in those cramped ships..."

"It never ends around here, does it?" I grumbled.

"Truly a bridge over turbulent waters is well traveled," Watanabi mused as he watched them go.

"Oy, so easy for you to say," Goldblum muttered.

"C'traBenla is trying to humiliate her?" I asked W'kiLap once they left. "Where did she ever get such an idea?"

"She has *quite* an imagination, doesn't she?" He gave me an amused ear twitch and a knowing smile, and left it at that, as did I.

§

The rest of the human fleet came limping home one by one, and they had suffered. Aside from the 'Zulu', lost with all hands, half the humans either died or suffered massive psychological trauma under the mental barrage, and their ships were all damaged by the aliens' defensive fire or by suicidal crew members. And although we hadn't told the humans, our casualties were nearly as severe. As brief as it was, our first interstellar war strained both fleets to the breaking point.

The Admiral was in the Singapore hospital for nearly a month, and was shaking and hollow-eyed when they discharged him. He promptly headed for Geneva despite his physical condition: the 'Marco Polo' had just returned with Captain Morgan and her report, so he came here so we could all attend the postwar briefing. The human physichs protested loudly, but he was nothing if not stubborn.

U'tdaPagrn reluctantly released us from house arrest since we were still part of the interspecies liaison herd, but he lectured us at length, and in no uncertain terms, that we were to be on the strictest good behavior. We didn't argue.

§

270

We gathered in the conference room at the Defense Ministry for the first time since returning from the battle. The place was grimly familiar, but comforting in an odd way. The mood was somber, but everyone showed a lot less of the tension and anxiety we lived with for nearly a year. The Admiral himself seemed weary and withdrawn. He sat in a chair at the head of the conference table, with his Aide fussing over him more than usual.

"Well, you four righteously stirred the shit-pot," he greeted us when we arrived. "More balls than brains, the entire lot of you."

"Sir?" I muttered in alarm.

MacKenna shook his head. "You blackmailed the Chancellor! If you don't take the brass ring, I don't know who could."

"They know everything," M'tinDegan muttered, aghast.

"I hope you at least realize what a chance you took. A fool stunt like that could have wrecked relations!"

"But..." I for one was shaken that the Admiral was on to their misguided scheme. We were in for trouble, and knowing his temper, the tail-knotting we were about to receive would be just the start of it.

"I *hope* you have a good explanation for this!"

"Admiral..."

"I am *sincerely* looking forward to hearing your excuses, mister!" His weary snout and posture gave me a horrid premonition that we would be responsible for the stroke which finally laid him low. One doesn't need to be an Arbiter to be appalled by *that* prospect!

"I can assure you..."

Just then the door opened, and Captain Morgan came in. She was frazzled and weary, with the haunted look in her eyes which everyone who endured the mind assault shared.

"Well, good timing, Captain," MacKenna greeted her. 'You arrived right at the dramatic climax."

She looked us over skeptically. "That bit with the Chancellor, sir?"

"Yep. Say hello to our fiendish conspirators." He waved a feeble gesture in our direction. "They nailed his hide to the barn door in grand fashion."

271

She pondered us again. "Good."

"*Good?* Is that all you have to say?"

"Personally, I would have them taken out and shot," she said severely. "But it had to be done, so I guess we'll live with it."

"But...but..."

The door opened again, and Commander Watanabi entered, followed by Honoré Dassault.

"What...?" I muttered in alarm. "Why are they here?"

MacKenna chuckled. "Relax, they're my men."

"Your...?"

"You don't *really* think we're fool enough to turn our backs on you for a second, do you?"

"You were spying on us!" I'eiBida protested. We were stunned by how the humans followed us every step of the way.

"Admiral, I can explain..."

"No explanations needed," Dassault said. "We watched the whole affair with considerable amusement."

"A stroke worthy of a Samurai," Watanabi added with an unabashed grin. He opened a paper sack, and handed each of us a slim book. "I have some tokens of our appreciation to give you."

"The Art Of War, by Sun Tsu," I'eiBida read the cover. "You used us to get at the Chancellor!"

"You four are charmingly naive, I must say." MacKenna jerked a thumb at Watanabi and Dassault. "It didn't take us long to hear of your little scheme, so we closed off a few blind alleys, opened up a few avenues, and let let you carry the ball."

"Indeed," Dassault said with a thin smile and a bow to C'traBenla. "You offered a most diverting chase."

"As I have mentioned in the past, a great leader wins without battle," Watanabi said. "Sun Tsu's First Principle."

"I *really* have to read this," I'eiBida muttered as he leafed through the slim volume.

"Well, enough fun for now." MacKenna shook an admonishing finger at us. "You'll skate on this one, but never again. Understand?"

"Yes, Admiral," we echoed.

"Right. Let's have your report, Captain."

We took our places at the conference table, with the Admiral at the head and us, feeling greatly embarrassed, down one side. "I've done some rough estimates, sir," Morgan said as she handed the Admiral a thin file of documents. "From what we've seen of the wreck, and making some rough guesses, we figured the population of that ship was somewhere around a million."

"Whoa!" MacKenna said. That number stunned us all.

"Thus far, we've found no evidence of a mass polarizer. On a ship that big, the capacitor would be the size of this city, easy. No way they could hide it, even if they wanted to. It appears they operated at sublight speeds, probably very low sublight."

"A generation ship," MacKenna said in disbelief. "I wouldn't have thought it possible."

"*That* would explain their behavior, sir!" M'tinDegan said. "A journey of who knows how many generations—hundreds, likely— would require a ruthless, rigidly enforced mindset."

"Religious zealots?"

"They'd have to be, if for no more than to keep their population in check and cull the inbreeding effects."

"You make it sound like we did them a favor by destroying them," I'eiBida said.

"You may be right."

"That so? Interesting." MacKenna mused on the matter for a bit. "Any evidence that there might be more of those monster ships around?" he asked the Captain at last.

"Nothing, sir. However our people did a rough estimate of the effort put into that thing, and they said it would take the entire resources of a major civilization well over five hundred years to build it."

"Likely a lot longer to construct booster systems to get it up to speed, sir," I'eiBida added.

MacKenna nodded. "So we won't be seeing another one soon."

"If they even managed to build another one," M'tinDegan said. We all turned to him curiously. "The only rational explanation I can see for such an effort would be as a stellar lifeboat. Their world may no longer exist." That produced a somber silence as we contemplated the extinction of an entire race, no matter how evil.

273

"Speaking of which, have you heard anything more from the Dreamsingers since the battle, Captain?" I asked.

"No, Arbiter, not a peep. I hope they're all right."

"J J was still functional enough to reach out to us after the battle," M'tinDegan said. "I imagine they will need a long time to recover from that attack, if what we went through is any indication."

MacKenna shuddered at the memory, even though J J blanked most of it out of his mind. "God, I hope so. It'd be a damned shame if they didn't make it, after all we went through."

It occurred to me it'd be a damned shame if we committed genocide for no good reason. The thought of it made me queasy; how do the humans live with that?

"Well thank God it's over." The Captain sagged in her chair with a weary sign, and after a moment took a drink from her mug of coffee. I didn't think anything of it until I noticed her stunned look as she examined the mug she was holding.

The Admiral did notice. "You all right, Captain?"

"Yes, sir." She sighed again and drained her coffee mug. "In fact, I feel pretty good. Tired, but I'm okay."

"You need a little R & R."

"We all do, sir." She stared at nothing for a moment, then took another sip from the mug she just drained. "I need to get back to Orbit Dock, Admiral. The 'Marco Polo' needs major repairs."

"The dock force can handle it for now. You need a little down time. Take the day and visit Geneva, at least."

She smiled. "I'd like that. The Spring Fest is on. I haven't been to a street carnival since, God, I don't know when."

"That's the spirit, Captain. In fact, let's make arrangements for your entire crew to have leave as soon as possible."

She frowned. "What's left of them." It would be some time before the 'Marco Polo' left the system again. She drained her mug once more, and left it on the table.

The meeting broke up, and the Captain and Hythe-Morrison helped MacKenna to his feet and guided his faltering footsteps out into the hall. "How soon will you be returning to Singapore, sir?" she asked.

MacKenna sighed. "As soon as possible. If I have to put up with that fool Hogarthy again, I might say a naughty word."

"It will be good to get back to routine, sir," Hythe-Morrison said.

"Lord, yes." MacKenna rubbed his eyes wearily.

"If you will excuse me, Admiral..."

"Yes, Captain. Enjoy the festival." He waved vaguely in response to her salute, then watched as she headed down the hall.

"She's changed, sir," Hythe-Morrison said, nodding in her direction. "Even more than before."

"Yeah." MacKenna considered her until she vanished around a corner. "Not so up-tight. Those contacts must be doing something for her. All to the good, I'd say." He shrugged the matter off and limped up the corridor toward his office. As he passed us, he was singing softly to himself.

Marching past, straight through to Hell,
The Infantry are seen,
Accompanied by the Engineers,
Artillery and Marines,
For none but the shades of Cavalrymen
Dismount at Fiddlers' Green.

§

We congregated in a side corridor near the elevators, since that was the one place we could be relatively undisturbed. So much history was made here: monumental decisions which changed the future of both races, and now a work detail of defenders was packing up the last of our furnishings, equipment, and supplies to take back to the embassy while a peacekeeper detail was putting this floor of the Defense Ministry back to sleep. Soon there would be nothing left but the echoes and a thin layer of dust.

"Did she bring that coffee in with her?" I asked.

"Eh?" I'eiBida paused reading Sun Tsu. "I...don't think so."

M'tinDegan and C'traBenla exchanged puzzled looks. "I don't recall," C'traBenla said. "But I don't think she did."

"No," M'tinDegan said. "She was carrying the briefing folder when she came in."

"Well then, it must have been there when we arrived."

"No," I said. "They didn't serve refreshments."

"And there would have been some for the Admiral and us," I'eiBida said. "A serious breach of protocol, otherwise."

"Then...where did that mug come from?" I was starting to *r'vebbe* at the thought. "Why was it always full?"

"Maybe *you* need a little 'R & R', K'deiTai," I'eiBida reproved me. "You're imagining things."

"Ancestors, yes." I rubbed my eyes and let out a weary groan. "I must have missed it when she brought it in."

"You don't really think she has some sort of magical powers, do you?" M'tinDegan asked with a skeptical look.

"You're right; foolish of me. I'll be *so* glad to get home again."

Captain Morgan came down the hall just then. The elevator doors opened as she approached, and she walked in without breaking stride.

§

As the humans say, time flies when you're having fun. Word of our losses in the space battle finally leaked out, and the result—predictably—was pandemonium. U'tdaPagrn expressly forbade us to get involved, and since Admiral MacKenna had returned to Singapore and the liaison office at the Defense Ministry was closed, he ordered us to remain at the embassy.

We spent the next ten days standing on our tails, watching the sensational news coverage on the big screen televisions in the Communication circle and fretting over our futures, while U'tdaPagrn struggled to sort through the diplomatic wreckage, which did nothing to improve his mood. And all through that time, the fate of the Dreamsingers haunted us.

"We can only hope they survived," I said during one of our frequent discussions on the subject.

"They were under attack for far longer than we were," I'eiBida said. "Their losses must have been terrible, if what we went through was any indication."

"We know J J survived," M'tinDegan said. "But if they lost even ten percent of their population, their civilization may have disintegrated. And I suspect their losses were even greater."

276

That was a grim image. We all knew of the horrors experienced here on earth during the Collapse.

"And yet they came to our help after the battle," I'eiBida said. "Who knows how many lives were saved by them?"

"A most admirable people," M'tinDegan sighed. "We could learn *so* much from them."

"Will we ever hear from them again?" C'traBenla asked.

M'tinDegan shook his head sadly. "It's impossible to say. All we can do is hope for the best."

§

U'tdaPagrn summoned us to his grotto a few days later, and he was in a grim mood as he showed us a thick stack of documents.

"These are the charges against the six of you. I want to give you copies so you can prepare your defenses." He handed out the folders, and we spent the next few minutes leafing through them. The specifics were extensive and damning.

"I was rather hoping we were past all this."

"K'deiTai, you of all people should know better. The rule of law applies to everyone, including you. I know you all meant well, but you've created a monumental mess. Bringing charges is the right thing to do, and it may help to placate the humans, so consider this as fitting justice for your folly."

"This will ruin our careers," M'tinDegan said, unhappily.

"You should have thought of it when you could still back down." He eyed us unsympathetically. "You will all be sent to Singapore on the next weekly flight. Our ship just arrived, so you need to pack up right away." Then he softened a bit. "I wish I didn't have to do this. Good luck to all of you."

§

We gathered in a loose circle outside his grotto to commiserate and try to buck up our spirits. None of us was in a talkative mood right then, but having each other there was a comfort at least.

"I...suppose we'll find employment in industry," W'kiLap said at last.

T'apiDien gave him a sour look. "Join the knotted tails? I was never meant to be a drone."

"Neither was I, but that's where we're headed."

277

"My interfering violated every standard of academic conduct," M'tinDegan muttered. "This will ruin my professional reputation." He glanced at me. "Which no doubt will apply to you as well, K'deiTai."

I nodded morosely. "I suppose I can say good bye to our Human Studies program." I looked at I'eiBida. "What about you?"

"The best I can hope for is to be reverted to the ranks," he said in despair. "They'll probably toss me out on my tail. What I'll do then, I have no idea."

C'traBenla wrapped her arm around his and nuzzled his ear. "No matter what, I'll stay by you, love." He patted her hand and nuzzled her cheek in appreciation.

"Well, we can comfort ourselves with the thought that we did what we had to," M'tinDegan said. "Which is why we came here to begin with. At least d'enchia is safe; that's what really matters."

That was cold comfort at best, seeing how my life's pursuit was about to come crashing down around my ears. Still, d'enchia was safe. M'tinDegan was right; that was what really mattered.

§

Antoine DuRochelle was waiting impatiently at the lobby desk when I came wandering by. "*Monsieur* K'deiTai, may I have a word with you?"

Right then I was too miserable and fed up to want to speak to anyone. "If you don't mind, *monsieur*, I am rather busy right now." I quickened my pace down the hall toward the cafeteria.

"One question, *monsieur*..."

"I really can't right now."

"Would you care to make a statement concerning the news about the Chancellor?" he called after me.

That brought me up short. "Ah..." My old reflexes for dealing with the news vultures kicked in. "It...seems a bit early to make any definitive statement," I answered cautiously as I racked my mind trying to recall anything which would set him off. There was nothing; which made me wonder if this was so new that word still hadn't gotten around. "We would prefer to see how things develop before offering any substantive statement."

278

"Do you think this will topple the government?"

That brought me up short again, and left me grasping for words. "That...is hard to say." All of a sudden, this mystery demanded attention; I tried urgently to coax some revelation out of him. "It would depend on how your people view the matter, of course."

He nodded, as if I just confirmed something. "So you feel this corruption is an internal affair?"

"That..." All of a sudden, it fell into place. Dassault released the blackmail files! "...is for your people to deal with. We would not presume to judge his actions."

"And how does your government feel about his interfering with the war effort?"

I suddenly wanted out of there in the worst way. "We have not had a chance to consult with the Ancients, but I suspect they will not take your government as a whole to task over it." Greatly daring, I said, "If I may ask in turn, how serious do you think this is for the Chancellor?"

"The opposition has hungered for *Monsieur Chical's* blood for a long time," he said with obvious satisfaction. "And now they finally have it. If *this* doesn't bring his government down, I can't imagine what would!"

§

"If *this* doesn't bring his government down, I can't imagine what would," I'eiBida told U'tdaPagrn a short time later in his grotto. "You know how DuRochelle will spin this. It will take care of any repercussions."

U'tdaPagrn fumed at him. "Even so, that doesn't excuse your actions!"

"No, sir, it doesn't. But since we won't take any backbeating over this, it should be quietly buried."

"If you think you'll get off easy by a bit of good luck..."

I'eiBida rode him down. "Any report will be scrutinized by the 'Dark Grays' and the Arbiters, and will certainly work its way up to the Chamber. Do you want them to learn about all that slime we uncovered? Just *imagine* what an unscrupulous faction could do with the network of bribery and corruption we uncovered!'

279

I jumped in quickly since there was nothing left to lose. "We can't let Z'keBalf get a taste of it. There's no telling *what* his hard-liners will do."

U'tdaPagrn faltered.

"L'datMparn doesn't know about this, does he?" I'eiBida said. "If you send us home under arrest, he'll run straight to Z'keBalf with it."

U'tdaPagrn slumped on his seat cushion and considered the documents in front of him unhappily.

"And think of the repercussions here on earth," I said. "You'll have enough on your hands with the wreckage of this war and building relations with a new régime without our being tied to this scandal. You don't need any more distractions."

"And we'll be off to Singapore and home tomorrow, so you'll be rid of us," I'eiBida added.

"All right, curse your Ancestors! Out!"

§

The diplomatic headaches surrounding this incident, which was already becoming known as the 'Dreamsingers' War', were in full flower when our transport arrived to take us to Singapore. Thankfully, I wasn't caught up in it, or with the rising clamor for the Chancellor's ears, but then I never wanted to be here in the first place. U'tdaPagrn was welcome to *all* the glory in *this* one, with my sympathies. Once again, I was lucky to get out of here with my ears, and thankful for it.

The embassy omnibus dropped I'eiBida, C'traBenla, and me, along with several staffers rotating home and a mountain of luggage at the Geneva terminal. The humans were talking about setting up an orbital shuttle service from Geneva, but nothing came of it thus far. And since none of the precious commercial P-wings were available, we were stuck with one of the lumbering propeller-driven peacekeeper C-wings. We were not looking forward to the dreary four day journey to Singapore.

The winter had given way to a lingering spring. It was raining steadily, and there was a decided nip in the air. I tugged my overcoat tighter as I was feeling a bit overheated, and wished we could get on the plane and go. More rain was forecast the next

280

day, so the peacekeeper air cargo service was anxious to get us out of here. But best efforts notwithstanding, we were stuck for hours in the drafty Geneva terminal while they serviced the aircraft.

W'kiLap, T'apiDien, and M'tinDegan were there to see us off.

"U'tdaPagrn made it plain that even if he isn't filing charges against us, he intends to request replacements, so we should be coming home in the not too distant future," M'tinDegan said. "I suppose it's for the best: we've all been here too long, and I for one have a lot of scientific papers to work up."

"And we've been thinking about cashing in on our time here," T'apiDien said. "We're going to open a software company."

"Well, good luck on that, to all of you."

"A little something to cheer C'traBenla up," W'kiLap said to I'eiBida with a smug grin. "I took a peek in the medical files: R'benTdan is expecting."

"Really?"

"It looks like C'tra won their little contest after all."

"That will please her no end," I'eiBida chuckled.

"Has there been any word from the Dreamsingers?" I asked.

They turned somber. "Nothing," M'tinDegan said. "No word from J J. The humans haven't heard anything either."

"That's the most frustrating part of this whole stampede," I grumbled. "I wish we could at least know whether they survived the attack or not."

"They don't seem to be talkative," I'eiBida said.

M'tinDegan sighed. "Such a fascinating culture. And J J seemed like a decent sort. I suspect we and the humans could both benefit from knowing them."

"I can't believe it," I'eiBida grumbled, "but I'm looking forward to getting back to duty at the Staff circle." His ears twitched in dismay. "I've been doing this too long."

"*You* should complain!" I said. "I have to go back to the wreckage of our Human Studies program. My Aide must be frantic by now."

I'eiBida gave me a wry grin. "Can't say as I blame him: he gets stuck at home trying to keep things from falling apart while you go galloping off on another high adventure."

I gave him an annoyed look. "An adventure..."

"...is when you're having a bad time in a nasty place far from home." We all enjoyed a rueful chuckle at that.

"He'll never speak to me again," I sighed. He might not, in fact, not that I could blame him.

"*There* you are, I'eiBida!" C'traBenla came stomping over, and she was in a foul mood since U'tdaPagrn didn't rescind his confinement order, preventing her from seeing *Señor* Vargas again. "These *Customs* humans are making a fuss about our luggage. The least you can do is help me!"

I'eiBida gave us a resigned glance. Ninety percent of their luggage was hers, and there was a mountain of it on two baggage carts. "Of course, love."

The others lingered for a bit, then made their journey wishes and headed back to the embassy. There was nothing better to do, so I stood watching the activity around me and musing on the past and future. The airport lounge was busy, with humans from several ethnic groups waiting for their flights. The airport officials were busy checking tickets and inspecting luggage, while the passengers waited impatiently or took advantage of the food vendors. There were hatchlings running loose amid stacks and carts of luggage, and the loudspeakers were drowned out by a civilian P-wing taxiing up to the loading ramp. I noticed I'eiBida and C'traBenla arguing again in the glassed-off luggage check-in, with a sorely harassed human Customs inspector caught between them. After what must have been a shrill debate, he confiscated some item out of their luggage and retreated, leaving the two to fight it out.

Now that I thought about it, I could see how emotionally fragile she was. It never occurred to me before, but her impulsiveness and her temper came from fear and frustration. I could see how she must feel looking in the mirror: her beauty was her one real asset, which she depended on all her life. She was still stunningly beautiful, but the years were creeping up on her, and the two eggs she'd had showed. I shook my head in dismay at that revelation. You have to be empathetic as an Arbiter; odd I hadn't understood before.

282

The two were arguing now, discreetly but furiously. I'eiBida began pacing back and forth as she unloaded a stinging diatribe on him, then he stalked off a few paces and the two sulked in angry silence.

I liked him from the start. He was brash and impulsive when first assigned to my diplomatic herd, but he matured into an excellent leader during our tour here. He was smart and hard working, and showed real potential. Odd, I never realized how fragile he was, too.

I stood there for some time, bemused by these revelations. It was almost like I was inside their heads hearing their thoughts and feeling their emotions. As I said, empathy is an important tool for an Arbiter; perhaps I never really took the time to contemplate them before.

I'eiBida turned and looked at her, then went over and began talking to her again. I couldn't hear what they were saying, but he was clearly trying to reestablish their dialog. I watched for a while, and wondered idly if the two of them could ever find peace with each other.

'Don' you worry 'bout it none,' a thought echoed through my mind. *'They'll be all right.'* As the presence faded, I caught a fleeting sensation of a knowing smile.

*****

The End

"Appendix"

"Fiddler's Green"

Published in the U. S. Army Cavalry manual, 1823

Halfway down the trail to Hell
in a shady meadow green,
are the souls of all dead troopers camped
near a good old-time canteen.
And this eternal resting place
Is known as Fiddler's Green.

Marching past, straight through to Hell,
the Infantry are seen,
accompanied by the Engineers,
Artillery and Marines,
for none but the shades of Cavalrymen
dismount at Fiddlers' Green.

Though some go curving down the trail
to seek a warmer scene,
no trooper ever gets to Hell
ere he's emptied his canteen,
and so rides back to drink again
with friends at Fiddlers' Green.

And so when man and horse go down
beneath a saber keen,
or in a roaring charge or fierce melee
you stop a bullet clean,
and the hostiles come to get your scalp,
just empty your canteen,
and put your pistol to your head
and go to Fiddlers' Green.

*****

"Dramatis Personnae"

Ic'nichi:

The Most Ancient continues to lead the Chamber Of Ancients, but is expected to retire shortly due to his declining health.

G'cetGian, chi B'nevd continues as head of the Arbiters' Service.

K'deiTai, sen V'ran, first Arbiter-To-Humans on earth, continues to teach Human Studies at a major Institute in the World Nest.

U'tdaPagrn, dro Mev'menk continues to serve as the second Arbiter or earth. He is presently working on the Third Accord negotiations.

R'benTdan, truo M'benbra continues to serve as the Cultural Attaché at the embassy. Agent Goldblum was recently instructed by the Agency not to file any more incident reports on her activities unless someone is seriously injured.

Learnéds W'kiLap and *T'apiDien* retired from intelligence work, and now run a small software business specializing in Ic'nichi-human interfacing products.

M'tinDegan, cro V'menba returned to d'enchia after the Dreamsingers' War, and published a series of sociological papers on alien cultures. Two of his significant works are an initial study of the Dreamsingers and an analysis of the sociological aftermath of the Ic'nichi's first interstellar war. His work was well received, and he is now Ki-Learnéd and head of Interstellar Studies at a major Institute.

N'detLeda, tan E'triin serves as an instructor and researcher at a major Institute in the World Nest, is part of a program to develop shielding against projected thought attacks, and does occasional psychological consulting for the defenders.

T'virDoma, ab Clas'nch continues her schooling in Human Studies, and is an assistant to Learnéd N'detLeda. At last notice, her application to 'Dark Grays' intelligence has been rejected again.

H'rhAtor, tem dre Fradash was incapacitated for several months after the battle, but has returned to duty as Fleet Eldest, where he pushes relentlessly to diversify the fleet's war-making capabilities.

I'eiBida, fan D'chr and his Worthy continue to serve at the 'Dark Grays' Academy and on the Staff as human experts.

L'datMparn, tii R'vebb continues to serve as head of security at the embassy despite ongoing attempts to have him removed.

C'traBenla, rani D'enta authors a regular column on human cultural affairs, gives frequent lectures, and is a fem rights activist. She is still troubled by severe possession syndrome, and undergoes periodic therapy.

Humans:

Jacek Hogarthy continues to serve as the human Defense Minister, to everyone's collective regret.

Admiral Brian MacKenna, the humans' most experienced war leader, continues to serve as Flag, Space Fleet. He is largely inactive after the trauma he received during the war.

Captain Loraine Morgan has been promoted to commodore as the field commander of the growing human space fleet.

Commander Ivan Rostokovich was promoted to captain (lower half) and commands the Ic'nichi liaison office at the Foreign Ministry.

Commander Lincoln Watanabi continues to serve as the space fleet liaison to the embassy.

Lieutenant Night Eagle was promoted to Lieutenant (upper half), and commands a company of the 5001st peacekeepers (space marines).

Agent Pierre Roubidoux, APA, was promoted to Inspector and now lives on d'enchia with his wife. He heads the security and intel office at the human embassy.

Agent Hyam Goldblum, APA, continues to head the human liaison office at the embassy. He is writing a book about his experiences there.

Honoré Dassault has vanished as mysteriously as he appeared. Whether he continues to work for the Admiral, or maintains his contacts in the embassy, or where he is in general is unknown.

J. J. Ballas, was an elderly Blues guitarist known by Captain Morgan when she was a child in the Champaign-Urbana refugee camps during the Collapse. Her child's-eye-view of him provided the memory image used by the Dreamsingers to communicate with humans. He has not been heard from since shortly after the Dreamsingers' War.

Ic'nichi phrases:

An empty egg
   A vulgar slang phase meaning to have nothing; comparable to the human term 'we don't have squat'.

Egg Testers
   Crèche workers who test newly laid eggs for genetic defects, and break the defective eggs with a small hammer, the symbol of their office; referenced as a symbol of fear, similar to the human BogeyMan.

First Finger
   A common slang term defining quality or achievement which refers to the Ic'nichis' four mutually opposed fingers: the highest quality is 'first' (index) finger, followed by 'second',

'third', and finally 'fourth finger'; barely passing. The human equivalent are grades 'A', 'B', 'C', and 'D', respectively. Commonly used in education.

Go back to the egg
To become senile; to give up in disgust; to fall asleep from boredom; to become severely drunk.

I'll have his ears
A euphemism for castration.

Stellar bomb
Ic'nichi term for the hydrogen bomb. They refer to atomic bombs as 'radioactive' bombs.

The set of his ears
Refers to the movements of Ic'nichi ears, indicating their emotions; euphemism for secret thoughts.

Tuck one's tail under
Slang for hiding from authority; to evade responsibility; to make a peace offering in a lovers' quarrel; slang for running for public office.

Uttermost Darkness
Ic'nichi belief that if their Ancestors judge them unworthy to join their bloodline, they will be cast out of the afterlife, dooming them to the formless void for eternity.

Ic'nichi words:

a'vemn'vb'li - The Ic'nichi vision of the afterlife based on the rich boglands their species evolved in. Ic'nichi belief is that after death, they will finally meet their Ancestors, and gallop with the ancestral herds in an idyllic eternity; similar in concept to the human 'Garden of Eden' belief.

Bna'vwep - literally 'an infested pile of your Ancestors' foul-smelling dung'; self explanatory.

bv'nunma - a popular light meal similar to tuna salad.

cc'v'renk - literally 'dishonored before ones' Ancestors'; acute embarrassment; disgraceful behavior; inability to make a decision; inability to see common sense; slang term for mental retardation.

er'trxxda - literally 'haunted by the Ancestors' voices'; obsession; insanity; delusion; raging temper; vulgar habits.

hro'n'nad - slang term meaning clueless or ignorant.

l'cc'vn - a vulgar adjective.

l'fru'ng - brazen audacity; annoying habits; body odor.

l'ni'ddi - a popular fast food similar to stew.

M'mendoch - literally 'someone who thinks fast'; slang term for a hustler; trying to get out of a hopeless situation; avoiding being cited by the peace wardens for a minor violation.

n'bna'nmn Slang term for an idiot; a vegetable pie; a bright color.

n'hroop - a common Ic'nichi language, spoken by about 8% of their population.

NmFargs - a food animal noted for their sexual prowess; a person whose sex drive is comically excessive.

r'vebbe - literally 'to feel one's Ancestors' disapproval'; slang term for being upset, shaken, or spooked by something strange.

'sti'eit - a popular brand of cheap liquor similar to ale.

t'pithm'ig - a showoff; an immature dandy; a vain person.

tra'taj - a prostitute; a slut; a person lacking scruples.

uf'thoka - a popular vegetarian dish analogous to bean sprouts with a spicy garnish.

un'brapta - cruel; heartless; self-centered; arrogant; the odor of unwashed linens.

un'tdar - a crude, vulgar person; a pig-like animal; bad breath.

V'liz - a popular beverage containing a mild stimulant which can be prepared either like coffee or soup.

'V'memb'Va - literally 'granted great vision in the egg'; natural ability; instinctive skill; a conclusion reached through long introspection; slang term for a know-it-all.

V'rima - bartering; black marketeering; a falsified invoice; con-artistry; seduction; to refuse to pay a debt.

vr'meol - someone who practices *V'rima*; a hustler; a compulsive liar; a sex maniac; slang term for terrible weather.

'v'thorble - slang term for someone with an exaggerated opinion of himself; roughly comparable to 'hot rock'.

x'mnnb' - literally 'dead fish'; slang for annoying, stupid behavior; comparable to the human term 'bullshit'.

*****

A Brief Note From The Author

Thank you for reading this novel, which continues my favorite work of my writing. I hope it was a good read for you. I would love to hear from you, my readers, to let me know how I am doing as an author. Every bit of input helps me to make my next effort a better product for your enjoyment.

All my best,

Bob Boyd

You can learn more about me, and keep up to date on my efforts through our Blog:

Facebook.com/The Written Wyrd

*****

An Excerpt From
Diplomacy's End: The d'enchia Incident
Part 3 of the Interstellar Concord Saga

Once again our ill-starred diplomats are caught up in crisis as a result of the late Dreamsingers' War: they are all becoming telepaths! As if the dangers of interstellar war and Chamber Of Ancients politics weren't bad enough...

*****

"Some Days It Just Doesn't Pay To Worry"
(Related by Learnéd M'tinDegan)

The next day *started out* more or less normally...

"Are you sure you want to be here, love?" I'eiBida asked as C'traBenla settled awkwardly on a seat cushion. "It's as boring as ever, and with you getting so close to delivery..." She arrived in mid-morning after a medical appointment, and he was understandably concerned for her.

She smiled, and gave him a happy ear twitch. "I feel fine, love! The physichs said I'm doing well, and I'm still a long way from due. Besides, my next interview isn't until late this afternoon, and I might as well be here as anywhere."

"Well, I guess, if you feel all right." He fetched a steaming bowl of *V'liz* for her as she settled in, which she accepted with a radiant smile and the happy aura she exhibited whenever she was the center of attention.

"You are in a fine mood this morning," I offered.

"Am I that obvious?" Her aura of pleasure took on a faintly embarrassed tone. She was a fount of happiness over her endless interviews and news programs since our appearance in the Chamber, and her aura helped lighten the psychic atmosphere.

"Yes, you are," H'rhAtor said. "It's good to see *someone* is happy to be here."

"You've all been so grumpy lately," she lectured us. "I swear it's enough to put a fem off." Not that anything could penetrate her blissful mood, it seemed.

292

"Honestly, I believe you have the the strongest and most advanced powers among us," I said. "I would think I'eiBida would be the strongest since he had so much exposure to the Dreamsingers."

"If I'm not mistaken, he comes in a close second," K'deiTai said. Our growing empathic powers were an obsession among us, and a lively topic of discussion was always welcome.

That tickled her no end. "What a breeding pair we make! Just *think* of the powers our hatchling will have! We should have more; they'll be the wave of the future."

I'eiBida flinched, which she, fortunately, didn't notice.

"Imagine it: a genuine second generation empath. She'll redefine our entire species. I'ei, this is *wonderful!*"

He eyed her doubtfully. "Well, for one thing, you don't know it's a 'she'...do you?"

She hesitated. "No..."

"So it could be a 'he', and who knows what powers, if any, might pass on to the next generation?"

"You are *so* negative," she scolded him. "Have a little faith. This is our hatchling! He, or she, will make history!"

"Well, he, or she, will have to be approved first..." Even as I'eiBida started ticking off points on his fingers, her mood shifted abruptly.

"...and we'll have no *end* of medical bills..." An icy psychic blast seemed to fill the room as she stared wide-eyed at him.

"...and there's the crèche fees, which I don't know *where* we'll..." He faltered as the building started to shake with a chorus of ominous creaking and groaning...

"Now you've done it," H'rhAtor mumbled.

"...ah...well, actually I meant..."

Then the building started trembling...

"...love...I didn't mean anything!" I'eiBida cried in alarm.

"I'ei?"

"C'tra!!!!"

"You can't let them hurt my egg!"

A pile of books on someone's desk toppled onto the floor. .

"Don't let your Possession Syndrome get to you!"

293

"*p'quas'tka*," U'tdaPagrn muttered as he dropped his little plastic cube and dove under his desk...

A shrill wind came up out of nowhere, blowing papers around like leaves as our staff cowered under their desks...

"They can't hurt my *hatchling!*"

"C'TRA! Get ahold of yourself!"

A window shattered. I felt my desk move, then all its drawers shot out across the room. The staff, as one, scrambled as far from her as they could amid a growing blizzard of papers and small items, cowering against the wall and behind filing cabinets.

"C'TRA!" I'eiBida tried to comfort her, but was knocked off his feet by a flying seat cushion.

"I'm sure the Egg Testers...have no protocols about...psychic abilities," I cried. "If anything..." I ducked a flying trash can. "...I'm sure they would..." A filing cabinet sailed over my head, collapsing in on itself as it bounced off the wall. "...they would rate them positively!"

A light fixture shattered...then another...

I looked to H'rhAtor, who was clinging to his desk. *'Say something before she explodes!'* I thought to him. We had a living stellar bomb ticking in our midst.

"An empath would...be priceless for the space program!" C'traBenla's head jerked around to focus on him, her eyes wide in panic. I realized she was feeding on the general alarm we all felt, trapping us all in a devastating psychic typhoon. "She'd be...she'd help com...munications..." H'rhAtor cringed as his desk flipped bodily upside down...

"A-and an empath would help the Arbiters!" K'deiTai cried. "Don't hurt meeee!!!!"

But by then she was in full-blown panic mode, beyond reason as per Possession Syndrome took over, her telekinetic powers feeding back on our alarm to wreck havoc.

"It's all right, C'tra!" I'eiBida bellowed over the rising storm. "Don't..." He ducked as a section of wall panel ripped away and went flying. "...get ahold of yourself!"

L'datMparn stuck his snout through the door just then, took one frightened look, and vanished as a section of the ceiling came crashing down. Two of our clerical staff bolted in panic, following him out the door.

"C'TRA!" I'eiBida tried to comfort her, but was smashed against the wall by some unseen force. One of the clericals dove head-first out a window, while another was knocked off his feet by flying debris.

"*Why* do my Ancestors do this to me?" K'deiTai moaned.

"C'TRA!!!" Another light fixture shattered, then the windows exploded. We all cowered under what cover we could find as the grotto was shredded around us.

Then J J Ballas was there, standing tall and solid amid the typhoon of flying wreckage. "Lawdy Baby-Chile!" he cried. "What's wrong wit yo?" He waded through the storm and laid both hands on the sides of her head. "Calm yo-self, chile!"

As suddenly as the storm erupted, it vanished amid a thunderous clatter as what was left of our furnishings and office equipment skidded to a halt.

"We're alive?" U'tdaPagrn gasped, then twitched anxiously as the building creaked around us.

"Now you calm down, Baby-Chile," J J said, sternly. "Yo' powers are too strong fo' you t' lose control like this."

"But...my egg..." C'traBenla seemed under control for the moment, but then I realized J J was holding her in check by main force. "...t-the egg testerrsss..." She slipped loose from his control enough to start bawling.

"Baby-Chile, there ain't nothin' you can do 'bout that by losing control this way. You—all-a you—need t' learn self control."

C'traBenla was a shivering wreck by that point. I'eiBida staggered to his feet and moved to comfort her. J J gingerly took his hands away, ready to grab her again if she lost it. She started sobbing, but managed not to panic as I'eiBida took her in his arms.

"Thas better. You really got to work on yo' self control, Baby-Chile." J J turned to us. "As fo' the rest of you, these powers ain't nothin' t' take lightly. You-all need t' learn self discipline."

"Ah...we're trying, J J," I said, uneasily.

"Well yo' need t' try harder! This-heah is th' sort of thing our young-uns do. You-all are grown-ups, you should know better!"

And with that, he vanished.

H'rhAtor was the first to recover his wits, poked his head up reluctantly and looked around. "Anyone hurt?"

Before anyone could answer, the door burst open, and Q'brnVen and two other Chamber Wardens charged in, with a medical team right behind. They ground to a halt, and took in the scene in dismay. "What happened?" Q'brnVen asked at last.

I'eiBida paused in comforting C'traBenla. "It...was nothing." He considered the shattered ruins in dismay. "Don't worry about it. We'll clean up the mess."

"*Don't worry about it?!*" Our office equipment and furnishings were mangled, our carefully filed records scattered and shredded, there were large pieces of wall material torn loose, and we could see daylight through a rent in the ceiling. "It looks like a stellar bomb went off in here!"

"Closer than you think," K'deiTai muttered. I made frantic hushing gestures at him, and he checked himself. "It was just a little misunderstanding, is all. It's over now."

"A little mis..." Q'brnVen was incredulous; understandable since the room looked like it was run through a trash compactor. "This hardly seems like a *little* misunderstanding!"

I made frantic hushing gestures at him. "It's all right. She's under control now."

"What? She...?"

"It was just a...well...she had a panic attack."

"A panic attack?" He stared at me blankly, then eyed C'traBenla with growing alarm.

H'rhAtor staggered to his feet and herded the Chamber Wardens out into the hall before Q'brnVen said something to set her off again. "Don't worry, we'll take care of it. Everything is under control for now."

"*How* am I going to write *this* one up?"

"You'll think of something; I have complete confidence in you." He forced the door shut, which took some doing, before Q'brnVen could protest.

*****

296

Titles from The Written Wyrd
2017

The Diplomacy Trilogy - Science fiction humor.

First contact from the aliens' perspective in a trio of lurid tell-all memoirs written by a team of alien diplomats sent to earth to open an embassy.

The MacKenna Trilogy - Science fiction military drama.

He was earth's greatest soldier; they needed his skills once more, but they didn't realize how wrong bringing him back from the dead was.

Nature's Way - Environmental disaster / apocalyptic horror.

This is the last day of our last stand against Nature out for revenge!

Trial - Science fiction political thriller.

The aliens demand justice for their murdered ambassador while right wing extremists plot revolution; which is the greater threat?

Overland - Period science fiction drama / romance.

He was trapped between a beautiful genetically enhanced revolutionary from the distant future and the inhuman monster sent to destroy her. Can he survive caught up in their titanic battle?

Playing God - Apocalyptic horror.

Brenda discovers she is the Dream Girl of a mad scientist capable of altering the past. Can she find a way to undo the disaster he wrought and prevent a nuclear holocaust?

The Big Snow - Environmental disaster / adventure.

A passenger train is wrecked at the top of Donner Pass in the worst storms in recorded history. Can the railroaders get the passengers to safety?

(continued)

Young Adult Demi-Novels:

Diplomacy's Children - YA humor / adventure.
A young alien space fleet recruit faces his greatest challenge in a self-centered, foul-tempered human youngling he is ordered to keep in check.

Star Flight - YA adventure.
She was an outcast, cursed with supernatural powers. She was offered a reprieve, a chance to start over, but could she survive the challenge?

Short Story Anthologies:

Deus Ex Machina - Humorous fantasy short story collection.
From bungling wizards to moronic barbarians to redneck elves, here are the old tales of epic adventure as we would love to see them told - just once.

Ghoulish Good Fun - Macabre short story collection.
Reality is a cruel practical joke. Laugh along with it if you dare!

*****

Available in print and Kindle from Amazon,
and in PDF and ePub downloads from Smashwords.
Visit our web site for details.

http://www.the-written-wyrd.org/shopping.shtml

www.ingramcontent.com/pod-product-compliance
Lightning Source LLC
Chambersburg PA
CBHW051525260626

47170CB00003B/782